CLOCKWORK CAIRO:
STEAMPUNK TALES
OF EGYPT

CLOCKWORK
STEAMPUNK·TALES·OF·EGYPT
CAIRO

EDITED BY MATTHEW BRIGHT

TWOPENNY
BOOKS

CLOCKWORK CAIRO

Published in 2017 by TWOPENNY BOOKS

ISBN: 9781527207776

COVER AND INTERIOR DESIGN: Inkspiral Design

FOR THE REAL CLEOPATRA BONNY
AND HER EVEN MORE FABULOUS MOTHER.

EDITOR'S NOTE

To me, Egypt was always the land of stories.

In England, where I grew up, the history of Ancient Egypt is normally taught in schools around about the age of eight, and I am far from unique in having been utterly captivated by the subject as a child. Those tales were so vivid: the pharaohs and gods, slaves and monarchs, the pyramids looming over the cities, the tombs and the treasures lost beneath the sands. They brimmed with wonder and imagination, beguiling and exotic.

Perhaps the steampunk genre is so appealing for precisely those same reasons: we can escape into a history that sounds like a grand story. Steampunk, at its best, fuses together elements of the Victorian pulp, the fantastical, the gothic; it boils them up in a magnificent machine made of pistons and clockwork, strains this chaotic brew through a filter of nostalgia, and spits out a heady mixture of roguish adventure and well-mannered derring-do. And though from this a casual reader might imagine that this would result in a genre that is pure confection, light and lacking in substance, the most cursory of glances across the milestones of steampunk demonstrates the capacity for quite the opposite.

But publishing in this particular era, in the wake of all of the changes an upheavals of the last few years, it's important to think about what exactly it means to say 'escaping into history'. After all, we all know who gets to write the history books.

Begging your forgiveness for the simplification of this description: steampunk springs from the pastiching of colonial-era pulp fiction. It's an easy genre to exaggerate, to write large, even to fetishize, extending right through the most potent iconography of the genre. London is frequently a central location in steampunk, being the heart of Victoriana, and when stories venture further afield it is often with the notion of exploring new lands, worlds foreign and—back to that word—*exotic*. And I'll confess, when I first struck upon the theme for this anthology, that was perhaps my first thought too; I was cast right back to those stories I was taught in school, my imagination immediately brimful of possibilities. I wanted to capture that with the collection, that spirit of exploration, of discovering the new and fascinating.

But then I thought a little harder about why that word 'exotic' sprang so easily to my mind, and realised that my heritage was what conjured that; I am, after all, British, and in that way of jokes-that-hide-the-truth, it's often said we miss our Empire. The more I examined this, the more I was spurred to consider what I wanted this collection to look like. Yes, I wanted the explorers, and the airship captains, yes I wanted ladies in corsets menaced by mummies, but I also wanted much more—I wanted voices that are often overlooked, voices so frequently untold, and voices often missing from history. Steampunk—and the science-fiction and fantasy genre as whole—has room from a wealth of diverse voices within it, and that was what I wanted from *Clockwork Cairo*.

The authors in this collection offer varied adventures worthy of the genre: pharaohs and gods, slaves and monarchs, the pyramids looming over the cities, the tombs and the treasures lost beneath the sands. The thieves and adventurers within these tales are more distinctive than any of the women and men who sought spoils for the Empire and Cairo, The City of a Thousand Minarets, remains a place of wonder.

MATTHEW BRIGHT, JUNE 2017

TABLES OF CONTENTS

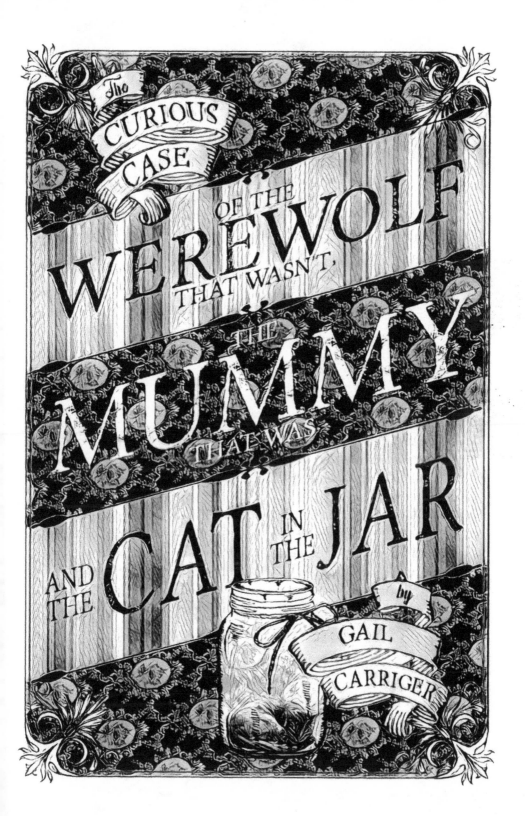

THE CURIOUS CASE OF THE WEREWOLF THAT WASN'T, THE MUMMY THAT WAS, AND THE CAT IN THE JAR

"Yoo-hoo!"

Alessandro Tarabotti's forehead crinkled under his grey top hat. Was that some peculiar birdsong?

"Yoo-hoo, Sandy!" No, it was a voice hallooing at him across the broiling humanity of the bazaar.

Mr. Tarabotti was so thoroughly distracted upon hearing such a name hollered at him in such a place and voice, that he relaxed his grip. The place was Luxor. The voice was just the kind that bled the inner ear, trumpeting out a nasal ode to abundant schooling and little attention toward the details of it. His loosened grip allowed the scrubby native boy with terrified fly-ridden eyes to rip himself away and scuttle down a convenient alleyway, vanishing round a pile of broken pottery.

"Well, that's torn it." Alessandro threw the scrap of material he was left holding onto the dirt street. He squinted into the alley, eyes adjusting slowly to the slatted light that crept through reed mats stretched far above. High houses and narrow streets—who would have thought Egypt a child of shadows and shade?

"Sandy, old chap!" The voice was getting closer.

"Who knows you here, sir?" asked Floote.

"More to the point, who would dare yoo-hoo at me?" Mr. Tarabotti turned away from the empty alleyway to glare at his valet as though the greeting were somehow Floote's fault.

Floote pivoted and gestured softly with his right hand. His left was occupied holding onto a large glass specimen jar.

The yoo-hooer hove into sight. Alessandro winced. The man wore the most remarkably bright blue frock coat, double breasted, with brass buttons up the front. He sported a pair of Rumnook's stained-glass binocular spectacles perched atop his tiny nose, and a limp cravat. In Mr. Tarabotti's world, nothing excused a limp cravat, even the dead heat of Egypt at high noon.

"Do I know that repulsive-looking blighter?"

Floote twisted his mouth slightly to one side.

"Quite right, quite right. Someone from my early days. Before I cultivated a brain. School, perhaps?" Mr. Tarabotti awaited his fate, brushing a non-existent speck of dust from the sleeve of his own gold frock coat. Single breasted, mind you, with pearl buttons and a deceptively simple cut.

"Blasted English, blemishing about the world. Is nowhere safe?"

Floote, who was himself an Englishman, did not point out that Alessandro Tarabotti, of a similarly unfortunate over-education as the man approaching, dressed and spoke like an Englishman. He didn't actually look like one, of course, boasting a long line of ancestors who had invested heavily in being dark, hook-nosed, and brooding.

Mr. Tarabotti continued grousing, right up until the yoo-hooer was in earshot. "I mean to say, Floote my man, what are your countrymen about these days? You'd think they'd leave at least one small corner of the planet to the rest of us. But no, here they are, shiny as all get up, ever expanding the Empire."

"We have benefited considerably from integration of the supernatural."

"Well it's hell on the rest of us. Do stop it, will you?"

"Very good, sir."

"You-hoo, you-hoo!" The man came to a wheezing halt before them, sounding like an exhausted steam engine, trailing some species of suitable young lady in his corpulent wake. "Sandy Dandy the Italian? By Jove, it is you! Fancy, fancy, fancy!"

Alessandro, who did not like the name Sandy Dandy the Italian, lifted his monocle and examined the man downwards through it.

The man said, to the monocle, "Baronet Percival Phinkerlington. How d'you do?"

At least he had the good grace to introduce himself. Mr. Tarabotti put down his eye piece pointedly. Really, what a thing to do to one's cravat.

"You knew my brother, I believe."

The face above the unfortunate neck cloth did have a familiar something about the eyes and mouth. "Good lord, old Pink's kid brother?"

The man grinned and doffed his top hat. "Right you are! Fancy I was a bit smaller back when you knew me last!"

"Practically half the man you are now."

"You remember our sister?"

The lady in question went red under Mr. Tarabotti's indifferent glance. He didn't bother with the monocle. She bobbed a trembling curtsy. Ladies always caught the blush-and-flutters upon meeting Alessandro Tarabotti.

He bowed. "Miss Phinkerlington."

"Leticia, you remember Sandy? Mr. Tarabotti, I should say. Italian chappy, went to Oxford with Eustace. Used to bowl for New College. Toddled down for a stopover one session break. The same time Daddy had himself that whole werewolf pack visiting." He turned back to Mr. Tarabotti. "Fancy meeting you here. In Egypt of all places!"

"Indeed." Alessandro tried to remember why he would bother visiting this man's family. Had it been an assignment? Investigating the werewolves? Or had he been there to kill someone? Perhaps just a mild maiming?

Sir Percival leaned in conspiratorially. "You ought to see to your man there, Sandy. You realize, he's got his arm 'round a jam jar of dead cat?"

"Mmm, yes, preserved in some of my best formaldehyde."

The baronet gave a nervous laugh. "Always were a bit peculiar, Sandy. Eustace seemed to like you well enough. I say, this may be Egypt, but trailing about dead cats—not the done thing."

"I have an eccentric Aunt," replied Mr. Tarabotti, as though that were explanation enough.

"Don't we all, my dear fellow? Don't we all?"

"It's her cat. Or it was her cat, I should say."

Miss Phinkerlington noticed the valet with the glass jar full of cat for the first time. She coloured a sandy sage and turned away, pretending interest in the bustling natives ebbing and flowing around them. A proper Englishwoman must find it a spectacle indeed, that tide of humanity in its multi-coloured robes, veiled or turbaned according to sex, loud and malodorous regardless.

"Floote," Alessandro used Miss Phinkerlington's discomfort as an excuse, "shove off, will you? Find out what happened to our young friend. I'll see you back at the hotel."

Floote nodded and disappeared across the bazaar, cat in hand.

Sir Percival seemed to take that as an end to the business. "Well, well, well, what a thing to see you here. Been a while, old chap. Came for the climate, myself. Wettest winter in donkey's years, decided on a bit of a change. Thought Egypt might suit."

"Imagine England having a wet winter, remarkable."

"Yes, yes, well, Egypt, here, a bit, eh, warmer, you understand, than I was expecting. But we've been taking the aether regular-like. Haven't we, Leticia? Keeps a body cool." The baronet jerked his head up at the three large balloons hovering high above Luxor. They were tethered by long cords to a landing platform dockside. Well, that explained the man's abysmal choice in eyewear. Tinted spectacles were recommended for high floating.

The baronet persisted in his social niceties. "And are you having an agreeable trip?"

"Can't stand travel," replied Mr. Tarabotti, "bad for the digestion and ruins one's clothes."

"Too true." The baronet looked suitably sombre. "Too true." Moving hurriedly on from a clearly distasteful topic, he asked, "Staying at Chumley's Inn, are you, Sandy?"

Alessandro nodded. It was the only place to stay in Luxor. Alexandria and Cairo provided a number of respectable hotels, but Luxor was still provincial. For example, it boasted a mere three balloons, and only one with a propeller. It was a small village, really, in an almost forgotten place, of interest primarily to those with an eye towards treasure hunting. Which didn't explain why Phinkerlington and his sister were in Luxor. Nor, of course, why Alessandro Tarabotti was.

"Catch a bite to eat later tonight, old man?"

Alessandro decided it was probably better for his image to be seen dining in the company of British tourists, than to be observed too frequently about his own private business. "Certainly. But now, I'm afraid, I must beg to be excused. My man, you understand, is gadding about Egypt with a dead cat."

"Of course, of course."

Mr. Tarabotti bowed to Miss Phinkerlington, who pinked once more at such direct attention. Not a bad looking chit, really.

As he walked away, he heard the baronet say, in tones of deep censure and insufficient softness, "Really, Leticia, an Italian is most inappropriate. You must stop blushing at him so significantly."

MR. TARABOTTI FOUND Floote exactly where Floote ought to be, at the centre of a milling whirl of dark limbs and bright fabric, engaged in a protracted bout of fisticuffs. It was unsurprising that Floote, who had fought werewolves in Scotland and vampires all along the French Riviera, was holding his own. What was surprising was that he did this while still clutching the jar.

Alessandro removed his jacket and laid it atop a low mud brick wall. He rested his hat carefully alongside. The jacket was tailored to perfection, flaring with just under enough fullness so as not to be thought dandified. It had three sets of invisible pockets in the lining, each housing a collection of sharp little sticks: silver, wood, and peppermint. The silver was for werewolves, the wood was for vampires, and the peppermint was for Mr. Tarabotti. Mr. Tarabotti was rather fond of peppermint. He was also fond of that jacket; it wouldn't do for it to be harmed, and he wouldn't need the weaponry, not in the middle of the day. He did transfer the letter of marque from the jacket to a waistcoat pocket next to his monocle and his miniature antikythera device, for extra security. Then he dove into the fray.

Alessandro was not burdened with Floote's sentimental British predilection towards proper violent comportment. When Mr. Tarabotti fought, he used both his fists and his feet, drawing on some spate of skills he'd learned in the Orient. He would have been summarily thrown out of White's, for his technique was, it must be admitted, most ungentlemanly.

He enjoyed himself immensely.

Mr. Tarabotti had always been fond of the occasional pugilistic endeavour, ever since he was a boy—revelling in that delicious slap and crush of flesh against flesh. He relished the heated blood buzzing through his brain, numbing all senses but those vital to security—sight and touch. Any pain was a boon, a reminder of watchfulness that he must keep his mind in play only so much as it did not hinder.

It was almost too easy. Floote's attackers were ill prepared for Mr. Tarabotti's sudden appearance. Soon enough, the swirling mix of appendages and colourful flowing robes resolved itself into three local malcontents: one fallen and two running away.

While Floote recovered his equanimity, Mr. Tarabotti sat astride the fallen man. He grabbed at the man's arms, pressing them to the ground.

"Who hired you?" he asked in English.

No response.

He repeated himself in Italian.

The man only looked up at him, dark eyes wide. He writhed about in the dirt, shaking his head frantically back and forth as though in the throes of some fit. Then, before Floote could put down the cat and render assistance, the man surged up, shook Alessandro off, and dashed away.

When Floote would have gone after, his master stayed him with a touch.

"No advantage in following. We won't extract any information from the likes of him—too frightened."

"Of us?"

"Of whoever paid them to engage the foreigner brandishing a dead cat."

"Hired by your contact, sir? Perhaps he changed his mind about notifying the government."

"No, no, I think not. There is someone else in play. Or several someones. Deuced inconvenient. Not to mention, insulting. As if I would gad about town dressed like a manservant."

He went to retrieve his jacket and hat.

"Who might be looking to stop you, sir?" Floote came over and straightened his master's lapel, checking the fit of the shoulders for good measure.

"Much good that blasted cat has done us. I thought it would provide quite the excuse for visiting Egypt. Now it's just making us easy to identify." The cat had caused quite the flutter at customs. Officials were used to dead animals being transported out of Egypt, usually of the mummy variety, but not in. Luckily for Mr. Tarabotti's aunt, gold worked regardless of country, and Mr. Tarabotti had the gold. The cat had served its purpose, until now. After all, why else would a rich Italian gentleman be travelling to Egypt during the high season of 1841?

"We must get rid of it, Floote."

Floote shifted his grip on the jar. "Shall I leave it in the street, sir?"

"Good God, no. Aunt Archangelica would never forgive me. Find someone to fix it up as she demanded, and quickly."

"Very good, sir."

SUNSET FOUND SIR Percival Phinkerlington and Miss Phinkerlington awaiting Mr. Tarabotti's presence at dinner in the hotel dining hall. Some crosses were meant to be borne during one's lifetime, Alessandro supposed. He joined them with a tight little smile, and helped himself to a glass of the mostly empty bottle of wine.

"Sandy, evening!" the baronet squawked.

Miss Phinkerlington blushed and nodded.

"Good lord, man." Mr. Tarabotti sipped the wine. It was cloyingly sweet. "Don't you own any other neck wear?"

The pleasantries disposed of, Mr. Tarabotti settled back languidly in his chair, waiting for the first course of what, he had no doubt, would be an utterly unsatisfactory meal. "What happened to old Pink?" He was only half interested. "I thought he was due for the title, not you."

Out of the corner of his eye, he caught someone watching him closely from a nearby table. He leaned his chair back on two legs, tilting his head about in an attitude of foppish boredom. The watcher was a military gentleman of some breed, stiff about the neck and long about the hair. The man noticed Mr. Tarabotti noticing him and returned to his food.

Baronet Phinkerlington frowned, troubled by the Italian's bluntness. "You didn't hear?"

"Married beneath his station, did he? Go into trade? Die?" Alessandro tut-tutted, and declined to remark that society gossip was not his focus during those few times he'd returned to England.

Miss Phinkerlington put a hand to her brother's arm. "Don't, Percy dear."

He patted her hand. "It's all right, Leticia. Sandy here's an old friend of Eustace's. Eustace always spoke highly of him. Played cricket together. Solid fellow." He leaned towards Alessandro, his breath redolent with the scent of cardamom and burnt aubergine. "Eustace tossed the title over. Gave it up to become claviger to some toothy old fluff of a lone werewolf."

"They always do take the smart ones from a family, don't they?"

"Mother was devastated but, between you and me, it's probably for the best. Wouldn't have got any grandkids out of old Eustace. If you get my meaning." The baronet waggled his eyebrows.

Mr. Tarabotti did. It also tickled his memory and explained why he'd visited the Phinkerlingtons all those years ago. Not an infiltration as it turned out, at least not an official one.

"Do I say felicitations?" Mr. Tarabotti sampled a rolled ball of some fried brown crispy substance that in appearance resembled meat and in taste resembled sawdust.

"Only if he makes it through the bite and change. You understand how it goes. Oh, silly me, you don't, do you? Poor man. Italian." The baronet shook his head sadly—demonstrating the pity of the one country that had accepted the supernatural for all the other poor ignorant countries that hadn't. Open acceptance of vampires and werewolves was the thing that kept the British Isles separate from the rest of Europe. Well, that and their cuisine.

Alessandro stroked thoughtfully at the indent above his upper lip. "Ah the English—confident in but two things."

"And what are those, Sandy my lad?"

"The supernatural and cricket."

Sir Percival laughed heartily then stuffed his face with a number of the most uninviting-looking little cakes imaginable.

"You insulting the national pastime, old chap?" he said, fortunately after he swallowed.

"Which, the supernatural or cricket?"

"Cricket, of course. You used to bowl a nicely lethal over yourself, if memory serves. Spinner, no?"

"Pace bowler."

The baronet nodded. "Ah yes, I remember Eustace crowing about how fast you were."

Alessandro raised both eyebrows at that, but didn't reply. Out of the corner of his eye, he observed the blond military man stand up from his table and make his way towards the door, moving behind and around the various chairs in the dining hall with precise little twists. He disappeared, not upstairs to his rooms as one might expect, but out into the cold night.

"Fancy a little stroll, Phinkerlington?" suggested Mr. Tarabotti, pushing his plate away petulantly.

The baronet, whose corpulence suggested he never fancied a stroll, little or otherwise, looked to his sister for salvation. She proved herself of no use whatsoever, a state evidently familiar to all around her, by saying, "Oh yes, Percy dear, do go. You know I shouldn't mind. Some of the other ladies were planning on a game of bridge in the drawing room. I shall be perfectly entertained there until your return."

Sir Percival Phinkerlington's only possible excuse thus occupied with cards, the poor chap could do nothing but join Mr. Tarabotti on his perambulation.

The hotel was situated near the northern edge of Luxor, the better to take in the view, such as it was: sand and dust on one side and the Nile on the other. They turned away from the verdant embankment, with its cultivated palm-groves, and headed towards the desert in all its burnt glory. A harvest moon hung low over two sets of limestone mountain ranges, one near and one far. Mr. Tarabotti pulled out his antikythera and confirmed his suspicions—full.

"Crikey, that darn moon's bigger than a bison's bottom."

"Very poetical turn of phrase, Sir Percival." Mr. Tarabotti put the antikythera away and searched the quiet streets. It was prayer time, so they were mostly deserted; yet he could not spot the missing military man.

They paused at the very edge of town. The baronet took out a large cigar, nipped the tip, and lit it with one of those new-fangled aetherospark distributors. "Tell you the truth, old man, we're here for Leticia's health."

"Can't she withstand the damp?"

"No, not that. Hers is a health that's not quite right about the head, if you comprehend my meaning. Ever since Eustace went over. Chit sees night crawlers everywhere and wakes up screaming. Thought we'd bring her here." He puffed on his cigar.

"Because there are no supernatural creatures in Egypt?" Mr. Tarabotti moved out of the smoke, coughing delicately. Cheap cigar.

"So they say, so they say. Like no snakes in Ireland. It's one of those things."

"True enough. There hasn't been a werewolf south of Alexandria in living memory." Alessandro thought of the papal letter of marque tucked securely in his waistcoat.

"Make a study of the supernatural, do you, Sandy?"

Mr. Tarabotti said nothing.

"Course you do. You Italians are all the same. Religious fanatics, the lot of you. Church says jump, you bounce about waving silver and wood, hoping it'll rid the world of all that goes chomp in the night."

"And yet I see acceptance of the supernatural has clearly done you and your family proud."

"Touché, touché. Fair enough. I'm not claiming to be a progressive, simply saying as how one extreme doesn't balance out the other. Far as I'm concerned, vampires and werewolves can do theirs, so long as I'm left alone to do mine. If you take my meaning." He removed the half finished cigar from his mouth and looked at the glowing tip thoughtfully.

"Would you be so magnanimous, Baronet, had you not inherited a title because your brother chose the supernatural over family obligation?"

"Now see here, that's hardly the thing to say!"

Mr. Tarabotti held up a hand sharply, cutting off any possible tirade. He cocked his dark head to one side, listening.

Far away, somewhere in the depths of a desert wadi, something howled.

"Damn this country with all its foreign beasts. I'm telling you, it's all very well for Leticia's peace of mind—not a vampire in sight—but all these snakes and camels and jackals are playing hell with my finer feelings." Phinkerlington turned away, snorting.

Alessandro frowned. The howl came again. "Werewolf."

The baronet tossed the butt-end of his cigar petulantly to the sandy ground. "That moon may be full, but don't be ridiculous, you just said, remember? There are no supernatural creatures in Egypt."

Floote was waiting for Mr. Tarabotti in their rooms.

"Message, sir." He held out a little wooden tray with two crisp pieces of papyrus on top. Scribbled on the top one was a message in Italian, the tiny, messy script bleeding in places along the lines of the fibrous paper. Alessandro deciphered it while Floote divested him of his coat and hat.

"I'm to go there tonight. He apologizes for the skittish messenger this morning. Apparently, the boy was supposed to deliver this, but was spooked by our cat. Imagine being raised amongst mummies and fearing modern scientific preservation techniques." He switched to the second sheet of papyrus. "And a map. How very thoughtful. I wonder if that's what those bully-boys were after this afternoon? This map."

Lowering his hand, he raised an eyebrow at his manservant. "Speaking of the cat."

Floote pointed to a wobbly reed dresser upon which lay a smallish cat mummy.

"Is that...?"

"Not your Aunt's feline, sir. The reports were perfectly correct; no one remembers how to mummify anymore. I found a willing apothecary, but the results were, regrettably..." a delicate pause, "...squishy. I managed to acquire that artefact, there, at a reasonable price and in excellent condition as a substitute."

Mr. Tarabotti peered at the specimen through his monocle. "It'll have to do. We'll tell Aunt Archangelica they made it look emaciated and ancient for the sake of fashion."

Floote went to hang up his master's outerwear.

"Don't bother, Floote. I'll need it again immediately."

"Sir?"

"Tonight, remember?" He wiggled the papyrus with the map on it at his valet.

"Of course, sir, but surely not the gold coat? Most inappropriate for one of your evening engagements."

"Silly me. You packed the burgundy?"

Floote gave him a look that suggested he was gravely insulted that Mr. Tarabotti should ever doubt such a thing.

The burgundy jacket was a comparatively stylish affair, but cut looser than the gold to better hide multiple pockets, and with a full skirt to mask any additional accoutrement secreted about a gentleman's waist. Alessandro slipped it on while Floote bustled about putting various items onto a large silver platter, which he then proffered politely to his master.

Mr. Tarabotti selected from the offerings, as a man will from a particularly delectable cheese plate: a nice bit of garrotte there, two vials of quality poison here, a tin of Germany's best phosphorus matches for extra zest, and a flask of turpentine to wash it all down. He chose one of the two pistols, the smallest and his personal favourite, checked that it was loaded, and stashed it inside a pocket over his left hip. After a pause to think, he took three cigars, the tidy little cheroots he preferred, and stashed them in the tin with the matches.

"Will you be requiring my company this evening, sir?"

"I shouldn't think so. After all, he is only an archaeologist."

Floote refrained from comment upon that statement. He had spent over ten years as valet to Mr. Tarabotti and, as yet, no one had turned out to be only anything. He smoothed down the sleeves of the burgundy coat and checked its armament carefully before buttoning it closed. He handed Mr. Tarabotti a matching top hat.

"Will there be anything else, sir?"

Alessandro tightened his lips over his teeth in thought. "Perhaps the other gun as well, if you would be so kind?"

Floote passed it to him. "Try not to kill anyone important, sir."

Stashing the gun up his sleeve in a special quick-release wrist holster, Alessandro grinned. It was an expression that did not sit comfortably on his patrician face.

"Any final orders, sir?"

"The usual, Floote. If I don't come back . . ."

"No record, no witnesses. I am aware of your standing instructions."

"Proceed then, Floote."

"Very good, sir."

THERE WERE MORE people in the streets when Mr. Tarabotti exited the hotel a second time. Alessandro wondered if nightlife had evolved in Egypt due to the lack of supernatural, much in the manner of peculiar animals evolving on islands without natural predators, if one were given to believe Mr. Darwin's outlandish theories. Then, again, perhaps it was simply the coolness of the air that encouraged wide-scale evening socialisation.

No one bothered him. No beggars whined for baksheesh. No tradesmen forced their goods in his direction. Alessandro Tarabotti had a way of walking that, even as a conspicuous foreigner in a foreign land, marked him as undesirable. Thus, he could move quickly through the narrow alleys that purported to be Luxor's main streets, passing whitewashed huts and undernourished obelisks, coming finally to a steep slope and sandy shore. Nearby, the three balloons were tied down, only one still inflated.

It took very little in the way of local currency or time to hire a stunted raft, piloted by a lacklustre youngster, to ferry him across the river. It took slightly more to convince the urchin to wait. At two gold coins and twenty minutes, Alessandro considered it quite economical. The boat-boy even pointed out the path he needed to take towards the tombs. Mr. Tarabotti had paid more for less in the past, and probably would again.

The map, it turned out, was not scaled as he might have hoped, and it was a long walk of some four miles before he noted any of the landmarks indicated there. He left behind the lushness of the floodplain for a long limestone canyon where little grew and less thrived. He was grateful for the moon, that he need not carry one of the ridiculous teapot-shaped oil lamps in order to see his way.

It should have been a pleasant walk, but Mr. Tarabotti, whom no one would ever insult by calling anxious, could not shake the feeling that he was being followed. Every time he jerked about and looked behind him, he saw nothing there. Nothing at all. This was compounded by another sensation, one of being repelled, as though he were a magnet too close to another of the same polarity. He'd felt it ever since Cairo but here it was worst of all, almost unbearable.

He happened upon the archaeological encampment eventually; a copse of canvas tents nestled at the base of a cliff. It appeared quite deserted, so he clambered up to the mouth of a rock-cut tomb, marked by an uninspired "x" on his little map. As he climbed, a new scent overlaid the clay musk of the cooling sands—tobacco and vanilla.

"I thought you hadn't received the message," said a voice in Italian when he reached the top. A figure resolved itself from gloom into a man by stepping forward out of the shadow of the rocks around the entranceway. Fragments of limestone crunched under sensible boots. "Trouble finding the place?"

"You sent a map. It had an 'x' on it."

The man gripped Alessandro's shoulders, kissing him on each cheek in the manner of old friends. "Giuseppe Caviglia."

"Alessandro Tarabotti." Mr. Tarabotti saw no harm in giving the archaeologist his name, though he objected to the intimacy of the rest of the greeting. "Show me what you found."

Mr. Caviglia tilted his head to one side and took a draw on his pipe. "You know I can't simply do that."

Mr. Tarabotti smiled tightly. "A rule player." He reached into his waistcoat pocket and pulled out the letter of marque, passing it over.

Giuseppe Caviglia unfolded and read it carefully by moonlight. "The government's full confidence? That must be nice."

"It has its benefits."

"You're authorised to take any action you deem necessary in conjunction with my findings here. What, exactly, does that mean?"

Alessandro ignored the question by asking one of his own. "You indicated in your original missive that this was a supernatural matter."

Mr. Caviglia nodded once, sharply.

"Well, you caught the antiquities ministry's interest. They brought your letter to government oversight, and oversight brought it to the Templars, and the Templars brought it to me."

The archaeologist sucked in on his pipe sharply at that revelation. Mr. Tarabotti waited with ill-disguised impatience while Mr. Caviglia coughed out puffs of vanilla-scented smoke.

Eyes watering, the man looked more closely at Alessandro's face. "You're one of them, aren't you? I thought they were all dead. Too susceptible to the poisonous humours."

Mr. Tarabotti, who was a bit of a poisonous humour, said sharply, "Interesting that you even know of my kind."

"My cousin is a Templar," Mr. Caviglia explained hastily.

Alessandro grimaced. That could make things difficult.

Mr. Caviglia recovered his equanimity. He handed back the letter of marque, openly evaluating his visitor's appearance. Alessandro knew what he saw: a man of lean build and patrician nose, tall, wearing a cleverly cut coat and trousers a little too tight. In short—a dandy. He would not see that the coat was cut to hide musculature, rather than exaggerate it, and that the tightness of the trousers was to distract from the smooth movements of the legs that wore them.

"You're not what I would have expected."

Alessandro cocked his head. "Well, at least one of us is surprised. You're exactly what I expected."

And the archaeologist was—unshaven, undersized, wearing round spectacles and a jacket no decent human would wish upon his worst enemy. He could be handsome under the grime, in a peevish scholarly way, but there were certain unforgivable flaws. Atop his head rested a battered object that might have started life as some species of hat many years ago and at the bottom of the ocean.

Mr. Tarabotti shuddered. "Shall we go in now?"

Mr. Caviglia nodded, tapping out his pipe on the side of the entranceway. "A remarkable discovery, really quite remarkable." He led the way inside the tomb.

Its ceiling was higher than Alessandro had anticipated. A smoking torch in the far corner cast a dim flickering light. It was as clean as could be expected from a place recently filled with rubble for thousands of years. There were few artefacts left—a broken column, several pottery bowls before an inset shrine, and a pile of digging tools nested at the base of the torch—but the walls were littered with carved and painted images. On one, a jackal-headed man sat at a vast banquet—bread, meat, and fruit laid out before him, a curly-tailed monkey crouched underneath his throne. On the other, the same man was shown undergoing various death rituals of a decidedly heathen nature.

"We found the tomb partly looted, of course. Most of them are. Oddly, the looters stopped half way through and not a single person has touched the tomb since. Until we came along." The archaeologist crossed the room, grabbed up the torch, and led the way through a carved opening into a short passageway.

Mr. Tarabotti followed.

The passage turned to the left, and before them stood a huge basalt statue of a mummy, threatening and protective.

The archaeologist ignored this, turning again and leading the way down a steep set of stairs, talking all the while.

"Once we saw the mummy we realized why. The natives are terribly superstitious about these kinds of things. Well, you would be too, if you grew up in a land entirely devoid of supernatural. I mean, our government has been trying for elimination ever since the Inquisition, but the hives and packs will keep springing up. Not here, though."

Mr. Tarabotti placed a hand against the tunnel wall to steady himself as he climbed down the dark stairs. "They're too strong and too well connected."

"Yet the Templars back home keep trying."

"They're believers." Mr. Tarabotti grimaced as his hand came away from the wall filthy with dark brown dust and a fine yellow powder.

"And you?"

Alessandro shrugged. He believed in very little beyond his job and the wealth it generated.

"Well, regardless, this excavation has been fascinating. The sarcophagus has unique hieroglyphics on it. And the mummy—excellent preservation, stunning condition, from flesh to fibre. There."

They emerged into a room slightly smaller than the first, and far less tidy. It was cluttered, with antiquities spread across the floor and nestled into niches in the painted walls. Everything was covered in a thick layer of dust and, while some artefacts had been knocked over and broken, most were intact. The preservation was amazing. Wooden furniture stood in the corners, draped in crumbling textiles with large stone statues of animal-headed gods resting on top. Pots in every shape and size lined the walls, nestled amongst crowds of tiny human statues, piles of copper weapons, and a myriad of other mundanities. In the middle of the jumble, next to the massive hole it had obviously been hauled out of, stood a large sarcophagus of red granite, its lid off and tilted against its side.

The archaeologist tugged Mr. Tarabotti over to it. Inside, a mummy lay partially unwrapped, the looters having started with its head, lusting after the precious amulets of gold and lapis tucked inside the linen bandages.

They'd stopped.

There was no doubt as to why.

"Remarkable," said Mr. Tarabotti in English.

The creature inside was human, almost, but the bones of its face were not. Teeth, jaw, shape of forehead all leaned more towards canine than man. There was even a light patterning of hair in the shrunken wrinkles of the dried brown skin.

"A werewolf."

"Undoubtedly."

"Mummified in half homo sapien, half homo lupis form." Alessandro pulled a small analogue aetheromechanical transducer from his jacket pocket and prodded delicately at the mummy, testing for remnant vital aetheromagnetism. Nothing. "They say alpha werewolves can maintain just such a state as this, half in, half out of human form. They use it in metamorphosis rituals. Can you imagine?" His fine upper lip curled. "Disgusting."

He investigated further. "Well, I commend you, Mr. Caviglia. If this is a hoax, it is a very good one."

The archaeologist puffed up in outrage. "I assure you, sir—!"

Mr. Tarabotti held up the transducer autocratically to stop any denunciation and continued examining the body. "Don't you think that head shape is a little odd?"

"Aside from it being attached to a human body?"

"We call it Anubis form," said a new voice in old-fashioned Italian flattened out by a British accent.

Out of the staircase entrance came the gleaming muzzle of a nasty double-barrelled pistol followed by a blond military-looking gentleman.

"Hello, Curse-breaker," he said to Mr. Tarabotti in English, gun steady.

"You were at dinner earlier this evening." Alessandro switched to the Queen's tongue, out of courtesy for their visitor, at the same time releasing his gun out of its wrist holster. The movement was so subtle as to be imperceptible. The gun slid down toward his hand, almost peeking out of the bottom of one burgundy sleeve.

The man nodded. "I followed you from the hotel. As you inconvenienced me by not allowing my agents to steal the map from you."

Mr. Caviglia raised both hands and straightened away from the sarcophagus. His eyes were fixed on the intruder's weapon.

Mr. Tarabotti sniffed. "I knew someone was following me. How did I miss you?"

"You never looked up." The man had a soldier's bearing and a young face, but his eyes were dulled by past lives.

"I'm too old to remember humans have taken to the skies." Alessandro shook his head at himself.

"You're a werewolf," accused the archaeologist, with more power of deduction than Alessandro would have given him credit for.

The man snorted. "Not here, I'm bloody well not." He glared at Mr. Tarabotti as though this fact were somehow his fault. "I hope you know what a bother it has been, travelling through Egypt after you these weeks. I had to learn to shave again, and every little cut takes donkey's years to heal. I don't know how you mortals do it. I really don't. I hope you appreciate the risk I'm taking."

Alessandro licked his lips. This was going to be fun. "Oh, I appreciate it."

The un-werewolf narrowed his eyes. "Don't you move." He glanced briefly at the archaeologist. "Is it true what you found? What he said? Is that there a mummy of a werewolf in Anubis form?"

"See for yourself," suggested Mr. Tarabotti, hoping the un-werewolf would come within striking distance.

The un-werewolf didn't take the bait, too old for that. "We used to rule this land. Did you know that?"

Mr. Caviglia gave a little snort of disbelief.

"You archaeologists haven't figured that one out yet, have you? They worshipped us as gods. Turned sour on us in the end. Most things do. The god-breaker plague swept the Two Lands and, within a generation, every werewolf had died. We've not been back since because this," he gestured to himself, "is what results."

"Mortality."

"And why would you risk everything to follow me here?"

The un-werewolf looked at Mr. Tarabotti. "Curse-breaker, this mummy is our ancestor. You daylighters," and he included the archaeologist in his contemptuous statement, "have no right. Especially not some crusading religious fanatics. That mummy is the property of the British Government, we have the concession, not the Italians. Ours to study and understand."

Mr. Tarabotti smiled his tight little smile. "Who said we wanted to study it?"

The archaeologist and the un-werewolf both looked to him in shock.

"But the Templars promised."

Mr. Tarabotti shrugged. "The Templars lied. And we can't very well have the English using it as some kind of pro-supernatural propaganda tool."

No record and no witnesses.

He slid the derringer smoothly the rest of the way out of his sleeve and into his hand, turned slightly in the same movement, and shot Mr. Caviglia in the chest at point blank range. The archaeologist fell with a tiny cry of surprise and lay still against the corner of the sarcophagus, slumped and limp.

"We can't allow you to go babbling about this to the antiquarian community either, I'm afraid." He looked thoughtfully down at the scholar's dead body. "Pity."

The un-werewolf started, but his gun remained trained on Mr. Tarabotti.

Alessandro tucked the now-useless pistol into his pocket casually, feeling about for his second one, and narrowed his eyes at the man.

"What it must be like, seeing that," he tilted his head at the fallen archaeologist, "and knowing you could so easily end up the same way."

"Do you really think, after hundreds of years, we immortals fear death?"

"Do the crazy ones, who have lived too long, travel to Egypt to die voluntarily?"

The un-werewolf shrugged. "Some."

"So, we find ourselves at an impasse."

"Mmm, please take your hand out of your jacket, Curse-breaker."

Mr. Tarabotti did so, tucking his second tiny gun up the end of his other sleeve in a manoeuvre he'd once learned from a street performer.

The un-werewolf gestured with his pistol for Mr. Tarabotti to move away from the mummy and towards the door. Cautiously, Alessandro did so. But, near to the entrance, as he passed close to his opponent, he pretended to stumble over a fallen urn, lurching violently to one side.

The un-werewolf growled at him and stepped threateningly forward.

Alessandro dove, shifting his weight and lashing up and out with his foot, striking the man's wrist where it held the gun.

The double barrel discharged a bullet, missing Mr. Tarabotti by a foot, the slug ploughing hard into a support column, spitting limestone shards at both men. The un-werewolf swore and rotated the chamber to load his second shot.

Alessandro rolled, as much as he could, over the small statues and artefacts littering the floor, coming into a crouch covered in thousands of years of dust but with his second gun clutched in his hand.

He fired, hitting the un-werewolf in the shoulder. The shot wasn't deadly, but it did cause the man to drop his own gun in surprise.

Mr. Tarabotti lunged for the fallen weapon at the same time as the un-werewolf, and the two of them scrabbled through the ancient offerings. Alessandro struck out viciously at his opponent, connecting where the shoulder wound seeped old blood, groping for the fallen gun with his other hand.

The un-werewolf backhanded Mr. Tarabotti, handicapped with only one working arm, and that odd British distaste for kicking in a fight.

Mr. Tarabotti had no such compunctions. Crawling as they both were after the fallen weapon, Alessandro kicked out with one foot and managed to shove the man over. Grabbing the gun, he came up triumphant, pointing the weapon at the un-werewolf, who now crouched amongst the wreckage looking as savage as he might have in his lupine state.

Mr. Tarabotti shot the last bullet. But the man was fast, even without supernatural speed, and managed to dodge. Frustrated, Alessandro threw the gun petulantly aside and pulled the flask of turpentine from his jacket.

He scattered it liberally about, making sure to coat the mummy in particular.

The un-werewolf lunged for him, seizing him by the waist and hurling him back to the floor. Mr. Tarabotti pushed against the man's chin, trying to wrench his neck. His opponent howled, an animalistic sound coming from such a human face.

"That was you howling earlier this evening?" Mr. Tarabotti panted out the question, clawing at the creature's eyes.

"Staying in practice, even if I can't change," came the hissed reply, as the un-werewolf struggled to hold Alessandro in a one-armed grip.

"That's rather perverse, you know that?" Mr. Tarabotti uppercut sharply with the palm of one hand, achieving just enough leverage to break the un-werewolf's nose.

Alessandro squirmed away. Coming panting to his feet, he brushed off his burgundy coat with fierce disgusted movements. "Is such dusty combat strictly necessary?"

The un-werewolf only bled at him.

Feeling deeply put upon, Mr. Tarabotti reached once more inside his jacket, pulling out the tin of phosphorus matches. He backed away until he was at the doorway. There, he struck a match and threw it at the turpentine-covered mummy.

Seeing this action, the un-werewolf decided on self-preservation and charged past him up the steps.

The flammable liquid caught easily, the fire quickly spreading to burn away happily at the wooden furniture and textiles scattered about. From the amount of smoke and flames flaring up from within the sarcophagus, Alessandro had no doubt the mummy was ablaze as well. He whirled and ran up the stairs and out of the tomb, coughing delicately.

Outside, things were not as they should be. The un-werewolf was getting away, dangling precariously off the edge of the gondola of a hot-air balloon, floating upwards. A tubby sort of personage was manning the balloon's thermo-transmitter and cranking up the hydrodine engine to get a steering propeller moving —a familiar tubby sort of personage, wearing a long scarf wrapped about his throat.

"Why, Sir Percival. I see you do own more than one item of neck wear."

"What ho, Mr. Tarabotti? Sad business, this. I did so hope it wasn't you."

"Working for the Crown, are we, Phlinkerlington? How menial."

"For the Glory of the Empire, Mr. Tarabotti. Can't expect a Templar's toady to understand, now can I?" As he spoke, the baronet succeeded in getting the propeller in motion, and then waddled over to assist the un-werewolf in flopping, fishlike, into the safety of the gondola.

The balloon began to rise upwards, its propeller whirling mighty gusts of steam. Soon it would be at sufficient height to set a steady course back to Luxor.

Alessandro flicked the air with the back of his hand, gesturing the men away as if they were mere irritations that had been bothering his evening's stroll.

No record and no witnesses.

He searched around his feet for a sharp fragment of limestone. The blaze from the lower part of the tomb had extended into the open room at the top. It lit the ridge-side on which he stood with flickering orange. It seemed the dust, itself, was flammable, and fresh air only encouraged the conflagration. He could hear the faint "poof" sound of limestone spalling in the heat.

He found a rock of adequate size. There was enough room on the hillside for him to run up his speed. Not exactly the perfect cricket pitch, but, then, one couldn't be too picky about such things. Mr. Tarabotti may have been born Italian, but he had bowled for New College, and been widely regarded as one of the fastest on record. The stone hit the balloon perfectly, tearing through the oiled canvas right above the engine feed, with immediate and catastrophic results.

The hot gas leaked out, deflating the balloon from one side and causing the whole contraption to list dramatically. The un-werewolf let out a howl of mixed anger and distress and Sir Percival swore, but there was nothing either man could do to salvage the situation. Moments later the balloon burst into flames, falling to the ground with a thudding crash.

Mr. Tarabotti paused to light a cheroot with one of his remaining phosphorus matches and then walked towards the wreckage.

Both men were lying face down in the sand. Mr. Tarabotti turned the un-werewolf over with his foot, puffing softly. Definitely dead. Then he heard a small moan.

"Still alive, Phinkerlington?" He pulled out his garrotte and tossed the end of the cheroot away.

No record and no witnesses.

The fallen baronet turned his head weakly and looked at Mr. Tarabotti.

"Looking less and less likely, Sandy my man," he croaked. "Nice bowl, by-the-by, perfectly aimed and you even got a bit of spin on it."

"I do what I can." Alessandro crouched over the fallen man and reached forward with the garrotte.

The baronet coughed, blood leaked out the side of his mouth. "No need, Sandy old chap, no need. Do me a bit of a turn, would you? For old Eustace's sake, if not mine."

Mr. Tarabotti sat back on his heels, surprised.

"See Leticia safely home to England, would you? Doesn't know a thing about this business, I assure you. She's only a slip of a thing, good chit, really, can't have her wandering about Egypt on her lonesome. You understand?"

Mr. Tarabotti considered. He'd have had to investigate the girl anyway. This gave him a good excuse to find out what she knew. He'd be terribly, terribly understanding and sympathetic. Tragic accident in the desert. What were they thinking, floating at night? He'd been out for a stroll and saw the balloon fall from afar. Dashed to the rescue but wasn't in time to save anyone. Old friend of the family, of course he'd be happy to escort her home.

Percival Phinkerlington's watery eyes bored into him. Alessandro pursed his lips and nodded curtly. The baronet sighed, closing his eyes. The sigh turned into a wet rattling gurgle, and then silence.

Alessandro Tarabotti lit another small cheroot off the burning balloon basket. What would he put in his report to the Templars? Such an incommodious bit of business. A dead un-werewolf was one thing, but a dead British aristocrat? He sighed, puffing out smoke. They'd not be pleased. Not pleased at all. And the mummy. Did his superiors need to know the truth of the mummy? For the truth was, that was no wolf's head at all. Alessandro Tarabotti had killed enough werewolves to know the difference, emaciated or fully fleshed. No, it had been far more dog-like, small, pointed. A jackal, perhaps?

He smoked his cigar. On the walls of that burning tomb, the jackal-headed god, Anubis, had been depicted assisting a jackal-headed man into the afterlife.

Werejackals? Surely not.

Alessandro snorted. But some twinge of fancy reminded him of the un-werewolf's words. They worshipped us as gods. And Ancient Egyptian gods had other animal heads. Lots of other animal heads. No wonder the Templars wanted to keep such information out of British hands.

Mr. Tarabotti turned to commence his long walk back to Luxor. Baronet Phinkerlington might be dead, but Alessandro had to escort Miss Phinkerlington back to England and deal with a mess of paperwork as a result. He wondered which one of them had got the better deal out of the arrangement. Probably Phinkerlington.

The Angel of Khan el-Khalili

If you want to find the Angel of Khan el-Khalili you have to make your way to the market at night. Not when the sun goes down, and Cairo's masses spill out into the opening shops, where soot smudged factory workers and well-groomed ministerial clerks mingle at open air coffeehouses to debate local politics. Not even after the first stars have appeared and, beneath the glare of gaslight, hawkers practice their best chat up lines to seduce idle wanderers to their stalls—where everything from counterfeit medieval antiques to drive shafts for automated wheel carriages are up for sale. No, to find the Angel of Khan el-Khalili means going to the market late at night, when most of the city have long retired to their beds, leaving the souk to the curious, the adventurous, and the desperate—like you.

For Aisha, you remind yourself. This is for Aisha.

You pass beneath one of the many stone arches that line the night bazar, and turn down the street of the chai-sellers, where young strapping men shoulder high-pressure steam urns and pour fragrant tea for their patrons into delicate porcelain cups. You pass through the shop of a gas lamp merchant, whose oval glass lanterns swirl with luminous alchemical vapors that cause them to float about like colorful airborne jellyfish. Exit through the back and you come out at a rounded yellow door divided into half-moons: the shop of the boiler eunuch mender. He is an unusually tall man, with thick set shoulders that seem unsuited to the gangly body you imagine lies beneath his sky-blue jellabiya. By his dark skin and the carpet of white whiskers creeping along his face, you guess he's Soudanese. Or perhaps simply Nubian. You can't tell.

He ignores your first words of greeting as you stand at the threshold of his shop, watching him use a hammer to beat a dented breastplate into shape. Perhaps it's because of who he thinks you are—a woman out alone at this time of night, unaccompanied by neither a husband or relative. If he could see behind your headscarf and white cotton veil, to the face of a girl barely fifteen, he would know it is worse than that. So, you stand up straighter, fighting the urge to draw the light black wrap more firmly about you or smooth down your green fringed dress, and speak with the authority you've seen used by some of the other girls at the dress factory. You think of your friend Zehra, the Turkish girl who's always going on about the exploitation of the masses and how we need to turn the tables on "the bosses."

Something in your tone catches his attention. Or maybe he's simply resting his hands. But the boiler eunuch mender finally stops his work long enough to fix you appraisingly with one eye—the other is hidden behind a silver tubular lens.

"Looking for a boilerplate eunuch?" he asks in a deep baritone that rumbles up from his chest. From the south or no, the accent is pure Cairene. "We have many to choose from, each no worse for the wear. In these modern times, every home in Cairo should enjoy the convenience of a boilerplate eunuch." His arms gesture about the room, where faceless metal automatons shaped in the likeness of men stand motionless: reminiscent of soldiers awaiting inspection—or corpses arrayed in their tomb. They are of decent quality, even if refurbished from older models and mismatched parts. But that's not why you've come.

"I'm here to see the Lady of the House, Usta," you say instead.

The boiler eunuch mender continues to stare at you in that appraising way. Sifting and weighing. "What is your name, daughter?" he asks at last.

Beneath your veil, you feel the heat rise in your cheeks. So, you hadn't fooled him then. You think of lying, but that measuring stare says he will see it right away. Besides, Aisha often warned that lying was one of the greater sins.

"Aliaa," you answer, careful not to give your full name. Cairo is a big city, but a family name could tell him everything he needs to know about you. His white eyebrows furrow at your evasion, but he only says: "The Lady of the House exacts a price. You are prepared to pay it?"

You respond with a stiff nod.

More weighing. More sifting. Finally, he stands up from his stool. Did you think this man was unusually tall? No, he is freakishly so, with arms that dangle to his thighs! He leads you past his silent creations, to a door at the back of his shop. It is made of weathered brown wood, like the ones you've seen in photos adorning temples in Luxor. You've dreamt of taking a tram line or airship to visit them one day, and seeing if they whisper with the voices of long dead infidels as many say. He produces a golden key from a leather apron at his waist, and fits it into a rectangular slot, pulling the door open. There are a set of stairs that lead down, illuminated by glowing lamps along the walls.

The boiler eunuch mender does not accompany you, but you offer him a little baksheesh for his troubles; it's only polite. As the door closes behind you, your mind wanders to stories of unfortunate servants, sealed alive in the tombs of ancient despots too selfish to make their own lonely journey into death. You are surprised at how long it takes to reach the bottom, and you wonder how this space came to be. Did the boiler eunuch mender dig it out himself? Perhaps his automatons did: the last slaves of Egypt destined to toil without respite. Or, more probably, as so much of Cairo, and the Khan in particular, this has always been here: built by some Fatimid caliph or Mamluk overlord for a long forgotten purpose.

Whatever the case, it now houses a different occupant.

The Angel of Khan el-Khalili is a towering giant. Even bowed as she is, her head near brushes the ceiling. Her body is wrought of iron and brass: a living statue in the form of a lithe woman constructed of clockwork machinery that hums and moves to its own metronomic rhythm. Shimmering silver wings lay folded on her back, a bundle of metallic feathers inscribed in turquoise script that shifts and writhes before your eyes. She sits amid a bed of brocaded cushions on a mammoth moss green divan, chin propped upon a fist in a thinker's repose. A draping skirt of gold conceals her legs and feet, falling in cascades to flow upon the ground below. You crane your neck to gape up at her, too taken at first to speak, and lost in her terrible beauty.

Angels arrived in Cairo some forty years past. Your parents had been children then, but they still tell you stories of al-Jahiz—the disappeared Soudanese mystic, scientist, madman—whose fantastic machines had sent magic pouring into the world with the force of an unstoppered sea. Djinn had been the first to appear, and were in many ways responsible for the great innovations of this age. Their kind you are accustomed to: creatures of flesh and blood, elements of wind and water (or whatever came from smokeless fire) who walk, live, work and interact among humans. Your family's apartment sits above the confectionery of an elderly onager-headed Sila. She's friendly enough, for a djinn, and hands out pink candy dolls to neighborhood children every Mawlid for as long as you can remember.

But angels are another matter. They are rarer things, ethereal beings who shroud their bodies behind contraptions of mechanical grandeur and hold themselves apart from mortals and djinn alike. None, not even the religious bodies of Cairo, have been able to discern the reason for their coming. And they have remained equally enigmatic. Some have taken up residence in old palaces and ruins. There are several, you have heard, who now occupy the Citadel outside the mosque of Muhammad Ali. Why this one has decided to shelter in a cellar beneath the Khan would probably befuddle the most learned scholar of the Ulama. All you know is that she calls herself Seeker.

They are not angels. All angels are in Heaven with God.

Aisha's admonishing voice comes to you even now. She could argue this subject at length, quoting from books you've never even heard about. She would explain that angels have no free will and so could not come among mortals of their own choosing. You don't understand it all yourself. But you try to remember as much and push away the awe that traps your tongue. At least some of it.

"The night's peace be with you, Lady of the House," you call up in greeting.

At your words, the angel's bowed head lifts up as if from slumber—though you doubt such beings can possibly be bothered with mere mundanities like sleep. You find yourself staring at a midnight blue mask glittering with flecks of gold. Brilliant light shines from crescent spaces where eyes should be, above a slight nose and full lips pursed in contemplation. The sound of working cogs accompanies four metal arms that unfold and spread out. Their palms open in greeting, as from beneath that fixed countenance comes a melodious and matronly, "Peace be with you, and welcome daughter."

That voice is more than you expect. Not at all like a machine, but decidedly real. More than real even. Aisha once bought you a doll that could say "mama" and "baba," and whose eyes rocked open and close. This is like that, only now you imagine the doll as a giant and you as its plaything. Somehow you keep your legs steady, and find the ability to speak again.

"I've come before you, Seeker, hoping to gain your wisdom." You remember to add, "If you'll grant it to me."

She studies you for a moment then replies: "Many claim to seek my wisdom. But in truth, it is my favors they hope to attain." Her tone is not harsh or even scolding. Still, you feel your face heat again. It is not a comfortable thing to hear that you are transparent. But you believe that gaze could strip any soul bare. "Forgive me Seeker," you try again. "I mean to say; I've come to ask a favor."

The angel tilts her head slightly, reminding you of a contemplative bird. "A favor asked by one so young? Are you certain, daughter, you would not prefer to inquire after a djinn? They deal as well in favors, with their wishes." That last word is said with a crisp distaste. "Perhaps you hope to catch the eye of a sweetheart? Or for great beauty? An assurance of a future with a well-to-do husband? Such mortal trivialities are more their domain, than mine."

You cannot help the frown that captures your face. A sweetheart? Beauty? A husband? Working girls your age dream of money enough to attend a university. Or the skills to pass a civil engineer job that might lift you out of the doldrums of factory work. The year is 1912, not 1812!

"I haven't come for a wish," you state adamantly. Wishes are risky business anyway—undependable and unpredictable. Never can tell what end of the bargain you'll come out on when dealing with djinn. You hesitate, but bring yourself to say it: "I've come looking for a miracle."

At this, Seeker straightens, so that a bit of light glints from one perfectly formed silver breast. "A miracle," she repeats. There is a savoring of the word. "Quite a favor to ask. You understand that such things come with a price."

You nod. This is Cairo after all. Everything comes with a price. You reach into the pockets of your dress and a draw out a bundle of folded notes. The money is all you've been able to save away, at least nine-months pay. There are dreams you have for this small fortune, all lost now. But you offer it forward, praying it's enough. Your heart falls as Seeker shakes her head.

"Such things are meaningless to me child," the angel chides. "What use have I for your mortal trifles?" You pull your hand back, feeling somewhat foolish. Of course. How could you expect that something as grand as a miracle could be bought with money? "I shall set the price of any favor to be granted," Seeker pronounces. "You accept this?"

"What will the price be?" you ask warily.

"That is for me to decide. Do you accept?"

"But how will I know that I can pay it?"

"All debts owed shall be paid," she states assuredly. "Do you accept? I shall not ask thrice."

Thrice? Who still talks like that? A dozen more pertinent questions sit poised on your tongue. Something about this feels even more precarious than dealing with djinn. But her words ring with a tone of finality. She will dismiss you as easily as a stray thought if you don't give answer. Of this you are certain. And you've come too far to turn back now.

"I accept," you say, and wait for something momentous to happen, some feeling seared across your soul of an unbreakable holy compact. But there is nothing of the sort.

Instead, the angel says simply: "Tell me then daughter, what is this miracle you seek?"

You let out a breath you don't remember holding. "I want you to save my sister Aisha. She's dying."

The words bring a flood of memories.

Aisha had worked at the dress factory years before you began. True enough she'd still hoped to go off to university, to study from all those books she liked quoting. Maybe she would become a historian. Or a barrister. There were women barristers now. There was always alchemy. But your family couldn't afford such things. So, she remained at the factory and tried to hold onto her dreams.

It was Aisha who'd gotten you your job when you came of age. Ever the doting big sister, she showed you how to work the loom machines without injuring your fingers. And helped you sew enough dresses to meet the demand of the floor bosses. The work was hard and long, with little breaks, sometimes for a whole half a day. But Aisha taught you how to push through it, to hum songs that made the tedious labor pass. How to keep it from your mind so you could sleep and start again the next morning.

She was something of a leader at the factory: looking out for those who couldn't work as fast, making certain everyone worked collectively to meet quotas. She'd convince others to cover the work of women who fell ill or who had to nurse sick children. She stood up for all of you, demanding things like safer machinery and threatening to stop work if someone was fired unjustly. She'd even begun talk about forming a union.

Until the fire.

Women would have died if not for Aisha. The fire that tore through the dress factory might have killed everyone in there, if she hadn't gone back into the flames. She dragged women out, one at a time, braving the worst of the blaze. You remember her carrying you to safety, your lungs filled with smoke and legs unable to stand. You'd looked up through stinging eyes to see her brown skin blistered and cracked. And her long black hair almost all singed away.

Aisha is a hero people say. A hero who now lays in a hospice bed dying. In a world of djinn and sorcery, your sister is dying. From something as ordinary and commonplace as a fire. The doctor who tended her claimed her injuries were beyond even what could be healed in this age of wonders. It would take a miracle, he'd said gravely. So, you came looking for one.

The angel listens in quiet as you relate all this, her radiant eyes unwavering and masked face as set as stone. When you finish she merely asks, "Why you?" Reading your confusion, she asks again. "Why have *you* come to me? Why has a girl, barely a woman, been set on this task?"

"Because no one else would," you answer plainly. What you do now is considered forbidden by many. Even your parents, who are not overly pious people, would balk. The angel stares down at you for a long moment before speaking.

"Do you know why I am called Seeker?" she asks.

You shake your head. Angels kept their true names secret, offering up only titles.

"I search for truth," she explains. "I seek it out. This is my purpose. The reason of my creation." You have little time to digest that before she continues. "You will be given three chances to give me what I seek. Do so to my satisfaction, and I will grant your miracle. This is the price I set."

You frown at that. Three chances? "You want me to tell you something...true?"

"A truth," she clarifies. "From the depths of your soul. Something hidden."

"You mean a secret?"

"More than that."

You dwell on that momentarily. When is a hidden truth more than a secret?

"A confession," you realize aloud.

Seeker gives a deep nod. "Those are the truths we hide most deeply," she states.

A confession? You have heard that Copts do such things, to their priests you believe. But you've never heard of anyone confessing to an angel. It is a strange request.

"How will I know if I'm giving you the right truth?" you ask.

"You will know," Seeker replies.

Nodding, you turn inward. A truth from the depths of your soul. Could this possibly be as easy as it sounds? Rummaging through your thoughts, you arrive at something. Perhaps it will be enough. At the least, it can be a test. You clear your throat.

"My first truth," you say. "I lied to my family to come here." Seeker receives this in silence. You continue. "They're all at the hospice, with Aisha. I told them I was going to stay with friends tonight. Instead, I came here." You feel a bit embarrassed at the admission. It is one thing to know it in your head, but another to speak aloud. "I'll likely have to lie to them again when I—"

Your words cut short as Seeker rears up abruptly. You watch, startled, as the breastplate covering her chest begins to move—sliding apart like pieces of a puzzle. Beneath it, nestled among a viscera of gears, is a circle of machinery: a spinning vortex of iron with teeth like an ever-moving mouth. From the center of that maw there is light, blinding and roiling like a violent sea. You step back, ready to cry out when something seizes you.

It is as if unseen hands have latched onto every part of you—limbs and bone, flesh and muscle, blood and nerves. Their fingers dig deep, pulling at you, prying loose some inner part of your being and wrenching it free from its mooring. The pain of that sudden severance consumes the whole of you, and it is while before you realize the shrieks filling your ears are your own. In your mind, you know it lasts only minutes, but it feels much longer. When the pain finally, mercifully, stops you fall to the stone floor, panting for breath. You blink up at Seeker who tilts her head curiously.

"An interesting offering," she murmurs.

"What?" you manage, trembling. "What did you do to me?"

"You gave me your truth," she answers in an obvious tone. "I accepted it in my embrace."

You stare dumbfounded. Her embrace. Those unseen hands no longer hold you, but a shade of their touch remains. "You didn't tell me it would be like that!"

"Confession is always painful," the angel states.

You glare, anger breaking through the hurt as you struggle to sit up. Your gaze goes to the rotating vortex set within the angel's exposed chest. "What is that thing?"

Seeker looks down, her metal fingers tracing along the rounded edges. "A construct of my own design. A more perfect way for my embrace to extract truth."

Extract. There is a feeling alongside the lingering pain. A sense of emptiness and loss. You remember something leaving you and you shudder. "What did… you take from me?" you whisper.

"Only a bit of your soul," Seeker replies. "Why do you look so? Truth, after all, resides in the soul."

You clutch at your breast, as if you can retrieve what you've lost. What was stolen! "That's not what we agreed!" you charge.

"It is everything we have agreed," the angel maintains. Her words have the hardness and care of stone. "And you have not yet met our bargain. That truth was by no means sufficient. Mortal lies are, after all, common. You have two chances still. Take care not to squander them."

Your eyes dart to the stairs. You can bolt from here. Flee the Khan and the bizarre bargain you've made with this callous creature. *But what about Aisha? You owe her this.* Squeezing your eyes shut, you whisper a prayer for strength before opening them again. It is an effort to rise to your feet. When you settle your stare on the angel you find her looking back, those bright eyes expectant.

You search your thoughts a second time, for a truth. It will have to be greater than the last. Something more than a lie. Something you wouldn't want known by anyone. A true confession. "I've stolen," you blurt out. That one truly fills you with shame. "From the factory. Some of the women know a man, who trades in the dresses we make. He pays half a week's salary for every bundle. I stole dresses for over four months and sold them to make money." You'd only stopped when Aisha grew suspicious. If she'd ever found out, you didn't think you'd be able to face the disappointment in her eyes. "I know it was wrong—"

The pain that comes is no less, for all that you have braced for it. There is that feeling again of being caught up by invisible hands, and something being torn out of you, stripped clean like meat from the bone. When it passes, you stumble up to your knees, fighting the urge not to empty your stomach. Your eyes wander back to Seeker. You find the angel staring down at you, that set face devoid of pleasure or pity.

"Not enough," she pronounces. "You have not yet met our bargain."

Your tortured body sags under the weight of that judgment. "I've given you all that I can," you breathe.

"No," the angel counters. "You have not. I seek truth, that which is hidden in the deepest recesses of the soul. Yet you have scarcely plumbed those depths. Instead you throw up what dross you skim from the surface. Lies and theft." There is derision in her voice. "You think I am impressed with the banalities of mortal existence? You think this is enough to win my favor?"

"What do you want?" It is a question wrapped in frustration.

"More," the angel demands.

You glare up in exasperation that fast blooms into anger. "I don't have more! I've given you all I can!"

Seeker surges forward then, bending down so low that her head comes only an arm's span from your own. The dazzling light behind those crescent eyes bathes you in their brilliance. You put a hand to your face, a feeble shield against that glare.

"I am Seeker," the angel declares, her voice thundering. "I search for truth. I am drawn to it. Do you think your small mortal soul can conceal itself from me? Do you think I cannot see what you keep secreted in its innermost chambers?"

A coldness forms like a dark pit in your stomach. "I don't know what—"

Seeker lets out a sharp hiss, cutting off your words with the ease of a blade slicing through poorly stitched cloth. "Do not lie to me." Each word bears a warning edge. "A girl, barely a woman, sets out to find me. To make a bargain for her dying sister. To ask for nothing less than a miracle. Why you?"

"Because no one else would," you stammer, that cold dark pit growing ever larger.

"A lie," Seeker pronounces. "Even if wrapped in the skin of truth, a lie all the same. I ask again, why you?"

Your eyes cast downward unable to meet the angel's scouring scrutiny. You fix on your hands and find them clenched so tight the nails bite into your palm. They are shaking. And the cold pit has grown to swallow every part of you, until your entire body trembles. The tip of a metal finger touches beneath your chin, gently tilting your head back up. The surface of Seeker's midnight blue mask is somehow reflective, and there you catch glimpse of your face—eyes seeping tears that glide down to coat your veil.

"Give me what I seek," the angel whispers—her voice now turned into a caress and a nudge. "Speak your truth. Allow my embrace."

The first words are hardest. "I started the fire." The rest rush out in a torrent.

Work at the factory has never been fair. You labor endlessly, for wages that are pittance at best. Because you are women, the company pays all of you less. And if you are younger, less still. The machines are dangerous. You've seen women scalded by ruptured steam valves or lacerated by weaving looms. The floor bosses don't care. The company demands they meet quotas and the lot of them wring every last bit of sweat and blood from each of you.

Aisha talked of creating a union, and asking for greater rights. But it was Zehra, the Turkish girl, who you thought had the right of it. The company was a machine, she often said, and it would ground all of you to bits if it wasn't stopped.

The idea to smash some of those machines was as much your idea as it was hers. You'd bring it all to a halt. The company would be forced to come to you, the workers who produced their wealth. And from a place of power, you'd make your bargains. The other women were sure to rise up if given that spark. You were convinced even Aisha would see the sense of it.

Only nothing had gone as planned.

The alchemical solution the two of you had cooked up was meant to melt through the gears of the loom machines. It wasn't supposed to catch fire, creating bright red flames that only spread the more you threw water on them. As you tried to flee, how could you know the floor bosses had locked the doors in the factory that day? They said later to the papers it was to protect against theft. But it was just another way to keep all of you churning out their damn quotas. That day, their greed and your rashness almost proved deadly. You can still hear the screams of the other women, banging on bolted doors that wouldn't open. You can still smell the smoke and the fire amid their fear. You can still hear your own screams.

The pain this final time is searing: those invisible fingers white-hot knives reaching into the heart of you, diving deep to draw out what you've tried to hide away. It feels as if you are being stretched within, almost to the point of tearing. You curl around that pain. You cling to it. And for a moment that seems a lifetime it is your entire world, blotting out your vision and leaving you in darkness. When your eyes flutter open again, your cheek is flush with the floor as you babble the same words in repetition. "I'm sorry Aisha. I'm sorry. I'll make it right. I'll make it right."

Slowly, you push yourself to a position of half-lying and half-sitting. You look up to find Seeker once more straight. Her breastplate is slowly closing, hiding that frightful machine mouth away. There is nothing to be revealed in the placid countenance of that carved mask. But when she speaks there is a tremor in her voice that can only be described as—satisfaction.

"You mortals are such frail things. Motes floating among more worlds than you can possibly imagine. Yet your souls hold the weight of stars. If you only knew..." She trails off, as if having spoken too much.

Angels and their secrets, you think scornfully. But you have no care for any of that. With gritted teeth, and more than some effort, you come to standing. Not steady, but at least standing. "Have I met our bargain?" you ask tightly, wiping your dampness from your face.

Seeker tilts her head in that contemplative way. "You are angered." She says the words with genuine surprise. "Are you not made glad in your confession? Is your soul not unburdened by speaking this truth? Atonement is painful, but are you not rendered the better for it?"

You stare at her in amazement. Does she think she's done you some courtesy?

"Atonement," you answer, "is gained through asking for forgiveness. And I pray for it every day. You can't give me that. Pain isn't absolution. Whatever you think you've taken from me, you haven't unburdened me of anything." You pause, willing yourself calm before starting again. "What I've come here for is restitution. Now, have I met our bargain?"

Seeker is silent for a moment, and you wonder what is going through that indecipherable mind. In your chest, your heart is pounding, but you meet that bright stare with head held high. And wait.

"Our bargain is met," she proclaims at last. The breath you release feels as if it comes from every part of you. The angel appears to pluck something from her lips. When her hand lowers to you it opens in offering. You take what she holds. A stone. Dull brown and unassuming, it is small enough to fit in your palm. You turn it over, running your fingers along its uneven smooth surface.

"A bezoar," Seeker explains. "Ground it to a fine powder for your sister to ingest."

"This will save Aisha?" you ask uncertainly. "This will heal her?"

"She will make a swift recovery," the angel replies. "Even her burns. Some might even call it, miraculous."

You glance up from the stone. Had that been a joke? But Seeker is already returning to her earlier repose.

"Farewell then daughter," she says in parting. "If ever you find your soul in need of unburdening, I might gladly welcome…savoring…your essence again." With that, she bows her head, propping her chin upon a closed fist and is once more still—all to be heard that peculiar metronomic rhythm.

"Not likely," you whisper. Turning your back on the Angel of Khan-el-Khalili (or whatever they are) you make your way up the stairs and back to the boiler eunuch mender's shop, taking Aisha's miracle—and your burdens—with you.

Mock the Midnight Bell

Act One

THIS IS A Robin Hood story. And also, it isn't. This is a story about taking things back; about the Bastet Gang and the twelve heists attributed to them by the international media. This is a story about names; after a small French-language regional paper in Shropshire made the connection between cat burglars and Egyptian goddesses and got it to stick, after a squalling baby was dropped off outside a Manchester orphanage, after two people called themselves cousins without a drop of shared blood between them. This is a revenge story, sticking to the back of your teeth like an old cough drop, getting under your skin like that newsprint ink, turning everything to murk and pea-souper and ambiguity. This is a story about the Bastet Gang, active from roughly August 1920 for eighteen months until they abruptly stopped and never resurfaced. This is about Tolerance and Understanding and a last unholy trinity who sent them on their way. This isn't a Robin Hood story, because at the end of it they called Robin a hero. At the end of it, Robin was praised by a lionhearted King, although it is said that Richard was named Lionheart not for his deeds, but his love for a nobleman. *Lyons-coeur.* That's French. But historians buried that. Academia is selective about what it brings up from the dirt and what it drops back down into an early grave. It's all in the telling, this story. It's all in the forgetting. *Oubliette.* That's also French. If not Robin Hood, with his bow and his arrow and his crusade and his king, then perhaps another. Perhaps this: Tolerance is William Tell and she has always gotten the apple.

"YOU SHOULDN'T SMOKE so much," Understanding says as she leans over his shoulder in the mortuary, "I know what your lungs look like when you do that. It makes me feel even more ill, that I know about all the tar in you."

She blows a stream of secondhand smoke past his deaf ear in response; he elbows her away without looking up, his hands being otherwise occupied.

"Are you stitching my shirt up with catgut?" Tolerance says, staunchly not budging and hooking her chin over his shoulder. Leaning forward like this, she is the silhouette of an apostrophe against Understanding's back. "Because you know, that makes me feel gross."

"If it's good enough for your skin, it's good enough for this," Understanding retorts. "Besides, I don't have anything else to hand. You're just going to have to make do."

"Story of my life," Tolerance sighs, and takes another drag of her cigarette. Understanding plucks it out of her hand, takes a drag himself, and hands it back.

"What about all the tar in you, then?"

"I only smoke when I'm stressed. Like now. You're stressing me."

At the ragged edge of Understanding's voice, Tolerance pushes her eyeglasses further up the bridge of her twice-broken nose and pulls a shilling from behind his ear. Understanding smiles at the magic trick, but the smile is piecemeal and unwholesome, half-present when Understanding is never anything but marvellously, entirely present. He worries, in this grinding, constant way Tolerance does not; Understanding worries in the very bones of him, alone here with his needles and his dead. She has never said *all we have is each other*; he has never said *if something were to happen to you*; they are family, and it's a truth that requires no telling. She holds the coin out to him and he puts down her torn shirt, puts down his needle and thread, and holds the coin up to the light.

"Look," she says, grinning as he flips the coin over and over in his hands, a blur of tails without end, like a ouroborus metaphor made mint, "No queens. All the queens are gone," and finally, Understanding grins.

TOLERANCE IS NAMED for the virtue; it's one of the reasons she says she turned to drink. This is not a place for ambitious girls, and they are always girls here;

Peter Pan, doe-eyed, nobody ever remembers Wendy-bird was shot down before anyone started to take her seriously. This is a place where ambition's spine is made of colonial pillars, where ambition is Christian and white and washes the blood from their hands before dinner. It is 1922, in a world where crashes are for cars not for currency, and everyone just keeps revving up faster. It's tempting fate. It's tempting retribution. It's tempting something. Tolerance is named for the virtue, but this is not a place for virtuous women. It is Cambridge, garlanded as it is with wreaths of golden spires, draped in artist's light, a garden of chiaroscuro amidst candlelight. It is 1922 and the boys in their vaulted libraries are boys no longer, or rather, lost boys. They are a generation of Abraham's sons walking through Jesus Green. They read of Troy, of the Odyssey, of lost men at sea or meat to burn for a nation's glory; their pronunciation is bloodlessly precise, but their eyes waver and you cannot tell what they are thinking. They have repainted the signs on the college doors to be both in English and German; this bilingualism is seen as treaty. This mutual transaction is seen as reparation. There is no victory, which leaves the whole thing feeling hollow as a hangover.

Then there is Tolerance, named by a penitent, perhaps, washed up on the shores of a Manchester orphanage to break against the tide. She sees herself as a Magdalene; she is seen as the Whore of Babylon. She compacts herself into neat collared dresses with drop-waists and paints her lips like sirensong. Tolerance has a typewriter, ambition and a longing not to feel quite so apart.

Tolerance is apart, though. It's not her fault. Ambition is ugly unless it's ordained to not be so by men written about in libraries; Tolerance is only the clerk tasked with keeping the books open and doors closed to the public. *Women should keep their legs open and their mouths shut.* Women should go back to where they came from; Tolerance is never sure if they mean the Manchester of her childhood, the India she has never seen, or the womb of the mother she has never known.

This is how we begin.

EACH DAY, TOLERANCE asks Understanding how he's feeling. He smiles, but doesn't lie.

"Tired," he says, with his lovely awake eyes, "and old. Nothing too unusual."

He carries a pill box in his pocket and you can hear the tumble of aspirin and manufactured laudanum powder inside and you can't hear the creak of his joints but she sees it in the wince of his face. He's twenty-six and walks with a cane and sleeps like a corpse. He was too young and too much of an invalid to have been called up for the Great War, on first name terms with his childhood doctor; his delicate wrists with the lavender veins, the frailty of his constitution, the nurses who suggested hotter portions of the Empire. Women should go back to where they came from; the ill should have the grace to exist quietly, if they are to exist at all. They shouldn't have stories of skinny dipping in the sanitorium grounds, stories of endless colouring books and staring up at ceilings, stories of existing loudly and bitterly and beyond the grace of God.

Understanding does. One day, Tolerance suggested they get married. Understanding glanced up, horrified, and said:

"But we're cousins."

That's been the story they've stuck to, easy habit after their first meeting, where a quiet Cambridge mortician wrapped an arm around the waist of an angry clerk in a speakeasy, glared at a smirking jackal of a man and said *we're cousins* to him in a tone that said *play along* to her.

"Not by blood," she said. They have never been related, but she understands what he means. "They wouldn't have me give up work anymore, even if they need the men. I can speak all the three tongues."

"Your French grammar is passable at best," Understanding said. His various ailments do not require him to be cerebral; but it was, perhaps, an inevitable side-effect of a life left in bed with nothing to do but burn his way through the hospital lending libraries. "Give me a real reason. Give me something real, Tolerance, and I'll think about it."

She said, eventually: "I'm frightened that they'll find out about Lucy and I want you as armour."

"I will always be your first line of defence," Understanding says, after a moment of rippling silence. "But I don't go to altars. I'm not the altar kind."

And that was that.

LET'S BACK UP for the backstory now:

The Great War ravaged Europe, as it always has done, as it always seemed it was meant to do, and nobody won. Not just in the metaphorical sense; the stalemate led to a concession of a final victory, and so the remnants of various Empires were sewn back together in a Germanic-Franco-British mess of an alliance. This is a generation of industrial trilinguals and all the licking of war wounds was done in the open, as though in publicising it the wounds would seal faster. That's not how flesh works, of course. There is no such thing as a brave new world; only a world that carries the deadweight of its history, ever heavier, and the slowest are left behind to gather up the slack in a cultural misunderstanding of Darwinian theory. Darwin never said only the strongest power survives. Darwin said *those who adapt fastest, and best; those are the ones who survive.* And so the very essence of life depends on malleability; Tolerance knows this, and yet looks at the world surrounding her and thinks *there are jellyfish with more spine.*

She isn't sure how it began, at what point she said *enough;* she knows all the points she wanted to say no but didn't culminated in a single glistening moment. Her Damascus. There was a late-night lecture being hosted at the newly-minted Faculty of Archaeology; due to its overwhelming popularity of attendance, they were outmanned staff-wise, and forced to resort to letting Tolerance steward instead of remaining at her post in the dusty Faculty library. She listened vaguely, for she had attended many such lectures before, and was not as keen-eyed as her earlier enthusiasm had led her to be, but she glanced up at the projection behind the lecturer, his face made invisible by the light of the image, and it hit her, just like that. Let there be light. *I am surrounded by a sarcophagi of stolen things.* The thought was so alien in its poetry she scarcely believed it to be hers; women like her were rarely elevated to the status of literature. And yet it remained, taut and certain in her head. *All of these things are out of time and out of place. This is not restoration. What did a pharaoh's death mask need saving from?*

The not-rightness, the injustice of it—that's it, that's the word—sits on her, heavy and familiar. It's hard to dance with the devil on your back, and when she sits up in Lucy's bed, saying *who gave them the right? Nothing divine, there's nothing but them saying righteousness to cover the sound of strongarming. There's nothing but them saying protection to cover the sound of broken bones.* Lucy had looked at her; Lucy, who was a tall blonde with Germanic cheekbones, soft pink areola, sky-veined skin, and she said *you make it sound like a war. The war's over, Tolerance. These are the best years of our lives.* Tolerance had fallen back into her kiss like a child being put to cradle; that is to say, because it was more comforting and familiar than being put out in the cold. She didn't bring it up again.

She kept her conversion quiet for weeks after that, until she turned on Understanding with the slightly vengeful zeal of the evangelist and said *but how can they?*

She meant *how can there be anything left for them to take* and she could see by the twist of Understanding's mouth that he'd heard her, he always heard her, better than anyone alive.

"They can because they can," Understanding said, "And because we never say stop in a language they understand. At least, that's what they say when they don't listen to us."

"We ought to make them listen," she said, something stinging in her teakettle eyes and the fuming set of her shoulders, her voice solidifying in the last act of the strange raging alchemy that had begun when she first took breath.

"And how would you manage that?" Understanding asked, sardonic without being unsympathetic.

And there's a metaphor to be found here, about crafting your tongue to be a double-edged sword, melding it into the shape of the oppressor's to cut them back, of spitting the scourge into their eyes for a change. About how Tolerance was fluent in all the three tongues, even though her French grammar remained only passable at best. About how she might have had other languages in her, like poetry, like extra souls, like a cat's nine lives, if she had been allowed her heritage.

"I'm going to do exactly what they always say to do with foreign objects," she said, her smile wide and steel and vicious, "I'm going to send them back to where they came from."

AND SO IT began. The first heist was small, a set of miniature shabti with delicate peeling paint, blue faience and seed-dark eyes; it was a matter of organising blueprints and memorising security schedules and wearing a coat as layered and heavily pocketed as her own soul. It was surprisingly, almost cruelly simple. She unscrewed a panel of the glass cabinet they were displayed in, slipped them out, and replaced the whole thing in under two minutes: thanks to years watching Understanding with the crates and coffins in his morgue. That is to say, thanks to his refusal to *let you attempt any part of this until you can rehearse it with your eyes closed*, his frown and an unpacked family of Russian dolls as understudy. Tolerance swaddled the shabti as carefully as she liked to imagine she had been. Understanding slipped them into the Moses basket of a dead man's bowels, emptied of acid and everything else from when there was life, placed the body in a shipping box filled with salts and sent the mummified artefacts back to a museum in Cairo. As easy as that. No, really, as easy as that. They had always seemed to be a two-headed creature, Tolerance and Understanding, two rent halves of a soul. And although Understanding was less than understanding, she could see the strange vicious twist of self-satisfaction when he hammered the last nail down on the coffin. And she knew then she had him, as she always did.

For three days after, they waited for the police, Understanding ashen-faced at his graveyard shift and Tolerance lighting up and lighting up and breathing in the tar at a rate of knots. She couldn't remember if they let women have cigarettes in prison. In the end, the theft wasn't even reported in the papers, and after a week, they relaxed; or rather, Understanding started to breathe easier. Tolerance wondered if they were trying to hush it up, and that made her take out the long black coat again.

"Oh, Christ," Understanding said, eyeing it morosely over his breakfast, which consisted of several cups of coffee, syrup-thick with sugar, and very little else. "Couldn't you take up flower-pressing? Steam engine spotting? Have you considered, perhaps, going to the Library?"

Tolerance made a derisive noise.

The next heists was equally simple. Nobody ever seemed to make the connection that a lockpick and a hairpin could be one and the same; nobody ever seemed to make the connection that a young woman could smile and be a thief. Nobody ever looked twice at the Indian library clerk with the red lipstick and the neat drop-waist dress. It was foolproof. They were foolproof. The newspapers started to sit up and take notice. They assumed it was a gang, and not a two-headed creature hiding in the shadow of a university city. And still nobody looked at them.

OF COURSE, THERE'S that saying about slippery slopes, about downward spirals, about the Fall and gravity and the tipping point that gives away the sleight of hand. There's that saying, about Icarus and tempting fate, about hubris and bringing down the wrath of the gods. Tolerance and Understanding are only two, and they're not even married. But the saying, that's the part we're forgetting. How does it go again?

Act Two

WHEN TOLERANCE OPENS the door, the first thing she wonders is if they've come to convert her to something. The second thing she wonders, looking at them, dark-skinned and beautiful on her doorstep just after dawn, is if there's something she's missed.

"Good morning," the young man says, lapis cufflinks in his white linen three-piece, lapis drop-earrings in his ears, lapis the colour of his eyes, kohl licking around the lids. His hair is slicked back and glistens in the light. "Are you the lady of the house?"

"The lady of the basement, more like," she says, taking the morning cigarette from her mouth. The flat she shares with Understanding is cheap and nobody says anything about cousins sharing. She thanks God again for that first shared lie, but the low rent means a definite lack of sunlight and so she blinks waspishly in the unusual brightness of early morning. "Who's asking?"

"Uh," the young man says eloquently. "I am—that is—that is to say—" He draws himself up to his full height, which is nothing on Tolerance.

Already losing patience, Tolerance's eyes flicker to the two stood with him; the woman puts a careful hand to the first young man's shoulder and says, "Darling, this is why I said it would be better if I did the introductions."

She is unusually lovely Tolerance notices with a pang somewhere in her chest. Her gloves have a hieroglyphic print on them, and her dress is embroidered with a replica of a wall frieze, thick with peacock silk and worshippers. Evil eyes wink from the back of her covered hands, and her hair is waved short. *Revivalists*, Tolerance thinks.

"I'm not interested," Tolerance says, and they all blink up at her on the top step. "Whatever it is. Try next door?"

But when she goes to shut the door, there is a breath of displaced air, lightning-swift and the sound of gales; her cigarette is blown out. When she blinks and realigns herself, there is a foot in the half-shut door and the third one, the young man stood at the back, is throwing it back open with all of his weight. The first young man and the woman slip in after him, the woman adjusted the small beaded scarab bag on her wrist in the half-lit dark of the hall.

Tolerance had left her gun on the kitchen table.

"Sorry," the third young man says cheerfully, not sounding in the least apologetic, "but we need to talk, and the neighbours do talk about you, and so we need to even though my brother doesn't seem to know how to talk for this century."

When he speaks, his voice rasps like sand in her hands, like the first sound of encroaching thunder. She has never heard a tornado siren, but she has read about them, and she imagines it now when he smiles with all his teeth.

"Hello, Bastet," the first young man bursts out, like he cannot help himself, dark eyes lit up, "Do you remember us?"

He steps forward, hesitant and excited. His eyes say: moving onwards, always onwards, nothing held back, all left behind razed to the ground. His smile is a horizon of white enamel. The woman just watches and the evil eyes on her gloves seem to watch Tolerance too. She swears they almost blink at her.

When she backs away from them both, she knocks into the third one, the young man who has moved to stand directly behind her. She can feel his breath hot on her neck. In her head, the siren only ratchets up in volume.

Tolerance does the only thing she can under the circumstances: she screams the house down.

"FUCK," THE THIRD one says, nursing the back of his head bitterly in Tolerance and Understanding's kitchen, "I've had better mornings. *Fuck*. I should curse you for this."

"Curse away," Understanding says, voice surprisingly calm for someone lev-elling a gun at someone's head. Tolerance is making coffee at the counter. "Sugar, please," Understanding called over his shoulder.

"What do you take me for," Tolerance replies, and puts in four.

The young woman and the first young man stay sitting in two chairs behind the third one. Although Understanding is not levelling his gun directly at their heads, they remain relatively still and placid. This is mostly to do with how Understanding had, until a short time ago, been pointing a gun at them whilst they were walked down to the basement flat, whilst Tolerance tied their ankles to the chair legs with rope, whilst the third one lay out unconscious on the parquet entrance hall floor and Understanding sat their with Tolerance's gun and waited for him to come back around.

"What did you call yourselves again?" Tolerance says, bringing the finished mug of coffee to Understanding's side. He drinks it without looking away from the third one, who leans back and looks all for the world like he's enjoying himself. At least, that is, until a twinge from the bruise on the back of his head has him wincing again. Understanding smiles wider.

"The name's Set," he says, "No surname, as of yet. What in the fucking hell did you hit me with?"

His eyes drift to the cane Understanding leans on, then look up. His eyes flash. Understanding shrugs.

"Does he always talk like this?" Tolerance asks the young woman over Set's shoulder. She sighs and arches one perfect, impossible eyebrow. It's painted gold, same as its sister, Tolerance realises suddenly, and wonders why that hadn't struck her earlier. Perhaps there is only so much of the bizarre a body can take in before it begins to upchuck it all.

"He always talks like this," she says. Set folds his arms behind his head and smirks at Understanding, showing all his teeth. Set's hands remain free, less because of any principle and more to do with the fact Understanding and Tolerance had run out of rope by the time it came to him. That, and Understanding was so fatigued by helping to drag Set down to their basement flat before their landlady came home for lunch; Tolerance so unnerved and stunned by the whole enterprise and by their own external mutual calm about the whole thing; that they hadn't tried to run to the corner shop for more. A small error. For want of a nail—

Understanding shifts from one foot to another, uncomfortable, like a subtle dance step slightly out of tune. Understanding had once told Tolerance that the pain was like the ache of a healing bone, something soft and throbbing, a gulping open maw. She sees it start up in the whites of his eyes; she sees Set and the young woman track his movement in theirs.

Tolerance holds her hand out for the gun. They make the exchange too quick for Set to take the advantage, and Understanding takes to the leftover chair. He cradles the cooling mug in his hands, a holy palmer's kiss of coffee, and lifts it to his mouth.

"You're used to this," the first young man pipes up, "but you haven't done this before."

He has been silent so long they'd almost forgotten he was there, faded into stillness like a statue, like, like the pattern of his friend's dress. When he tilts his head to look at them, a little birdlike, the lapis earring on his left side dangles precariously in the air. The right one rests on his cheek. There's a faint scar by his jaw, as though from stitches.

"Well?" he asks. "Am I right?"

Tolerance and Understanding exchange a look. This look says: did you watch him watching us? I was too busy watching for the belladonna in Set's eyes. I was too busy watching for her to speak. How naked have we been to him?

"We're used to each other," Understanding says finally. Tolerance readjusts her grip on the pistol.

"Cousins," Tolerance says, at the same time Understanding says, "Friends." They glance at each other, askance, whilst Set snickers and the first young man smiles and the young woman watches and watches, her eyes an ivory weight.

"Ah, blood brothers," he says, "I see. I have a wife and a brother," he adds, still smiling softly. It's almost sad. "They are not the same."

"We're right here," Set snaps, turning around to look at him.

"You usually are," the first young man retorts, peaceable. His eyeliner glimmers a little in the low light.

"May I do the introductions this time?" the young woman asks. It's the first time she has spoken since they brought this unholy trinity down to the basement. Her voice is rich and clear and makes Tolerance think of how it is to be loved.

Tolerance watches the dip of the earring in the first young man's ear as he very slowly nods, and half-listens to that voice, wondering how much the earrings would cost. She starts listening properly at Understanding's first derisive noise, and keeps on listening, her grip slackening on the pistol in surprise, right up until the young woman stops.

"Are you done?" Understanding asks, terse.

"Yes," she says, settling back in the chair. "Quite done." She looks towards the first young man, who she claims is called Osiris. "Thank you, my dear."

In front of them, Set pulls a face.

"Do we believe them?" Tolerance says, crammed into the tiny water closet with Understanding, the door ajar so they can keep an eye on the kitchen's newest residents.

"Obviously not," Understanding snaps, glancing towards the kitchen out of the corner of his eye. "Reincarnated Egyptian gods? Called up from the abyss due to a resurgence in belief? They could at least be intimidated enough to come up with a better story."

He looks at Tolerance; Tolerance feels it and quickly rips her eyes away from where Isis sits with her eyes half-lidded, listening to them without being obtrusive about the fact. Isis. As in, Isis, goddess, wife of Osiris, mother of Egypt, worshipped as truth made flesh over a span of several hundred lifetimes.

"Really," Understanding says, his voice heavy on the syllables, and Tolerance suppresses a wince. Understanding at his most scathing is scalding, and she feels her skin go prickly-hot in response.

"They let us tie them up."

"After they forced they way in!" Understanding hisses.

"Tying people up is hardly the basis for most major decisions," Set says, before meeting the eyes of everyone else in the room. "What did I say?"

"We were having the good grace to pretend we couldn't hear them," Osiris says. Briefly, Tolerance closes her eyes, feeling a bastard of a headache solidifying at the back of her skull.

"You can't honestly be considering—"

"I am honestly considering," Tolerance retorts.

"Five minutes ago, he thought you might be Bastet reincarnated, Tolerance," Understanding sounds weary. "Because of the newspapers. He believes the *newspapers*, Tolerance. I don't buy any of this."

"No," Set calls over. "We're the ones trying to buy you."

"I'm an atheist," Understanding says without looking over his shoulder. Trying to have a private conversation about the likelihood of their guests being con artists masquerading as reincarnated deities was proving increasingly difficult.

"We have money," Osiris says, finally. "A lot of money."

Tolerance and Understanding look at each other for a moment. Tolerance raises her eyebrows. She knows they are both thinking of next week's rent.

"We had thought to appeal to your better nature—"

"Poverty," Tolerance replies, "is our better nature."

She keeps on looking at Understanding.

"Don't give me those eyes," he mutters, bracing one hand on the doorframe for support. He looks away and Tolerance takes him in; the soft down of his eyebrows, the fringe of his eyelashes, the angle of his nose.

She looks over his shoulder, at the three would-be, could-be gods sat at her kitchen table.

"How much money are we talking?" she asks, and ignores Set's slow-reaching smile.

"Untie my brother and his wife," Set says, "And then we'll talk."

IT'S AN OBSCENE amount of money.

Furthermore, it should be clarified Understanding is not at all surprised that their racket has been discovered. The Sword of Damocles has hung over them so long, the weight of the wait for discovery, that for it to finally happen, for the someone to kick the guillotine and send the blade rushing down—it is all an odd sort of relief. He has been to this kind of place before, when his body hovers on the tipping point of agony, and he has lived through it. He always lives through it. Having the worst come to worst is something Understanding prepares his life in accordance with, so when it turns out Tolerance and himself are being half-bribed, half-blackmailed to steal a dead priestess' fancy and frankly priceless hair comb from its current resting place in a glass case, he simply leans back in his chair. The pressure of the back of the chair eases the knots in his shoulders, just a little, just like pressing down on a bruise, but he'll take it.

"A lot of trouble for a dead man," he says, and watches Osiris' eyes flicker, wounded and dangerous.

"It was a gift from Osiris," Isis says, "Carved by his own hands out of bone."

She looks to Tolerance as though appealing to her. It's probably working, bone-carving aside. Tolerance has a weakness for the pretty ones, even though it's been a good few years since she's been stupid enough to go after a married one. Understanding still remembers that last disaster. They'd had to move flats over it all.

"And what, it has some kind of untold power?" Tolerance asks, folding her arms and looking skeptical. The colour on the cupid's bow of her lip shines, half the lipstick and half sweat. It's summer here in England, and all the best sinners are boiling alive.

"No," Osiris says calmly, "Well, I don't know. Very probably. I do know, however, that I have loved five people in as many centuries, my wife included in that, and I want what I gave away back."

"Wasn't he my priest?" Set drawls. "From one of my temples? That's if I remember right. Always taking what isn't yours, brother dear."

"You took one of mine," Osiri snaps, "At least thirty years before I took him. You set precedent."

"Like you appreciated Nakht," Set sneers, "You only learnt his name when he stopped singing yours."

Osiris turns to look at Set and they stare at each other for a moment, poised and seething, Set's jawline tensing and the cruel angle of Osiris' kohl glittering, before Isis says, "Sometimes, I believe we have grown out of this ugly teething stage, and then one of you opens your mouth again."

"It's hereditary," Set snarls, but throws himself back in his chair.

"Let me check," Tolerance says, "You want us to steal this for you?"

"No," Isis says, "We want you to take it back. We've followed what we could distinguish of your careers, and we noticed you don't seem to selling anything on the black market that you steal."

"Don't we?" Understanding deadpans.

"We would know." Isis puts her hands in her lap. "Which leaves us with the question of motive for your good deeds that do no good for yourselves."

"Oh," Set murmurs, "I do love the righteous thieves. Always so settled in your causes."

"Tell us why you want it," Tolerance says, and Understanding feels them look past him to her. "Tell us why you want it, and make it better than a love story."

In the end, it is Isis who tells them. She talks about forgetting, about the sleepy tip of the hourglass, how for a god of transition memories dissipate. She talks about how a young god who had already died once, who was weighted with the fear of what time might do to mortal lovers and his own mind, carved his own memories into bone and gave them away. They had been in their youth and had believed in a legacy that would stretch out, unfurled and unbroken, across the sea. In a country of sand, they had forgotten that sand erodes.

"Anything to add, brother?" Set taunts when she is done, but he lacks his usual bite.

"No. I'm trying to listen to Isis more," Osiris says. "Being buried alive by your brother, after you failed to listen to your wife the first time, does give you a certain degree of perspective."

A FEW DAYS later, they ready the harness and gears in silence. There's only ever been one harness. They will have to have other escape routes; the trio insist on joining in on the heist, they say out of curiosity. Understanding and Tolerance both know that, for all their talk about higher motives, the three of them are afraid the two of them will renege on a deal hesitantly struck. They line up the lockpicks like cutlery for a last supper, and:

"So we're doing this, then," Understanding says, and Tolerance looks up at him like she only can when she's knelt on the floor in a tangle of their equipment and he's standing in the doorway, and she says:

"We're doing this then."

Her eyes say: we can't turn down that money. I wish we could but we can't. Her eyes say: they haven't talked about the police yet, but they will. Her eyes say: for all my higher callings, I am only human, and we are not wealthy, and I am afraid of what may happen to us.

Her eyes say: I believe them. I want to believe them. Please understand.

And she puts every last lockpick into her hair.

THE PLAN IS this: at 4:35p.m. precisely, Tolerance, Isis and Osiris all enter the museum's main entrance separately. Osiris leaves his coat in the cloakroom, and flirts with the boy checking the coats, and Tolerance and Isis cut down the staff corridor. If they are stopped, they will say they are looking for the bathroom. They ghost past into the Archives, past reams of catalogued boxes, grinning animal skulls faintly white in the half-dark, and packing crates. They slip into a wardrobe in one of the Archives, picking it based on size and and jam it shut from the inside. Outside, the museum shuts its doors for the day. Osiris, making eyes at the coat boy, makes a point of leaving by the same main entrance, after which he goes to the basement flat, collects a suitcase and returns several hours later to keep an early lookout along the top of the street. Understanding and Set take up watch by the guards' exit with guard uniforms underneath raincoats. There have been a series of summer storms these past weeks. Meanwhile, Isis and Tolerance wait amongst the animal skulls to be set free.

There is absolutely no way this should work, so of course, it doesn't.

THEY SIT IN the wardrobe and wait to be told it's safe to be let out. The darkness with them feels living, feels tangible, feels like they are encompassed by a set of blacklit lungs and the lungs are breathing.

"I sometimes wonder," Isis says, very softly, "if this is what it was like for my husband. Before he died the first time. He doesn't like to talk about it. I do not like to ask."

Her voice does not tremble; it is too rich for that. It ripples. Their arms press together in the dark, flesh against flesh, cold and marbled without light to glean it. Tolerance breathes them through it.

"I'm sorry," she says; Tolerance, who has never apologised for a damn thing in her life. The words drop between them, empty and hollow, cracked eggshells against the weight of whole lives and deaths. *I'm sorry* is not enough. They both know it.

Tolerance, her eyes adjusting in the dark, sees the faint sliver of Isis smile.

"You're very kind," she says. "We were rich and young and drunk. It is easy to believe you are too much for the world to swallow you up, under those circumstances."

Tolerance knows the myth. Set, in a fit of jealousy, builds a jewelled coffin made to his brother's exact measurements and holds a banquet, lets the wine overflow and says: *look at this beautiful thing I have made. Anyone who is brave enough to step inside, let them. If it fits, it will be theirs.* Isis, seeing how the rubies glittered in the reflection of her husband Osiris' eyes like blood, said: *husband, don't be stupid. Set has always looked at you and seen a lamb to lead to slaughter.* Osiris said: *wife, don't be a fool. We are brothers.*

Osiris suffocated in the coffin made perfectly to his size; Set cut him in seven pieces and poured the remains into the Nile, just to make certain. Isis, alone and grieving and furious with the men she had loved, the men who had betrayed her, gathered up her skirts and dredged the banks of the Nile, sewed Osiris back into life so he could lie in her arms again, and everyone said: what an excellent example of womanhood. What a virtuous goddess. What a wife!

"It was his hand that I found first," she says, "And I was not fond of the dark after that. The dark waters seemed like an open mouth to me. That is all I see when I look into the empty. A jawbone, waiting to snap shut." She smiles again, and the sickle of it is waning. "But Osiris dislikes cramped spaces. He is a nightmare in elevators. And so here I am."

"Here we are," Tolerance reminds her, and fumbles in the dark for Isis' hand. She takes it slowly, not wanting to startle, feeling the pulse rabbit-snared in Isis' mortal wrist.

"Yes," Isis says, voice low. Her fingers catch around Tolerance's. "Here we are."

"This," Understanding says, for at least the tenth time, "is an incredibly, irrevocably, irresponsibly stupid idea."

"Nice alliteration," Set grins, but something is slightly awry with his whole expression. It's unsettling. That is to say, Set's usual smile is unsettling. It's always bloodthirsty, always lit gasoline, *panem et circuses* with the flicker of the burning martyrs glistening in his eyes. Right now, he looks almost subdued. Understanding offers him a cigarette.

"There are quicker ways to kill yourself," Set says.

"Like climbing into my own coffin?" Understanding retorts. He doesn't regret it exactly, but Set inclines his head.

"Touche," he says quietly, turning to keep an eye on the guards' exit, "You know, I never expected to meet someone who had less faith in my brother's plans than I did."

"I'm your standard heretic," Understanding says. "Blame the church schools."

Set laughs under his breath, low and hot and real. Understanding concentrates on how his shoulder aches and thinks about his cousin that is not his cousin, thinks about safety and existing loudly beyond the grace of God.

"Do you know why we're all back together again?" Set asks abruptly. He keeps his eyes fixed on the guards' exit as he speaks; they flash opaque in the streetlamps' glare. "My brother, my brother's wife, and I?"

"Power of three?" Understanding suggests. Set shakes his head.

"We're born when a generation believes in us. Not just in what we were— not the wall friezes or mummy curses or fascination with long-dead organs in jars. We are only what we represent. It's when a generation falls in love with an ideal. Somewhere, they break us out of the pantry again, like forgotten wedding china from a marriage gone sour, and they put us out to play at believing again."

"I feel like you're trying to say something," Understanding says, "And you'd better just go on and say it."

"Osiris," Set says. He counts them off on his fingers, long and slender and choked with silver rings. "Everyone believes in death, don't they? But this century believes in progress. The machines are turning. So, Osiris. And nothing like new enterprise to bring back the backlash. Where are all our virgins gone, they're asking. All our sweet wives and the mothers of our children? All gone to the dogs with cheap lipstick. So, Isis. People love a good paragon."

"Is Isis a paragon?" Understanding asks. Set's smile turns thin.

"People want her to be. Isn't that enough?"

"And you?"

Set snorts, and looks up at the moths flickering about the street lamp's glare.

"You live in this world, and you ask me if people believe in breaking bones? Half your enterprise is geared to murder and half your culture is geared to bleeding the other half dry. Trilingual or not, this empire will see a lot of tongues die out this century."

Set looks at him then, under the white light, and their skin leaves them nowhere to hide. For a moment Understanding is caught, is flayed open.

"It doesn't always take gas to make good men stop talking," Set says.

"You don't have to tell me that," Understanding replies. "You don't have to tell me this like it's a story. I know it's not a story."

Set opens his mouth to say something. He almost looks chagrined. Understanding doesn't particularly care. There is very little he feels able to say when it comes to this sort of affinity with strangers.

"Why stick with your brother, when you tried to—"

"Kill him. You can say it. And I didn't try. I did." Set shrugs, the gesture liquid. "Blood ties, I suppose. What's a little lasting hatred, between family?"

He sounds weary. Understanding thinks of Tolerance, of her tired eyes and her crooked nose, broken falling down the stairs, never healing right. He thinks of how he wouldn't marry her when she asked, but if she'd asked for anything else, if she'd asked for his own right arm, he'd have taken out the knife himself. He thinks of trying to explain that there is more to family than the weight of shared years, more than a method of insulating yourself against solitude.

But then the church bell chimes and Set says, "It's time to go," so Understanding stops talking riddles with the Devil and goes to find his cousin.

OSIRIS WALKS ALONG the street with his empty suitcase and listens to the ebb of nighttime laughter out of windows. He walks along the street and listens to lovers moan in cheap upstairs rooms and pint glasses shattering where they are thrown to the floor in a brawl. He listens to the rattle of breath in a dying woman's throat and he feels the bruises form after a blow to the face in the boxing ring. He sees every electric synapse as a Fellow solves one last theorem and hears every ticking moment of his decaying spine all at once.

The faint scars along his jaw and throat, visible in every reincarnation so far, sting. He thinks of them less as a mark of coming back and more as a mark of coming home. Every new century is so interesting. People often mistake them for stretch marks, or wounds from whatever recent war, but if you look closely and in the right light, as you could now, you can see where there must have been stitches and sealing flesh once.

In the dark of a vault, a comb Osiris once gave to a man he loved sings out.

He can hear it. He has only loved five people in as many centuries. He wants what he gave back.

Osiris walks.

THE HEIST GOES wrong. The heist goes catastrophically wrong and nobody's quite sure who is to blame. Tolerance has accounted for everything; every guard, every door, every alarm. She has not, however, accounted for the effect a trinity of reincarnated deities might have on a room of objects dedicated to sacred worship.

When the vague ethereal wailing from the shabtis starts, Tolerance realises exactly how much she's bitten off, and how much she's expected to chew, and turns wildly to Osiris.

"Make them stop!" she hisses, as the wailing goes up a notch. Several notches. The plural of notches. It ratchets up her spine like panic.

"I didn't make them start," Osiris insists. The whites of his eyes are huge in the faint moonlight. "I don't know what I did. I'm a manifestation! This has never happened before."

"This didn't happen earlier," she bites out, sweat slicking down the small of her back. She imagines the lights flickering on in the houses nearby as the wailing reaches fever pitch. It's like every imagining she ever had of the professional mourners of old Egypt, misery in the baking heat of an English summer, all echoing out of the mouths of a miniature army of stone-eyed dolls.

"I was busy," Osiris snaps back, "With the coat boy. I never actually set foot in this gallery."

"Make it fucking stop!"

Understanding is supposed to be holding the back gate open for them. Tolerance hopes he has the good sense to run, because he does; but knows he has the loyalty to stay, because he does. At this point the real fear of the law kicks in, and the shabti are still screaming.

She wonders, almost idly, the horror of it slow like glue, how long it will take the police to arrive.

"It's belief," Isis says, and when Tolerance turns to her, Isis' eyes are dark and faraway. "Don't you feel it, husband? It's been a long time since we were known by name."

"Alright," Tolerance says, scrambling to gather all the equipment-that-would-be-evidence into her arms. It's ungainly and heavy and an attempt to keep them all together. "Four minutes before we hear a siren, three to the back gate. We need to move."

Later, she will wonder at how her voice stayed so level. She itches to turn on the electric light, see if there's anything incriminating that she needs to save, but she thinks they've attracted rather too much attention to the museum building after-hours as it is.

Osiris turns to her, his eyes sparking.

"Leave?" he asks slowly. "But the comb."

"Our lives for a bit of bone?"

His face hardens, angry and impetuous, and Tolerance has never thought of him as cruel until this very moment, not even when he was crowding her in her own house.

"Our lives," Set says, "For a bit of bone. That's the bargain you would make?"

He is framed in the doorway, out of breath. He looks at Tolerance, and Tolerance has always thought of him as cruel until this very moment.

"Help me," she says.

"Your cousin is waiting," he replies. "Take care of your own. I'll take care of mine," and brushes past her so fast she sees a blur.

Tolerance makes for the door, and does not look at Isis. This has never been a choice. At the sound of crashing glass, though, she starts and looks back, like Lot's wife, and what she sees nearly crumbles her legs to salt.

Osiris has plunged his hand through the glass vault and stands there, reamed in glass, fingers bleeding and clutched around the comb. Isis has him by the collar, Set by the shoulder. They are tableau of a story that began long before Tolerance was born, fixed like the frieze on a temple where men believed in them and called them by name.

"For all you say you loved him," Isis says softly, "For all you say he passed through your gates, for all you say you wept blood for days when he died, you do not say his name, and it is only a comb."

The screaming, Tolerance notices, has stopped, so suddenly her ears still ring with it as though they cry still. But the shabti are dead once more, and Set looks at Isis, at Osiris' bent head, and says:

"Just because we're shit at staying dead, doesn't mean you can drag all of history back up with you. Get his other shoulder."

"Don't," Osiris says, so quietly it might be denied. Isis' knuckles go white on his other shoulder, and she doesn't look away for Set. She nods.

"I've killed you once," Set says. "Call this balancing the scales," and Tolerance watches as Isis and Set drag Osiris back from the vault, the last of the glass collapsing around his arm, around them, so much Tolerance wonders how it isn't in their eyes, in their mouths.

And here's the thing: Tolerance will live past this night. Tolerance will live to be old, will live to have greying hair and crow's feet. Tolerance will never be arrested for her life as one half of the Bastet Gang, and neither will Understanding. Both of them escape relatively unscathed from this last escapade, with regards to the law of the Empire at least. Tolerance will watch them carrying a bleeding god through the night, and watch Understanding get out his catgut like he did for her blouses and for dead men, and Understanding will sew up Osiris' arm, and Isis will slowly retrieve the comb, now snapped in half, from clenched fingers. Set will sit, hunched, by the kitchen table like an overgrown crow, until Understanding snaps at him to get some hot water, and then Set will keep asking about morphine.

Tolerance will live past this night. Tolerance will live to be old. But Tolerance will not forget what it meant to be young and to hear a god of death scream. Tolerance will not forget the phantom taste of glass on her tongue.

SOME SAY IT takes a coven to make a religion. No, that's wrong. It only takes twelve. It only takes an even number, and you can splice that down the middle just fine. It only takes five to make an act of faith go bad, and it only takes two to make history; one to say *are we doing this then?* and one to sigh. It only takes two to make a bet. It only takes one to win a bet. It only takes one to lose, and Understanding stands at the train station to see Tolerance off into the arms of a reincarnated goddess. The goddess' husband stands nearby, hands in his linen pockets, and they have come to some kind of arrangement. Understanding doesn't bother to understand; Tolerance is lit from within despite everything. Two nights ago, he saw Isis take Tolerance's hand at the kitchen table and saw the light happen, saw it travel through her veins like a reverse bloodletting and finish behind her eyes.

"You're getting tomorrow's train," she reminds him, sternly. Her eyes are shimmering. She'll say it's the heat.

"I'm getting tomorrow's train," Understanding repeats back, solemnly. His bones are aching and he has no desire to go to Luxembourg. They look at each other for a long moment.

"Don't forget," she says.

"As if I could."

When they part, it is quick as snapping someone's wrist if you know the bones right. A flash of hair and eye in the rising steam, the swing of a lacquered door, a whistle and gone. Understanding waits until the train is far beyond his sight.

"I've seen lovers part with less of the long glances," Set says, hovering behind him, and Understanding turns to face him. He raises his eyebrows. "What? Something I said?"

"I think you've lived with blood family so long you've forgotten what it is to find your own," he replies. He sees a flicker of something in Set's irises, but his bones are aching and he turns for his last night in his old bed.

"So," Set says, "There's a train leaving in an hour."

"Of course there is," Understanding says, "There always is. Going where?"

"I don't know," Set says. "Somewhere."

"Not Luxembourg."

"No," Set agrees, "Not Luxembourg. Not yet."

"I thought the lure of the horizon was your brother's calling."

"Well," Set says, with suspicious mildness, "we are related. Similarities are to be expected."

He walks beside Understanding and the click of Understanding's cane against the pavement denotes heartbeats, exhales, the wavering of uncertainty. He looks down at the ground. *Step on a crack and break your mother's back.* But the pavement is riddled with them. Understanding stepped on the wrong ground long ago. He calculates the cost.

"Let me get my coat," Understanding says, and turns away from a last worst god's slow-reaching smile.

WORTHLESS REMAINS

BY
JONATHAN GREEN

A PAX BRITANNIA STORY

Worthless Remains

June 1998

I—Lifeless Things

THE MAN RAN pell-mell into the maze formed by the dusty backstreets of Giza as if all the dead of Egypt were after him. Reaching a street corner he stumbled to a halt, collapsing against a mudbrick wall, gasping for breath. Desperate eyes peered out of a gaunt face from behind round wire-frame spectacles, scouring the alleyway behind him, but he could see nothing there by the glowing orb of the moon that bathed the desert in its monochrome light.

The Ancient Egyptians had imagined the moon god Khonsu as a falcon, carrying the moon-disk upon his head as he soared over the desert, lifted high by the thermals that rose from the sun-baked sands as they gave back their borrowed heat.

Narouz peered now with hawkish interest at the sand-dusted street but still he could not see anything. He could not hear anything either, other than for the ever-present whisper of the wind coming off the western desert, and the hiss of sand grains blown by the breath of Shu, the god of the air.

Taking a deep breath, he set off again at a slower, steadier jog. With the pyramid complex behind him, he began to convince himself that his audacious plan might actually work: he would make it to the river, and board a boat that would carry him to Alexandria—far away from the corrupt officials in Cairo—and from there catch an airship that would carry him all the way to Londinium Maximum. There he would finally be able to safely inform the authorities of what was going on, without fearing that he might receive an assassin's poisoned thorn-dart in the back of his neck at any moment.

He knew the backstreets of Giza as well as he knew the intricate maze of code he had helped develop for the Osiris Corporation. He would have to send his daughter a message, once he was clear of Cairo, to let her know he was safe, but first he had to reach the river and find a boat.

He turned another corner, his heart full of hope, and found them already there, waiting for him.

They came towards him in a shambling mass, stiff-limbed, their bandaged feet shuffling through the sand. By the unforgiving moonlight he could see desiccated black-green faces drawn tight across the skull bones beneath. None of them had eyes anymore; those had dried up and turned to dust centuries ago.

Stifling a cry of horror, Narouz turned, his feet slipping on the sand as he struggled to find purchase, before skidding back around the bend in the street.

They were waiting for him there too. His pursuers might not be fast, but they were relentless. And there were far more of them than there were of him, but then the Ancient Egyptians had practised the art of mummification for so many millennia and there were a lot of them lying around in their desert tombs, if you knew where to look or who to ask. There had been a healthy black market trade in mummies long before the Osiris Corporation appeared on the scene.

Grey fingers, made bony talons by the preservation process, reached for him.

Narouz briefly considered trying to barge his way through the mass of mummies, but deep down he already knew such an escape attempt was futile. He turned his attention to the enclosing walls of the small windowed buildings round about him.

In his desperation to get away, Narouz threw himself at the wall of a house, using the sill of a tiny window in the mudbrick wall to pull himself up. But his upper body strength was not what it might have been and the adrenalin rush that had brought him this far was starting to wear off, leaving his body so drained of energy that his legs could barely even bear his weight anymore, let along aid him in climbing up onto the flat roofs of the town to get away.

A hand closed like a steel clamp around an ankle and yanked hard. Narouz was dragged down the wall, fingernails tearing as he tried to keep his purchase in a feeble attempt to save himself.

The press of mummies closed in on him, the stink of their salted bandages and acrid unguents filling his nostrils as they grabbed at him with hungry hands.

The last thing Narouz was aware of—before his soul took flight to join Osiris, the King of the Underworld, beyond the western desert—were the dry fingers of the dead about his neck, as they throttled him to death.

II—A Traveller From An Antique Land

"WAS THIS REALLY the best you could do, Nimrod?" Ulysses Quicksilver complained as the contraption that passed for a car bumped and jolted along what was little more than a dirt track skirting the edge of the desert.

"Yes, sir," his gentleman's gentleman-cum-personal bodyguard-cum-chauffeur replied. "It was short notice, sir."

"Well thank God we're almost there." Ulysses peered over the top of the folded paper map he was struggling with at the looming silhouettes of the three great pyramids that stood out like black paper cut-outs against the burnished gold of the endless Egyptian sky. The tip of the largest structure shone in the sun. "Or should that be gods?"

"Was it really necessary to come all this way on a whim?" Nimrod asked, fighting the steering of the old jalopy.

"The murder of an eminent Earl and reality television star hardly qualifies as 'a whim', old chap," Ulysses said defensively, still struggling with the map, which now looked like an over-sized piece of origami akin to the kind that the staff at the Ritz were prone to make out of what were simple serviettes, much to Ulysses' chagrin.

"I thought the press reported that it was caused by a malfunctioning domestic appliance," Nimrod said, his face as expressionless as a sphinx.

"That's the best euphemism I've heard for someone being killed by an Egyptian mummy," Ulysses laughed.

"But where did it come from, sir?"

"Well the Earl of Grantham's grandfather was part of the great Egyptology explosion of the 1920s. The mummy was one of the treasures he brought back with him to England. It was the late Earl—the 13th, appropriately enough— who sent it away to have the shabti slave module fitted."

"So how did it happen?" Nimrod asked, his interest piqued despite his best efforts not to express any interest in the story whatsoever.

"It was during breakfast at Downton Abbey. According to the report in *The Times*, the mummy had just delivered the kedgeree from the kitchen. Grantham was halfway through his kippers when the mummy ran him through with a grapefruit spoon."

"How inconvenient, sir."

"Well, quite."

"But I'm still not clear why such a state of affairs, unfortunate as they are, meant that we had to hop on the first airship travelling from London to Cairo," Nimrod persisted as he continued to wrestle the battered, desert-dusted vehicle, bouncing and bumping over the stony track.

"Don't you remember, Nimrod? Robert Grantham and I were at Eton together."

"I'm sorry, sir, but what I meant to say is that although such an accident is undoubtedly tragic, it is not unheard of. Automata malfunction all the time."

"Don't I just know it," Ulysses sighed with exaggerated exasperation. "In fact, I would go so far as to say that I'm some kind of malfunction magnet, because they do so with alarming frequency in my presence. Besides, the automata accidents you're referring to don't all involve robotic products of the Osiris Corporation, which just happens to be owned and run by one Ramesses Faron."

"Let me guess, sir. You were at school with him as well."

Fighting the map down into his lap, Ulysses clapped his hands in delight. "We'll make a detective of you yet, Nimrod!"

"Why, thank you, sir."

"Although he went by the name Ramesses McQueen back then."

"Giza, up ahead, sir," Nimrod suddenly announced.

"Is it?" Ulysses replied, still struggling to orientate the map correctly.

"According to that road sign we just passed, sir."

Ulysses ran a hand through his wind-ruffled mop of hair. "Well, I feel a stop at the nearest souk is called for. After our sojourn in the desert, I feel the need to visit a tailor and quaff a glass of mint tea. I don't know about you but I'm parched!"

III—A Shattered Visage

"THE FACE OF the Sphinx is generally believed to represent the face of the Pharaoh Khafra," Nimrod stated. The two men gazed at the impassive stone expression of the edifice. "It was built in approximately 2500 BC and faces directly west to east."

"And who was Khafra when he was at home?"

"Pharaoh of the Fourth Dynasty during the Old Kingdom. He was the son of Khufu and the throne successor of Djedefre," Nimrod replied in a disinterested monotone.

"What happened to its nose?" Ulysses asked, shielding his eyes against both the sun and the relentless desert wind. He was decked out in a smart cream linen suit and a white shirt of Egyptian cotton, which was offset by a yellow silk cravat, held in place by a gold pin sporting an enamel scarabeus, the cuffs of the shirt kept in order by matching scarab cufflinks.

"It doesn't say," his batman said, turning the promotional pamphlet over in his hand.

"I heard a story back at school that it was broken off by a cannonball fired by Napoleon's soldiers."

"Iconoclasts, sir?"

"Bless you, old chap," Ulysses quipped, "but no. Just ruddy poor shots, I believe."

A polite clearing of the throat drew their attention back to the Egyptian, dressed in traditional gallebaya and fez. "This way please, sirs," the porter said, indicating a doorway that had been cut into the stone between the Sphinx's legs.

"And how do we enter?" Ulysses asked, a wry smile curling his lips. "Do we just toot and come in?"

Nimrod gave a weary sigh and approached the grand, carved entrance. An Ankh rose in bas-relief from the lintel above the door. As Ulysses' batman neared, the heavy stone doors they slid open with a hydraulic gasp. "It's automatic, sir."

The door attendant ushered them through and the doors hissed shut behind them again. Inside the two men found themselves in a tunnel lit by flickering torches and braziers. An attractive young woman dressed as Isis—or some other Ancient Egyptian goddess, Ulysses wasn't entirely sure—welcomed them, directing them onto the moving walkway that travelled the length of the tunnel. As they set off along, the flickering light illuminated carved and painted murals—either borrowed from some dead pharaoh's tomb, or recreated in the same style—depicting the soul's journey into the afterlife, embellished with hieroglyphic extracts from various Coffin Texts and the Book of the Dead. As they passed certain pertinent scenes, a soft-spoken commentary—in English, French and Egyptian—explained what they were seeing.

"Before they could reach the Field of Reeds," the commentary explained as they passed images of a man in white robes being led by the hand by a jackal-faced god, "our ancient ancestors believed that the soul had to pass a series of tests."

The travellator moved on through the belly of the Sphinx and the scene changed accordingly.

"First they had to cross the River of Death, then pass through the Twelve Gates, guarded by serpents."

The man in white was now standing before a huge set of scales upon which the same jackal-headed figure was weighing a canopic jar against a stylised white ostrich feather, watched by a pharaonic figure wrapped up like a mummy, with a severe face, and what visible skin there was painted green.

"It's like something out of the funny pages," Ulysses said, keeping his voice low, in case he disturbed the spirits of the dead that must surely haunt this place.

"Finally their deeds in life were judged by Osiris, God of the Dead, in the Hall of Judgement," the commentary intoned. "Here the dead person's heart was weighed against the Feather of Truth by Anubis, Guardian of the Necropolis and the supplicant's guide through the Underworld. If the heart and the feather were in balance, the person had led a good life and could reside in Duat, the Kingdom of the Dead, forevermore."

The walkway moved on.

"But if the heart tipped the scales, then the person's evil deeds weighed heavily upon their soul and they were fed to Ammit the Devourer."

A spotlight flashed on, illuminating a hideous monster that was part lion and part hippopotamus, with the head of a crocodile.

"I'm glad this is all a work of fiction by Ancient Egyptian scribes," Ulysses muttered, "otherwise I wouldn't fancy my chances."

"But now, inspired by the myths of old, the Osiris Corporation has married the latest in cutting edge cybernetic design with the legacy of our ancient ancestors to bring you the ultimate domestic servant. Resurrecting the dead to serve the living."

Ulysses tuned out as the marketing spiel kicked in and, reaching the end of the tunnel, he and Nimrod stepped off the end of the travellator to be met by a Cleopatra clone, who ushered them into a high-ceilinged, hypostyle hall. It looked to Ulysses like it might once have been part of a funerary temple but the addition of various robotic creations on plinths, a few potted palm trees and papyrus plants contained within large, glazed Moorish vases, and a dusty crimson carpet had transformed the space into a grand showroom.

There were bandaged mummies standing in the spot-lit spaces between the painted limestone pillars, alongside wood and stone statues, clearly 'recovered' from sites across Egypt and upgraded, thanks to the addition of an internal, robotic shabti armature, then sold on to the lucrative Magna Britannian market and the the oligarchs of cities across Europe. There were even entirely mechanical devices, one in the form of a huge black serpent, but the most impressive was a sphinx.

The construct's leonine body was twice the size of an actual desert lion, its mechanical parts hidden beneath a veneer of carefully carved alabaster plates. The automaton's head had been fashioned in the form of a golden sabretooth's skull, with long ivory fangs implanted within the gleaming jaws, the whole surmounted by a pharaonic headdress. An alternative human head—carved from a single block of peach-veined alabaster—had been placed on a stand beside the sphinx.

"Is there something you have your eye on?" another Nefertiti doppelganger asked, approaching them.

"No, thank you—" Nimrod began.

"Actually, yes there is," Ulysses countered, giving the young woman a lascivious smile.

IV—My Name Is Ozymandias

HALF AN HOUR later, master and manservant were led from the exhibition hall into another bas-relief-decorated gallery for Ulysses to conclude his transaction.

Tables were dotted around the chamber, surrounded by clusters of chairs. If the previous space had been the showroom, then this was most definitely the salesroom. There were even some other customers present, being tended to by over-zealous salesmen, keen to earn themselves a tidy commission employing the sort of bargaining skills that wouldn't be out of place in the markets and bazaars back in Cairo.

They had left the entrance beneath the Sphinx far behind them. The travellator had steadily carried them deeper underground until they must now be under the desert, although still within the former funerary complex.

"That's yours," the Nefertiti lookalike said, passing Ulysses a hemispherical object that glimmered under the artificial lights, "and now if you'll just bear with me…" and with that she got up and left them.

"We must be close to the Great Pyramid of Khufu," Ulysses said, gazing up at the painted ceiling far above his head, his voice almost a whisper in the sepulchral space, as he waited for the woman to finish processing his payment. It was painted with an elongated image of a woman that stretched the entire length of the hall—a sky goddess perhaps, seeing as how she was painted lapis lazuli blue, her naked body adorned with simplistic yellow stars.

"Why, if it isn't Ulysses Quicksilver!"

Ulysses turned to see a man dressed in a cream linen suit approaching him from the far side of the hall. His black hair was slicked back from his face, and kept in place with copious amounts of hair cream. Striking almond-shaped eyes fixed Ulysses with their glittering stare from the midst of a face that looked like it had been carved from sandstone.

"My, oh my, you haven't changed a bit." The man sounded like a Cambridge graduate, although he had the chiselled features of a prince of Egypt.

"*You* have," Ulysses said. The teenage podginess had gone, along with the angry red spots, as had the glasses, but through this newly-handsome façade he could still see the youth he had known at Eton.

Nimrod cleared his throat emphatically.

"But where are my manners?" Ulysses said, catching himself. "This is my manservant Nimrod. Nimrod this is my old school chum Ramesses McQueen."

The man's face twitched—the unguarded lapse of a moment, nothing more—but Ulysses registered it nonetheless.

"Please, Ramesses Faron," the man corrected him.

"Oh yes, that's right, you took your maternal grandfather's name after you left England. I had forgotten," Ulysses lied. He turned to address Nimrod again: "Mr Faron is the founder and CEO of the Osiris Corporation." He turned back to Faron. "You've been busy since we were at school together."

"Well you know what they say: the Devil makes work for idle hands. Besides, from what I see in the papers and the newscasts you've hardly been idle yourself since you returned from the afterlife." Faron was referring, of course, to the eighteen months during which Ulysses Quicksilver had been missing, presumed dead, after battling his nemesis the Black Mamba above the Himalayas, their hot air balloons becoming entwined before both plummeted onto the frozen peaks. But more than a year had passed since Ulysses had miraculously returned from the dead and resumed his complicated life as a bon viveur, occasional consulting detective and agent for the throne of Magna Britannia.

"Oh, you know what they say, it's good to have a hobby. And yours appears to be turning mummies into robotic slaves."

"Better than grinding them up to make paint, don't you think?" Faron said, the ingratiating smile never once leaving his face.

"Well quite. And that's the magic of what you do here, isn't it? Turning the dead into a commercial product to turn a tidy profit."

"Don't tell me that an agent of the throne of Magna Britannia is a socialist!" Faron laughed.

Ulysses smiled coldly. "Well seeing as how we're clearly done with the social niceties, I'll get straight to the point, shall I?"

"I wish you would! I take it you're not here to purchase a piece for yourself?"

Ulysses sensed Nimrod assume a sturdy fighter's stance at his shoulder.

"Oh, I wouldn't be so hasty in your assumptions. But no—the real reason I'm here is because the 13th Earl of Grantham was murdered by one of your shabti-adapted mummies."

"Really?"

"Yes, really. It appears the shabti module malfunctioned."

"That's terrible!" Faron's face was a mask of appalled horror, no doubt picturing all the potential lawsuits coming his way and the subsequent compensation payments the Osiris Corporation would be forced to make. "Perhaps we should continue this conversation in my office," he said, eyeing the paying customers present in the salesroom.

"Perhaps we should," agreed Ulysses.

Faron led them to the back of the hall and through an entrance into yet another chamber, this one flanked by two huge stone colossi, their faces those of millennia-dead desert kings.

A number of mummies stood around the room, some in sarcophagi, some on stone plinths, but Ulysses couldn't tell it they were there merely for decoration or to be at Faron's beck and call.

"So what happened?" Faron asked, taking a seat behind a large, gold-lacquered desk that looked like it might once have been part of the contents of a pharaoh's tomb.

Ulysses sat down in a chair opposite him, while Nimrod waited at his shoulder. "Like I said, the unit malfunctioned and stabbed its owner through the heart with a grapefruit spoon."

"But what makes you think it was a malfunction?"

Ulysses hesitated, wrong-footed by the man's last remark. "What do you mean?"

He only became aware of the mummy approaching him from behind when the undead Ancient Egyptian seized him in a vice-like clinch, pinning his arms to his sides, and trapping him in his seat, while another of the automaton mummies grabbed Nimrod. Even the former champion bare-knuckle boxer was unable to break free of the mummy's steely grasp.

"What are you doing, Faron?"

"What does it look like?" the other laughed. "I'm taking you prisoner!"

V—King Of Kings

"ACTUALLY, YOU'RE RIGHT," Faron conceded, "it must have been a malfunction, the unit shouldn't have executed that part of its programming—if you'll excuse the pun—until triggered from here, but the underlying subroutine in the Lovelace code was certainly no accident."

"You mean you had the unit programmed to kill the Earl?" Ulysses could not believe the audacity of the man!

A burst of hearty laughter from Ramesses Faron echoed from the carved stone walls of the funerary temple-cum-CEO's office.

"Of course not! You are so small-minded," Faron chuckled, "your concerns so parochial. You can't see the bigger picture."

"If the Earl's death wasn't an accident, but he wasn't the specific target either, then..." Realisation dawned on Ulysses like the sun god Ra rising over the eastern hills. "You mean to say that *all* of the shabti units have murder encoded into their algorithms?"

"That's right!" Faron exclaimed gleefully, clasping his hands in delight.

"But... But..." Ulysses struggled. The man was a multi-millionaire, with an empire built upon the enormous success of converting mummies into household slave-droids. And that meant—

"A mummy in every home!" Faron laughed. "But not just in every home—in every hotel, café, restaurant, shop and museum from here to Londinium Maximum!"

"But... Why?"

"Because the blood of pharaohs runs in my veins!" Faron declared. "Because Egypt was once the greatest nation in the world, and shall be again. Because why rule one corporation when you can rule the world? Because –"

"You're insane?" Ulysses helpfully finished the sentence for him. "You always were one camel short of a caravan, McQueen."

"My name is Faron!"

"But it was McQueen once, wasn't it?"

"McQueen was my father's name. It is not *my* name!"

"But McQueen was the name you were christened with, wasn't it? Which also means that only half the blood in your veins is that of the pharaohs. I would imagine the other half is neat Scotch whiskey!"

The twitch had returned to the left side of Faron's face with a vengeance.

"Ramesses McQueen was pathetic!" he spat. "Ramesses McQueen was bullied at school, bullied by his father. It was Ramesses McQueen who just stood by and watched as the old drunk beat his beautiful Egyptian mother, standing there shaking in a puddle of his own piss.

"Ramesses McQueen died the same day his Scottish father did. But he took his inheritance and remade himself as Ramesses Faron, the descendant of pharaohs. And now the final pieces are in place and I am ready to play my endgame."

"So all this"—Ulysses took in the chamber, and by extension the entire Osiris Corporation beyond, with a twist of his head—"is simply to satisfy some little boy's need for revenge?"

"You don't know what it was like!" Faron railed.

Ulysses scowled. "Maybe I don't. But we've all known pain and loss. It's what we do with those feelings, those experiences that matters. The abused doesn't have to become the abuser. At some point in your adult life you have to come to terms with the fact that you can't keep using the privations of your childhood as some feeble excuse. One day, you have to wake up and make a conscious decision as to what kind of man you're going to be."

The words were barely out of his mouth when Faron was on his feet. Leaning across the desk, he smacked Ulysses across the face with the flat of his hand.

Ulysses gave a chuckle. "You're going to have to do better than that."

And so Faron did, with a vicious punch, accompanied by a scream of rage, that jerked Ulysses' head backwards, knocking him clean out.

VI—Look On My Works, Ye Mighty, And Despair!

ULYSSES OPENED HIS eyes, blinking several times until the blurred images before him resolved into distinguishable shapes, and sat up.

He took in four stone walls, broken mortuary temple statuary, and a vid-cast screen—one of the few indications he had that this was the twentieth century AD and not the twentieth century BC.

And Nimrod was there; ever dependable Nimrod.

"Where are we?" he slurred through bruised and bloodied lips.

"Another part of the complex, sir," his faithful manservant replied. "We were brought here after your altercation with Mr Faron. Are you alright, sir? That was quite some punch he delivered, and I should know, I'm something of an expert."

Ulysses thought of all the injuries he had suffered at the hands of disgruntled ne'er-do-wells. He tested his teeth with the tip of his tongue. "Nothing a trip to the dentist won't fix."

Ulysses swung his legs round and got up from the stone plinth. The ancient stone chamber was lit by the very modern electric lights, placed in alcoves around the walls. There was a stone door in one wall but when Ulysses tried it—even going so far as to put all his weight behind it—it would not budge.

"It's locked," Nimrod told him helpfully. "I've tried forcing it already."

"Very well," Ulysses said, continuing his circuitous examination of the room as if in the hope that he might find a hidden secret exit Nimrod had missed. "But why put us in here at all?"

"I was wondering the same thing, sir."

"I mean, why not get one of his shabti mummies to kill us? Faron's clearly not squeamish about ordering the deaths of others, when you consider the plan he's about to put into action."

Ulysses sat down again on the plinth and stared at the screen.

"Ah," he said, as understanding came to his aching head at last, "of course."

"Of course, sir?"

"Yes, Nimrod, isn't it obvious?"

"Isn't what obvious?"

"To have devised such an audacious plan isn't enough. Faron's crowning glory will be putting it into action with us knowing that's what he's doing, and yet unable to do anything to stop him."

"I see, sir."

"The man needs an audience. Simple as that."

Just then, as if Faron had been listening in on their conversation—which he probably had—the screen came on with a squeak of static, and the image of a very definitely twentieth century control room appeared, full of banks of Babbage Engines and Turing machines attended by a team of technicians.

And then Faron's face appeared, calm and composed once again.

"Ah, I see you are awake," he said. "Such impeccable timing."

Ulysses scanned the room for any sign of a camera.

"It's in the screen in front of you," Faron said, reading his body language rather than his mind.

Ulysses picked up a piece of broken stone from the sandy floor of the chamber and moved towards the screen, the hand holding the rock raised.

"Don't you want to know what's going to happen next?"

Ulysses froze.

"Of course you do."

Ulysses knew Faron was goading him, but he would permit him to do so, for the time being at least. "You've got your audience, so spill the beans."

"Very well," said Faron, the self-satisfied smile firmly ensconced upon his face. "When I give the word a signal will be broadcast from our location that will activate the hidden code buried within each shabti unit—the Osiris Algorithm, if you like—effectively turning every single automaton-adapted mummy and statue over to my direct control."

"But surely that will only activate the units within—what?—a fifty mile radius at most," Ulysses pointed out, hastily trying to work out the maths in his head. "Without a satellite network to support the signal, you won't be able to reach those units you've sent abroad, to places like Paris and London."

"You're quite right, and therein lies the true genius of my plan," Faron boasted. "Each unit acts as a relay station. As well as receiving the signal from Pyramid Control, each one also boosts it, broadcasting it over another fifty miles. People have been collecting my antiquities for years. They're in every rich family's household from here to Monaco!"

"You're insane!" Ulysses railed at the screen.

"Typical bully," Faron sneered. "When you can't use your fists you're reduced to hurling abuse. Sticks and stones may break my bones but words will never hurt me!"

Ulysses hurled the rock at the screen.

RAMESSES FARON TURNED to the technician seated next to him at the control desk. "Activate the beacon," he growled. "Send the signal."

Turing engines galvanised and the pre-coded series of zeroes and ones coursed through the maze of motherboards, finally finding egress via the circuits bound into the fabric of the great golden cap of the Great Pyramid of Khufu.

From there it took flight into the ether, beaming out in powerful pulses until it came into contact with an Osiris Corporation shabti unit. And within each docile and obedient mummy-droid and statue-automaton, it wrought a startling change. Where before there had been a submissive slave, in its place there was now an implacable invader, working for a new master.

In the echoing halls of the Cairo Museum, a host of exhibits animated, turning on their unsuspecting spectators, indiscriminately killing the museum's human staff and visitors before finally herding the survivors into one gallery, where they then stood guard over their terrified prisoners.

In souks and restaurants throughout the city, drinkers and diners fell foul of the traitorous dead, the enemy having been hiding in plain sight all this time, waiting patiently for the moment when they would be called upon to fulfil the would-be pharaoh's bidding.

On pleasure cruisers travelling up and down the Nile, at temple ruins and in the tombs of the Valley of the Kings, people succumbed to the curse of the mummy again and again and again.

And within the chamber that had been hollowed out of the heart of the Great Pyramid of Khufu, at the centre of his Osiris operation, Faron watched the horror unfolding across the country on visual feeds relayed to the control room by the shabti units themselves, his eyes alive with insane glee.

"My name is Ozymandias, King of Kings," he muttered under his breath. "Look on my works, ye mighty, and despair!"

"WE HAVE TO shut off that transmitter, wherever it is!" Ulysses declared.

"Forgive me if I am being impertinent, sir," Nimrod said, "but how do you propose to do that when we are still locked in here?"

"It's alright." Ulysses smiled a wry smile. "We have a friend on the outside."

Putting a hand into a pocket, Ulysses pulled out the device that the sales assistant had given him. It looked, at first sight, not unlike a highly-polished alabaster scarab. Cradling it in the palm of his hand, he depressed the button secreted in its base.

Nothing happened.

Nimrod looked at him expectantly. "Is it broken?" he asked.

"Just give it a minute, will you?"

Nimrod waited, while his employer kept his eyes on the door. And then Ulysses felt a shiver of electricity dance down his spine and a moment later they could both hear the echo of pounding footsteps from beyond the stone walls of their prison cell.

There was a moment of eerie quiet and then with a tearing of steel hinges, the stone door was forced open from the outside by titanium-toughened claws.

Crouching there in the passageway beyond was an automaton twice the size of a lion, its piston-powered legs gently rising and falling on their hydraulic suspension units as it waited for its next instruction, its motor purring. The machine seemed to watch them with predatory analytical interest through the shining lenses of its eye-cameras, although it was the curved, scimitar canines—razor-sharp and deadly—that drew one's gaze.

"Good lord, sir!" Nimrod exclaimed.

"Magnificent, isn't she?" Ulysses stepped through the forced door to pat the robot sphinx on the top of its gleaming sabretooth skull.

"That's one way of describing it," his manservant conceded. "But won't it be susceptible to Faron's resurrection code, or whatever he called it?"

"You'd think so, wouldn't you? But apparently not!" Ulysses declared, giving Nimrod the sort of grin he usually reserved for talking about his Mark IV Rolls Royce Silver Phantom. "Turns out the sphinx has a different operating system entirely. It uses a different source code from the shabti units. On top of that, each one is gene-coded to its owner"—he held up the scarab-like remote—"so from now on it responds to me and me only."

Ulysses hopped into the saddle built into the automaton's back as Nimrod approached with caution. An electronic growl emitted from the rumbling mechanisms of the sphinx.

"Care to come for a ride? After all, we have a megalomaniac to thwart."

VII—That Colossal Wreck

"Sir? The prisoners are getting away," one of the technicians in the central control room of the pyramid said.

"I can see that," Faron hissed with all the menace of Apophis, the Ancient Egyptian demon snake-god of chaos.

He turned his attention from the feed from the cell to the other screens, scouring them for any sign of the fugitives.

"Where are they?" he demanded. "Find them for me!"

He was so close now, he could not allow Quicksilver to thwart his plans. Besides, the idiot was too late; the signal had been sent and was, right at this very moment, being relayed across Northern Africa and on into Europe. Soon even the hallowed halls of Londinium Maximum would feel his cold, bandaged touch.

But nonetheless Ramesses Faron wasn't going to risk Quicksilver's interference and would deal with him here and now, once and for all. After all, he had read the news reports about the sort of situations Ulysses Quicksilver usually got himself into and how he always managed to get himself out of them again, even if it was habitually by the skin of his teeth.

"They're in the factory, sir," one of the technicians suddenly announced.

"Direct all units in the area to engage and destroy," Faron commanded.

"But they have a sphinx," another technician said, speaking without thinking. "It'll make mincemeat out of them."

An uncomfortable atmosphere descended over the chamber; the other technicians turned away to pay great interest in the Babbage engine consoles in front of them.

"I know that, idiot!" Faron snarled. "I don't expect the shabtis to stop them, merely to slow them down until I can get there."

"You're going–?"

The technician saw the look in the CEO's eyes then and fell silent.

Faron said nothing. Turning from the bank of screens and thinking machines, he moved to the centre of the control room where there stood a sarcophagus-like object carved out of black granite that reflected the lights of the chamber from its polished, obsidian-smooth surface. Golden circuitry covered it in a geometric pattern worthy of a pharaoh's final resting place.

Hung on a cradle inside the sarcophagus-like booth was a headpiece, adorned with gold and lapis lazuli, looking not unlike the death-mask of King Tut himself. This one, however, was connected to the sarcophagus by a snaking bundle of cables.

Lifting the death-mask from its cradle, Faron carefully put it on.

Closing his eyes he uttered a single word: "Engage."

There was sensation like a rush of electricity and adrenaline and he gave an involuntary gasp.

He opened his eyes again and overlaid upon the control chamber before him he saw another chamber; a mix of ancient stones and modern technology. As he focused his mind, the control chamber faded away altogether to be replaced by the other gallery-cum-storage hangar.

He was gazing down upon rows of benches covered in mummies and pilfered statues in the process of having their shabti units fitted.

He tensed his arms and felt strength such as the pharaohs of ancient times must have felt, when the word of one man was interpreted as that of a god. He turned this way and that to survey the hangar and was aware of the grating sound of his own head turning left and right.

"Now is the moment of our ascension!" he declared, and took a colossal step forward.

THE SPHINX BOUNDED along a walkway running alongside a clanking conveyor upon which reclaimed robot parts and other pieces of metal detritus jolted as they were carried towards a mighty collecting hopper at the end of the vast factory. The complex had taken over the whole mortuary temple, buried beneath the Giza sands, and the interior of the Great Pyramid of Khufu as well.

"Look out, sir!" Nimrod exclaimed as a mummy threw itself from a gantry above them.

Ulysses' sword-cane was in his hand in a moment, and he ran the undead robot through, sparks flying from the back of the device as Ulysses severed the slim spinal column connector rod. His hands back on the controls, he pulled hard left and the sphinx skidded sideways, leaping the conveyor—coming perilously close to colliding with it and becoming entangled in its workings—before landing gracefully on the far side.

More mummies crowded the gangway ahead of them.

"Who knew there were so many mummies in Ancient Egypt?" Ulysses exclaimed.

"Well, it was the most long-lasting of all the ancient civilisations, sir," Nimrod pointed out informatively.

"Have you still got that pamphlet with you?" Ulysses enquired, as the sphinx bounded towards the advancing pack of artificially-animated undead.

Ulysses took the subsequent silence as confirmation of his suspicions.

A thunderous crash drew their attention away from the lumbering mummies and towards the end of the subterranean factory complex.

"Good lord!" Ulysses gasped as something massive burst its way into the machinery-filled hall, an entire wall giving way before it.

It was as if one of the pantheon of Ancient Egypt had returned to the Land of the Pharaohs, ready to smite all those who stood in the way of Ramesses Faron, one of the huge statues of Abu Simbel reanimated and bent on meting out its divine retribution. The stone colossus strode towards them, smashing through the winding structure of conveyor belts, heedless of the damage it was causing in its determination to reach the fleeing fugitives.

"Mummies are one thing," Ulysses declared breathlessly, as the sphinx crushed another bandaged body beneath its iron claws, "but stone giants are something else altogether!"

"Might I suggest we abandon our plan to find the control room?" Nimrod began.

"And take out the transmitter itself," Ulysses finished. "Good thinking, old chap."

Ulysses pulled hard on the controls and, in response, the sphinx leapt over another rumbling conveyor, heading for a grilled vent, set between two ram-headed stone guardians.

"Duck!" Ulysses shouted, as the sphinx smashed through the grille, its steel claws slipping on the smooth metal floor of the ventilation duct beyond, before it crashed through another grille at the other end and they emerged into the searing light of Ra.

Ulysses recoiled for a moment, as the sphinx found its footing on the steep slope of stepped limestone blocks that formed the face of the pyramid, throwing an arm up to shield his eyes from the glare of the Sun God. His sunglasses were in his jacket, which he only then remembered was still in the cell, and after the relative gloom of the factory the bright sunlight was a contrast so stark as to be blinding.

It took him a moment to realise they were near the bottom of the Great Pyramid of Khufu. Above them, blazing like white-hot molten metal, shone the golden tip of the pyramid.

"Up there!" Ulysses pointed. "That has to be the transmitter."

"And I would have to agree with you, sir," his faithful manservant replied.

Before either of them could move, the side of the pyramid erupted outwards. Great blocks of stone were flung out into the desert, crashing down on the sand and the rudimentary road that ran through the pyramid-factory complex. One crushed an automaton dromedary parked at the foot of the cyclopean structure.

The head and shoulders of the enormous statue emerged from the hole, the huge, carved face turning its impassive granite gaze upon them—but the sphinx and its passengers were already gone, racing away up the side of the man-made mountain.

The automaton bounded up the steep steps of the pyramid's exposed inner structure, its steel claws giving it purchase on the sand-slicked surface of the stones. But the colossus had them in its sights now. It clawed its way up the pyramid after them, crushing stones in its granite-hard grip, the same tight-lipped, emotionless expression meeting Ulysses' gaze when he glanced back over his shoulder, despite the grinding of its mechanical innards that issued from it like a rasping roar.

RAMESSES COULD SEE his quarry now, via the visual feed being sent from the robotised colossus to the sarcophagus headset, and from there stimulating the visual centres in his own brain.

He was as a god. Where he smote his fists solid rock cracked and crumbled.

Where he trod the ground shook. And those he deemed his enemies would not escape his vengeful wrath.

While his body remained contained within the black sarcophagus, his mind was free to inhabit the effigy of his ancient ancestor Ramesses the Second. Carved out of red granite, over thirty feet tall and weighing over eighty tons, nothing could stand against him.

Hauling his huge body clear of the hole he had mindlessly smashed in the side of the pyramid, he picked up one of the broken blocks in his powerful hands, stone joints grinding as he did so, and hurled it at the sphinx that was heading for the golden transmitter at the top.

The projectile tumbled slowly through the air before crashing down where the sphinx had been only a split second before.

Roaring in frustration—his bellow of primeval rage echoing from the walls of the sepulchral control room, as well as from a vox relay in the statue's chest—Ramesses climbed the pyramid in pursuit of the fleeing sphinx, the edifice shaking beneath him with every seismic footfall.

SCRABBLING ON THE stones, the sphinx reached the golden cap at the summit of the pyramid. It was pyramidal in form itself, but with columns of ancient hieroglyphs replaced by the geometric patterns of complicated circuitry instead.

"That has to be the transmitter," Ulysses said, jumping down from the saddle.

Ulysses glanced back down the pyramid at the colossus continuing its climb towards them. It still had some way to go, but in reality he didn't have long.

"It's a shame I don't have some of Spring-Heeled Jack's limpet-mines," he muttered. He looked at Nimrod: "You keep an eye on that thing's progress while I try find a way to deactivate the transmitter."

From the peak of the pyramid Ulysses could see for miles in every direction—from the depths of the Saharan wilderness to the west, to the lush green lands bordering the Nile and the life-giving river itself, and on to the Sinai Heights away to the east. But Ulysses Quicksilver's attention was wholly on the golden transmitter. Regardless, he could see no obvious way of accessing its inner workings or even removing the device.

Feeling impotent, Ulysses pulled the rapier blade from its cane casing once more, as if that was the answer to all his problems, only to put it away again a matter of moments later.

"Sir!" Nimrod shouted from the saddle of the sphinx.

The colossus was closing rapidly, red granite hands bunched into bludgeoning fists. Shooting one last frustrated glance at the golden pinnacle, Ulysses leapt back into the seat behind the sphinx's head, the leonine-automaton immediately hunkering down in a crouch.

"So what do we do now?" Nimrod enquired. "How do we stop the transmission?"

Ramesses the Second loomed over them. "Brute force," Ulysses said.

A fist as heavy and as powerful as a pile-driver smashed into the blocks at the top of the pyramid as Ulysses steered the sphinx sideways, Nimrod clutching Ulysses' seat back to keep from falling out of his seat altogether. The colossus's rage rumbled like the thunder of Set himself, and it lunged at the sphinx again. Again it missed, as Ulysses sent the automaton dancing back down the side of the towering edifice. Two huge fists grabbed hold of the golden peak of the pyramid as the sphinx escaped its clutches.

The feline machine landed and took a moment to find its footing again as the carefully-laid stones shifted beneath it.

"Almost there!" Ulysses gasped, before sending the sphinx back up the pyramid and within reach of the flailing giant.

They were behind the colossus now. Ulysses hesitated for a moment, understanding the dire consequences that would follow if the sphinx was actually struck by the stone giant, and then committed them to whatever fate had in store nonetheless.

The sphinx leapt onto the stone pharaoh's back, even as the giant twisted to meet their assault. The weight and force of the automaton hitting it unbalanced it even more, and the colossus fell across the apex of the pyramid, the sphinx leaping clear again.

As the big cat-droid landed, and Ulysses and Nimrod were thrown forward precariously in their seats, they heard the groan of the ancient structure giving up at long last after enduring such a battering.

Under the weight of the colossus, the golden transmitter sank a few inches. It wasn't much, but it attested to a much more serious architectural failure elsewhere. As the giant struggled to rise again, to mete out its divine retribution against its enemies once and for all, the stones and metal framework supporting the transmitter gave way.

RAMESSES FARON WATCHED the drama unfold through the stone eyes of the statue as the colossus tumbled into the void beneath the top of the pyramid—a space that had been constructed to house the factory control room. As the shattered tip and the brilliant blue sky beyond fell away into the distance before his eyes, Ramesses broke the link as the artificial lighting inside the control room was overwhelmed by the sunlight streaming in through the hole above.

Casting the headpiece aside, he threw himself forwards, out of the sarcophagus, the tip of the transmitter hitting him and smashing his head clean from his body. Mere moments later, the giant stone automaton crashed down into the chamber, crushing the obsidian sarcophagus beneath it, wrecking many of the other Turing engines, and—coming apart in a hail of shrapnel beneath its weight—completely crushing the transmitter.

At that instant, in a thousand locations throughout Africa and Europe, shabti-adapted mummy automata froze in their assaults, as the signal from the Osiris Corporation headquarters ceased transmitting.

There was a moment's inaction while the units rebooted themselves, looming over their cowering victims, and then, one by one, the mummies and statues reached out gentle hands to help the very people they had been threatened only seconds before.

Cautiously, Ulysses peered over the lip of the hole, steadying himself against the stones, ready to run at a moment's notice should one of them start to shift under him.

"Sir?" said Nimrod, from his place beside the sphinx, the automaton's idling engine causing its body to gently rise and fall on its sprung legs, as if recovering its breath after its exertions. "Can you see anything?"

"Yes," Ulysses replied, "wonderful things. I can see...a shattered visage," he said, as he gazed down upon the unmoved features of Ramesses the Second, the stone head having broken free, exposing the articulated metal spine beneath, "whose frown and wrinkled lip and sneer of cold command tell that its sculptor well those passions read."

He paused in his recitation of Shelley as he considered how quickly and how easily Ramesses Faron's plans for revenge and global domination had come to naught.

"My name is Ozymandias, King of Kings," he continued, as a cold wind blew in over the lone and level sands of the western desert. "Look on my works, ye mighty, and despair!"

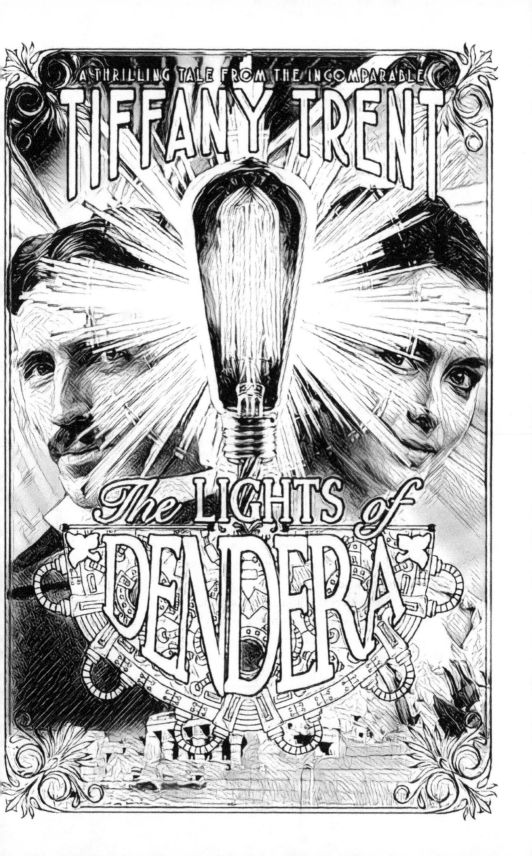

The Lights of Dendera

I first saw him in the Metropolitan Opera House. Someone had invited him to the Washingtonian ball, and I, along with other members of the opera troupe, had paid to be in the gallery to see the finery of New York's elite as they feasted and danced below. He caught my eye immediately. I wrestled the opera glasses away from Francine to view him—lean, tall, black hair greying around the temples, coat in the most becoming and masculine fashion. He was too old for dapper. He was far removed from that—no, he was the epitome of intellectual beauty in a way I had found no other to be, despite many men's attempts to convince me otherwise.

And because we were forbidden from moving from our seats in the gallery— we could not mingle with such aristocracy, only entertain them—I looked at him as long as I liked, wondering if my glass-eyed gaze would burn a hole in his neck.

Francine said as much when she noticed me staring. "Good thing you ain't the sun, Miss Ames! You'd burn the poor man!"

I hissed at her, but gave the glasses back and pretended to talk to the person to my right. I still have no idea who that kind, dull soul was.

It was in the papers next morning—NIKOLA TESLA ATTENDS WASHING-TONIAN BALL AT THE MET!!! A coup for the society man or woman who had managed his attendance; I had heard his appearance at social gatherings was quite rare these days. The article went on at great length about his achievements and the lasting conundrum of his bachelorhood—"Can no woman win the heart of this Wizard of Science?" Under his portrait—taken when he was many years younger—the caption: "I can in no wise commit myself to any lady, however deserving, for in doing so I would repudiate the true Muse to whom I am eternally Bound—Science."

I had a notion to break that perception of his. Science could take a long walk off a short pier.

But as I looked in my mirror, readying myself for the next performance, I could hardly countenance my wild imaginings. I folded up the paper and threw it in the rubbish bin. "Such fancies," I whispered to myself.

The truth was that anything I might do romantically would jeopardize my career unless I found a true manager who would finally bring me to my pinnacle. I had brought myself far, as far as I could. But now I needed more. Love was not part of that equation. I rouged my lips—Jezebel-scarlet, as Francine liked to call it—and powdered my nose. My hair, crimped and oiled and pressed, was behaving, and Cecilia the company seamstress had done a wonderful job of fitting the white, pleated gown to my curves. I slid the gold serpent armbands up my arms and arranged the pharaonic headdress over my hair.

I stood, admiring myself as surely Amneris, the Egyptian princess, would have. I was still peeved that I had not been given the role of Aida. Never mind that my voice was perfect for it; Adelaide Chambers could never understand the heart of Aida the Nubian slave as I could.

Francine entered; she never had the manners to knock.

"Lordamercy, Miss Ames!" she said, looking me up and down. "Every man in that theater gone pop his drawers when he see you!" She rumbled appreciatively. Unlike me, Francine had never lost her Louisiana accent. I had softened mine to a pleasing patois that many easily mistook as originating from Quebec or France. I never dissuaded anyone of that notion when they voiced their thoughts about my origins. Better to be full French than a quadroon from the French Quarter trying to pass.

"Hssssh, Francine," I demurred, though I caught my own eye in the mirror and silently told my reflection: *that is the entire point*. Still, that didn't mean I had to admit it; I certainly didn't have to like it.

"Whatever the costume, it's all about the singing," I said. I looked in the mirror at my hollow dark eyes, my full lips and powdered cheekbones. Everything in order. Everything in place. "All about the singing," I whispered to myself.

I SANG MY heart out that night. That night and every night. I was singing the sorrows of Amneris; I was pouring my heart out to Radames, bewitching him with my voice. All my yearning, all my love went into my arias to him. Never mind that I saw Nikola Tesla's face when I sang.

But of course no one noticed. All the accolades, all the roses, were for Adelaide Chambers. Not me.

It happened in a strange way, as all chance does. I'd said I was looking for a manager, and on my few off days, I frequented the places where I thought one might be. If only I could bend an ear like P.T. Barnum's. Would he do for me what he had done for Jenny Lind, the Swedish Nightingale?

But no one of that ilk frequented the places I did. As far as I'd come, it was not far enough. I began to think I would always remain in the gallery of that Washingtonian gala, watching the diamond-encrusted primadonnas waltz across the floor.

That all changed when Mr. Dark came to see me.

HE WAS A man small in stature but large in presence; ushered in by an uncommonly nervous and supplicatory Francine, he filled the room without seeming to move at all. He wore a gray suit that he appeared to find deeply discomfiting. When he looked up at me from under the brim of his hat, his eyes flashed gold.

"Good evening, ma'am," he said, removing his derby. His hair was plastered down with hair oil, and I noted that he sported a pencil-thin mustache, which almost looked drawn on. His eyes were dark and seemed lined, like the men in the opera. I must have been mistaken about the gold.

I nodded slightly.

"I'm Mr. Dark." He extended his hand. I merely looked at it, clasping my hands together firmly.

"An ungloved lady does not shake hands with a stranger," I reminded him.

He looked almost frightened then, and that strange gold slid through his eyes. "But of course." He nodded and cleared his throat. "Well, then, Miss Ames, I am here to offer you a proposition."

I raised a brow, and he cleared his throat again. His nervousness seemed incongruous with what hid in his eyes—something ferocious and ancient, a spirit that seemed to match my own.

"It's fairly simple," he said, and I heard an accent slide into his voice, one he'd obviously been working hard to hide. Recognition filled me. He was like me, this one. Passing for something he wasn't. He would likely claim French ancestry as I did, when anyone might wish to intimate otherwise.

"Go on." I allowed a small, confidential smile, and that seemed to calm him somewhat.

"The charity I work for is putting on a gala in celebration of the new Egyptian exhibit at the new art museum. Since you've been singing in Aida this season, we thought perhaps you might be interested in performing there."

I picked up a nearby peacock feather fan to give myself time to think of how to say what needed saying. "Are you certain it isn't Miss Chambers you've come to see? Her dressing room is down the hall." I pointed with the fan toward the door.

He smiled. "I am not mistaken in coming to see you, Miss Ames." He did not move closer but fixed me with a gaze both considering and slightly mischievous. "It is you I want, not that *poseur*. There is magic in your voice. There is none in hers."

I hid my smile behind my fan. "I see."

"There will be remuneration involved, Miss Ames. You needn't fear that. And it's good work done in the name of the new collection—I think you can see how important a contribution your voice would be."

"Well, then," I said. "You have endeared me to your cause, sir. Certainly, Mr. Dark. Do give my assistant Francine the particulars."

I reached for him this time with my ungloved hand and he seemed surprised when I took his hand warmly in mine. "Thank you for seeking me out." I hoped that somehow my touch communicated my happiness at finding kin in this city wilderness, even if I could never speak it aloud.

Now it was his turn to nod and withdraw. "Of course, Miss Ames. I look forward to your debut on the museum stage."

He smiled then. As he left, something caught my eye, a dark shadow slipping through one of my many mirrors. I turned to look.

What walked out of my dressing room was not a man. It was shaped like a coyote, but taller, more slender, its muzzle tapering to a sharper point. But this creature's fur was black as pitch. He regarded me with great golden eyes and bowed his head.

I whirled back to face him, only to have the door latch shut in my face.

I SANG THREE more shows. Each night I looked out beyond the footlights and swore I saw Mr. Dark sitting there, but when I would send Francine out to invite him to my dressing room—a thing I'd never done before—he was nowhere to be found. Regardless, every night after his inquest, a bouquet arrived, delivered by an unseen courier and bearing no trace of its origins. It was filled with roses, jasmine, lotuses, anemones, and chrysanthemums. The roses were dark as dried blood, the mums bright gold as the eyes of that strange creature that had walked out of my dressing room.

I shuddered, but still inhaled them, and their freshness stirred strange images in my mind, made me think almost that I was not that jilted princess I played at night, but a queen of that very Egypt of which I sang.

It is perhaps important here that I mention I had forgotten all about Tesla by this time, except as a drifting fancy presented occasionally by the papers. He was a face in the crowd that had stirred me once, nothing more. So much had the strangeness of Mr. Dark's invitation infiltrated my mind that I did not think of much else when I was awake. At night, I took laudanum so I would not dream.

The hansom cab came for me on an evening when I'd pleaded illness from a cast party the manager was holding. I snuck out, my heavy black velvet cloak hiding my gold Amneris costume, the gown she wears in her last attempt to bring Radames back to her side. The bite of October was in the air, and I found myself longing for my wool coat and ermine muff.

Mr. Dark was waiting for me by the curb. As he helped me alight, he saw the golden shimmer beneath the velvet and his lips quirked in a canine grin. "They will adore you, my dear."

"Thank you for the flowers."

"The flowers?" He spoke as if distracted, though he kept hold of my hand on his arm as we walked toward the Met entrance.

"I assume you have been sending them—the roses and lotuses and mums. Quite a strange combination. If I were a devotee of the language of flowers I would be very perplexed as to your meaning."

He glanced at me, and again something wild and golden slid through his eyes.

"All things have meaning, but not always what you might think. Those flowers were once grown in the gardens of ancient Egypt. I sent them in remembrance of what you do. Nothing more."

I nodded, but something about his words set a trembling in my limbs. This was a charity event. A paying gig for me, a little bit of notoriety perhaps. Nothing more. Why did it feel like the weight of Time pressed down upon my shoulders as I walked with Mr. Dark up the stairs and the glass doors were opened for us?

The Great Hall was filled with light and music. I stopped for a moment, stunned by the sound and brilliance of it all. Columns had been painted like those in the temples of ancient Egypt, and sarcophagi and statues of the gods rose between them. At the far end, chairs surrounded a stage over which loomed a great statue, of which god I could not quite make out at this distance and angle.

Through the play of lights on the fountains, a familiar face caught my attention.

Tesla. Nikola Tesla.

I was to sing for this Wizard of Science.

I stopped, my hand slipping away from Mr. Dark's arm.

"There is some problem?" he said. Again that patois slipping between his words. I was no longer certain he was from the bayou. I was beginning to think he might be from somewhere else entirely.

I swallowed and raised my chin, looking away. Tesla's dark eyes had slid over and past me, as they did all women. I would sing for him, and that was all.

I could feel the red heat in my face at the thought that I had ever imagined anything more than that, even for a moment. Perhaps I'd had too much gin that night when Francine and I had stood in the gallery gazing down at the stars.

Mr. Dark seemed to notice my attention. "You know him?" he murmured.

"Of course," I fluttered. "Everyone knows him, don't they? He is Mr. Tesla, the Wizard of Science."

"Indeed," Mr. Dark said. He licked his lips in an almost canine way. "But I meant—do you *know* him?"

"Personally?"

"Intimately."

"Mr. Dark, I am offended that you might even suggest such a thing! Do you wish me to sing tonight or not?" I very nearly stamped my foot against the marble in protest of such a rude question. I stepped away from him.

"I am sorry," he said, turning fully toward me. There was great strain on his face. "It would go better thus if you had been…ah…more intimately acquainted with him is all."

"What? What would go better?"

Mr. Dark shook his head. He pulled a folded paper from his pocket and placed it in my hands. "This is what you will sing. And you must be sure to be near Mr. Tesla when you do it."

"Why? What do you mean?"

"Just…please trust in this. You are needed. None will forget this night, I promise."

I smoothed the paper in my hands, glancing at the title. *Harper's Song for the Dead.*

He made as if to leave.

"Wait," I said. "How am I to sing this?"

He turned, the lights of the fountain weaving golden sheaves across his face. His eyes were gold, too, that knowing gold I remembered from the creature in my mirror. "However you feel it sounds best, Miss Ames. You will be called when the time is right." With that, he bowed to me and departed.

Left to my own devices, I wandered from the Hall into the new gallery, worried that I shouldn't stray too far. In particular I was entranced by the *shabti*, the little figurines placed in the tombs of royals which were meant to represent servants, pets, and even ordinary objects the deceased favored. It was believed that in the afterlife, these objects would come to life, stretch in size, and aid the royal dead in their daily tasks in the Beyond. Charming notion.

In fact…I bent closer to one particular *shabti*, a carving of a young woman. Her curves, the necklace at her throat, the tiny painted face with its lips wide as if singing for all eternity…The deep familiarity roiled my stomach.

I turned wildly, about to flee, when a woman clicked toward me urgently in her sharp little boots. "Miss Ames?" she said. "You are needed!"

Museum pages went around dimming lights. Behind the stage was ominously dark, save for the great statue of the jackal-headed god, Anubis.

Jackal.

The trembling began the moment my eyes fell upon his black head and gold-painted eyes. I thought I might faint. I thought I might run away, but then I turned and found sharp, dark eyes upon me. Curious eyes, wondering why I hesitated, measuring me and finding me wanting.

Tesla was seated at the far end of stage left.

Mr. Dark was right behind him.

Someone introduced me—the irritable woman who had fetched me a moment ago. I kept my head bowed; I had allowed myself to be distracted by the museum exhibits, and I had not warmed up. Furthermore, I had no idea how to sing this song. Mr. Dark had left me in the dark, as far as I was concerned. For the first time in a long time, I was worried this performance might go very badly.

"I give you Miss Thomasina Ames!"

I lifted my head and smiled in a way Amneris would have.

The musical accompaniment was simple, almost primitive—harp, flute, and drum. I could not see from whence it came, somewhere in the outer darkness. I listened for a while to catch the rhythm—slow, pure, meandering through the notes like an ancient river.

Show me the man who is pure in the eyes of the West
Show me his sister, his beloved who has gone before
Let him rejoice in the evening of the second life
Let him rise up on the morning of his rebirth...

The statue of Anubis loomed behind me. The light grew stronger. Tesla's mouth opened; he spoke soundlessly. A jackal paced between the seats as they receded from view. Time stretched, snapped. My voice hung on the last note and shattered.

The stage was pulled from beneath me and replaced with flagstones as swiftly and neatly as a set change. But my feet could not manage the switch quite so neatly, and I fell.

Tesla was beside me then, helping me up.

"Miss Ames." I had never before heard the burr in his voice, that Serbian rumble that so many women found utterly charming. "I do not think we are where we were." The smile he gave me was not reflected in his eyes. Though there was courtesy and the deftness of a gentleman in his aid to me, there was nothing more. In fact, as I stood, dusting off my costume, I saw him try to surreptitiously wipe his gloved hands down the front of his trousers, as if touching me had somehow tainted him.

I would ignore that. For now.

"No," I answered, looking around at the painted colonnades topped by wide, grinning faces. "I believe we are somewhere else entirely."

Mr. Dark, I thought. *Anubis. What have you done?*

"Do you think this is some other part of the museum?" he asked. "You see, already I am trying to figure how they managed this and who must have made the device that enabled them to do it. It must have some kind of mechanism..." He crouched down, feeling with his long, slender fingers along the edges of the flagstones.

Someone stepped forth from the shadows, though I knew nothing had been there a moment before. I covered my gasp with a hand, as Anubis stepped forth from the shadows. Anubis in his true form.

Mr. Tesla was busying himself with the flagstones, trying to find the mechanism beneath them. He did not see until the jackal-headed shadow fell over him.

"Nikola Tesla." The resonance of his voice made my bones ache from heels to crown. Here was the god fully in his element.

I lowered my eyes. I had heard of such beings in the French Quarter in my youth, but I had tried to avoid all of it as superstitious nonsense the old grannies used to grasp at power. Voodoo women with their roots and possessions. Nothing to fear or concern myself with. I was, after all, getting out.

Tesla looked over his shoulder. I saw the fear cross his face for one second, and then he stood, walked over to the jackal god, reached up and pinched him on his black-furred cheek.

Anubis snapped at him, but Tesla seemed unphased. "Remarkable detail," he murmured, dusting his hand on his trousers again. "Whatever it is that you want of us, you've spared no expense to make it so."

"Indeed I have not. I have paid a greater price to bring you here, O Wizard of Science, than you could ever guess."

His words were laced with the jackal-song of the twilit desert. In his true voice, I could finally understand the things I had not understood before.

"I suspect you paid a great deal for that costume," Tesla said. He walked round behind the god. "How is it put together?"

Anubis swiveled, snarling at him.

I sighed. "He is Anubis, sir, the messenger-god of the old Egyptians." I had at least done some of my homework before singing in Aida. From what I had read, Anubis escorted the dead to be judged before Osiris, and he held the scales that weighted their hearts while they awaited their fates.

Tesla laughed out loud. It was an unpleasant, wheezing sound for one with a voice ordinarily so rich and smooth. "If indeed there are gods, there is only One…"

I gestured toward the god who seemed to be swelling even taller and darker in his wrath. "I think this one disproves that theory."

Tesla eyed him, undaunted. "Let us just accept this thought experiment as true for a moment. If he is hypothetically a god of ancient Egypt, walking about enfleshed, and we are presumably not where we were, then…would it be right to suppose that we have somehow been transported back in time?"

Anubis nodded, with a tension that I read as exasperation, if gods are prone to such a thing. I imagined they must be exasperated with us much of the time.

"But how is that possible? The laws of physics…."

At the actual growl that emerged from Anubis's snout, Tesla fell silent.

"Magic," Anubis said.

Tesla had the grace not to laugh this time, saying rather sharply, "Magic is just another word for technology yet to be discovered."

"As you like," Anubis said. "You were brought here by a technology you could not possibly understand." When Tesla opened his mouth to refute, Anubis snapped, "Not even you, Wizard of Science. But I need your knowledge nonetheless, even if it is paltry compared to that of the gods. Some things we can engineer. Some we cannot."

"What do you want of us, then?" I asked.

Anubis looked at me. "You were the opener of the way. I was trapped in New York in your time trying to find Mr. Tesla, until you were able to sing open the gates. I told you there was magic in your voice. I am seldom wrong." He dipped his head in the direction of Tesla. "But as for him... I need him to light the lights of Dendera."

HE DREW US out onto the porch of the temple. We looked across the dusk-laden Nile Valley. Little villages clustered around temples like this one. Irrigated fields drew the great river into furrows and canals where crops waved in the freshening wind. Farther off, the ramparts of palaces or temples rose in the twilight. The smell of desert blew in strongly—salt and sand and...menace. A storm brewed to the north and east, rolling clouds that promised only lightning but no life-giving rain.

And under the storm, we saw waves of dark riders, pikes bristling like a vast, thorny hedge above them, approaching the unprotected, fertile valley where most were bedding down for sleep.

"I show you what is coming," Anubis said, gesturing toward the storm. "The Hyksos bring the rage and warmongering of my brother Set upon this land. He has sent his null magic down through the river. I was able to get out beforehand, but not back on my own recognizance. Thus, I am sorry to say, I had to trick Miss Ames into helping me bring Mr. Tesla back to Dendera. If the lights here can be lit, they will warn others to prepare."

Tesla looked for a moment across the Valley, as if for the first time he realized what he was seeing. We did not have to guess as to what would happen if he refused to help.

"For certain," Anubis said softly, "we cannot stop them forever. But we can soften the blow now." Love of the land, of the deep, muddy river where the lotuses grew, even the rot of the shallows and their whispering reeds, was in his voice. Care for the dead who had hallowed this land for their children was also there. I had never imagined a god so kind; in my darkest hours, I had been sure God as I knew Him did not exist at all.

"There is a system I've long held dear," Tesla said. "A system by which electricity could be generated and transmitted wirelessly. If the proper equipment was raised in the places you wish to protect, we might be able to send the signal instantaneously."

Anubis nodded. "That is what I had in mind, but I cannot raise that much magic, I fear." He grimaced, and his sharp jackal teeth made me shudder.

There was a sweet, rattling chime from within the temple, and Anubis looked back into the dim interior. "The sistrum. My sister Hathor summons me," he said. "I will send someone to fetch you."

In one breath, he vanished.

Soon enough, a kilted man came and led us to what we presumed to be our lodgings. He did not speak. I theorized that perhaps he could not speak to us as Anubis had. I had sensed that the god could make himself known to us in ways that an ordinary mortal could not.

We were treated well as guests by a small assembly of servants, and slowly I began learning to speak with them. I learned that what we called Egypt, they called Kemet. I learned that they were careful of us because we were favored of Anapa, their name for Anubis.

It was a revelation to be among dark-skinned people all the time, to no longer have to pass. There were many gradations of skin color, from darkest midnight to the cool olive of my skin; I no longer felt the need to lighten myself with powder, or hide from the sun. They were also the first people who understood how to care for my hair. For the first time, I wore it down freely, in the long ringlets they best knew how to make, though I saw that many of them went with shaven heads and wigs, which they scented with a heavy pomade.

Tesla I saw but rarely, mostly at meal times. We were given to understand that the urgency of our mission meant that we were not to leave the House, but Tesla they took to a workshop each day where he was to accomplish the work Anubis had set for him, though I was not made privy to its location. And so, though my contact with him was as fleeting as it had ever been in the century we had left behind, in a strange way we clung to one another, as those will who have been exiled from their own land and time. We had been adjured by gesture and charade not to stray.

In the evenings, Tesla would return for a meal, and afterwards we stood together out on the portico of the House of the Lotus. We had not seen Anubis since he had brought us here days ago, and I suspected that was by design. We leaned together on the balustrade, looking out over the peace of the night.

"I trust you are well, Miss Ames?" Tesla asked. He seemed more relaxed here than I had ever noticed in the brief encounters we had had in New York.

"I am," I said. Even the clothes agreed with me here, comfortable and cool in the heat of Kemet. The heavy *wesekh* collar of faience beads I wore glowed against my skin; they had belonged to the Lady of the House before she passed, and she had bequeathed them to her daughter (or at least that was how I had understood the pantomime), who now loaned them to me.

I noticed Tesla would not look at me, though. Devoid of the mutton-leg sleeves and wide skirts that were proper for our time, I supposed to him I seemed nearly naked.

In fact, he had not traded his clothes for those of Kemet, preferring instead to wear the same trousers, shirt, and coat he had worn the night of the gala. I did not know how he was not positively rank from the sweat or what he did for clothing on laundry day, but close as I was to him now, I smelled nothing offensive.

"And you, sir?"

"Quite well, though still baffled by this enterprise. It is hard to believe New York as we know it does not yet exist."

I nodded. I had been thinking on that, too. It was even harder to believe that my ancestors had come from a place like this, perhaps—a place so serene and civilized, a place brimming with food and culture. Among the many things I had realized was that I had felt a deep shame, which I masked with defiance, back in New York for who and what I was. In my depths, I had bought into the message that my people were savages and that I would have to be the most civilized of all to make up for the lack of my ancestors.

Now, I saw differently, though I of course could say none of this to Mr. Tesla. To him, I was still an opera singer of questionable virtue, who could protect what little integrity she possessed by saying nothing of her true thoughts.

"Miss Ames?" He noted that my thoughts had strayed.

"Yes, sir," I said. "It is a strange and wondrous thought indeed."

"Stranger still," he said, "that all of the things we were celebrating that night in the museum as antiquities are now part of our present. It fills me with interesting notions about Time."

He looked out over the Nile, with the many lights of barges and night-fisherman floating upon it like stars. "Perhaps Time does not only flow one direction," he mused. "Perhaps Anubis was able to bring us back here because there are eddies and currents beneath the surface. Still—how did he accomplish it?"

That was a mystery I doubted we'd ever be privy to. As a scientist, though, he surely could not resist trying to solve it.

"And how goes your work?" I asked.

"Excellently," he said. There was joy in his voice that I hadn't expected. Joy that seemed a bit out of step with the task at hand. "I am testing a principle that I was never able to convince my backers at home to allow me to test within the confines of the city. Wireless electricity. A means for electricity to cross the entire world without cables or wires, without companies controlling it."

"You are that thrilled with turning on lights, Mr. Tesla?"

"Yes, as a matter of fact. But I have discovered other things here that I never would have expected."

"Ah, yes?" I was hoping that he would invite me to his workshop. I edged closer to him, and he moved away discreetly, pretending he had seen something beyond my line of sight that interested him. Still solicitous of my virtue, I presumed. I at least thought he might tell me of the secrets he'd discovered, but apparently he was not interested in confiding them.

"What's that?" I gripped his sleeve and pointed toward a line of fire zigzagging down the river toward us. The boats it touched burst into flame. When it came to the Temple of Hathor by the water, the light reared upwards, resolving into a golden snake.

I saw Anubis on the temple steps, towering into the night. Beside him stood his sister Hathor, her horned head encompassing the moon. They merely stood while the snake threatened, testing their defenses. Eventually, the snake receded, its hectic light disappearing far in the north.

Anubis was with us, then. He looked worn around the edges; I could have sworn his muzzle showed gray in the torchlight.

"You saw him," he said.

"What was he?" Tesla asked.

"That is Apep. He is Seth's instrument, the bearer of Chaos. We must hurry in our task. Lower Egypt is falling. Upper Egypt will not be prepared."

Tesla nodded. "I will work through the night," he said. "I bid you good evening, Miss Ames, sir," he said.

He presented me and the god with a deep bow of the style those here in Kemet used to one they honored. There was a gleam in his eye that made me think perhaps I ought to seek out his workshop after all.

"Good evening, Mr. Tesla," Anubis said.

THE NEXT MORNING saw me determined to discover the whereabouts of Tesla's workshop and to see the progress made. I had heard miraculous things of his laboratory in New York, how something he had done had caused an earthquake that nearly brought the entire building in which it was housed to rubble. I had read, after seeing him at the Washingtonian gala, of speculations surrounding his experiments at Wardenclyffe, which was off-limits to the public and shrouded in great secrecy.

I explained to the servants through charades that I would like to go for a walk in the garden, which was a partial truth. From there, I hoped to scout or perhaps draw from my escort where Tesla's workshop might be hidden.

Servants came, bearing fans to swat away the biting flies and mosquitoes that hungered for our flesh in the sun. I walked along the byways of the garden, enchanted. Here grew the very flowers Anubis had sent me, not so long ago. I gathered them in my arms, the lotuses and scented lilies, even the roses with their thorns and pressed them to my bosom, not caring that they dampened the linen of my dress. I hoped that some of their scent might wear off on me—though I was already richly perfumed with the oil of lime the Lady of the House favored.

Then, I looked down, and saw the pointed head of an asp. Its tongue flicked between the thorns. I staggered back, thinking of the great golden serpent that had challenged Anubis and Hathor the night before.

An explosion came then from the northern corner of the garden, and it felt strangely bound up with the asp, the golden serpent, and the terror that had begun tapping at the back of my mind. We raced to the northern edge to see what had happened.

The servants and I looked down past the walled veranda toward another building; I would have presumed it a storehouse based on its sparse design and simple features. Smoke flowed from the doors and birds ascended from the roof at the noise. Tesla came out arm in arm with someone, a boy pale as alabaster, both of them coughing. Tesla's hair was wild. The boy seemed hairless.

I judged the distance and how I might reach it by scaling the wall or walking round. One of the servants ran back to the House, presumably to tell them that Tesla might be in need of assistance.

I pantomimed that perhaps we should scale the wall and go to his aid, but the remaining servants shook their heads. They brought me to the edge and showed me. There was a terribly steep drop and sharp rocks at the bottom. There was no ladder. Someone wanted to make sure we stayed put.

I nodded. "Another way?" I gestured. They looked at one another, then took me to the southwest corner of the garden. Concealed under vines was a door, a rusty thing that could likely be forced with some exertion. By the looks of it, it was often used, and by the way the servants were grinning, I suspected I knew exactly what for.

They had read me truly. I blushed and fanned myself with the woven palm they offered. They patted me on the arm as if they knew perfectly well my affliction, as if they would keep it our secret.

That night, I paid the door a visit, and there was none, not even an asp, to bar my way. I was fairly certain I had calculated the path correctly, and Tesla had not been at the evening meal. He was working hard now, obsessed with finding the answer. The Hyksos drew near.

I remembered his deep bow the other night. I had focused on that instead of his aversion. This night, the servants had brought me a lovely gown of the same undyed linen but of a cut that strove to reveal all my heretofore hidden charms. They adorned my arms and wrists with gold, my feet with sandals of the lightest and softest leather. They painted my eyes in their style, lining them with kohl and spangling the lids with green malachite. They knew my quest. In New York, I would have been embarrassed and certainly much more discreet. Here, it seemed perfectly natural that a lady would bedeck herself to go out and seek her lover. Of course, the forms had to be obeyed—I could not simply walk out of the House, but I could sneak out, and they had been kind enough to show me the way. I felt certain if I did not arrive again before dawn, the servants would not make known my whereabouts, either.

Along the alley and down the place I'd seen Tesla earlier I walked, my sandals making music against the flagstones, the heat of the evening pulling sweat from my shoulders and back.

The portico was lit with torches, which flickered and smoked in the night breeze. I smelled the heavy mud of the river, heard the distant calling of insects and frogs down by water's edge. The doors were not latched; I supposed they would have to be bolted from the inside for them to be locked. Pushing and pulling, I was at last able to slip inside, but the sound of the door opening certainly would have woken the dead, or so it seemed to me.

No one came; it did not occur to me to fear for myself. There were no servants here, though I heard two voices in the room just off the main foyer—perhaps guards who were playing a game of *senet*, the most popular game in Kemet, to pass the time.

I crept past them, though a glimpse confirmed my suspicion. One of them raised his head as I passed, perhaps alerted by the whisper of my presence, but I hurried on, bent on my mission. I hoped to Anubis these people were not the only protection we had against the Hyksos when they came.

In what would normally have been the main storage area loomed tall shapes, some joined by slender braids of beaten copper wire. Others were freestanding, though, and I guessed this was part of the major experiment. I was a bit surprised—I had expected to find Tesla here working feverishly, as he was reputed to do in New York.

For the first time, a little doubt crept into my heart, but then I conjured his face in my mind; the dark spark in his eyes, the half-hidden tug of his lips beneath his mustache, compelled me onward.

I heard what sounded like a low humming noise in a room off the main laboratory. A shadow moved beyond the reed mat that curtained the doorway, Tesla's familiar tall form, though I saw no edges of collar or coat.

I hesitated again. Perhaps he was making ready for bed. Perhaps I should not disturb him. In truth, if he had blown out the oil lamp then, I might have gone back the way I'd come.

But the light remained on, the humming increased in intensity—almost, as I approached, it seemed more of a moan than a song. Perhaps he was in pain? Perhaps a scorpion or an asp...?

"Oh God," I heard him whisper, his voice cracking, straining. I pushed back the reed mat just a fraction to see if he had indeed hurt himself.

What I saw—the sensations of it—were hard to describe. The flickering shadows made a mosaic of light and dark. The boy rose from where he knelt before Tesla, his naked body seemingly sculpted of marble. Tesla's rigid fingers dug into his shoulders, as if the boy was all that held him upright. The boy turned aside a bit, wiping his mouth on the back of his hand.

It must have been then that the gasp slipped from me. The boy turned, his white nostrils flaring. His eyes were red as demon-fire.

I dropped the mat. I walked back to the house, my feet no longer singing on the stones, and collapsed onto my pallet like a wounded bird.

IN A FEW more days, the trial was ready. By then, I was able to look at Tesla again without seeing what I had seen that night in his workshop. I was not horrified— oh no, not in the least. I was ashamed that I had imagined the outcome of that night in my favor, certainly, and embarrassed that I had intruded so brazenly on the man's privacy. But my deeper shame was that I was fascinated—nay, utterly titillated—by what I had seen. I could not stop imagining it to myself. The heat it produced in my body sent me rushing to splash my face with cool water in the garden many a time. I thought in fact of sneaking down again, but the boy had very sharp ears, and I did not want to risk him alerting Tesla, if indeed he already had not.

I had seen what I had seen. Seeing more would serve no purpose.

On the evening of the trial, Tesla was nervous and fretting. The boy murmured to him as they worked and that seemed to soothe him.

The priests of Anubis had come to the temple to summon the god, but he was there almost before the first incense was lit.

"Miss Ames," he said, bowing to me. I found myself blushing as if he could read all the secrets of my heart, as if he weighed them. I did not know if he found them wanting. "Mr. Tesla," he said. "The priests in my sister's northern temple have received disturbing visions. Apep rallies the Hyksos. Are you ready?"

"I think so." Tesla looked to his assistant, who nodded. His pink eyes flashed above his grin. I was still unused to them. I had not forgotten the way they'd glowed at me in the dark, but the grin I very much liked.

The grin was evidently infectious, for I saw the widest smile I'd ever seen Tesla give. "And you, sir?" he asked Anubis. "Are you ready?"

Anubis nodded. "What little power is left to me I will feed into your machine. And if it should work, I imagine it will give me enough strength to send you on your way back to your own time in New York." He eyed me, that flash of gold reminding me of all I'd left behind.

How strange it was then to feel a cold shaft of denial pierce me, even as I saw Anubis stretch forth his clawed hands. I contemplated coming between him and the machine to prevent the outcome he suggested, even as I knew it would likely spell the swifter ruin of Kemet. Perhaps, I thought wildly, we were wrong to alter history. But the deep truth was that I just wanted to stay.

The god gave of himself, filling the coils with power. All the hair on my body lifted as the coils surged to life and the sparks flew through the gap, igniting the coils and the copper-topped lights of Dendera. They flared with a holy fire that leapt through the temple doors and out into the night. We followed it, those of us who could.

We stood on the temple steps and watched as the beacons flared to life north to Abydos and beyond, south to Luxor, Karnak, and the great temple of Edfu. All along the Nile, the lights of Dendera shone. And though it was still night, somehow the dark receded, uncloaking the long river of the Milky Way, the heavenly twin of the great River below.

Miss Ames.

Anubis called me back to the inner sanctum. Between the coils, a gate of light hovered. Through it, I saw the streets of Manhattan, bustling with people who now seemed terribly overdressed to me. I heard the noise of thousands of carriages and horses, the steamers and high wheelers of the wealthy.

Tesla looked at me. Then, he grabbed the hand of the albino boy and ran toward the flickering gate.

Anubis cried out, but he could not move, so fixed was he by his own power.

I could not hear the words he said, but as the lovers leapt the divide, I saw the boy's hand dissolve into feathers. I saw Tesla tumbling into the street, followed by the fluttering of a pure white dove.

Tesla sobbed on his knees, and the sound of his weeping filled the quiet sanctuary. "Horus," he whispered. But already, people had seen him and were helping him up. The dove and what became of him I could not see.

Anubis turned to look at me, the strain of holding the gate clear by his rictus grin. *You should go, if you are going.*

"Must I?" I said. I took an uncertain step forward.

Anubis considered. *Though mortals cannot move forward in time, there is no law against moving backward to what has already been lived.*

I nodded, watching the lights flickering across his bare chest and kilted legs.

And I think, Miss Ames, you have already been here before.

I thought of the *shabti* I had seen in the exhibit hall and realized that the face it had born that seemed so familiar was indeed my own. The horror of it had left me, replaced by a certainty I was now willing to claim.

"Then I will stay," I said.

The gate closed with a thunderclap, though the air still felt charged and volatile.

"Then," grinned the jackal-god, "we welcome you, my long-lost daughter."

"Call me Amneris."

Ushabti

"Are they not lifelike, oh my greatness?" A drop of sweat crept down Sennefer's back.

Normally, there would have been no need to ask Pharaoh for an opinion. In the three years that Sennefer had worked on his tomb, Pharaoh had always been eager to discuss the details that would glorify him in the afterlife—the gold leaf in the antechamber, or the lapis on the sarcophagus, or the ebony canopic jars that would contain Pharaoh's organs after embalming. But today, Pharaoh just stared at the brown waters of the Nile swirling against the reed-covered banks outside the palace. His crippled body was hunched over in a golden chair. To Sennefer's dismay, Pharaoh had needed his guards to carry him into the vast, columned hall. He had not even acknowledged Sennefer when they had set him down.

"I brought your ushabtis, your greatness," Sennefer said, raising his voice. "You had asked to see them."

Pharaoh swiveled to look at the thousand, knee-high human figures made of clay, gold, faience, and alabaster. Sennefer had lined them up carefully on the marble floor, like a tiny army waiting for Pharaoh's command.

"Yes, yes. Very lifelike." Pharaoh took a deep breath and pushed himself up from his chair.

Sennefer resisted the impulse to help him. Pharaoh wasn't an elderly grand-

father dozing in the sun; he was the son of a god, the ruler of the Double Kingdom, and the conqueror of the Hittites. He wasn't to be touched by a commoner,
even a wealthy and respected one like Sennefer. Sennefer could lose a hand, or
worse, for such an infraction.

Pharaoh limped over to the ushabtis, dragging his deformed foot behind
him. Although Pharaoh had come into the world with a crooked spine and a foot
that folded back in on itself, he had still managed to rule with vigor and guile for
twenty-five years. As a child, Sennefer could remember Pharaoh hobbling from
one end of the capitol to the other, waving his serpent-headed walking stick and
shouting orders. Build this temple! Plant these crops!

Now, Pharaoh looked like the shed skin of a locust. He even shivered in the
summer heat.

Another drop of sweat slithered down Sennefer's back. Sennefer bowed his
head towards Pharaoh, trying to hide his pride in his work behind deference.
"I based them on your servants, oh greatness. Here is your gardener—you'll
recognize him from his large earlobes. Your cook—the one who makes honey
cakes. And your favorite maids."

Sennefer's hands hovered above the girls' ushabtis. "Maids," of course, meant
concubines, and so Sennefer's artisans had painted the ushabtis' lips red with
vermillion and their skin white with powdered lead. Sliced obsidian disks made
up the shining black of their eyes.

Bracing himself on his cane, Pharaoh picked up a concubine's ushabti.
Sennefer held his breath. The clay was fragile, though Sennefer didn't know
which was more in danger of breaking—Pharaoh or the figure.

"Beautiful." Pharaoh held the ushabti out to Sennefer.

With relief, Sennefer took the smooth weight of it into his arms. "Thank
you, oh greatness. They will serve you throughout eternity, I swear. As well as
your living servants do now."

There were stories from long ago of pharaohs who had cruelly taken their
entire households with them into death. Sometimes the servants would be
drugged, so when the tomb closed they would pass peacefully onwards. But
Sennefer had also heard tales of screams echoing from under the desert after a
burial, and hyenas scrabbling in the sand. Those horrors, thankfully, were from
barbaric times, before ushabtis had been fashioned to fill the role of servants in
the land of the dead.

Pharaoh swung his head up. His smile was bitter. "Eternity will come all too
soon. I am dying, you see."

"No, my lord. You are still full of life!" Sennefer stammered.

Pharaoh hawked and spit a glob of mucus onto the marble floor, where it gleamed next to one of the columns that held up the high palace roof. "Do not lie to me, Sennefer. Haven't you and I been planning for my death, all these years? You have designed so many luxuries for me to take into the next world." He looked at the army of ushabtis. His mouth twisted. "Now, as I grow weaker, I know they are all useless."

Without warning, Pharaoh lifted his cane and swept it through the first row of clay figurines. They shattered on the marble floor, the sound echoing through the hall.

Sennefer recoiled as shards of clay spattered against his legs.

"Think of it, Sennefer! An eternity in this broken body? Always in pain.... Oh, to be young again. To be healthy." Pharaoh's eyes rested on the concubine's ushabti, still cradled in Sennefer's arms. His face softened. "It is a good likeness of her, Sennefer. What a pity you can't make such a ushabti of me."

Then Pharaoh froze. His eyes darted back up to Sennefer.

"Sennefer."

"Your greatness?"

Pharaoh took a dragging step toward Sennefer, then another, until Sennefer could feel Pharaoh's breath on his cheek. It smelled like stagnant water.

"Could you make a figurine to replace my own body? Something tall and strong and straight? Something *young*?"

"It has never been done, oh my greatness."

"Then you will be the first."

"But...."

Pharaoh drew himself up as straight as he could. His eyebrows arched. "Have I hired the wrong man to fashion my tomb?"

"Of course not, my greatness."

Pharaoh coughed again, wetly. He shook his serpent-headed cane at Sennefer. "You have three days."

WHEN SENNEFER DUCKED his head under the low doorway of their house, Amunet was sitting at the wooden table, the ingredients for their dinner spread around her. Sennefer could smell sharp, bitter greens and the tang of salt.

"You should let a servant do that now," he told her.

"They never get the spices right. And if I don't keep busy, I'll get even fatter." Amunet sat back. Her belly seemed bigger than it had that morning, and her linen shift stretched tightly across her dark, glowing skin. She pointed. "What is that?"

Sennefer realized he still held the ushabti, cradled in his arms like a baby.

"One of Pharaoh's ushabti."

He looked down at the jeweled eyes and painted lips of the figure. He remembered the unnerving ferocity of Pharaoh's anger and shivered.

Amunet frowned up at him. "Is something wrong?"

"No, of course not. Everything's fine."

Sennefer took down his linen work bag and put the ushabti inside. Then he sat next to Amunet and told her about his morning. He left out Pharaoh's final threat. He made the task sound like an interesting problem to solve, nothing more.

Amunet narrowed her eyes, as if she could see right through his efforts to shelter her.

"A replacement body. Wouldn't that be blasphemy?"

Sennefer cast his memory back to the papyrus rolls in his workshop, the spells in *The Book of Coming into the Light*, which the peasants called *The Book of the Dead*. He'd studied the spells carefully, to ensure that the tombs he designed would help their owners pass through the difficult trials of the afterlife. A dead man's soul would face dark caverns and narrow passages, beasts such as He Who Lives on Snakes and He Who Dances in Blood. The most difficult challenge of all, of course, was the final judgment of the dead man's deeds, in which Osiris weighed the heart on a scale against the feather of Ma'at. A heavy heart would condemn the dead man to oblivion instead of paradise among The Field of Reeds.

Even Sennefer could do nothing about that trial, except to ensure that the embalmed heart was protected with a carved, jeweled scarab placed over the chest cavity.

"There's no prohibition against a replacement body in the scrolls," he told Amunet. "The real question is whether it's possible. The figure doesn't need to breathe, or talk, or think. But the texts do say that it must be One Who Walks Through Life."

"Oh, is that all? Just a ushabti that walks? Pharaoh asks for a lot."

"I think Pharaoh is afraid of death," Sennefer said, softly. "And that fear has changed him."

Amunet rubbed her hand under her belly. The rest of her hadn't rounded out at all, and her legs seemed too slender to carry her new weight. Just the day before, she'd unpicked all the long braids she usually wore in her hair. Everyone knew that knots in clothing or hair could hamper a baby's birth.

"Fear doesn't change a person," she said, softly. "Fear shows who a person truly is."

"Now who is talking blasphemy? He's Pharaoh. A god."

"A god who is going to die, just like a man."

"Amunet!" Sennefer glanced over his shoulder, as if Pharaoh could hear.

Amunet tilted her head to one side. "Why won't you tell me what's wrong, Sennefer?"

Sennefer quickly put his hand on her stomach to distract her. He made himself smile at her. "The only thing that's wrong is that I haven't mentioned today how beautiful you look."

"I look like a hippo."

"It's good luck to resemble Tawaret, protector of childbirth."

After a moment, Amunet smiled. She allowed Sennefer to draw her close to him.

Sennefer ran his fingers over Amunet's smooth, warm skin. He'd been so proud when her father had chosen him, from among all her suitors. At the thought of those suitors—one in particular—Sennefer frowned. He'd always known that Amunet's father had been swayed in his choice by Sennefer's position. Pharaoh's new tomb builder! What a prize.

But...Sennefer had always feared that Amunet herself might have chosen differently. If she'd been asked. Oh, she'd never hinted that she wasn't delighted with him. Occasionally, however, Sennefer had seen a wistful look in her eyes, and he'd wondered.

So he'd bought her this fine house—two stories high, with stone floors and a reed-covered terrace on the roof. He'd hired servants and ordered a bed made of ornately carved ivory and bone.

If Pharaoh dismissed him, he'd have to take any work he could get. They'd have to let the servants go, move to a smaller house. And then how would Amunet feel about him?

"Sennefer?" The light from the reed lamp slid over Amunet's smooth face. "Pharaoh's demand...you know, you could always...."

"What?"

She hesitated.

Suddenly afraid of what she might say, Sennefer gently put his finger on her lips.

"I will find a solution," he promised her.

SENNEFER ORDERED HIS artisans to begin with stone, but the life-size statue they presented was far too heavy. Its arms and legs would never move, let alone walk.

Next, he ordered his workers to make bodies of clay. But forming such a large figure proved impossible. Some of the clay wouldn't harden in the summer's heat. Other figures cracked as they dried. Others shattered after they were fired in the kiln.

The body of wax just melted.

Finally, the night before he needed to meet Pharoah, Sennefer turned to wood. Wood was rare in water-starved Egypt. But because this project was for Pharoah, Sennefer only had to snap his fingers, and Pharaoh's servants scurried in with a tree trunk so vast it took ten men to carry it. It had come by ship, all the way across the ocean from a distant country.

Time was short, so Sennefer sent his artisans away to other tasks. He tried not to notice their shocked looks. It had been years since he'd needed to work with his own hands, like a lowly worker instead of their master.

He cut into the trunk, the spicy, earthy scent filling his workroom. The wood carved easily.

By morning, he had a body.

BUT PHARAOH, CRUMPLED in his golden chair, recoiled when Sennefer uncovered the figure.

"*That* is what you have made for me? That...*abomination?*"

The figure stared stiffly ahead, its carved eyes blank.

"It isn't finished," Sennefer said, desperately. "It needs paint, clothing...."

Wheezing, Pharaoh stretched out his serpent-headed cane and pushed on the figure's shoulder. The figure swayed to one side, then stilled again.

"It needs to *walk*," Pharaoh reminded him. "Do you think Osiris will permit me into the Fields of Reeds as an unmoving block of wood?"

"With just a little more time, I'm sure I can...."

Pharaoh lifted a trembling, bony hand, and Sennefer fell silent.

"Time? I also would like more time. No, perhaps you need more... motivation."

Pharaoh looked back and forth between Sennefer and the wooden figure. For the first time, Sennefer saw cruelty as well as fear in his eyes.

"You have two more days," Pharaoh said. "Or else, when I die, you will join me in my tomb, to carry my useless body into the afterlife. You will serve me forever."

SENNEFER WORKED LATE into the night. The sweat on his back turned to ice whenever he remembered Pharaoh's words.

During all the time Sennefer had spent in the stone chambers of tombs, he'd never been afraid.

Now, he was afraid.

He hollowed out the figure's limbs and created joints and joists and left space for the mechanics to fit inside. But when he tried to construct the weights and pulleys necessary to move it, he failed.

"Carvings and drawings I can do," he told Amunet the next morning, trying to keep the despair out of his voice. "I can make the figure *look* real. But I can't make it move."

It was so hot that Amunet's white shift was transparent with sweat, her belly button poking out under the linen. She had finally let the servant prepare their breakfast, and sure enough, it was bland and inedible.

Sennefer put his spoon down and sighed.

"I've never seen you so worried before," Amunet said, sounding worried herself. "Usually working on a tomb makes you happy."

It sounded strange, but Sennefer knew it was true.

He'd worked on over a hundred tombs, each one more praised and magnificent than the one before. Each time he'd done his best, not just from pride, but because he saw that the tombs brought comfort both to the people dying and to the people left alive.

He had caught Pharaoh's attention after creating a massive funerary complex for an entire family killed by the weeping sickness. The family's sole survivor—an elderly official—had spent an entire year criticizing Sennefer's every decision. He'd demanded that each detail be redone and then redone again. Most tomb designers would have thrown up their hands and abandoned the project. But Sennefer had understood. When the tomb was finally completed, the man had wept. "Now they are really gone," he'd told Sennefer.

What would Amunet and the baby do if Sennefer were gone? She could return to her father's house, he supposed. But what kind of life would that be for her?

Amunet rubbed her stomach, absently, the way she might pet a cat. Finally, she sighed.

"You could ask Inut-raten for advice."

Sennefer pressed his lips together.

"He could help you. I know he could."

Sennefer clenched his fist. Somehow, he knew that this was what Amunet had been about to say on the night he'd told her about Pharaoh's task. How easily Inut-raten's name fell from her lips! Sennefer had been right. She had been thinking about him, perhaps ever since they'd been married.

If he died, would Amunet go to Inut-raten?

Amunet gasped. Her stomach bunched up under her sweat-soaked dress. The baby was moving, like a fish cresting underwater.

"He's ready to jump out and meet us!" Sennefer exclaimed, his hand relaxing.

"Or she." Amunet's smile was an apology for mentioning Inut-raten.

"Or she," Sennefer agreed, after a moment.

AMUNET WAS RIGHT about one thing—Sennefer needed advice. The next morning, he slung his work bag over his shoulder, the weight of Pharaoh's ushabti a reminder of his threat. He strode through the clean, straight streets of his neighborhood and across the city. He walked until the streets became narrow and winding and dusty, heaped with garbage and filled with children running naked through pools of sewage. Like the people he passed, Sennefer wrapped a band of linen around his nose and mouth.

Even so, the stench as he approached the low, mud-colored building made him pause at the entrance. The smell clawed at his throat, acid and rot mixed together. He would have to change his clothes and scrape his skin clean with oil before he returned to Amunet.

The embalming room was low-ceilinged and brightly lit. Stone tables lined the room, a body face-up on each, all in different stages of preservation. Men hunched over the bodies, working.

Theshen stood over a body near the back, a shining knife in his hand.

The other workers looked away as Sennefer threaded between the stone slabs. With the linen bands hiding the lower parts of their faces, they didn't look quite human. Most people, in fact, didn't think of them as human. Sennefer had always been careful to follow the proper restrictions, too. He'd never shaken hands with a preparer, or eaten food with them, or greeted one on the street. Of course, it had been years since he'd needed to come here himself; that was a task for a lowly apprentice.

"We are honored, sir," Threshen said, bowing low. "It is rare for someone of your status to visit us."

He was a short man, slender to the point of emaciation, with a nose like a hawk's beak. When Sennefer had been an apprentice, Threshen had been the one to tell him about a shortage of myrrh, to warn him when a nobleman's body would swell too large for his sarcophagus, and to advise him on the proper shape of canopic jar for each organ. They hadn't been friends, of course, because who could be friends with a preparer? But perhaps they had been something that came as near to friendship as circumstance allowed.

So Sennefer nodded curtly. "I'd like a demonstration of how muscles work, especially in the legs and arms."

"Of course, sir." Threshen bowed again and led him to the body of a young man.

The skin of the man's torso had been torn off, shreds of it still clinging wetly to his bones.

Sennefer had to swallow several times. "Did you do that to his skin?"

"Us? No. We could have, of course," Threshen replied. "The lye in one of our tubs can slough the skin clean off a body and leave it like a coat for someone else to put on. But this man died building a new pulley system for Pharaoh's dam. He slipped and fell down a rough stone embankment. He was naked, of course. It's a pity—if Pharaoh gave his workers better clothes, his skin would have been spared. He'd still be dead, of course. But at least he would have been whole for the next life."

Sennefer took a step back from the body in surprise. "You are allowed to work on the poor here? Among the nobles?"

Threshen exchanged a quick glance with another worker, their eyes sliding toward each other over their linen masks. "No, sir. I'm sorry, sir. Please do not mention this infraction. I do it out of charity."

"Charity?"

"I do not mean to overreach, sir. But even in the afterworld, the rich have everything, and the poor have nothing. This man will not even be buried with a single amulet to safeguard his passage. I felt...sorry for him."

Sennefer had never thought about what happened to the poor after death. His own tomb and Amunet's was going to be modest but beautiful. He'd planned it already, down to the last stone, but with room for improvements if his wealth should increase.

Threshen cleared his throat, nervously, his breath puffing out his mask. "Now, sir. You wanted to look at the workings of the muscles?"

AFTER HIS VISIT to Threshen, the interactions between muscles, ligaments, and bone made more sense to Sennefer. They were simply the same as pulleys, levers, and ropes. And what was the body except a mechanism? One thing pulling on another. A balance.

He sat back from his work and rubbed his hand over his face. His artisans had gone home long before, glancing uneasily toward the corner where he hammered wires and threaded them through ivory sockets he'd created to mimic bone.

Now, Sennefer leaned forward to slide the wooden ribcage over the chest. He'd left a space underneath it for Pharaoh's heart, a dark, secretive hollow. Then he fit the wooden chest structure over the rib cage and fastened it with golden clasps, like the front of a cabinet.

Holding his breath, Sennefer pulled on one arm.

It moved.

He'd done it.

Something crashed to the ground behind him.

Sennefer whirled around and saw Amunet, her hands covering her mouth, her eyes frightened. Shards of pottery lay at her feet among olives, squares of white cheese, and pieces of bread. She'd walked all the way to the workroom to bring him dinner.

He rushed over to her, but she waved him away.

"It looks just like *him*."

"He does?" Sennefer felt a spurt of pleasure.

"You call it a *he*? It's not a he." She stared at the figure. Then she turned away, squeezing her eyes closed. Sennefer felt chilled, as if Amunet were turning away from him as well.

"Of course it's not a *he*," he said. "Now, go and rest. I'll clean up the mess and make my own dinner tonight."

IN THE TWO days since he'd last seen him, Pharaoh had shrunk down even more. His head was slumped forward on his narrow chest, like an unbearable weight.

"Wait until you see it move, oh my greatness!"

Sennefer pulled the figure forward, like a father teaching his child to walk. Haltingly, creakily, it took one step, and then another.

Sennefer looked at Pharaoh hopefully.

But Pharaoh frowned. He took a deep breath. Something liquid and thick burbled in his lungs. He coughed and spat in fury. "I am Pharaoh, not a puppet to be pushed one way and another. I want to walk on my own. I want to run, the way I've never been able to do in this life! You were supposed to make me a better self."

Exhausted, Pharaoh sank lower in his chair. His eyes drifted toward the Nile, as if he'd forgotten Sennefer was there.

"Because...what if, in the afterlife, I am not Pharaoh? What if I am only myself?"

Sennefer hesitated. He was struck by the question. In the afterworld, there would be many Pharaohs, from thousands of years of rule, stretching back through time the way the sand dunes stretched to the horizon. Who among them would rule the others? Surely not this hunched old man.

Pharaoh turned and flinched at the expression on Sennefer's face. "You pity me? How dare you!"

Sennefer fell to his knees. "My lord, I would not...."

Pharaoh tried to rise and failed. Even more angrily, he snapped, "By tomorrow, you will make me a body fit for a Pharaoh. And if you do not, I'll...." Pharaoh paused, his eyes roaming the room as if seeking terrible inspiration. "I'll sell your wife into slavery. I'll take your new baby and leave it in the desert for the vultures to feast on."

SENNEFER'S KNEES TREMBLED as he climbed down the steps of the island's tower.

How could Pharaoh have threatened Amunet? Amunet, who had never harmed Pharaoh in any way! And the baby....

Sennefer remembered Threshen's tale of the worker who had lost his skin because Pharaoh had not bothered to give his slaves clothes. Had fear of death changed Pharaoh, as he'd told Amunet? Or had Sennefer simply never seen this side of him?

Now, Sennefer's legs shook so badly that he had to pause for a moment, his hand braced against the tower's stone wall.

The island pointed from the capitol into upper Egypt, like the commanding finger of Pharaoh. The tower stood at the very tip of the island, so the Nile flowed past it on either side. The horizontal lines carved into the tower's sides were used to measure the height of the annual Nile floods during the season of *akhet*, and therefore the amount of crops that could be grown in the fertile upper valleys, and therefore the taxes that each region owed.

Inut-raten stood waist deep in the water at the base of the tower, squinting at a device of some kind. Wheels and cogs turned and ground against each other, churning the brown water around them into a frothy white.

At the sight of him, Sennefer's stomach curdled as well. He'd made a mistake, coming here. Fear and pride rose up inside of him, and despite everything— Pharaoh's threat, the danger to Amunet and the baby—he took a step back, ready to flee and abandon their last hope.

At that moment, however, Inut-raten looked up. His whole body stilled.

Then he raised a hand in acknowledgment and waded out of the water.

Sennefer waited for him, his heart pounding.

Inut-raten had aged well, as much as Sennefer hated to admit it. He was still taller than Sennefer. His shoulders were broader and his legs more muscular.

Would Amunet still find him handsome?

"I heard that Amunet is pregnant," Inut-raten said, not bothering to dry off the water that pooled around his feet. "You must be pleased."

Sennefer pressed his lips together.

During Sennefer's courtship of Amunet three years before, Inut-raten had been his greatest competitor. While Sennefer's work was buried beneath the sands, Inut-raten's dams, bridges, and temples were on display for all to admire. When Amunet's father needed a new well dug, Inut-raten had rigged up a device that accomplished it in a single day. Inut-raten had even fashioned a toy ibis out of metal that had strutted across the floor, flapping its wings, without being touched. Sennefer could still remember Amunet's delighted laughter.

Worst of all had been the night that Sennefer had learned he'd been chosen to work on Pharaoh's tomb. He'd hurried to give the news to Amunet's father, hoping it would sway his decision. But her father had just nodded thoughtfully.

As Sennefer had left the house, convinced his suit had been refused, he'd seen a man slip out the back door.

Inut-raten.

Amunet's bedroom was at the back of the house.

Sennefer had never asked Amunet about that, not even after her father had announced that Sennefer had won her as a wife. He'd been too afraid to threaten the happiness that had filled him during their wedding and the first years of their marriage. And now it was too late. What could he say? That he worried his wife loved someone else?

The memory of Inut-raten's shadow sliding across the darkened passageway still choked him with jealousy.

Jealousy wouldn't help Amunet and the baby.

So Sennefer looked at Inut-raten and managed to force the words from his lips. "I need your help."

Inut-raten narrowed his eyes at him. "Tell me," he said, warily.

Sennefer led Inut-raten back up the narrow stone stairs to the cart where he'd placed the figure. Inut-raten blinked when he saw it. He pulled the limbs, prodded the chest, and then nodded.

"You did good work," he finally admitted.

"Not good enough. Pharaoh wants it to move on its own. To run and jump." Sennefer couldn't keep the bitterness out of his words. "I remembered the toy ibis you made for Amunet. And I wondered...."

"That was just a toy! But this?" Inut-raten shook his head.

Sennefer's chest clenched up.

"I do have an idea," Inut-raten said, slowly. "I've been...experimenting. With steam."

"Steam?"

Inut-raten nodded. "When water is heated, the steam takes up more space than the water does, pushing everything around it outwards. I've been working on a way to get that pressure to force a lever to work. Or a wheel." He glanced over his shoulder at the mechanism in the water. "I have an idea for a dam that could raise and lower itself. Pharaoh could decide which parts of his kingdom could receive water, and when. His tax revenue would multiply ten-fold."

Sennefer remembered the lines carved into the base of the tower. "What would happen to the people deprived of water?"

Inut-raten blinked. "I never thought about that. My task is only to solve the problem. Isn't that enough?"

Sennefer frowned. How could Inut-raten so easily dismiss the fate of the farmers in the upper Nile, who needed floods to deposit the rich silt for their crops?

He suddenly wondered whether the worker he'd seen in Threshen's workshop had been working on Inut-raten's dam when he died. Somehow, Sennefer knew that Inut-raten wouldn't know. Or care.

"Steam might work here, as well."

Slowly, Sennefer turned away from the Nile as Inut-raten matter-of-factly opened the figure's chest cavity and stared down into the dark space where the heart would go.

"I'd need to put some small metal boxes inside, looped together by metal tubes. We would light wood chips in one, like an oven. Then the water in the other container would heat up. As the water expands, it would pull on the wires and pulleys."

"Can you come to my workshop tonight? There's no time to lose."

Inut-raten blinked at him. "I sense there is something you have not yet told me."

Sennefer hesitated. "There is. If this doesn't work, would you hide Amunet and the baby? Keep them safe?"

Behind them, the Nile churned through the wheels of Inut-raten's device. An ibis—a real one—soared overhead, its wings outstretched against the blue sky.

Slowly, Inut-raten nodded.

Sennefer let out a breath he hadn't realized he'd been holding. "Thank you." He found himself wiping tears from his eyes. He took a deep breath. "Amunet's father...he should have chosen you, instead of me."

Inut-raten's eyes widened. "Her father? Her father didn't choose you. Amunet chose you herself."

"What?"

"I even stole into her room one night, to change her mind. But it was no use. She said she didn't want a man who was all thought and no heart." Inut-raten frowned. "That made no sense to me. I told her I was proud of what I had accomplished. Then she recounted some tale about a tomb you'd made for an elderly official. I must admit I didn't understand that, either." He shrugged and busied himself inside the figure's chest cavity.

Sennefer remembered telling Amunet about the tomb, and the elderly official weeping.

His heart was suddenly as light as the bird winging above them.

Inut-raten looked up.

"You didn't know, did you? And still, you came here, to ask me...."

After a moment, Inut-raten sighed and put one hand on Sennefer's shoulder. "Perhaps I'm starting to realize why she chose you."

WHEN SENNEFER GOT home late that night, Amunet was too busy to do anything more than kiss his cheek. She was cleaning house, an ungainly whirlwind directing the servants to dust behind the wall hangings, rearrange the bed, and knock the cobwebs down from the reed roof.

"You should rest." Sennefer wished the servants weren't there, so he could tell her what he and Inut-raten were doing. That now he knew she truly loved him.

"The house needs to be clean before the baby comes."

"The baby won't care about cobwebs."

"But I will! Now go. Finish your...."

She didn't know what to call it. Neither did Sennefer.

So Amunet turned away and kept on cleaning.

THE NEXT MORNING, Pharaoh was lying down, his head cradled in an ivory and gold head rest. He was so weak that he simply waved a hand at Sennefer and croaked, "Show me."

Sennefer and Inut-raten had worked through the night. While Inut-raten had fashioned the device inside the chest cavity, Sennefer had made the skin from papyrus, molding it carefully to the arms and legs. He'd painted the face to resemble a younger, more handsome Pharaoh.

It was more than a ushabti, but less than a man. A creature, perhaps. Alive and not alive.

Trembling, Sennefer pressed the button that Inut-raten had helped him fashion. The creature rose smoothly and walked toward Pharaoh's bedside.

Pharaoh gasped in delight. "It moves as I would move!" He spoke to the creature, as if it would understand him. "Come to me!"

Sennefer's heart fluttered as the creature bent down over Pharaoh.

Pharaoh smiled up at it.

Sennefer sent up a prayer of thanks to Osiris, to Horus, and to all the gods and goddesses who walked the world and the afterworld. Amunet and the baby would be safe.

Then Pharaoh reached up and caressed the creature's cheek.

His hand sprang back as if he had touched fire.

"What is that?" he hissed. "That is not skin! It is rough and dry. Scaly!"

"It is papyrus, oh my greatness," Sennefer stammered. "The finest, most intricately layered...."

Pharaoh interrupted him. "I cannot have skin like a crocodile." He pushed the creature away.

Sennefer desperately thought of the materials in his workshop. "I can use a gold mask, with lapis eyes, oh my lord. Or the purest, whitest alabaster, so you will glow in the afterlife!"

Pharaoh frowned petulantly. A string of drool slipped down his chin, unnoticed. "Gold and alabaster are cold. I'm always cold. In the afterlife, I want to be warm. I want to touch and be touched."

Sennefer thought of the maids' ushabtis and shuddered. What if Pharaoh decided to take others down into the darkness with him, as well as Sennefer?

"Then goat skin, oh greatness! I will scrape and tan it until it is as soft as a baby's...."

"Goat!" Pharaoh's mouth twisted. "How dare you! Osiris will never permit me into the land of the dead wearing the skin of an animal. No, you must find something better. May I remind you what is at stake for you if you don't?"

"Yes, oh my greatness," Sennefer whispered.

Pharaoh had already closed his eyes. A faint snore issued from between his dried lips.

SENNEFER LOADED THE creature onto its cart and pushed it out of Pharaoh's room. The servants sweeping the marble floor of the vast hallway cast nervous looks at him, as if they could see his fate written on his face. His body was leaden with terror, his mind darting from idea to idea, none of them what Pharaoh wanted.

He needed to take Amunet to Inut-raten immediately.

"Sennefer!"

Sennefer turned. One of Pharaoh's concubines was hurrying toward him, the one whose ushabti still lay in his work bag. Her linen dress swirled around her body, and her black braids swung around her face.

"It's your wife," she told him. "They sent word for you, but I didn't dare interrupt your visit with Pharaoh. You must go home. Now!"

THE SOUND OF a crying baby filled the house. Sennefer's heart contracted with joy as he saw one of his servants rocking a squirming bundle of cloth. A tiny hand thrust out from it, as if waving at him.

But the serving woman's face was ashen. "She is in the bedroom, sir," she said, over the child's cries. "I am sorry. We did all we could."

Amunet lay on the bed he'd been so proud of, her dark hair matted around her face. The enormous swell of her stomach was gone. Without it, her body seemed grotesquely flat. The cotton-stuffed mat under her was soaked with sweat and blood. The room stank of it. Sennefer remembered the smell of Threshen's workshop.

"Amunet!" he gasped.

Her eyelids fluttered open. Her lips smiled. "Sennefer. My love. We have a daughter." She tried to sit up.

Sennefer sank onto his knees and gently pushed her shoulders down. He was sobbing. She was still alive! Why had the servant said she was sorry?

"You must rest, Amunet. Keep your strength."

Amunet shook her head. She looked at him, hard. "We don't have much time."

"No! You'll be fine. I'll get Pharaoh's physician himself. He will come and..."

She coughed. The wet sound of it reminded Sennefer of Pharaoh.

"Shush," Amunet said, as if he were a baby himself. "I'm getting weaker. So now you must finally tell me everything that troubles you."

Sennefer bowed his head over their clasped hands. As her rasping breath filled the room, he told her of Pharaoh's threats, the visit to Threshen, his old fears of Inut-raten and their reconciliation. He even told her about Pharaoh's final, unanswerable demand. All the things he had ever wished to say to her but had been afraid to.

"Ah," Amunet said. "All this, you kept from me?"

"I'm so sorry," Sennefer whispered. "I was afraid...."

She shook her head. To his horror, a thin stream of blood ran out of her nostril. "I believe what I said to you—that fear shows what a man truly is. Look at what you did! You created something the world has never seen. You tried to shelter me. You went to Inut-raten. You faced your own fear." She put her hand on his chest. "Your heart is as light as a feather, Sennefer." A spasm of pain distorted her face. "And now you must save our daughter and yourself from Pharaoh."

Sennefer wanted to tell her that he would. Instead, he spoke the complete, frightening truth. "I don't know how."

She smiled again. "I do."

THE SUN IN Pharaoh's room warmed the springs inside the creature's arms, and the fingers curled. As if it were alive. It looked down at Pharaoh's bed with eyes as dark and gleaming as Pharaoh's own. Sennefer had fashioned them from the same obsidian he'd used on the concubine's ushabti.

Slowly, Pharaoh reached up and grasped the creature's hand. Joy spread across his face. "At last," he muttered. "Soft." His head sank back down on his head rest. "Good."

He could have been holding the hand of a young and healthy version of himself, with a straight back and soft, glowing skin.

When Amunet had taken her last breath, Sennefer had left the baby with the servant maid, to be fed on a mixture of water buffalo milk and honey. He'd lifted his wife's body in his arms and placed her on the cart next to the creature. He'd pushed them both through the streets, weeping, until he reached Threshen's workshop.

"Can you help me?" he asked Threshen, as if Threshen was his friend.

Threshen and Sennefer lifted Amunet's body into the tub filled with lye. They removed her skin and draped it over the creature's body, sewing and gluing until it looked as though it had grown there.

Sennefer painted Pharaoh's face over Amunet's, obliterating her forever. He covered her empty eyeholes with obsidian.

Threshen took the red, skinless horror of Sennefer's wife and laid her gently on a stone slab. "We will cover her with the finest linen," he promised Sennefer. "But, sir? You could have commanded me to use the skin of another. Perhaps one of the poor, who have no relatives to speak for them."

Sennefer looked around the workroom at the bodies on the slabs surrounding him. All of them equal in death.

"And rob that person of the only thing they might have to take into the afterlife? No, my wife…" His voice broke. "My wife offered herself willingly."

And then Sennefer had reached into his work bag and pulled out the concubine's ushabti. "That worker, the one you showed me last time I was here? Bury this with him, so he will have at least one servant to help him with his passage."

Now, looking at Pharaoh and the creature, Sennefer felt as though he'd been hollowed out and filled with all the elements of the world and the afterworld, just as Pharaoh soon would be, alien and raging inside him—a storm of grief, sharp bursts of lightning love for his new child, a deep muddy flow of horror at what he'd just done with Amunet's body.

He was still terrified of Pharaoh's threat. And yet, somehow, he also felt compassion. Because Pharaoh was, after all, a man close to death.

Pharaoh's eyes closed, his fingers still clutching the creature's hand.

WHEN HE GOT home, Sennefer took his daughter into his arms for the first time. He hefted the surprising weight of her, marveling at her strength as her tiny hands gripped his finger.

"Hold the child all night," the serving maid instructed him. "She needs to feel your skin on hers."

Sennefer flinched as he held her against his chest. Then, for a long time, he wept.

That night, as Sennefer slept, he was gifted with a vision of the boat of the sun, sailing across the river of the underworld. He could not see Pharaoh yet, but Amunet was standing in the prow, surrounded by all the other recently dead. He knew her instantly, because she had no skin. Her body glistened red in the strange light over the boat, neither sun nor moon, and her lidless eyes turned as if she could see him watching her. Somehow, she was still beautiful.

She lifted her hand and waved. She was smiling.

Thermodynamics; and/or The Remittance Men

Alexandria is where we go; Cairo is what we come back to.

There's a truth in there, a resonance deeper than the simple facts of travel, of journey and return. Alexandria, city of poets and exiles, stranger in a strange land, in exile itself from its own proper country: of course we'd want to go there. How not?

Cairo, though: Cairo is where we belong, what we belong to. What we were made for, made from. Both. And made by, that too. Cairo is the blood and the stink and the bone of us; Alexandria can only ever be the dream and the hope and the yearning. Cairo is a state of being, where Alexandria is merely a state of mind.

Cairo is the colonial city, the very expression of empire. The British—I should say *we British*, of course, but I will not—stroll about with their swagger-sticks and their bristling moustaches, their uniforms of serge or crumpled linen or crisp white cotton duck, their parasols and their pets. Dogs and monkeys and mocking clinging birds, the British will make a pet of anything that moves. And take fond possession of anything that does not. Except Alexandria, perhaps. It lies within their ambit, beneath their aegis, under their control and yet never quite within their reach or understanding.

Here in Cairo, they press an alien order into the heart of the city. Streets and structures, steam lines and railway lines, queues and currency and church parade on Sundays, ten thousand little British days played out under a Cairene sun.

GOD BE THANKED, I never was a part of that great enterprise. I can look the part and act the part, but it has only ever been a performance. I can don the skin of the Englishman abroad, and doff it just as easily. Underneath—well, I am still and always irredeemably an Englishman, and still and always irrefutably abroad, and yet. Not one of them.

Sometimes I wonder if that isn't true of us all. Stand on any street corner in what we laughingly call the British Quarter and see the nursemaids go to and fro with their charges, the corporals and the memsahibs, the schoolboys and the bankers, the bureaucrats from the Colonial Office: perhaps every one of them wears their label as superficially as I would. Inside, perhaps they all know they're playing a role in this grand absurd theatre that we call an Empire, and ours.

Nothing here is truly ours, any more than we are truly us.

THE VOYAGERS' CLUB might have been lifted wholesale from Pall Mall and deposited discreetly just off Soliman Pasha Square. Down a side-street so narrow it's an alley by another name the club stands, behind its classic Georgian facade and its curtained windows. If gentlemen have to abandon their steam-fiacres in the square and walk fifty yards to the door, so be it. The club servants keep the path swept clean and the gas-lamps lit above the door, and tip a street-boy to chase off the inevitable stray dogs. Stray cats, of course, are as welcome as anyone.

More welcome than we ever were, I and my kind: strays ourselves, who have the right of entry by virtue of our birth, and but few rights else. Few virtues else, that too.

This particular night, I came light-footed up the steps from the street, to be greeted by the doorman with his usual resentful nod.

"All well, Barrows?"

"As well as might be expected, sir." *Not very well at all, so long as the true gentlemen continue to tolerate your sort.* Not that he actually said so, of course; he liked his job too well for honesty. Like any London club, the Voyagers' offers its members and their guests all the comforts of Home: British food and drink, British newspapers in the library, British beds in narrow rooms, and British servants to judge you where even God would not.

My friends and I were born to this, to all of this, but we seldom ascended to the penetralia of the Voyagers'. Members in good standing we might be; unwelcome none the less. One grows tired of sidelong glances in the dining hall, the disapproving rustle of papers in the library, the sudden heavy silence in the billiard room.

Still we came, for stubbornness and convenience and an excellent port. For the most part we chose to congregate in the basement, and keep the servants trotting up and down those narrow stairs all night.

Properly, we met in the Silence Room, which was meant for study and private contemplation. We had long since turned out the scholars, though, and made over the room to our own desires and designs. A rug and easy chairs, convenient low tables, coals for the fire—a weapon against damp as much as chill, with the Nile such a very close neighbour—and a bell to bring those sullen servants down.

This day, I opened the door to the Silence Room and was met by a fug of smoke and a buzz of quarrelsome voices. Bellaire's pipe, I diagnosed, two rival cigars and a cigarette; Creighton's voice and Mallenby's, with interjections from one Smith or the other, both. Smith Major would be one of the cigars; Smith Minor—no relation—was careful of his wind, and didn't smoke. Creighton was the cigarette, certainly. I recognised the sulphur of his hand-rolled street tobacco. Which meant that either Mallenby was smoking tonight, not likely where the possibility of port came into play, or—

"Tattersall, man—the handle stands by you, sir! In God's name, use the thing. I can hear Minor's wheezing from here, and I can see nothing at all."

"To be strictly accurate," came his voice from the miasma, "I stand by the handle; but I take your meaning. One moment."

I heard a metallic cranking, backed by the swift busy rasp of a ratchet imparting load to a spring. After that came a soft, scrupulous ticking, somewhere within the walls, and the air began to clear in short order. Being subterranean, of course we have no window; Bellaire had fashioned an ingenious mechanical flue in lieu. He called it his aerator, and spoke of a patent application. That would never happen. Bellaire's inventions all tended the same way: a working prototype that he would fiddle into convenient usability, and then no more. His own house was a wondrous engine, devices of every sort all powered by a steam-driven clock, but it was also a premature museum, a monument to unrecognised endeavour.

At least we could all enjoy the effects of his aerator—so long as someone remembered to pump the handle every hour or so. Tattersall applied himself to the task, then looked me up and down and said, "My dear Chapman, I rejoice in your good news."

"I have shared no news," I said bluntly, irritated. It was none of his business, and besides: how could he know?

"Your very clothes betray you. All last week you were walking here, those dreary miles from your digs. Today you have no dust in your turn-ups, no camel-dung on your Oxford brogues. Indeed, you are quite nattily turned out; from which I deduce a recent pleasant call upon your banker, followed by your arrival here in the fiacre you haven't been able to afford for a month or more. In short, sir, you have received your quarterly subvention, and are in funds."

"Damn your eyes, Tattersall!" I took swift rein on my temper, and went on more moderately, "Are you always right?"

He shrugged elegantly, and I felt briefly envious of his tailoring.

"Detective tricks," came a growl from the wing-chair. "Chose the wrong path in life, didn't you, Tatters?"

"Not noticeably," Tattersall murmured, shooting his very expensive cuffs. Perhaps my envy was not so much brief as ongoing. If clothes make the man, he was very much the better-made. "I know what a detective earns. I have done... significantly better. And don't need to pester my banker every quarter-day to learn if my distant and disgusted relatives have kept their word once more."

"I'm hardly the only one here who has taken money to leave his country for his country's good," I said, as mildly as I could manage. "Indeed, you might be the only one who has not. Though I hear you were barely a step ahead of Scotland Yard when you took your own departure."

"There but for the grace of God, old boy. We all have our histories that drove or dragged us here." His gaze strayed idly around the room, and mine followed as by nature, as he meant it to. The debtor, the runaway bridegroom, the defrocked priest, the cashiered cavalry captain: England allows so little leeway to its disreputable. Happily, the colonies are less nice.

On a table beside the hearth, bottle and soda-syphon stood waiting, alongside a jug of beer. I filled a glass with whisky and seltzer-water, and looked about more purposefully. I was last of the likely arrivals; everyone had a drink; I lifted mine and said, "A toast, then. I give you the Remittance Men—and long may our families continue to remit."

We were a club within a club, and disliked for that as much as for our individual reprehensible pasts, our current seedy, shady tenancy and our likely future shame.

Still, no one on the committee had ever offered to blackball us. Provisions were made; we had our bolt-hole here, we had our drinks and licence to wander upstairs when we must. I sank into my place on the ottoman beside Smith Minor, touched my glass against his beer mug in a quiet, private toast, then gazed more closely at the boy.

"You're looking a little peaky, old lad. How's the chest?"

"Nothing to worry about," he said stoutly. "It's this beastly weather, that's all."

Last month, it had been *this beastly heat*. The first rains had already broken that excuse.

I said, "Dr Murchison is safe to be upstairs at this hour. I could hale him down, to have a look at you."

He pulled a face, like the child he almost still was. "Not tonight." Children always seek to bargain with the inevitable. "I'll see him tomorrow, when I don't have to do it in the club."

"You'd rather go to that clinic he runs by the souk?" Murchison was a genuinely good man, which is why we rarely saw him in the Silence Room. Definitively, not one of us.

"Frankly, yes."

"He'll charge you the same. And say the same, and send the same nurse to see you follow orders."

"Nevertheless."

Nevertheless, he'd rather wait among the dispossessed in the noise and dust of the market than make an exhibition of himself under the members' eyes. Of course he would.

"All right, but I'll come with you. Just to be sure that you do."

He shrugged, smiled. We left it at that.

"I'll tell you what, Bellaire," Tattersall said, speaking supposedly to one but actually to us all. "I've a curio here I picked up, which I think might tickle your fancy. Yours too, Padre."

Creighton looked aggrieved, as he always did when we used that title; but we were fond of it. And a man may lose his living, but not the curiosity that cost it him. Of course he rose and came to see what Tattersall had laid down on the sideboard. So did Bellaire, and so did we all.

"A scarab, surely?" Creighton said. "In the style of the heart scarabs of the New Kingdom, but—"

"Contemporary," from Bellaire. "Unquestionably. Brass, largely, with steel banding. Cast, not carved. Fine work, too: not a tool-mark to be seen, and these coloured patinas are not easy to—I say!"

His startlement was echoed in all of us, gasps and cries and more. I think we all took a step back, except of course for Tattersall. Then—reassured, perhaps, by his stillness—we pressed forward again, to see just what this thing was doing.

It was a toy, a mechanism, the simulacrum of a scarab beetle. It had opened its wing-cases when Bellaire poked at it; the sudden movement and the sharp buzzing sound were wholly unexpected and disturbingly lifelike. Not one of us thought the thing an actual living creature, but if devices could harbour life, it would have been utterly persuasive.

It fluttered those enamelled wing-cases at us, and rose up on needle staccato legs, and scuttled about on the mahogany. Something in it could seemingly sense an edge; its movements seemed quite random, but it never fell off the sideboard. Nor, when we laid obstacles in its path, did it run into them. Those jewelled eyes could not possibly see, but something greater than the laws of chance was turning it away from trouble.

"Is it clockwork?" Creighton breathed. I think we were all moved by the beauty and the mystery of the thing, but that would never stop us seeking to anatomise it. Taking things apart was what we did.

"Oh, surely," Bellaire said. "How else would you motivate it? The workings must be a marvel, though: so complex, so delicate, and silent too."

In motion, the thing was anything but silent. Its dagger-feet clicked on the varnish, its wing-cases rattled aggressively, I thought some tiny bellows-action was giving it a voice, a hint of whistle. But there was no resolute ticking of a clock-action in its interior.

Bellaire was our man of science, though, our ingenious engineer; we took his word for it unquestioningly. Tattersall said not a word, he only held up one finger: *wait*.

Every clockwork toy has a cycle that it runs through, before it runs down. This had one trick more to show us. It stood abruptly still, so that we'd have thought it done if not for Tattersall's alert anticipation; and then it unfolded wings of tender filigree, the finest gold and silver wire. They trembled so credibly in the still air, I do believe we all expected to see it lift and fly.

Of course it did no such thing. It stretched those wings and agitated them, as if to hint of more; and then it put them away again and closed its shell, folded its legs beneath it and was still.

"May I...?"

In response to Tattersall's nod, Bellaire snatched the gadget up and examined it minutely. Baffled, he said, "I can find no hole for a key."

"There is none," Tattersall replied. "No hole, no key. I had it up till dawn, running through its little repertoire over and over; and then again a dozen times today. It has had small rest and no refreshment, and yet it is as bright and busy as it ever was, no sign of depletion in its energies. I thought that might be a matter of some interest."

"Indeed, indeed. It's not powered by steam, clearly; so if not clockwork, then what? I can find no screws either, that might allow access to its interior." Bellaire screwed a jeweller's loupe into his eye and continued to turn the thing over in his hands, seeking and seeking, unrewarded. He muttered to himself as he peered, repeating the laws of thermodynamics and conservation of energy, "heat is work and yet it's not even warm to the touch..."

We knew all about the laws of thermodynamics. I ignored him. "Tattersall? Whence came this trinket?"

"I told you, I picked it up."

"Yes, but in whose house?"

"Shepheard's," he said nonchalantly.

"They still let you through the door?"

He raised an eloquent eyebrow. "My dear man! I have the entrée to some of the most exclusive salons on the Continent. I hardly think the doorman of a busy hotel is going to bar my way. Nor the manager issue a ukase against me. As it happens, I am *persona grata* with the staff of Shepheard's at every level; they won't hear a word against me."

"Just as well, in the circumstances," Smith Major growled. Minor snickered softly, where he was hanging over my shoulder, hoping for another sight of the wonder.

"Be that as it may," Creighton said, with not a note of censure in his voice. "You were let into Shepheard's on the nod; you let yourself into some other man's room, and helped yourself to this—I am going to call it a puzzle, because I am not sure what words else to use—among other goods, no doubt."

"No doubt," Tattersall agreed dryly.

"Very well, then. The question remains, whose room? Who had possession of this before you, and how did he come by it, and where?"

"It didn't exactly come with a provenance attached," Tattersall murmured. "I did look about quite carefully"—I believe we all felt sure of that already—"and I found nothing else remotely like it. Nor the tools and templates of a craftsman, the designs of a draftsman. He's no more an artificer in secret, an amateur of the craft, than he is in public."

"Perhaps he leaves all that behind him," Minor suggested, "in his workshop at home. Do you travel with your lockpicks and safebreaking tools?"

For answer, Tattersall simply shook his jacket pocket. The resultant rattle was enough to leave Minor gasping and wheezing—it was never good to make him laugh, when his chest was bad—and holding his hands up in apology, abashed.

"You still haven't put a name to him," Mallenby observed.

"No. There is that within me which would prefer not to do so, even now. I no more choose to boast my activities here than I do to apologise for them. However," he went on swiftly to stem our rising protest, "tonight—well, tonight the man himself has taken that choice out of my hands. His name is Sir Edward Bolsover."

Possibly that name meant something to each of us, except perhaps to Smith Minor, who's a heedless young devil. In the digestive silence after Tattersall let drop the name, Creighton said, "Sir Edward Bolsover has a room in the club here tonight, at my invitation."

"I know it," said Tattersall. "That's why I couldn't keep him anonymous, and why the choice is no longer mine to make. You know the man, Padre. What can you tell us, beyond what we read in the newspapers and hear in the tap-room?"

"Well, for one thing, you're right that he could not have made this, or anything like it. He no more has the skill in his fingers than he has the understanding in his head, or the invention in his soul. He could not conceive of such a thing; if he were given the conception, he could not design it; if he were given the designs, he could not achieve it. No, if this was found in his possession, the kindest thought I have is that he bought it. More likely—well, I will not say. It's still possible that he's an honest man."

"Padre?" Mallenby spoke for us all. "How do you come to know the Great Wen?"

"Oh, don't call him that, it's too ridiculous—and we were at school and university together. Five years at Rugby and then Oxford after, though I was Keble, of course, and he was Magdalen."

"Why do you call him the Great Wen?" Minor asked, all innocence. "I thought that was London?"

"And so it is—but Bolsover owns great swathes from the City to the East End, and so I suppose the name stuck."

"Come, Padre, you're too good to the man. He's a grotesque swelling on the face of humanity, Minor, and *so* the name stuck." That was Smith Major, making even Creighton smile, albeit reluctantly.

"Well. He is a boor, certainly. A loud boor, and a bully. I tried to see less of him at Oxford, and he wouldn't stand for that. If any man was ever bullied into a social circle, that man would be myself. Sounds absurd, doesn't it? But I believe he liked to show me off, as though my credentials could add to his credibility. So long as he had such a great intellectual in his train, in his *eager* train, then no one could accuse him of vapidity or worse, do you see?"

"Oh, I think we see," Tattersall said, smiling. "Truth now, Padre—just how eager were you?"

"Well, the food at Keble was particularly diabolical in my time, so..." The end of that sentence was lost in a shout of sympathetic laughter

"So, Padre." Smith Major again, determined. "Vapidity, or worse? What *would* you accuse him of?"

"Oh, worse. Far worse, since he's been loosed on the world. I hesitate to speak ill of my alma maters—almae matres, I suppose that should be—but neither Rugby nor Oxford did him any good at all. He inherited money, too much and too young; he's made much more since, by means I prefer not to think about. If he's in Egypt now, it's because he's found some way to exploit a new country."

"Oh, be fair, Padre," Mallenby said, only half joking, "we all do that. Even those of us who only live here because we're not wanted at home. We exploit that distance, and the opportunity it gives us to live in our own little mockery of English life without penalty of English law. It's shameful, really."

"It is shameful, but the weather's better." That was Minor, trying to lighten the mood.

"It is shameful," Creighton went on, "and we are the least of it, the least worst of all the Empire means and does. Britannia wouldn't believe it, but it's true. Her rule is...not benign, for any of the native peoples. We see that best, perhaps, who live here on the margins of empire, less engaged with it; disinterested observers, if you like, merely taking advantage. Bolsover is the other thing, deeply invested and cruelly disposed. He owns diamond mines on the other side of the continent, and he treats his people barbarously. Barbarously. I would fear for the *fellahin*, if he saw and seized an opportunity here."

"Well," I said, "and this is the man you have invited in among us? I'm hurt, Padre. We might count as members more by default than acclamation, but nevertheless. Do you despise us so very much?"

"Don't be absurd. You can't imagine that I want him here. He sent a boy with a note this morning, saying that his hotel room had been burgled"—with a pause to glower at Tattersall—"and he no longer felt his property or his person safe at Shepheard's. He has a berth on the airship tomorrow, but in the meantime could I recommend him somewhere? I was his only friend in Cairo, and he didn't at all trust the men who had enticed him here, etc etc. It was all nonsense, of course—he is no kind of milksop, to be alarmed by an intruder, nor yet by the shady creatures he does business with—but he will have enjoyed tracking me down and obliging me to offer assistance. If I'd ignored the note, he'd have turned up himself, and—well, you know my domestic situation."

We did. The last thing poor Creighton could ever hope to see on his doorstep would be a wealthy acquaintance from his former life. Not that he actually had a doorstep. He barely had a door to call his own, sharing his quarters with an excommunicate Copt and a Jain who had somehow wandered here from Portuguese India. We called them the Three Seekers. They occupied a grim hut at the desert's edge and pooled all their resources, funds from England and alms from the charitable and letter-writing fees from the illiterate. Some nights, I knew, they went to bed hungry and called it a fast.

"The club was the best I could think of," Creighton went on. "Where he could be answered, accommodated, and evaded, all at once. I wrote that I was unable to join him for dinner, due to a previous engagement. He'll be upstairs right now, I expect, making some other member's life a misery, thank God." He lifted his glass to us, his previous engagement, and tried to look suitably ashamed of himself.

"He is," Tattersall confirmed. "He's found himself a table of cronies already. I'll give him this much, the man's a fast worker. Happily, so am I."

He looked at us meaningfully; we gazed back at him, a little aghast. He was impossible to misunderstand, and almost impossible to credit. It was the laws of thermodynamics that had kept us friends—or his interpretation of those laws, rather, a particular sense of honour that transmuted them into laws of hospitality. *The virtuous thief does not steal from those poorer than himself.* That was the Second Law, and the one that allowed his welcome into our variously shabby homes. The First Law stated that *The virtuous thief does not steal from his host*; any roof that offered him shelter was safe from his depredations.

That had always included the Voyagers'. Until, apparently, tonight.

"Gentlemen—does any man among you believe that he came by this... trinket...honestly or honourably?"

Silence.

"No. Well, then: we have one last chance to learn whence he had it, and what else he had. I've already taken as much as I want of his wealth; this is a quest for information. If you can be quick and quiet, you are welcome to assist."

That was unprecedented. Tattersall did his work alone, and never discussed it. We had all respected that discretion—which is not to say that we were incurious. At first mention of this opportunity, we rose to our feet *en masse*.

"What, all of you? Well, so be it. Mob-handed it is. Quick and quiet, mind. Do as I tell you, and touch nothing until I say. Bring your smokes, by all means; leave your glasses here."

BARROWS MUST HAVE been startled to see us troop up from the basement, file through his demesne and head on into the club proper. As a servant of the house, he was owed no explanation; nevertheless, Tattersall tossed him a glance as we passed. "Villeforte using his telescope this evening, d'ye know, Barrows?"

"I believe Sir Marcus is at dinner, sir."

"Is he? Splendid. Then he won't mind if we spend an hour peering at the native beauties, will he?"

"Sir Marcus did give me to understand, sir, that he was...increasingly frustrated to find that his instrument had been meddled with in his absence."

"Gave you to understand, did he? Well, well. Did he give you two bob at the same time?"

"Sir, I cannot—"

"No. No, of course not. But I can. Tuppence is more in his line, I believe. Tell you what, Barrows: here's half a sovereign," and a flicker of gold passed between them, barely appearing in the one hand before it had vanished into the other. "That's to make up for all those times we've kept you running up and down the stairs, above and beyond the call of duty. All serene?"

"That is very generous, sir." The man's face was a mask, professional to the core. No device known to man would have been adequate to measure the depth of his surprise. Still, we knew: and it was certain sure that if, as a result of our activities tonight, some unholy detective were to interrogate him about the members' doings, he would remember only that we six had been playing with another man's property, turning the magnificent astronomical telescope on the roof to more mundane pursuits, hoping to focus those highly polished lenses on heavenly bodies somewhat closer to hand.

We proceeded in single file up the stairs, Tattersall keeping the rear like a sheepdog herding an unwieldy flock. Past the first floor, library and billiard-room and dining hall, the steady buzz-and-clatter of a male congregation at the trough; past the second floor, members' bedrooms and bathrooms. Minor was somehow in the lead, and he led us all the way up through the attics—servants' bedrooms, boxrooms and the like—to a narrow door out onto the flat roof.

We gathered there in the air and the lowering dusk, and he said, "I thought, if we'd said we were coming up here, we probably should."

He sounded uncertain, but Tattersall clapped him on the shoulder and said, "Quite right. Always establish an alibi first. We said we'd make a nuisance of ourselves with Villeforte's precious telescope; let us nuise. Is that a word? Never mind. Take five minutes, gentlemen. Stroll about, scatter your ash widely, enjoy the view and leave your cigar stubs in inappropriate places. That'll confirm our occupation here, if matters should come so far. And meanwhile..."

He stripped the oilcloth cover from Villeforte's magnificent brass tube, dropping that carelessly at the foot of a chimney. The telescope was pointed at the heavens; he twisted it about and tilted it crudely downwards, towards the low rooftops where young Cairene women were accustomed to take their evening baths, their voices shrill as crickets as they called to each other through the gloaming.

The lens caps followed the oilcloth into obscurity, in a gesture guaranteed to enrage Sir Marcus. There were no other guarantees. When men such as we turn to downright larceny, we cross a border that we have no more than stalked before. That side of the line was *terra incognita* to all of us, bar Tattersall.

He took me by the elbow now and drew me to the parapet. "I love to watch the city as the sun sets," he murmured. "It's like a change of master, or at least of oversight. The light goes, the Empire salutes the flag as it comes down, soldiers are confined to barracks and the night city marches in to reclaim its own."

It was happening as he spoke, eerily as it seemed in response to his words. Hazelights in the streets, more traditional lamps showing through windows and on rooftops and the vicious furnace flare of ironworks, the smudged glow of smokestacks and steamships on the river, locomotives oozing like fireworms through and through the city, the slow drift of bright-lit airships overhead, and all backed by the uncanny unlight that invested the pyramids on our horizon, on every horizon, so that those three stolen tombs stood out even more boldly after dark than they did throughout the day: even with so many and so varied lights all about, they served only to herald and enforce the dark as it closed in upon us, as it transposed our Cairo from one reality to another.

We are creatures of the margin, we Remittance Men, belonging not quite anywhere. Which was another way to see that Tattersall was really not quite one of us, because he held himself a full subject of both worlds, light and shadow. The idle companionable sardonic man-about-town slipped away with the sun, and standing beside me in his place was the Tattersall I'd never seen till now, brisk and businesslike, competent, experienced and careful. He gathered us all with a whistle and a jerk of his head, and led us across the roof to another doorway, another staircase down.

Of course he had prospected this route ahead of time. Down one floor, along a corridor to one numbered door among a dozen such; a brisk tap, a brief pause, and he drew a sinister set of steel hooks from his pocket.

"Are those...?"

"Yes. Be quiet."

Minor subsided, abashed. I touched his shoulder for comfort, won myself a sidelong smile that warmed my heart for a moment before we both turned back to watch Tattersall at work.

There was little enough to see. Perhaps he'd practised this too, on this very door; perhaps he had tested himself against every door, every lock in the club, just in case. He slipped one shaft into the keyhole, fiddled briefly, followed it with a second, a third. There was no fuss or drama, only a sudden anticlimactic click and the door was open.

He withdrew his instruments and oiled his way inside, staying us with a gesture. I don't suppose I was the only one to wonder what we'd say if someone came along the corridor now, or which one of us would be bold enough to say it.

It can't honestly have been more than a few seconds, though it seemed so very much longer, before he appeared again in the doorway.

"All serene," he said in a murmur. "Even so: don't speak unless you have to, and keep your voices down. Try not to touch anything. Just hover. When I need you, I'll let you know."

So we stood in a cluster in the middle of the rug, and watched him go to work. Creighton might have murmured a prayer, to a god that none of us was quite sure he believed in; Minor might have slipped his arm through mine and rested his chin upon my shoulder, wheezing softly into my ear. That boy never could keep still or quiet, without drawing on someone else's strength. His captaincy was purchased, never earned; a less military soul would be hard to imagine. Though I'm sure he looked a picture in his uniform, on his horse.

It had not occurred to me that there might be an art to burglary. A science, of course: Tattersall's speed and skill with the picklocks was impressive, but not really surprising. But he went around that room with a particular grace that spoke to a deep understanding of the human psyche, the very work we commonly look to art to provide.

From hat-boxes to shoe-trees, he looked at everything with swift fingers and sharp eyes. Through the wardrobe, through the drawers of the dressing table, through the suitcases—two, and both quite empty, which had him pausing for a moment, gazing towards the door, unexpectedly thoughtful and out of his rhythm—before he said, "Very well, then. I was hoping for something, anything physical that might have yielded a clue as to the scarab's provenance. Even if it only served to deepen the mystery, to confirm that we're looking in the right place." Another glance at the mute and unrevealing door. "Lacking that—and I've looked twice and found nothing—then here's where you come in, gentlemen. I'm afraid it's noses to the grindstone and devil take the hindmost. Devil take us all, if we're caught here before the hindmost is done with his reading."

So saying, he hauled a leather case out from under the bed, deposited it on the covers and flipped open the lid. Papers spilled out, and he distributed them by the handful.

"Quick as you can," he said crisply. "If we learn what his business is here, where he's been and who he's been dealing with, we'll have a better chance of tracking this thing down to its source."

Honestly, I thought he was clutching at straws now, and we were all of us men of straw. Other men made a go of colonial life, made fortunes indeed; we merely floated in increasing anxiety from one grudging payment to the next. Tattersall was the only one among us who took his living from the teeming city that we called our home.

Still: Remittance Men know when to pull together, before the world entire pulls apart. That thing in Tattersall's pocket gave me a chill deep in my bones, where all of Egypt's heat could never penetrate. We of the modern world are used to wonders, be they clockwork or steam-driven or more arcane yet. This, though—this was something other. It came from somewhere other, I was sure; no mortal hand—or at least, no human hand—had made it. There was no such science known to man. If it baffled the Empire, it baffled us all; and between us, creatures of shadow though we were, we could more or less represent the Empire. Or at least her sum of knowledge. Bellaire spoke for science and engineering, Creighton for philosophy and religion. Smith Major was somehow a poor gambler but a fine mathematician; he said that he could calculate probabilities, but that luck always forsook him in the end. Mallenby was our linguist, a school usher before love betrayed him. And I?—Well, I had my uses. If you needed a précis of any novel within the Oxford syllabus, or a more thoughtful essay on the effect of the Romantic poets on the English landscape—or vice versa—I was your man. No good asking me to write a poem—never seek me in Alexandria, for you will always find me here—but if a critic's what you're after, look no further.

I flicked through the sheaf of notes that Tattersall had handed me, and was first to hand them back. "Bills, notes of tender, notes of hand," I said briskly. "He seems to be mounting an expedition. And paying for everything in advance, which is...unusual."

"'Unprecedented' would be closer to the mark," Tattersall said. "He must be very confident. Not only of discoveries, but market value. Major, would you care to cast your eye across these, in case there's something hidden in the numbers?"

"No need," Smith Major rasped. "I've numbers here of my own. I can tell you this, it's not a expedition he's outfitting, it's a small army. Whatever he thinks he's on to, he intends to take it by force. Likely a place, not an artefact; this manifest is enough to stock a siegetown for the winter."

"Or a campsite," Minor murmured, "that he thinks he'll need to defend all season long, while they dig out whatever artefact he's after. I've names here that I recognise, from regimental gossip. Old soldiers, cashiered for worse sins than my own."

"Does anyone have a map?"

No. No one had a map.

"Very well. All the papers back in the case, please, gentlemen. Don't worry about original order; that had been disturbed already, for I tipped everything out haphazardly on my first incursion. And found the scarab buried beneath, for what that's worth. We have what we came for, more or less. Bolsover knows something, the whereabouts of something, or believes that he does. We have learned no more of the location than we have of the target; either he knows neither himself yet, or else he's holding those secret in his head. It's a fair guess that the scarab is connected, but not a certainty. We—"

We all turned our heads as one, at the sound of a key in the door.

HAD TATTERSALL LOCKED it again behind us? It didn't matter, either way. A moment's delay for us, a moment's warning for the new arrival: the door was going to open in any case, and there was neither time nor room to hide. We stood where we were, six men grouped around the bed. I felt Minor's hand on the small of my back, firm and reassuring. Perhaps he drew strength from the touch, just as I did: the whole may be greater than the sum of its parts, though that too would be a breach in the laws of thermodynamics.

A figure, a man stood in the doorway, momentarily still, gazing at us each in turn, it seemed; then he took a slow, careful pace into the room, and closed the door equally carefully behind him. "There is no need for that, sir."

I was briefly puzzled, till I saw Tattersall put away the revolver I had not seen him draw. His dinner jacket must be remarkably well-cut, to conceal such a weight. Once more I envied him his tailor.

The man before us was far more modestly dressed, and most certainly not the man whose secrets we were here to burgle. He was thin, sallow, almost nondescript in his clean but faded linen suit.

"We forget," Tattersall said slowly into the silence, "we who live this life in exile from the norms of society—but of course a gentleman travelling abroad would have a man to attend him. I knew it, the moment I saw that he was unpacked here, for just the one night's stay. He would never have done so much himself. And of course you'd use the dinner hour to lay out his night-things and see that all was as he liked it. However, I do have to say, you don't look much like an Englishman's valet."

"No, sir. Sir Edward's own man was...unable to continue in his service, after falling ill last week. I was the local contact, acting as dragoman so long as Sir Edward remained in Egypt; I said I would be happy to attend to his personal needs also. I am not inexperienced in these matters."

"No, I daresay not." Smith Major gave him the once-over with an impeccably jaundiced eye. "Dismissed—for what, for drinking, was it? or for petty thieving?— well, no matter. No more a gentleman's gentleman, anyway. So you make shift as best you can, eh? And find your way to Cairo because this is where all the dregs of Empire wash up at the last."

"Indeed, sir." His voice was bland, his gaze was indirect; his insolence was absolute, and absolutely telling. Remittance men all, we had not a word to say in our own defence. "And now, if I may ask...?"

"Oh, I don't think you need to ask, do you?" Tattersall was the coolest of us all. "You know very well why we're here. In fact, you know better than we do. Why don't you explain it to us?"

"Sir?"

"Oh, come. His valet didn't fall so conveniently ill without help, did he? With you so handily situated to stand in? My guess is, your masters had you in place from the beginning just to keep an eye on Bolsover because he's dangerous; then you saw what he had, or what he meant, and acted straight away. With the valet out of the picture and you to substitute, you could—well, what? Disrupt his plans or share them, steal his fame or his achievement, what?"

"No, we would steal nothing," the man said, open at last in the face of openness. "Stop him, rather, from stealing what he has no right to."

"Yes, I thought that might be the case. But what? Something to do with this?"

Tattersall took the scarab from his pocket, and tossed it casually onto the bed.

The hiss of air through the man's teeth was answer enough. The device itself lay inert on the coverlet, as though it had no thought of movement.

"I never should have thought it his, now should I?" Tattersall went on musingly. "Master and man: when you're travelling, the boundaries get rubbed away. In a hotel like Shepheard's, you share the same quarters, more or less. I didn't bother to search the connecting valet's room, while I was robbing Sir Edward. It's a point of principle with me," *the honourable thief does not steal from those poorer than himself.* "Perhaps I should have forgone that principle, just for once."

"You would have found nothing worth your attention," the man said bitterly. "Sir Edward had found it already. I do not know what right he had, to be rootling among my things."

"Perhaps the same right you had," Creighton suggested, "to be insinuating yourself into his service, in lieu of the valet you had—what, suborned? Poisoned? Abducted?"

"Oh, nothing grievous. A little ipecac in his dinner, followed by a doctor of our own; the man believes himself far sicker than actually we made him. He is taking a slow recuperative sea-voyage home, with the promise on arrival of a place in a household less...abrasive than Sir Edward's. You're right, of course, it was a liberty or worse, to be playing games with someone else's life, even if he comes out of it better than before—but Sir Edward plays a different kind of game, and really cannot be allowed at the table. We felt that he bore watching."

"Who is 'we', sir, in this argument? Whom do you represent?"

The man smiled thinly. "Men such as yourselves, sir: a caste apart, who look at the world a little differently and perhaps see more than our neighbours do. Men who can see the danger of a Sir Edward Bolsover, and are prepared to take risks to forestall that danger."

"Wait," Bellaire said, sounding bewildered. "What in the world can you know of us?"

"Obviously, we know that Mr Tattersall rifled Sir Edward's rooms at Shepheard's, and came away with more than a comfortable profit." His eyes moved inexorably to the scarab, seemingly against his own intent. "In fact, though, we know a good deal about each one of you. The work of the Remittance Men is...not entirely unnoticed in this city."

"Well." He spoke softly, almost in a drawl, and I may never have heard

Tattersall sound more dangerous. "You have the advantage of us, seemingly. Despite our best endeavours. So, what's next? Will you make us known to your principals?"

"I will not. I don't have that authority."

"Ah, yes. Just a lowly dragoman, I remember: and not above standing in as a body-servant, where required."

"Just so, sir. I am a dragoman; I have been a valet. I can probably never go home. To be fair, I don't know that I would want to. The life suits me, I find— and here I can be of service to more than the occasional needy gentleman, or a party of sightseers. Here I can do work that counts for something."

"And that is—?"

This time it wasn't only his eyes that moved. He stepped towards the bed, somehow contriving to seem small and self-effacing and yet purposeful, all at once.

We made room, watchfully. This time I think we were all aware—the newcomer included—that Tattersall's hand was in his pocket again. At least he kept the revolver out of sight this time.

Unexpectedly, it was Minor who stalled the man. "May we know your name? Sir?"

The man hesitated. "My name?—Yes, I suppose so. My name is Hegarty."

"I expect that's the name of Sir Edward's supposed dragoman, isn't it?" I had not known Minor so perceptive, nor so stubborn. "I was asking for your own name. As you claim to be privy to all of ours."

The man might have been twice Minor's age. His mouth quirked a little at the corner; then, quite straightforwardly, he said, "As you wish, Captain Smith. My own name is Parsons, Melchior Parsons. Though I'm not sure how well you will find it serve you. It is...very little known, here in Cairo."

"No matter for that. It's known to us, now. Don't worry, we'll treat it kindly." Minor stepped back—conveniently into my embrace, as he knew full well—to allow Parsons to go that last yard.

He stepped, he reached, he lifted the scarab from the coverlet. He was almost reverential, holding it cupped in the palm of his hand, touching its back lightly with a finger. The wing-cases seemed to shiver, but it lay static otherwise.

"Will you tell us what it is?" That was Creighton, one enquiring mind speaking for us all.

"Come. I will show you."

The room was small and narrow, but even so: french windows led out to a tiny balcony. There was just room for Parsons to stand out in the air and set the scarab on the balustrade, while the rest of us massed in the opening.

Then his hand dipped into his pocket, and emerged with something that gleamed darkly, that lay heavy in his hand, that matched our scarab exactly when he laid them side by side.

He barely had time to take his hand away before the two of them were moving: rising up on those needle legs, rattling their wing-cases at each other, extending their fragile wings.

I thought at first that they would fight like crickets, that this after all was the point of them: mechanical gladiators, the one pointless and purposeless without the other. But all they did was mop and mow like two disdainful courtiers, fluttering wings and bobbing up and down on spindly limbs, waving antennae in complex patterns.

"What are they doing?" Minor asked softly.

"Talking." The man was succinct, so matter-of-fact we could almost take it unquestioned. "Or we think it may be more like dictation, an exchange of information, so that each learns what the other has registered. Bring any two together, they will do this. And in greater numbers, too. They pair off with one after another until their observations have been shared by all. At least, that's what we believe."

"How many of them are there?" Major asked.

"Untold. We know of...many. In our keeping, and kept elsewhere, and abroad, on their own occasions."

"But what are they for?"

"For this. For data-gathering, and sharing, and reporting in. Wait. Watch now."

Night or day, the light in Cairo is not like light anywhere else in the known world. Night or day, the human eye can't help but turn towards the pyramids and what nests within them, leaking its effluence into the sordid air. Even under the baked glare of a Cairo noon it can be seen, something like a shimmer if shadow shimmered, if an incomprehensible overcast beneath a clear sky could somehow disperse its own corruption of what light is, if it could spread a luminous kind of darkness through the day. Night is its true time, though. Under a blaze of stars in a perennially cloudless sky, the pyramids radiate black light against a black background: visible, almost tangible, a pulse from otherwhere.

It ran over the scarabs' shells like tidal water, lapping, reaching, claiming. When they were done with each other, whatever strange form of mechanical communication that was, they turned as one to face the source of that unlight, the jutting peaks on our horizon that loom over all the city and all our lives.

They raised their wing-cases again, unfurled their wings again and now squatted motionless on bent legs, almost like worshippers at a shrine.

No one had to ask; Parsons knew well enough what was in our minds. "They all do this," he said, "whenever they have clear line of sight. It is in our minds again that they are communicating, reporting to their masters, and perhaps receiving new instructions. If those wings were wireless aerials of some kind, if they could transmit and receive like miniature mobile Marconi stations..."

"Yes," Bellaire murmured, "but how? In so small a device: how is it energised, how engineered? Communicate what, and by what means, what code, what intelligence? And to whom?"

"Such questions are our stock-in-trade," Parsons said, with a sad smile. "As to the energy, we theorise that they draw it somehow from the pyramids, that they are doing so now: that those wings act as receivers also. As to the rest, to the best of our belief, the pharaoh's tombs have been parasitised by creatures from another world. Cuckoos have nested in the pyramids, and these are their servants, gathering what information their masters might require. Before they emerge, perhaps? Reborn, perhaps? It may be that the pyramids play the role of a chrysalis, sheltering the invader through its metamorphosis into a creature that can survive this world. Or it may be that they are a tomb again, that the invaders are dead and that all this is mechanical residue, service to a long-lost lord. Faith and guesswork, these are all we have to offer, where answers are impossible to come by."

"Say faith and deduction, rather," Creighton intervened, "employed within a theoretical framework. Many an answer can be found—has been found, indeed—with such an approach."

"Mr Creighton, yes—but how are we to know when we are right? If we are ever right? Faith is all very well, but it will not actually move mountains. Neither open them."

A soft chime came from Parsons' pocket. He glanced at his watch, flipped a switch, then put it away again. "Sir Edward is a man of regular habits. He will be moving now from the dining hall to the library, from claret to port—but unless his company is congenial, he won't stay above one glass and a smoke."

I could hear the sound of Mallenby's blink, I swear, in the silence that we left ready for him. I daresay we all could; certainly I felt Minor's delight, his indrawn breath and the quiver of anticipation that coursed all through his body.

"The port here is...exceptional," Mallenby said carefully. "Surely he will not smoke?"

"Ah, but he will, Mr Mallenby. He will smoke, and orate—and he will recruit. It's a coarse kind of charisma, but effective."

"Tell us, then, swiftly: what is he recruiting for? An expedition of some sort, clearly—and nothing to do with our pyramids. He could be there in an hour, but he's budgeting for months. I take it those plans have not changed, despite our colleague's infiltration yesternight?"

"I'm afraid not. He had plans to visit London anyway, for business reasons. He always intended to return to Egypt after the rains, with everything in place for an immediate departure into the desert. I see no hope of those plans being changed. Even the loss of the scarab has not really shifted him, it only makes his arguments more difficult to establish."

"And his arguments—and his intentions—are—?"

"Are my fault, largely." He suppressed a smile, and then a sigh; and went on, "In truth, I found this scarab through a rumour in the bazaar. It is known that they are looked for, and will be paid for. We usually hear indirectly, when another turns up in the city. I was sent to track this one down; I found my way to an elderly widow, whose husband had dug it up and was afraid of it, thinking it possessed by the spirit of a djinni, and so sealed it in a pot. With him dead, she was keen to sell. That's all the story, but I was already engaged by Sir Edward, and had no time to take it to my masters. I thought it would be safe among my things, for true darkness always keeps them quiescent. I thought I could pursue my other responsibility, to keep a watchful eye on a figure known to be dangerous and keep him perhaps from doing too much harm, or growing too interested in places we have protected, with cause, for a long time now.

"It was a mistake, of course. I underestimated his coarseness, or his curiosity. Or else I did something to arouse his suspicions, that I might be more than I seemed: what employer goes through his valet's bags as a matter of course? At any rate, he did it, and found the scarab. And kept it, and interrogated me at length, and threatened me with dire consequences if I didn't reveal its provenance. He didn't ask me about its meaning; what could I know? He called me a greasy sponger, a half-caste, all kinds of names. He threatened my person, my family, my future.

"I resisted long enough to be credible, I hope; then I told him what he most wanted to hear, a fantastical tale about an oasis in the desert, a people unknown to the Empire, discoveries unknown—or long lost—to science. I hinted at a lost tribe of Israel."

"And he fell for this farrago? Even under this—corpselight," with a broad wave towards the pyramids, "where any sensible man's inquiry would first turn?" If Bellaire was outraged, it was at this obvious neglect of scientific principles and the rule of Occam's Razor.

"Hook, line and sinker," Parsons confirmed, not without a note of pride at having carried off such a conceit. "Nothing would satisfy him but to plan an expedition, which as you have noted reads more like an invasion force. He is leaving me in charge of implementing his plans, while he flies back to London."

"He's not worried that you'll just vanish in his absence?" God knew, there would be opportunity aplenty: upriver, or to Alexandria, or simply into the city's slums where a man like Parsons could find shelter that a man like Bolsover would never breach.

"He's not, because he thinks he knows too many ways to hurt me, even in my absence. And in fact I won't, because left to himself, raging through the city with tales of lost toys, he might blunder into worse trouble than he's made already. No, I will submissively follow his orders, and have his people ready to march on his return. I will guide them into the high desert, and..."

"And leave him there?" Minor suggested, with an edge of hopeful cruelty that always surprised me when it showed itself. One forgets, perhaps, how savage the young can be. I quieted him with a touch, as Parsons shook his head.

"I dare not; he'll have men with him who could bring him safely out again. And there would be too many questions asked, in any case. No, I thought I'd just lead him in circles as long as I can, and then admit that I have no idea where the blessed oasis can be found. Let him do with me as he will; with any luck, he'll spend his time, his fortune and his life on a wild goose chase, far and far beyond any chance of harm."

"Except to yourself. And your family thereby, if they depend on you or hope for your safe return." That was Creighton, inevitably concerned for the man, for the individual soul.

"Yes, sir. I've a wife and child here, and parents still back home, and nevertheless, I see no way, otherwise. The issue is too important. My responsibility—"

His sense of responsibility was breaking him, seemingly. We none of us thought that he could see his project through, even if any of us had thought that he ought to.

"Oh," said Tattersall, "I think we can take that responsibility from you. How say you, fellows?"

"Least we can do," grunted Smith Major.

"Best we can do," chimed in Minor.

"It may be the most we can do," said Mallenby, "but it'll have to be enough. Padre?"

"My guest," said Creighton firmly, "my responsibility. We'll take it from here, Mr Parsons. You do your work for Sir Edward, tonight. Tomorrow, deal with the scarabs as your conscience and your duty require, and have an eye to your family. Leave the rest to us."

"I don't think I can do that, sir. With all respect. I am sworn to—"

"I think you are sworn to many things, Mr Parsons. Too many things, and they are tearing you apart. We can shift some of that burden from your shoulders. This...will not be the first time. Do you tidy up here and lay out your master's pyjamas; by the time he comes to bed, you should have no more than that to concern you. Just lend us those scarabs for an hour, though. You shall have them back after your valeting is done, my word on it."

IT WAS A tall order, but not one beyond our reach. This was our city, our tribe—in the final analysis, our club, however unwelcome we might be within its purlieus.

Nor was this the first time we had rallied in defence of something nebulous, out of our reach, perhaps beyond our understanding. We are citizens of no mean or quotidian city; here where East meets West, where science and more ancient lore lean hard upon each other, where the boot of Empire presses into soft river-mud and barely leaves a mark that lasts. There may be nothing new under the sun, but there is much in Cairo that is very old indeed, and we modern folk must struggle constantly to keep it down, or else keep others from disturbing it.

We trooped out of the room, along the corridor and down the stairs, almost without discussion. On the first floor, we divided our forces, this way and that. Minor clattered off down the servants' stairs to the nether regions, kitchen and scullery; Creighton stepped into the card-room, empty at this hour, for a moment's private reflection that he preferred not to call a prayer. Tattersall vanished, as is his wont.

Mallenby stood back, in a niche that held a group portrait of the Voyagers' founding spirits. He'd wait for the padre, but not join him. Mallenby wasn't much of a joiner; really it was a surprise that we Remittance Men had managed to catch and keep hold of him.

Myself, I thrust open the library doors and held them wide for Smith Major. I was already talking.

We call it the library, and it is shelved as is traditional with many and many a book that's never read; but in honesty, it's far more a tale of easy chairs and lamplight and firelight in season, of brandy-snifters and cigars and that legendary port, with a club servant ever on call to bring you more. It's not at all the sort of library where people hush you for speaking out; that's what the Silence Room is for.

Used to be for, before we annexed it for our very own, our club-within-a-club.

"...So HERE, SIT yourself down and I'll show you, it really is the most extraordinary thing..."

Library or not, it's still a place for quiet after-dinner converse, mulling over your preferred glass and your smokes, in your preferred company. My voice deliberately shattered that calm, turning every head.

I did try not to look, I tried to be oblivious, but even so: there was a group of half a dozen in the most favoured seats around the fireplace, and I recognised all the faces bar one in that brief glimpse that I couldn't quite restrain.

I guided Major to a lamp-lit alcove and a table for two, where we could sit hunched and mysterious about our doings. Not too close to the fire, not too far away: I could pitch my voice to be heard across the silence of broken conversations, while still seeming to speak privately to Major alone.

"Take a pew. The boy'll be over in a minute with the decanter, they know what I like hereabouts. Light up if you want to smoke, that's the way. But look, here's what I meant to show you. I call it my magic beetle. No need to wind it up, no need to stoke it, d'ye see? It just runs and runs, and stretches out those pretty wings, and waves its whatchamacallits, its feelers, and never ever topples over the edge of the table..."

I had set the scarab on the table between us, and nudged it into life. It was running through all its repertoire of party tricks, with all their unfathomable purpose; I fancied even the clicking of its feet on polished wood must be carrying to my intended audience.

True enough. I was still warming to my patter when a heavy hand closed crushingly on my shoulder, and a voice thick with fury said, "Sir, how do you come by my property?"

"I beg your pardon?" For sheer fastidious contempt, there's nothing to touch a prefect in an English public school, faced with an impertinent junior. I put all my remembered lessons into effect, rising to meet him face to face, giving him the benefit of my finest supercilious eyebrow and the coldest, crispest accent at my command.

Inwardly, I might perhaps have felt a little daunted, if I'd been in truth the solitary swindler that I seemed. Even with my cohort at hand, he was a hard man to face: half a head taller than I, bull-necked and bull-tempered, the shadow of his beard already darkening his jaw though I knew Parsons would have shaved him before dinner.

"That," he said, pointing at the scarab with one huge hand, while the other still kept a grip on my shoulder, "belongs to me. And was stolen from my room just yesterday. Are you a thief, sir, or do you merely consort with thieves?"

"Oh, here, I say!" That was Mallenby, escorting Creighton in with exquisite timing. "You can't sling words like that about in here. Not to members. It's just not on, old man."

"You mind your own business," Bolsover snarled, "and leave me to mind mine."

"Well, but you're making it everybody's business, if you start a dust-up in the library. What's it all about, anyway, what's Farrant done to have you accuse him like this?" Somehow, Mallenby managed to say *what's Farrant done?* and make it sound like *what's Farrant done now?*, which was just right for the occasion.

"That's mine," Bolsover said unequivocally, pointing again at the scuttling scarab. "It was taken from my room at Shepheard's last night, along with a quantity of cash and cufflinks and such—but it was this I valued most. And now I find him playing with it here, trying to sell it to this customer," a gesture at Smith Major, "unless I miss my guess."

"Well, that would be in character," Mallenby confirmed—a little maliciously, I thought—speaking over Major's spluttered protest that no one had mentioned money, it was just a curio he was being shown for interest's sake. "But, oh lord, sir—Sir Edward, isn't it? I heard you were to be our guest tonight—don't you know what you have there?"

"I know it to be a mystery of the highest order, and a precursor of great discoveries to come."

"Oh, dear. I am sorry, Sir Edward, I shouldn't laugh—but truly, it's just a gimcrack bazaar toy, designed to catch the eye and the pocket of the gullible. Heavens, you carry one yourself, don't you, Padre?"

"I do indeed," Creighton confirmed, pulling Parsons' second scarab from his pocket and setting it down beside the first. "I had it from a beggar for a broken sixpence. I use it to amuse the children in the poor ward, and sometimes as an object lesson in hollowness and show. These trinkets seem mysterious and wonderful, but in the end they don't actually amount to anything."

Our two on the table there were conducting their courtly dance, like two dowagers bringing each other up to date on the latest happenings in Society. Which—if Parsons and his masters were right—was a tolerably accurate summation, I supposed.

I had no leisure then to wonder about the devices' makers, or by what science they were powered and instructed, or by what means or language they communicated with each other or with the pyramids. Here in Cairo, we grow used to unanswered questions and permeable borders between what is or can be known and what lies entirely beyond our reach, even when it sits in the palm of our hand. Strangers to our city have more rigid attitudes and expectations. Sometimes our task is merely to distract them; sometimes actually, actively to deceive.

I said, "I really must protest—" but I said it softly, like a man already exposed, and Creighton simply talked right over me. I suppose possession of a pulpit in a draughty church teaches the clergy all the gifts of oratory; certainly for a quiet and self-effacing man he has a hidden power in his voice.

"I was curious to learn where they came from," he said, "there are so many cropping up all across the city. I asked questions in the bazaar, and made myself quite unpopular among the trading classes; but in the end I tracked the source down to a warehouse full of Chinese coolies. It's quite wonderful, in a way, watching how they work. Each man has a specific task, and the skills and tools required for that and that alone. It's the opposite of craftsman work; no one man made either of these, or any. Still, they turn them out by the crateload. Many go straight onto ships, bound for every port in the Empire; more are sold at the door to any beggar or street dealer with a few piastres in hand and a plausible manner. I'm sorry to see a gentleman engaged in the trade, though—or the club being used in such a way. It is all rather sordid. Especially living where we do, in the light of something legitimately esoteric. These things are mere fribble, but the unethical amongst us have been known to use them as bait for much larger deceptions. Whole expeditions have been financed and their funds misappropriated; or the principals have been led directly into the hands of bandits and held for ransom—"

"Oh, no, really, that's too much!" I expostulated, unconvincingly. "I have this charming little artefact, which I wanted to show off to my new friend here, and suddenly I'm accused of banditry and peculation and all sorts!"

"Well, it's hardly the first time, is it, Farrant? I believe the Chief of Police has been in here asking questions about you, more than once." That was Mallenby, being as insinuating as he knew how.

"He is a member, after all," I murmured vaguely, looking about as though for rescue—and instead finding Tattersall, as brisk to appear as he often is to vanish, with the club's president in tow.

"Again, Mr Farrant?" Parfitt rules the Voyagers' with a will of steel, wrapped in a voice of silk. "What is it this time, a case of simple fraud? Well, as I believe I heard you mention on my way in, that really is too much. If we'd only known you better, you should have been blackballed from the start. As it is—well, I can do that *post facto*, *ex parte* and *ex officio*. The rules allow it, and I believe the occasion insists. Remove yourself, if you please, and don't trouble to return."

"I'll do no such thing!" I protested vehemently.

"No? Then I must have you removed. If you would, Smith..."

Smith Major, still the gullible victim, startled at the mention of his name, but didn't move else. There was no need. I felt strong young hands close upon my person, and a bare glance behind showed me Smith Minor, now in the get-up of a club servant, complete with apron buttoned over his waistcoat.

"This way, sir. *If* you please..."

I struggled, partly for show and partly for the pleasure of being manhandled by a lean and wiry youth who was enjoying it as much as I. We're not often licensed to sport in public, but we made a splendid spectacle of ourselves, all the way out of the library and down the staircase.

Assured that Parfitt had detained Bolsover above—with apologies, certainly, and alcohol no doubt—we unhanded each other in the hallway and pulled our clothing straight, all under Barrows' disapproving eye. Disapproving, but experienced: this was hardly the first time we'd played out this scene, or others like it.

"I have to say, I do quite like you in uniform," I murmured, reaching out to tweak Minor's collar straight.

"You say that every time. And its corollary."

"Well, both are equally true. I do quite like you out of uniform as well."

Minor snorted, and pushed me towards the basement stairs. Barrows looked on, the very embodiment of distaste. He loved none of us, but Minor and me he loved the least of all.

Alas for him, we thrived under his antipathy. Ensconced once more in the Silence Room, we poured ourselves glasses of port—I refrained from smoking, in deference to Minor's sensitivities, though of course he asserted it was rather in deference to Mallenby's: "You care more about his opinions than you do about my lungs, and that's all there is to it"—and settled back to wait for the others.

One by one, they manifested. I had already set the aerator in motion, in anticipation of Major's cigar; he nodded at me, and stood courteously by the flue with his pint of ale. Creighton and Mallenby were full of the joys of deception; Tattersall came in last and late, with the president still in tow.

"Gentlemen. I am to suppose that tonight's—theatre—had a purpose behind it, yes?"

"Yes, sir." Smith Major was taciturn as ever; the others were too elevated to make sense. It fell to me to be the rational one, and make our case. "Bolsover was indeed planning an expedition, on the basis of one scarab. He...had been misled, and it would have availed him nothing; but he was out to recruit, and he would have dragged club members and the club's good name into quicksand before he was done. We deemed it better to intervene early, and discourage him from the start."

"Well, that much you've done. He's still headed home in the morning, and he says he won't be back. These fly-by-night entrepreneurs are quick to see an advantage, but quick too to revoke under pressure. In the club's interest, gentlemen, I believe I have to thank you once again. Despite certain disruptions in the even progress of our ways."

We apologised for that, profusely; and insisted that he share a glass of his own port with us, and kept him amused with tales that fell barely the right side of decency, until he took his departure and left us to our revels.

Almost as soon as he was gone, Parsons slipped in. Tattersall dipped hands into pockets, and restored two scarabs to the man.

"All serene," he said blithely. "He was so upset at being so nearly taken for a fool, I don't believe he even noticed these had vanished again. That was well done, by the way, Padre, leaving your own as if it were of no account."

"Oh—in honesty, I just forgot it in all the kerfuffle. Still, if that helped..."

"We all helped, I believe. It was a splendid caper, one and all. We have one bully fewer to trouble the country, and one secret more to tackle—because you do understand, Parsons, that we shall be prying under every rock until we can find out just who your mysterious masters are, and what exactly they intend? Cairo is our city of choice, for all that we talk so much about Alexandria; the instinct to defend her is strong within us all."

"Oh, sir, I understand you perfectly. And I wish you joy of the hunt." Parsons smiled knowingly, slipped the scarabs into his own pockets and departed, very much with the air of a man who never expected to be troubled with us again.

"Alexandria sounds good to me," I murmured into Minor's ear. "Maybe I could set up as a poet after all, at least for a month or two."

"You'd never stick it," he said sorrowfully. "You'd be wanting to come back in a week, just to take soundings in the club here, just to check that nothing newly awful was going on and you not here to mend it."

And he was right, of course: which is why we are and will remain tolerated at the Voyagers', at least until the pyramids crank open to give up their unlawful dead.

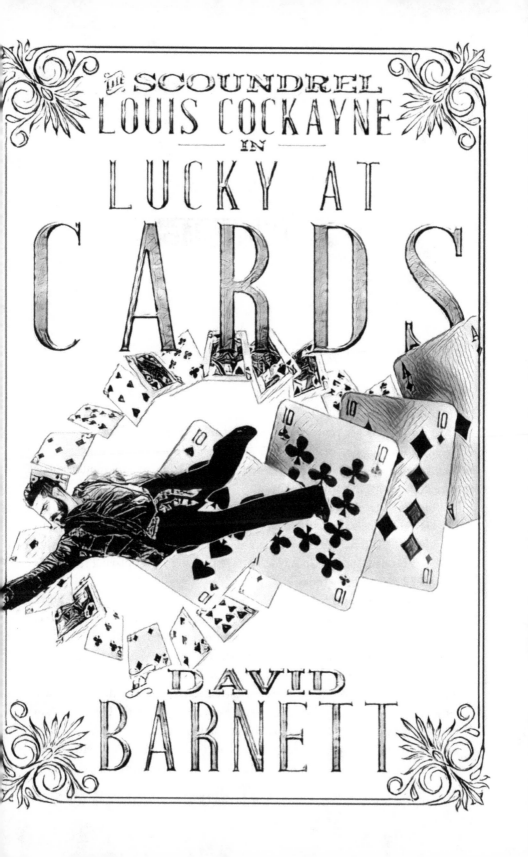

THE SCOUNDREL
LOUIS COCKAYNE
IN
LUCKY AT
CARDS

DAVID
BARNETT

LUCKY AT CARDS

✦-DAVID-BARNETT-✦

"You ought to get yourself over to Madame Choo-Choo's," said Thaddeus Pinch, saliva dribbling down his dull metal jaw as he chewed on his cigar. Pus oozed from the yellowing sores at his neck where the bolts from his modifications were driven clumsily into his flesh.

He slammed the clanking, hissing tangle of steel, cables and pistons that was his right arm on the table, making the dirty shot-glasses jump, and with his good hand he laid his fan of cards face up on the warped woodwork. "I mean, you gotta be lucky in love, Cockayne, 'cause you're sure as shit playing your cards like a dead man walking today."

Louis Cockayne puffed on his cheroot and looked with narrowed eyes over the rim of his own cards at the hand Pinch had spread on the table. Flush. He looked up at the self-declared King of Steamtown, surrounded by his deputies and lieutenants, as the white Texan sun poled in fractured beams through the ragged old bullet-holes in the window shades of the bar. He wondered briefly whether he could shoot his way out of the saloon, make it to the *Yellow Rose* tethered a quarter of a mile away at the edge of town, and get the hell out of San Antonio before Thaddeus Pinch put a bullet in his ass.

He decided not, and with a sigh fanned out his hand. Pinch began to wheeze and rock backwards and forwards, pale, viscous liquid spurting from the fleshy wounds where his replacement limbs plunged into his red and swollen skin, steam rising in thin exhalations from the joints of his huge metal arm. Thaddeus Pinch was laughing, Cockayne realized, and like the King of Steamtown himself it was not what anyone might call a pretty sight.

Pinch threw a glass-load of bourbon into his mouth, ignoring the fact most of it dribbled down his metal lower jaw, and he slapped the table with his good hand. "And that, unless I'm very much mistaken Louis, is you broke as a bitch." He leaned over the table, his foul breath a cocktail of rotting teeth, cheap booze and engine oil, and smiled grotesquely. "That means your ass is mine, Cockayne."

Cockayne smoothed his mustache with his thumb and forefinger and drained his own glass. He felt the eyes of Pinch's thugs on him, shifted in his chair until he registered the reassuring weight of his pearl-handled revolvers snug in their holsters at his hips. There was a pile of IOUs on the smooth-worn felt of the table between him and Pinch. Cockayne had promised the earth and would have put his own grandma on one of those scraps of paper if she'd still been alive.

Pinch rose with effort and noise from his chair. "Let's take a walk, Louis."

In the merciless sun that beat down on the main street of San Antonio— pretty much known as Steamtown to anyone who had the misfortune to end up there since Pinch took over as tyrant-in-perpetuity from his daddy, who'd been one of the many British American governors in Texas who'd seceded from Crown control and decided to run things down below the Mason-Dixon Wall just as they liked them, not as some toffee-nosed Brits wanted things to be—Louis Cockayne paused to light a cheroot. Thaddeus Pinch lumbered alongside him, his mechanical left leg dragging heavily through the dust. Everyone knew all the stories about how Thaddeus Pinch lost his arm (chewed off by a coyote), his leg (an accident in one of the Steamcrawlers, Pinch's tracked vehicles used to cover great distances across the Texas deserts and prairies) and his jaw (shot off by a bounty hunter whose corpse still swung in a gibbet at the main gates into San Antonio). Pinch paused alongside him, steam hissing from the pipes on his arm and leg.

"Gonna get right to the point, Louis. You owe me a fuck-load of money."

Close to the mines the *Yellow Rose* was tethered, and Cockayne could see the tantalizing shape of her balloon bobbing above the low rooftops. Pinch followed his gaze and said, "Mighty fine airship you got there. You really think I'm going to let you fly out of here to earn my money? I'd never see you again, Louis, like they ain't seen you in Houston since you took that dirigible off Trey McFarlane."

Cockayne started to protest but Pinch silenced him with a wave of his good hand. "You're a coward, a crook and a bastard, Louis Cockayne. And that's why I like you. And that's also why I got a proposition for you."

From between two tall wooden buildings a pair of Pinch's thugs armed with shotguns strode, and Cockayne heard a rising swell of song and the rhythmic clanking of chains before he saw the column of men, almost all of them black and shirtless and shackled ankle-to-ankle, their bodies glistening with sweat and coal-dust. They walked like dogs whipped to exhaustion, but held their heads high, the man at the head of the column singing in a low, vibrating tone, "Hoe Emma Hoe, you turn around, dig a hole in the ground, Hoe Emma Hoe..."

As he finished each line the men behind repeated the chorus to him in a harmonious unison that was so beautiful Cockayne had to stare at his boots until the slaves had passed. Not for the first time he wondered what was wrong with him, that he'd fly all the way from the civilised towns of the British Americas near New York and Boston just to get loaded on strong bourbon, sleep with dull-eyed women and lose his shirt at poker to Thaddeus Pinch in this shit-hole.

"I need more Negroes," said Pinch flatly. "For the mines. This summer's been a bastard, Louis, and it's hot work digging out that coal."

Cockayne said, "What's that got to do with me, Thaddeus?"

Pinch smiled again. Cockayne wished he wouldn't do that. "Mighty big ship, the Yellow Rose. Bet it's got a real roomy hold, right?"

Cockayne stared at him. "You want me to go slaving for you?"

"Not alone. I'm not so stupid." Pinch clicked the fingers of his good hand and Inkerman wobbled up. "Get half a dozen of the boys. Bo, maybe, his brother Luke, a handful others. Tell them they're going for Negroes with Mr Louis Cockayne in his fancy airship. And get some supplies in. It's a long way to Africa."

Cockayne looked at him. "Africa?" He'd thought maybe they'd be looking for stragglers north of the Mason-Dixon Wall, or escapees from the Confederacy trying to get to Free Florida. "Africa?"

"The Ivory Coast, to be exact," said Pinch, spitting in the dust, webs of stringy saliva clinging to his metal jaw. "Mighty fine hunting ground, Louis. Mighty fine indeed. Now why don't you get yourself over to Madame Choo-Choo's? On the house, Louis. Like I said, you're so goddamned unlucky at cards, you got to be lucky in love."

Mr Okoth clicked his tongue absently as he scanned the columns of neat figures in the leather-bound ledger open on his wide desk, then leaned backwards in the rickety chair that looked as though it could barely hold the mass of his immense frame.

"Mori!" he called, stretching his long arms towards the whitewashed ceiling. "Tea!"

There was no answer from the kitchen, through a curtain of beads behind him. Mr Okoth sighed and stood, stretching again. It was such hard work doing the monthly books, though he should not complain. Work was steady; better than steady. Every day, it seemed, someone was knocking on the door wanting Okoth's help with this or a guide to somewhere, some information about that or the map to somewhere else. His wife Kissa, may she rest quiet in her grave, would be proud of him, he was sure of it. Proud that he was such a success, building a life and business in Alexandria. His gaze fell on the tattered map of Africa pinned to the wall by his desk, the countries and states colored and re-colored with sticks of chalk as they fell to one European power or another, generally the English or French these days, though the Portuguese, Spanish and Germans each had their own favorites. Everyone wanted a bit of Africa, it seemed, though no-one ever thought to ask the Africans what they thought about it. If Okoth traced the course of the great river with his square fingertip he could follow it from Egypt and into The Sudan, along its divergence into the White Nile straight to Uganda, where he had been born and Kissa had died after being taken by the fever when Mori was little more than a baby. Yes, thought Okoth, she would be proud of him. What she would think of their son, however, he had no idea.

The bell rang twice, signifying that someone was climbing the whitewashed stone steps from the bustling souk to the offices of Okoth and Son. Okoth raised his head, expecting Mori to come through it, perhaps returning late from the souk where Okoth had sent him to buy spices. Okoth was winding up to unleash a stream of complaints at the boy—*your lateness! your loincloth! your laziness!*—in the manner that Mori liked to call his 'Mr Tom' routine, so-named for the book that Mori had left pointedly by Okoth's bedside. But the man who entered was not Mori.

As soon as he saw his dour face, Okoto rose to greet Soumaila, the purveyor of gold trinkets, silver chains and frankly poorly-crafted woven rugs who struggled to maintain a respectable trade on his stall three rows over from Okoth's office in the souk. In Okoth's opinion there were two very easy measures which Soumaila could take to improve the fortunes of his ailing business. One was not perpetually wearing an expression that put people in mind of a hippopotamus simultaneously suffering toothache in all its teeth while a crocodile chewed off its back leg. The other was to set his daughter Yasmina to work on the stall, a daughter Okoth had not seen for some time and who now sat before him beside her father, her lustrous hair covered with bright silks. She must have been twenty-one or twenty-two now, and was quite the most beautiful woman Okoth had seen in a long time.

Evidently Okoth was not the only one of this opinion, for suddenly the absent Mori had appeared from a back room bringing tray after tray of steaming tea to the desk, trying and failing to catch Yasmina's disdainful eye.

Not that it would have made any difference, as Okoth swiftly found out. Soumaila, looking like he had lost a gazelle's head and found a boar's trotter, outlined the reason for his visit. "I want you to take Yasmina back to Sia. She is betrothed to the son of a very powerful *wakomo* who is the head of an extremely strong lineage. It is a very good match."

Okoth rubbed his chin. "And lucrative?"

Yasmina glanced at her father but Soumaila did not meet her eyes. He stared at the hands knotted in his lap and said, "There will be a dowry from the *wakomo* to us, yes. For our inconvenience. Yasmina knows her duty to her parents and her brothers and sisters. It is a hard living for us in Alexandria and this is a good opportunity for her to marry into a good family back in Sia, improving our fortunes here in Egypt and paving the way for our eventual return."

The look on Yasmina's face suggested she was less than entirely thrilled with the whole arrangement. Okoth stood and inspected his map. Sia was one of the largest two settlements on that strip of godsforsaken land south of Mali. The French would take it in six, perhaps seven years at the most, so Soumaila better be quick if he wanted to retire back to the old country. Okoth followed the coastline from Alexandria west along the Strait of Gibraltar and down the Atlantic coast. A ship could put in on the Ivory Coast, though landing points were few and far between and the going inland was not easy. No-one owned the Ivory Coast, though both the French and Portuguese had dabbled there. Well, no-one owned it save the people who had lived on the Ivory Coast for countless generations, of course, but they didn't seem to count to the Europeans. That meant it was also one of the few remaining places the Texan slavers frequented. The neighboring Gold Coast was a better, and safer, option. Calculating swiftly in his head, Okoth turned and said, "Twenty-one days by boat. If the going is smooth."

Yasmina's brow crinkled and Okoth felt suddenly sorry for her. Soumaila narrowed his eyes. "Would an airship not be quicker?"

Okoth raised an eyebrow. "You are not footing the bill, I take it?"

"It will be cash on delivery," said Soumaila. "With the dowry to be brought back on the return trip."

If Yasmina objected to being discussed as though she was a rolled carpet Okoth could not tell from her downcast eyes. He rubbed his chin again. Finding someone reputable who would take Yasmina more than 2,500 miles without payment until they landed at Sia, deliver her unmolested and return with a chest of dowry money for Soumaila was going to be nigh impossible.

Still, that was why people came to Mr Okoth.

He broke out into his widest grin. "Soumaila, my friend, leave this with me."

Louis Cockayne strode through the bustling Alexandria souk in the welcome shade afforded by the silk verandahs strung out over the myriad of stalls selling fruits and spices, textiles and pottery, sides of meat buzzing with flies and glittering jewels in rainbow colors. In the darker shadows of the sprawling market there were other things for sale, herbs to raise your consciousness and lower your inhibitions, flesh that was still alive, dark-eyed and inviting. After negotiating the maze of bureaucracy to allow them to berth at the dusty airfield north of the city and organizing for fresh water and provisions to be delivered to the *Yellow Rose*, he'd sent the crew off for some shore leave, knowing that they'd be heading straight for the more forbidden fruits on offer. He'd kept with him the sandy-haired boy called Bo; or rather, Bo had elected to stick with Louis. He guessed the Steamtowner had been given strict instructions by Thaddeus Pinch not to leave Cockayne alone lest he try to welch out on his debt.

"Where the hell are we going?" said Bo, clutching his hat and twisting to watch a young woman with a pot balanced on her head walk by. "Can't we go whoring with the others?"

"You can, if you like," said Cockayne. "I got business."

Bo's face twisted in indecision, then he evidently decided Pinch's instructions carried more weight than the desire in his trousers. "What sort of business? Where?"

"Here," said Cockayne, stopping by a whitewashed building between the stalls. He led Bo up a flight of stairs to a dark wooden door, and pulled on the bell rope.

"If you are visiting Okoth and Son with a business proposition please enter," boomed a voice from within. "If you are a debt collector or other scurrilous rogue, then there is no-one at home."

Cockayne grinned and opened the door, beckoning Bo to follow him. "Okoth," he said.

"Mr Louis Cockayne!" called the large man seated behind the desk, framed by a map of Africa on the wall. "How utterly astonishing! Come in, come in! Mori! Tea!"

Cockayne sat heavily in one of the wooden chairs Okoth pulled up to the desk, relieved to be in the cool office. As the boy Mori brought a pot of steaming tea and three cracked mugs Okoth said, "And what brings you to Africa, Mr Cockayne? Not hot enough for you in America?"

"There's plenty heat in Texas," said Cockayne, glancing sidelong at Bo, who regarded the cup of tea as though it was piss or poison. "Here on business, Okoth, after a bit of information. Heading south and wondered if there are any local difficulties I should be aware of."

"This is Africa!" laughed Okoth. "There are *always* difficulties! " He stood and looked at his map. "South, you say? The Boer Republics? Not that they call them that anymore, not since the British campaigns there. Astonishing it was, Mr Cockayne, all those airships! Still, a lot to fight for. Astonishing amounts of diamonds there, and gold too." He tapped the map. "The Germans are making a lot of inroads around here, too. Out of Zanzibar and nibbling at the British borders. There will be trouble there, mark my words."

Cockayne waved at him dismissively. "Pshaw. Trouble between the Germans and the British? They're thick as thieves after the Germans helped the Brits put down the rebellion in the Americas back in 1775."

Okoth tapped the side of his nose. "Mark my words, Mr Cockayne. Perhaps ten years, perhaps twenty, twenty-five maybe. But there will be trouble between Germany and Britain. Those old alliances, they only hold so long."

Cockayne shrugged. "Anyway, I'm not going so far. Ivory Coast's where we're headed."

Okoth inspected Bo, who stared coldly back at him. "And how are you traveling, Mr Cockayne? And who are your friends?"

"Airship, Okoth. The *Yellow Rose*." Cockayne grinned. "I'm a 'stat pilot now. She's just getting a refill of lifting gas and a clean-up back at the airfield. We flew straight over from Texas."

Okoth clapped his hands. "How astonishing! An airship pilot! And you and your crew...the Ivory Coast, you say?"

Bo spat his tea suddenly back into his cup. "Jesus Christ, I can't drink this shit. Ain't you got any liquor?"

Okoth appraised him mildly, and signaled to Mori who was lurking by the door into the kitchen. "Take Mr Cockayne's friend into the back room, find him some whisky."

Mori nodded and Bo scraped back his chair and followed. As soon as he was out of sight Okoth narrowed his eyes. "Ivory Coast, Mr Cockayne? Slave hunter territory?"

Cockayne stared at his fingers. "Bit of business, is all."

"With Texans?"

Cockayne finally met Okoth's eyes. "Yes. Business with Texans."

The big man shrugged. "None of *my* business, Mr Cockayne. I had thought you made of stronger stuff, but..."

"Like you said, none of your business, Okoth," said Cockayne briskly. "Thanks for the tea, we should be getting off. Want to be airborne at first light." He met Okoth's gaze once more and sighed heavily, suddenly sick to his stomach. Must have been the tea.

DAWN BROKE HOT and brutal, and Cockayne was sweating as soon as he stepped out into the glare of the sun. They'd slept in their cabins on the *Yellow Rose*, or rather he had. Bo had gone off to find the rest of the crew a little before midnight, and Cockayne did consider just untethering the 'stat and getting the hell out of there. But a man like Thaddeus Pinch wouldn't let something like that lie; he might never spend much time out of Steamtown but he had enough money to put a handsome price on Cockayne's head. It wasn't worth looking over his shoulder for the rest of his life. Besides, he had another duty to perform now.

The boys had returned in the early hours, clattering about the airship and whooping and hollering until Cockayne yelled from the stateroom for them to shut the fuck up. Now, as the morning heat rose intolerably, they came down the ladders in ones and twos, red-eyed and stinking of hooch.

Bo sipped at a tin cup of black coffee and squinted into the sun. "Hell of a night."

Cockayne grunted and smoothed the sweat from his moustache. He could pick out two figures walking across the dusty airfield towards them. Bo clocked them too and said, unnecessarily, "Negroes."

Cockayne spat into the dust. "Jesus shit, you going to say that every time you see one? Don't know if it's escaped your notice, but you *are* in Africa."

Bo shrugged, running a hand through his blond hair and peering at the new arrivals. Cockayne felt him perk up beside him, letting loose a low whistle.

The man was dressed in cool white robes and had a face like a horse with a nail in its hoof. But the young woman he protectively gripped by the arm... Cockayne felt the breath leave his body as though he'd been punched. She was the most beautiful woman he'd ever seen. Her white eyes burned like the noonday sun and her thick black hair hung in plaits over the brightly-coloured silks that entwined around her body.

"Mr Cockayne?" said the man hesitantly, looking with doubt from Louis to Bo to the other Steamtowners staring slack-mouthed at the girl.

"Soumaila," said Cockayne, holding out his hand. The other man took it tentatively and said, "Mr Okoth..."

"Okoth has employed my services to take your daughter to Sia," he said, as reassuringly as he could. "I will deliver her safely."

Soumaila didn't seem too convinced. "She is most precious to me..." he said.

The girl, Yasmina, made a lout tutting noise and looked away.

Cockayne clapped him on the shoulder. "You have my word, Soumaila. No harm will befall her."

The man muttered something in a tongue Cockayne didn't recognize to the girl, who shrugged and folded her arms. He spoke again, more pleadingly, and she finally relented, and allowed him to embrace her. Then she looked coldly at Cockayne and said, "We are to depart soon?"

"Immediately, miss," said Cockayne. Soumaila kissed his fingertips and waved them at his daughter, and as he departed back across the dusty airfield Cockayne held out a hand to help her up the ladder to the swaying gondola.

"I am not an invalid," she said coolly, and climbed herself, ignoring the appreciative whistle from Bo's dark-haired brother Luke, greeted by a volley of cackles.

"One for Madame Choo-Choo's," said Bo with a grin as she disappeared through the hatch.

Cockayne stared at him. "What?"

"Madame Choo-Choo's. The brothel."

"I know what it is. What are you talking about?"

Bo gestured helplessly at the gondola. "We're taking her back to Steamtown, right? One down, a hold-full to go. Maybe we could break her in on the journey, huh?"

Cockayne turned to face him full on. "That girl doesn't get so much as looked at by you boys, you got that? We're making a little side trip and taking her to her father's village. And that's that."

Bo frowned. "But we're here to round up—"

"I know what we're here for," said Cockayne through gritted teeth. "But I'm the skipper of this airship and I say she gets safe passage to Sia. Now load up and let's get the hell—"

Cockayne felt a rough hand clamp on his shoulder. He turned to see an angry, bearded face up against his, a man in a fez and a waistcoat, gesticulating wildly at a young woman behind him, eyes to the ground, wrapped in a blanket.

"What the hell is going on?" said Cockayne, shaking off the man's hand.

The man scanned the crew and pointed at a young red-head who barely spoke, and who was leaning against the ladders with a canteen of water in his hand. "That one! That man! He has assaulted my daughter!"

Cockayne looked at the red-head—Pete, he thought his name was, though he hadn't made much effort to get to know the Steamtowners too well on the flight over—and back at the woman, who he saw was little more than a girl. Jesus. He said, "You know what this guy's talking about?"

Pete shrugged. "We went whoring. We ran out of money. I was still horny."

"She was out like a good girl getting fruit from the market for my stall in the souk!" shouted the man. "This beast of yours he—he—"

The girl began to sob and her father turned to comfort her. Cockayne glared at Pete and said to Bo, "Get 'em all back on the 'stat. Quick." He turned to the man, digging in his pocket for the roll of pound notes. "Sir, I am very sorry. I will, of course, admonish—"

The man slapped the money out of Cockayne's hand. "Admonish!" He spat into Cockayne's face. "He should be hanged like a dog. You are animals. All of you."

Then he turned and with an arm around his daughter's shoulder, ushered her away from the *Yellow Rose*.

ONCE AIRBORNE, THE *Yellow Rose* practically flew itself, as Cockayne had swiftly found out to his delight after taking possession of her. On the bridge he charted a course—2,500 miles in a straight line overland—and locked the wheel into position. Bo, who Cockayne had instructed to take the first shift on the bridge, stood beside him as he ran through the controls.

"Mr Pinch is going to be pissed at you when he finds out about that little chickadee," said Bo with a self-satisfied grin.

Cockayne scowled at him. "Thaddeus Pinch isn't here."

"No, but we are," said Bo with that same maddening smirk. "And you can't talk to me like that. You're paying off a debt, you know. Who the hell do you think you are?"

Before the Texan even had time to curl up his mouth into another smile, Cockayne had him by the front of his shirt and had whipped out the pearl-handled revolver that hung in his right holster, pushing the cold metal of the barrel up into the underside of Bo's suddenly quivering jaw.

"I'm Louis goddam Cockayne, and don't you fucking forget it," he whispered. Bo blinked and nodded. Cockayne said, "I can't hear you, asshole."

"Sir, yes sir," said Bo.

Cockayne smiled and holstered the gun. "Good boy. Now you keep an eye on those instruments and try not to crash the airship, OK?"

"WHY ARE YOU here, Mr Cockayne? In Africa?"

Cockayne chewed the mint-flavoured lamb he'd bought in the souk, cooked up himself in the galley and served with some startlingly bright green beans and a heap of couscous. Louis Cockayne had lived alone and on his wits for long enough to know how to serve up a decent dish or two when required, and besides, there was no way he was going to eat anything rustled up by Pinch's idiots.

He looked across the table at Yasmina, who sat straight in the wooden chair and took small forkfuls of the couscous. He had insisted she stay for the overnight journey in his stateroom, which could be locked from the inside and as well as the large bed had other opulent fittings such as the dining table and well-stocked drinks cabinet. Yasmina had agreed, especially after hearing the raucous shouts of Bo and the boys in the galley as they filleted the *Yellow Rose's* rum supplies, and had also nodded her head to Cockayne's suggestion that they have dinner together. He had lit candles and watched her through the flickering flames while he considered his answer. The yellow flames reflected in her skin and her eyes as she watched him. He felt uncomfortable and awkward, and kept thinking he had food in his mustache or slivers of bean between his teeth.

She's bewitching you, Louis. Watch out!

"Mr Cockayne?"

"Business," he said abruptly, looking down at his meal. It was good lamb, if a little well-salted, but he couldn't find his appetite.

He looked up and Yasmina still had her eyes on him, drilling into him. What age had Okoth said she was? Twenty or twenty-one? He shook his head slightly. Those eyes were ancient.

"Slaving business," she said, more of a statement than a question. Ancient *and* wise.

"I'm not a slaver," said Cockayne, too quickly.

Yasmina smiled minutely, and Cockayne's stomach flipped. Get a grip, he told himself. You're going gaga over some slip of a girl. She said, "You are not a slaver, yet here you are slaving." She held his gaze. "I am not an idiot, Mr Cockayne."

"No," he said softly. "No you are not." He wiped his mouth with his napkin and laid it over his half-finished meal. "And you are right, I am slaving. I have a... debt to discharge. A duty to perform. I haven't really much choice."

"We all have a choice," said Yasmina, cutting into the lamb.

He raised an eyebrow. "We all have a choice, yet here you are, being married off."

She frowned sharply. "You are making fun of me."

He held up his hands in surrender. "No, I'm not. Well, maybe a little. But I am interested...you seem intelligent. And capable..."

She snorted, somewhat deliciously. "My father will not be able to run his business without me. He has no idea how much I do. He would have been ruined a year ago had I not taken over many things without his knowledge."

Cockayne took a sip of the Seventy-eight Bordeaux, pretty much the last of the stocks on the airship that McFarlane had left on board when he lost the *Yellow Rose*. Cockayne would have to restock soon, but it would be rum and bourbon, not this fancy French stuff. He said, "So why is he packing you off to the ass-end of nowhere to marry a man you've never met?"

Yasmina—her own drink untouched on the table—cast her eyes down and Cockayne reckoned he'd guessed right that she'd never even clapped eyes on her intended. After a long pause, in which sudden hot winds gently buffeted the gondola, she said, "What do you know of duty, Mr Cockayne?"

He shrugged. "That it generally involves doing something you'd rather not."

She smiled, those beautiful eyes suddenly wet, and sad. "Yes. You are right. I had thought my life was to be something different. I have been taking lessons in all kinds of things—English, economics, history—at the free school set up by the Christian missionaries. I thought to perhaps take over my father's business, allow him to retire back to Sia."

"And you've told him this?"

She shook her head tightly. "No. He has already promised to hand over the stall to my eldest brother." She made a dismissive gesture with her thin hand. "He is almost as much of an idiot in business as my father. It is not a woman's role. My destiny is to make a good marriage, and one that brings much-needed funds into my father's business." She laid her cutlery neatly on her barely-touched food. "That is my duty."

Cockayne tidied up the plates on to a tray to take back to the galley. The rays of sunshine that fell through the portholes were deep and golden, heralding approaching nightfall. He gestured to the bed. "I'll leave you to prepare for the night. There are books over there if you're of a mind to read."

She nodded as he picked up the tray, and opened the door for him. He said, "Lock it behind me and stay here until I knock for you in the morning."

As he elbowed his way through the narrow doorway she bit her lip—he felt his heart lurch in a most uncharacteristic manner—and said, "Mr Cockayne? You go where you wish in this airship? Have adventures?"

He shrugged. "Pretty much."

Yasmina smiled. "How lucky you are."

PETE WAS ON the bridge, staring at the black sky and the moon-dappled surface of the wide Nile beneath them, when Cockayne climbed up to relieve him. He hated the red-head for what he'd done to that girl, for making her father lump him in with the rest of them. Louis Cockayne was many things, but he'd never forced himself on a woman. As Pete, weary from studying the unfolding African landscape, headed to his bunk, Cockayne said quietly, "And you so much as even try the handle of my stateroom door on your way past, I'll blow your nuts off."

Pete nodded, refusing to meet Cockayne's eye. Word had obviously spread about his earlier run-in with Bo; good. Maybe those boys would show him a little more respect now.

Cockayne checked the charts and the instruments, adjusted their altitude slightly and turned them a degree or two south-west. They should hit Sia sometime around early evening tomorrow. And then he would deliver Yasmina to her new family, and pick up the dowry payment to take back to her feckless father on the return run.

And he'd never see her again.

What the fuck is wrong with you, Louis? Yasmina had been right. Barring slight hitches like Thaddeus Pinch, Louis Cockayne went and did what the hell he liked. He could have been married a hundred times over—hell, he bet even Rowena Fanshawe, the Belle of the Airways, the tough-as-nails 'stat pilot from London, would walk down the aisle with him if he asked. Love 'em and leave 'em, that was Louis Cockayne. He knew the names of maybe half the girls he'd bedded and remembered the faces of only a quarter of those. He was Louis Cockayne! It was a *privilege* for them to lie with him!

So why was this Yasmina lodged so firmly in his head? She was beautiful, yes, but the world was full of beautiful women. She was intelligent, but so were half of the debutantes in New York. She was strong and go-getting yet modest and demure. And all that, plus a ha'penny, would buy a cup of coffee. So what the hell was it about Yasmina?

He pondered long into the night, until a sleepy-eyed Luke, his dark hair mussed from his bed, yawned his way on to the bridge for the last few hours of darkness.

OVER A BREAKFAST of bread, olives and a salty, white cheese bought from the souk Yasmina said, "You slept outside the door last night. I heard you breathing."

Cockayne nodded. "I think the boys would have left you alone, but..."

Yasmina placed an olive between her full lips. "Thank you."

His heart swelled like a dog thrown a bone. She tossed him another: "You seem a decent man, Mr Cockayne."

He shrugged. "I am."

"So why are you stealing people from Africa to work until they die in the mines of Texas?"

He withered under her patient stare, picking at his bread. "You spoke of duty last night. This is mine."

She raised one eyebrow. "A duty to Texas?"

"A duty to not having my neck stretched by a rope tied to a tree branch," he said, then finally met her eyes. "I'm discharging a debt. If I didn't do this my life would be forfeit."

He was sure she'd understand that, at least. Yasmina inspected another olive. "And you consider your life to be worth more than those of the free men and women you will kidnap, is that it?"

Cockayne opened his mouth to answer then closed it again. He'd suddenly realized what it was about Yasmina. He'd slept with milk-maids and princesses, whores and nuns. And every single one of them had thanked him and begged him to stay, even as he was pulling on his boots and gun-belt.

Yasmina...she was the only woman Louis Cockayne had ever met who, he was somewhat shocked to acutely understand, he just wasn't good enough for.

COCKAYNE WAS GUIDING the *Yellow Rose* towards the square of orange dust— nominally Sia's airfield, though the town itself was little more than a jumped up village, so he couldn't expect the facilities to be of the standard of Highgate or North Beach Aerodromes—when Yasmina announced herself on the bridge with a scent of spice and a tiny cough.

"We're here," said Cockayne as the shadow of the airship's balloon grew larger and larger on the ground, swallowing a knot of thin black shapes on the edge of the airfield. "I think there's a welcoming committee. Looks like some kind of cow pulling a wagon." He glanced sidelong at Yasmina. "Must be the in-laws."

"Mr Cockayne," said Yasmina, staring out of the window ahead. He looked at her profile, inked against the setting sun, her midnight skin on fire with blazing orange. "Mr Cockayne, you seem to have been on the verge of asking me something all day."

They both knew what it was, and it went something like this: *Why don't I shoot these Texan idiots, dump their bodies over-board, you can blow out this arranged marriage and we'll follow the sunset wherever it leads us, for ever and ever and ever?*

On the ground Sia's languid stevedores burst into activity to snatch at the trailing tether cables, and they hauled the *Yellow Rose* to a jarring halt. The gondola steadied and began to sink as the ground-crew pulled on the tethers.

"What would you have said?" he asked.

The shouts from below told them that the airship was secure. Yasmina turned away from him. "We shall never know, because you didn't ask." He felt her at his back, as though waiting for him to say something, but he had no clue what to say. He looked over his shoulder but she had silently gone.

Cockayne stayed on the bridge until Bo and Luke dragged up a heavy sack, its neck tied with chains. "The Negro girl's dowry payment from her rich new husband." He didn't say anything, not even to threaten them if there was so much as a bean missing. He waited for the ground-crew to wave at him that the tethers had been released, and took the *Yellow Rose* up without a backward glance.

Louis Cockayne stayed on the bridge all night and into the next morning, when he put the airship down in a heat-baked valley by a small village of ramshackle huts, surrounded by a sea of long grass. They were over the border into the Ivory Coast. He just wanted to get this over and done with. Before he'd even got the *Yellow Rose* in a landing pattern, a couple of the boys had broken out the personal blimps—small helium-filled balloons fixed to harnesses—and were already floating over the fields, laughing as the villagers fled into the long grasses. Cockayne brought the ship down with a bump.

"You coming?" said Bo. "Rounding up Negroes is always fun."

Cockayne just glared at him until he shrugged and went away. Outside he could hear whoops from the boys, as though they were at a rodeo, the crack of gunshots, and the screams of men, women and children. He went to the galley for a bottle of rum and found a moth-eaten deck which he shuffled as he walked back to the bridge, the rum in his coat pocket.

Yasmina's words came back to him, mingling with the screams and yells. "And you consider your life to be worth more than those of the free men and women you will kidnap, is that it?"

He began to sing softly to himself, that song he'd heard the slaves intoning in Steamtown. "*Hoe Emma Hoe, you turn around, dig a hole in the ground, Hoe Emma Hoe...*" It drowned out the noise from outside, but didn't make him feel any better. Instead, he felt sick to his stomach. And there was only one cure for that.

Drinking straight from the bottle, Louis Cockayne pushed aside the charts and map-books and started to deal himself a Klondike solitaire spread. Unlucky in love....Maybe that meant he was lucky at cards again. What was it Yasmina had said? *We all have a choice.* He looked out at the blue African sky. He felt the thrumming of the engines in the soles of his feet. *We all have a choice.* Louise Cockayne cut the remainder of the deck, face-down on the table, and split it into two piles. It was all on the next card. Red, he stayed, discharged his debt to Thaddeus Pinch, took those poor bastards being rounded up and stolen from their homes all the way to Texas to die in Steamtown's mines. But at least he was a free man again. Black, he freed the tethers, took off in the *Yellow Rose* and let Bo and those bastards rot down there. And Thaddeus Pinch would put a price on his head so big Louis Cockayne would never get a good night's sleep again.

We all have a choice.

Hand hovering first over one pile of cards, and then the other, Louis Cockayne made his.

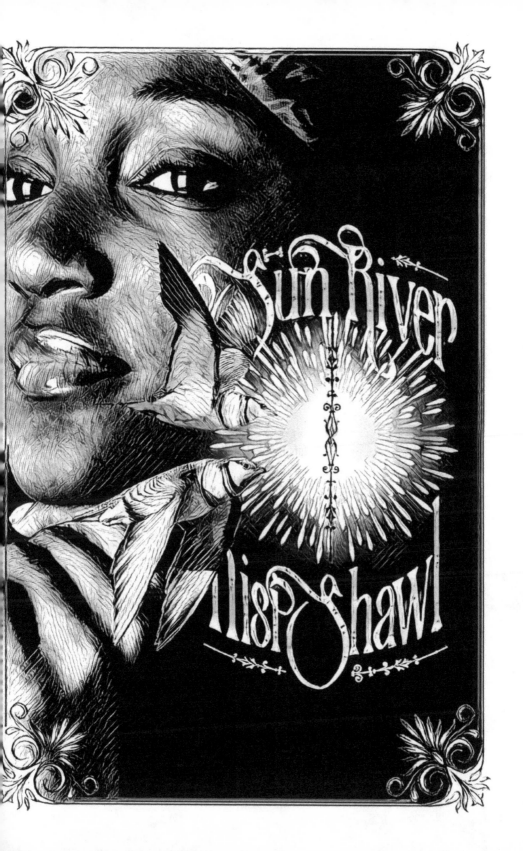

Sun River

Nisi Shawl

Sun River

PRINCESS MWADI WHEELED gracefully above the Nile. She flew in two birds, turning them in upward spirals to catch the last thermals of the day. Soon the sun would set, the air cool. But shortly before that she would be home.

She could have cut hours off her time. The desert route between Alexandria and Cairo was far shorter than this one. But Mwadi was kind to her mounts and didn't often ask them to betray their true natures, and then not by much. Far easier to persuade seabirds to travel along a river than to force them to abandon the water entirely.

Far easier to make these periodic journeys to the coast by occult means than to persuade her buffalo-headed brother Prince Ilunga to "allow" her to go there alone, in her own body.

She switched her eyesight entirely over to the younger of the gulls she rode, then swooped that one ahead of its elder. A barge piled high with bales of white cotton floated toward her, passed beneath her. They traveled in opposite directions and in opposite conditions: the boat was headed north to Rashit, loaded full of merchandise to sell in foreign lands across the Mediterranean; the princess south to Al-Maadi, the aristocratic enclave outside Cairo, and sailed through the sky empty-clawed, delivered of the reports her birds had carried to visiting spies.

At last! The sharp downstream spit of Gezira Island appeared ahead, swelling as she glided on southward. A change in the river's course had exposed this highly valuable land, Mwadi's sources informed her. So then greedy Cairo had expanded to cover it. Greying shadows filled the wide new boulevards erected here in the opening years of this nineteenth century by the British, and over there on banks reclaimed by Egypt's previous rulers, the Turks. But the low stone wall of the Corniche still gleamed as if made of gold, reflecting the sinking light of the sun for which, by many accounts, the city had been named.

From behind a raucous cry pierced her four ears, stirred her two hearts. Mwadi cried out too, struggling against both birds' urge to dive. Fragrant garbage tossed from the decks of low houseboats called to her, bobbing temptingly up and down on the suddenly murky waters. Below the surface a flash of silver—a fish? But she had anticipated this.

Firmly she imagined the brackish, half-salt pond she had ordered to be installed in her villa's garden, the schools of carp she raised there—picturing not just their bright colors but the barely visible tracks of their sinuous wakes, and more: the smell of their soft droppings falling to the pond's silty bottom, the dampness rising off the water's warm surface to cloud the air with their perfume. The birds' attraction to the trash immediately available lessened sufficiently for Princess Mwadi to conclude her flight home.

Alighting on the tall spire of limestone she'd had the builders place in the pond's center, Mwadi turned four beady orange eyes toward the pavilion on its shore. Yes. Her body lay where she'd left it, apparently drowsing on a divan. She turned her mounts' fidgeting attempts to plunge into the pond beak-first into a double arc passing over her body's head, and let go. And fell into herself.

Darkness. These eyes—the eyes she'd been born with—were shut. She kept them that way a moment more. Listening, she heard brisk footsteps—but far off. Good. Her instructions to the women who waited on her were to protect these special slumbers from intrusion. She stretched and moved her feet so they hung over the divan's edge and sat up slowly. In the evening dimness, the pavilion's silk awning and shadowy netting resembled the walls of a room in the "palace" where she'd spent several years of her childhood—the hotel her father, King Mwenda, had commandeered from Leopold II's European thugs. The hotel's gardens had crept in everywhere, green life seizing avidly on crumbling stucco and cement. And since her mother, Queen Josina, seemed to welcome it in, and also to prefer the garden's nooks to her royal chambers, Princess Mwadi had joined her there back then. She found comfort now in those memories....

Well, but that was long ago—before she'd learned to ride the birds, before Mademoiselle Lisette and Lady Fwendi taught her the rudiments of her craft. They would be glad to receive her latest intelligence report, but it would worry them. Perhaps they'd need her to act quickly—to hinder Ilunga in his idiotic flirtation with Britain before it bloomed into a formal relationship. Would the prince inherit their father's throne only to become Victoria's puppet? If so, how could she cut the strings?

Best to prepare for any likelihood. Mwadi stood, smoothing out her creased skirt. She pushed through the netting to the path that would take her to the terraces and up—and paused.

Above the rustling leaves stirred by the evening's rising breeze came another, similar sound: a rhythmic swish of fabric, the fluttering back and forth of another woman's clothes. Whose?

Sudden as a storm, Rima Bailey swept around the path's gentle curve and flung her bare arms wide. "Look at you! Ain't you grown, now? Litta bitty Bo-La turned into a fine young woman for sure." Rather than prostrating herself on the ground before the princess like the tiresome Egyptians, the actress seized Mwadi by her shoulders and pulled her into a tight embrace. In Everfair they'd been equals despite Mwadi's royal rank—troupers in Sir Jamison's play <u>Wendi-La</u>. Bo-La was Mwadi's role.

But the production was on tour. The last she'd heard they'd finished three months of engagements in Brazil.

Released from the actress's strong brown arms as swiftly as she'd been gathered into them, Mwadi shook herself straight. "How did you get past my serving women?"

Miss Bailey threw back her head and laughed. "Them cobwebs? They couldn't hold back a spider. They'll be followin me down here soon, though, if we don't head on up to your house mighty quick. I told them I had a short private message to deliver you from Queen Josina."

"You do?" It had been nearly a season since her mother had contacted Mwadi.

"Naw, not actually." The berry-dark lips quirked downwards.

"Well, why say what you said, then? Why say anything? And what is it brings you here if you're not coming from my father's favorite?" Who could have sent whatever word she desired to send via a dozen other routes, now Mwadi considered the idea dispassionately.

Miss Bailey laughed again, an entirely different sound. Half a choke. "Child, you know my job is makin people believe lies."

The princess was no longer a child. "Take a holiday from your work, then. We'll join the rest of my household now, as you suggest, and on the way you can tell me the truth."

"Yeah."

They walked together to the arbor at the bottom of the terrace steps. As they climbed upward night descended, closing the blossoms of the jasmine bushes planted on either side. Moths and mosquitos came near, attracted by oil lamps along the paths being lighted by small, self-effacing boys. Some of these lamps bore the pierced brass shades popular in the country of the princess's birth.

They reached the terraces' third level in annoying silence. One more to go. Vexed, Mwadi stopped, and tugged on Miss Bailey's wrist to make her stop too. They stood in clear sight of the balcony where Ilunga customarily held a lax court with his friends, other students at Victoria College. The balcony was obviously occupied: drunken voices slurred indistinctly from its tobacco-scented shadows. There could be no excuse for her overzealous attendants interrupting her tête-a-tête with the beautiful actress here. But it was also doubtful she'd be overheard. "Why did you need to speak to me alone?"

"They said you was sleepin."

Not an answer. "Why?"

"But I know better. You ride anything besides seagulls?"

Even less of one. How should Miss Bailey know about that? Had Lady Fwendi—or her husband, Sir Jamison—been indiscreet?

The princess found to her irritation that she held Miss Bailey's hand. She released it. Her mother had taught her that power lay always with the questioner, never with the questioned. She tried again. "What do you want with me?"

The hand had somehow found its way back to hers, claiming it now as the other woman's possession. "You know, Brother Mo-La is kinda stupid, but he can see plain enough if we only talkin. An then he's gonna wanna know what's bein said. Better make him think we makin love." She suited action to words, kissing Mwadi's rosy palm, stroking her wrist, rucking up her loose sleeve to reach the shivery skin that paled at the fold inside the bend of her elbow...

"No!" Mwadi drew away. Hard as it was.

"So you go with men?"

She shouldn't answer that. "With *you!*"

"Ah!" Miss Bailey's hands and mouth returned. They moved to the thin cloth over Princess Mwadi's armpit and nestled in. They—didn't tickle. Not really. No, not at all. A barrier she'd never before been aware of broke. Pleasure poured through it.

The princess fought to surface from the flood. "But I have to know *where*." That must make sense. She didn't trust her voice for anything longer.

Miss Bailey's head rose. Her tongue carved a riverbed beneath Mwadi's shoulder blade. Beside her spine. Flirting with the back of the girl's tingling head, the actress buried her face in the naked crook of Mwadi's neck. Then lifted her lips and murmured low: "You wanna know where you goin with me?"

Mwadi nodded, a response which would be felt if not seen.

"I was plannin on a little jaunt to a buildin site."

That seemed more like Mademoiselle Lisette's sort of excitement.

Mademoiselle had been Miss Bailey's lover once. For some time. Perhaps an attachment still lingered on the part of the actress. Mwadi set her steady hands on the actress's smooth-brushed hair and moved her away. Gently. But firmly.

The actress smiled confidently. "Come on. Sir Jamison heard from his Lady Fwendi you learnt to ride gulls so fast you asked how many other sortsa birds you could study for mounts. You ever try on any around here?"

Was that all this was? The dalliance a cover for whatever scheme Miss Bailey wanted Mwadi involved in? She had said so. Shame pricked the princess's eyelids, stinging them. To be used so, fooled so—

"Bo-La? You rather I invite you more formally? In front of your brother and all? As princess? I thought this would be nicer—"

"Hullo! What sport! Nigger hoors! Loongee, you're the right sort, you are— No? Positive?" The jovial cries from the villa's balcony ceased, hushed by others of her brother's white friends. The unlucky merrymaker's ebullience subsided as these repeated their assurances that the women on the lawn below had not been hired for his entertainment.

"Pardon me! So awfully sorry!" The apologies grew louder as Mwadi walked quickly toward the library's french doors, then ceased abruptly as the women waiting there to open them swung them shut behind her. The noise revived briefly when, at the urging of Miss Bailey's polite rap on the glass, the doors reopened.

The actress slipped into the room with the offhand grace Mwadi remembered admiring at rehearsals. "Aloli, ain't it?" she asked the tall maiden on the door's right. Who bowed almost as deeply as she had to the princess. "Sweet name. Juicy."

"You would like water? Beer?" Many Egyptian Muslims frowned on alcohol, but Prince Ilunga's retinue expected and got plenty of exceptions to this custom of his adopted country's upper classes.

"I'll take whatever you're havin'."

After a day of fasting, her body ravened. She ordered a supper such as the queen would have offered to guests arriving from an embassy. Primarily Everfairer delicacies: well-spiced soups served alongside heaps of stolid grains. A course of freshwater fish, to which she had added shelled creatures from the river's highest reaches. Perhaps this was owing to her mounts' lingering influence? The whole was to be followed by iced fruit. And to begin, beancakes and a gourdful of the local, peasant-made barley brew. And two cups.

Upon these appetizers' arrival the princess dismissed all her women but one. She ordered Aloli to stay, determined not to show any jealousy. Though she poured Miss Bailey's beer herself.

The actress took a healthy swig. "Good as I remember from Everfair." They sat on spindle-legged benches with curving backs, British furniture supposedly modeled on Egyptian antiquities. Ilunga treated these sorts of objects carelessly, so Mwadi had gathered as many she could into her private apartments, protecting and maintaining them. She took a strip of linen hung over that Aloli's arm and arranged it on the little table between them, then poured her own beer and set the gourd on the cloth. She drained her cup in one gulp. She hadn't meant to. She poured more, but held off from drinking it. She ate a bean cake instead, dipping it in a fiery red sauce that did nothing to assuage her thirst.

A scratch at the door signaled the advent of the first course. The servant woman Aloli went to usher it in. Mwadi bent close to the table and leaned forward so Miss Bailey would hear her soft speech more easily. Or did she speak softly so she could lean forward?

"I've experimented to expand my reach, living so far inland as I do here. I found a flock of *kattar-kattar*—"

"What you call them?"

"That's the locals' name: *kattar-kattar*—after their call. They're desert birds resembling pigeons, but far better fliers. I've ridden several at a time."

"You think you can get em to go where—"

The servant Aloli returned bearing a tray of covered dishes. She transferred them to the table with fluid motions more careful than Miss Bailey's, but just as pleasing to watch. If Mwadi had been in a mood to be pleased by them.

A loud knock came from the door. Swirling her shoulder scarf as if it were a cape the servant turned to answer it, but before she took two steps it opened. Mwadi's brother entered, face shining with an inner heat. "So sorry to disturb you," he enunciated with too much precision. Behind him hesitated another man, his skin and clothing white against the passageway's gloom. "Scranners insists on apologizing to you as well as to me. Personally. And to your guest."

The white man followed the prince in then, crushing what looked like a slouch hat in his fidgeting hands. A shamed grin stretched his thin lips. "Deveril Scranforth at your service. Must beg your forgiveness for my very silly mistake a few minutes ago. I ought to have known—at any rate, abject abasement and all that. Are we quits?" One hand released his hat and was offered to the princess— to shake? Presumptuous of him.

"You served in Kenya?"

Scranforth started as if he'd overlooked Miss Bailey's sprawling beauty till she questioned him. "Ma'am?"

"Rima Bailey. The other 'nigger hoor.'"

White became red. "You oughtn't say such words."

"You did."

"Completely different cases." Her brother's friend appealed to Mwadi with his rough-lidded eyes. "Aren't they, Miss, umm—Miss?" The ungrasped hand dropped.

"Thank you for your apology." Mwadi rose to curtsey stiffly, without inclining her head one inch. Would he go now?

"You ain't answered me." Miss Bailey stood and stalked off from the table where Ilunga swayed over her neglected food, lifting the dishes' covers.

"I what?"

"I asked did you serve in Kenya. Because of your hat—the kind they used to wear there in the police force. 'Scuse me; the Army. So?"

"Ah—no! It was my cousin's. Grandison Sprague. He wore it when they were putting in the rail line under Lord Delamere. The Lion Killer?"

Lady Fwendi hated Delamere.

"Your cousin get eaten by one a them giant lions?" Looming now over Ilunga's friend.

"As a—as a matter of fact he did. Look here, Loongee, you want to pack it in and talk about selling off those shares in the morning?"

"I'll be fine once I have a bite. Fine. Need to soak up the excess spirits." The prince picked up Miss Bailey's abandoned porcelain spoon and helped himself to her groundnut stew. "Fine."

"But—the ladies? That is, we don't need to discuss business in your presence, Miss—boorish behavior by any standards."

More boorish than labeling them prostitutes and thus businesswomen themselves? Mwadi took note.

The second course had arrived, barely noticed. The serving woman fitted more dishes on the already crowded table. Ilunga plopped down in Miss Bailey's place and lifted another lid. A large fish stared up from its platter with one cloudy eye. Brown breading glistened with fat.

"This will only take a moment. I swear. When I'm done we'll retire to my rooms. Finish the deal there." The prince stabbed a three-tined fork into the fish and flaked off a bite. "Wait, though—Didi has shares to get rid of too. Don't you?"

How Mwadi loathed her brother's new habit of calling everyone by these "nicknames" he came up with. But as with his other and often more troubling habits—his Western dress, his immoderate consumption of alcohol, his gambling, his reckless abandonment of tradition-minded counselors for scions of Europe's upper classes such as this very Scranforth—she practiced a pacific tolerance. For the moment.

So she answered him. "Yes, I have several shares in the Great Sun River Collector Company. Gifts from you. Why are they to be gotten rid of?"

Her brother gestured to his mouth, too full to talk, then to Scranforth.

The white man obliged with an attempt at explanation. "Well, the, er, the construction of the collector tube has hit a few snags. Delays, that sort of thing— reminiscent, actually, of Delamere's Kenyan railway project, and of course the contractors your brother recommended aren't to blame in the least. Though I'm led to understand cost overruns here have—Hang it! Difficult to describe the details of these things to a lady, don't you know!" Scranforth twisted his mouth into a line as irregular as the brim of his nervously wrung hat. Mwadi wondered if what kept him from talking clearly about the situation was his own lack of understanding.

"No need," her brother announced, shoving a bolus of boiled millet aside with his tongue. "Didi will dump any stocks I tell her to. Tell her tonight." He swallowed, wiped his brow, and returned his attention to the fish.

"What's your hurry, though?" Miss Bailey asked. "You got the Cairo Bourse right next door—" It was several miles away, in fact. "—and you can be there soon as it opens just by leavin here first thing in the mornin."

With a groan, Ilunga pushed the fish away. "I feel unwell." Grabbing the platter's cover from the bench pads beside him he inverted it and vomited into its shallow depths. As he slumped back, letting it tip dangerously, the serving woman ran to snatch it from the prince's loosening hands. As she passed a sour reek wafting from the improvised basin threatened to turn Mwadi's half-filled stomach inside out.

"P'raps—" The white man shuffled backwards to the door. "—p'raps that's a better idea." The prince rolled onto his side and emitted a series of moaning gasps. His arms waved in the suddenly thick air like the tentacles of a desperate octopus.

Miss Bailey plucked a brass vase from the hearth and dumped out the dried bulrushes it had held. "Here you are." She thrust it at the hapless prince. Ilunga seized and used it.

No longer hungry, Mwadi ordered the food cleared away, climbed the stairs to her brother's rooms, and sent his Egyptian valet to him. Then she walked the rich carpets to her own rooms.

Behind the door to her boudoir waited Miss Bailey.

"WHERE IS MY maid?" Not visible through the wide archway leading to her bed. Perhaps in the closet? Yet the louvres of the closet doors were dark.

"Hasina? I sent her away."

Mwadi smiled. "Why don't you ring for her to return, then?" Or move away from the bellpull.

"Awright. If you want. But I was thinkin we could learn to know each other better without company." The actress got up from the gilt-armed chair where she'd been poised, uncrossing her pyjama'd legs. "Like I could show you my gun and my camera and tell you what I need you to do for me."

"Gun?"

"Oh, I ain't offerin violence. Look—I laid it down over there, on your vanity."

Its curves interrupted by half a dozen shining crystal bottles a brass silhouette showed on the vanity's cluttered surface, familiar from Mwadi's training as a spy: a shongun, the Everfair invention that flung poisoned blades at your targets in place of bullets.

"Sir Jamison give it to me in New York. Said I might need protection on our tour out west." Miss Bailey shook her head and chuckled lightly, bitterly. "From Indians, I guess. Came in handy but not cause a them. Some cities ain't so hot on mixed-race casts. Most of em."

Mwadi picked the shongun up, checked the breech. Loaded. To be sure, it would be useless otherwise. She aimed it at her unexpected guest but immediately lowered its muzzle. After all, Miss Bailey could have shot her just moments ago, or poisoned her earlier, or—This was not about killing. "What are you doing? Why?"

"You don't think I'd hurt you, do ya? I brought the gun to show how I'm serious about this."

"About what?"

"About what the Lincolns hired me for. Stoppin the sabotage at the collector site."

A few snags. "Is that the building site you wanted to take me to?" Princess Mwadi didn't remember moving after she reached the vanity but here she was, within an arm's length of Miss Bailey. She could smell the woman's make-up cream. She could count the pulses throbbing in the hollow beneath her exposed collarbone. "And—and what was my job going to be?"

"You know the Lincolns, right? Hotel owners from Baltimore? They invested in the new production of Sir Jamison's—"

"Of course I know them. I own Great Sun River stock."

"Right—I hope you bought it cheap, back when they inherited the plans from the inventor—not them, but the daughter's husband who worked for Mr. Shuman did, and it was practically worthless? Well, it's been fallin lately till now it's just about the same level of no good. They say they can put more money in another new show, somethin of mine if I—Bo-La, you need to sit down? This is a complicated story."

Mwadi laid the shongun aside. With her emptied hand she reached for Miss Bailey and found that even the arm's length between them had gone. She touched the beautiful actress at the juncture of hip and thigh. Taut muscles covered in pale yellow satin slid beneath her palm. "No. I don't want to sit."

"There's a pitcher with water on the windowsill. Or maybe you cold? I seen a brazier in the corner."

"No. Yes. Don't be so obtuse. Come to bed. Isn't that why you're here?" She dared to hope. Despite the claim as to what was really wanted: work.

"Yeah, Bo-La, but—"

Mwadi surged against the maddening woman's warmth, threw her arms around her high neck and clasped them behind that perfect column's dark, near-iridescent sheen. Leaned up to kiss those berry-looking lips. Miss Bailey rocked back to avoid that but recovered her balance.

"But Bo-La, you—"

"In the garden you wanted me. What's different now?" Mwadi began to tremble: little shivering crests of desire and troughs of doubt.

"Come on." Irresistible arms guided the princess to the vanity's bench. Away from the bed. Unyielding hands pushed her shoulders down so she sat there.

"Someone has to-to watch?" *What sport!*

"Naw."

"I c-c-can get one of the servants—"

"*Naw!* Aw, don't look so sad. Scoot over." Sitting beside her, Miss Bailey took Mwadi's hands in her own. But then did nothing with them.

"Listen. How old are you, Bo-La?"

"I had my birthday markets and markets ago." In the month the British called July. This was October.

"How old?"

"Thirty-three seasons."

"Sixteen years. Where I come from that's barely big enough to do what we already done. Let alone what more we imaginin."

What *we* want. Mwadi stopped her shivering. So was her age all that bothered Miss Bailey? "But you aren't where you come from—you're here! My father ruled our country when he'd lived just a season longer than I!" She grasped the hands that had held hers. "I'm grown! A woman!"

"Yeah. Sure. I can believe that. If I work on it. And I been tryna make myself 100 per cent certain you understand I ain't in love with you. I figure sayin it straight out's best. Best for both of us."

"Love!" Mwadi laughed, a little wildly. "That's none of *my* concern!"

"Ain't it? You young." The actress sighed. "And lyin. I got no time for that." She stood and strode to the door.

"Wait!" Mwadi followed her. Caught her by one slippery beige sleeve. "If I did—if I decided to be in love with you and expected you to love me back, what—what then?"

"Then I would tell you, 'Not yet.'"

Not yet. "Then when?" Mwadi gathered the pyjama sleeve tighter.

"When I'm free." Disentangling herself from Mwadi's clutching fist, Miss Bailey paced slowly back to the room's center. "When I'm done with this assignment.

"Which is why I called myself comin here tonight to tell you what I gotta do. And gettin your help."

Turning, Miss Bailey went to the bookcase next to the boudoir's entrance and came back to the bench carrying a black box. Not plain—latches and a strap decorated its top and sides. Glass-covered holes pierced one end. "My Brownie," she said proudly. "A witness everyone trusts. Because everyone uses them."

"You'll catch the saboteurs with this?"

"You seen cameras before?"

"Yes, but—"

"I ain't gotta catch em, just show what they doin in a photograph. Lincolns will bring the law into the picture."

Mwadi eyed the camera box askance. "And you want me to do what? Fetch it to you? Fetch it away? I'll need more than one bird to lift such an awkward thing as that."

For answer, the actress pulled a small spool from her pyjama pocket and held it up between finger and thumb. "Think you can handle a couple of these, though?"

AT DAWN FLOCKS of kattar-kattars gathered by a waterhole miles to the house's east. Under the awning which had yesterday been erected behind the villa, Princess Mwadi stretched out on her divan. Sleep would have been welcome after the restless night she'd spent in Miss Bailey's—Rima's—embrace. But she had agreed to remain awake and enter her chosen mounts.

Cool air stirred—the sun's breath blowing across the waking desert, entering the tent where the southern wall had been rolled up. Filling her lungs with it she sang, high and pure as light from heaven, falling, sliding, gliding down to the sand before her open door. Chicks fluttered nearer to her, nearer to their mother, gathered their courage and strutted all the way in, bodies brown and grey and black and buff, barred with yellow orange and olive green. Preening heads bobbed once, twice, then stopped, transfixed by her stare.

Without stirring an inch Mwadi leapt into their eyes.

After that the supine form on the divan called to them no more. Her four kattar-kattars rejoined the rest of their flock. Together they swooped above the Cadillac saloon in which Rima waited, parked alone on the rough track back to the rough road. Though they kept flying with their fellows they dived lowest, braked hardest, and flirted nearest the actress's scarfed head. She waved to signal her understanding of the princess's success and drove off.

Last night—this morning? Sometime during the tender hours of darkness, Rima had drawn a map showing where the seemingly ill-starred Great Sun River Collector rose and slumped and rose again. The princess had memorized that map, then burnt it in the brazier furnished to perfume her sleep. The sandalwood normally used to fuel it she left untouched. Another, saltier smell had driven out the bitterness of the map paper's smoke. Now, though she kept pace with the Cadillac, she recognized the winding route it traveled.

Soon the sun rose. Bright beams broke widening gaps in the dispersing clouds. Her mounts split once more from the rest of the birds—normal behavior for this time of day. But they wanted to go west, toward the promise of green shoots sprouting in the wheat fields nearer the Nile, while Rima swung off on a graveled track to the east, following it deeper into the desert.

She changed the birds' contrary impulses into a circle. Spreading her feathers, she caught the spiral currents of gradually heating air and cupped them beneath her wings. Not high—no higher than they'd go normally. But high enough that she saw what Rima must have missed: Ilunga's lilac and grey Napier speeding toward them through the sparse morning traffic.

How far away? A mile? Two? Hovering over the crossroads, Mwadi couldn't decide what to do. Should she shadow Rima and if necessary retrieve the film she shot, as they'd planned? Or switch to watching Ilunga, to see what he was up to? Or—

Both. With a nauseating wrench Mwadi tore her mind in half, riding three birds east and one north. Though she'd long ago gotten used to how the land tilted and whirled beneath her when she flew, the vertigo caused by heading two ways at once threatened to toss her headfirst from the sky.

She'd done it before, going in different directions like this. Once. In a pair of gulls. She shut her panicked beaks on confused cries of "ga-ga-ga!" and continued to come apart.

Strongest were the blinding shards of sun spearing her eyes as she floated above the Cadillac's dusty wake, but simultaneously she plunged up the map toward her brother's swift approach while wondering why he'd come, was he still suffering from the evening's overindulgence, which it was best not to remember or she'd spew the contents of her crops like droppings on the sand—the road— the sand—the road, and she was past him! Bank with these wings, not with those, and come around flapping hard to catch up, but not so fast because the Cadillac had stopped. Rima jumped out. Lay flat. *Undulated* along the ground, like a snake, to disappear below the rim of a long-gone stream's dry bed.

Where had Ilunga's motor car gotten to? Paying too much attention to Rima's movements, Mwadi'd lost control of her fourth bird. She prayed those remaining would be enough to provide any necessary back-up. But how to arrange them so their presence would seem natural?

Her mounts proved attracted to a large patch of asphodel nearby. She let them settle, and as they gorged on the plants' buds she caught glimpses of Rima's goal: a sort of staging area from what she could judge, perhaps in the shape of a semicircle. Piles of pipes marked its approximate edges, some winking and glinting metallically in the morning sun, some a dull black.

The grinding roar of an engine grew louder and louder. It sounded nothing like Ilunga's Napier. Easy to take her mounts aloft again; they wanted to scatter, but Mwadi held them loosely yet effectively, keeping their restless circuits confined to the staging area. Beyond, rows of empty wooden cradles lined the grey sand.

A freight truck—source of the engine noise—became visible. It stopped in the staging area and two strangers opened its doors and clambered out. They spoke in Arabic, too rapidly for Mwadi to understand more than a few words. Something about finishing their task before the builders ripened. Opening the gate of the truck's rear compartment they laughed and greeted a third man, who cursed them. Probably. But he laughed too when the crate he shoved off the truck's bed exploded open at their feet. Shattered glass tumbled out of its broken sides. More cursing. More laughter, shared by all the men now. The two from the truck's cab climbed up to join their coworker in tossing the entire shipment out to smash on the ground.

Mwadi's mounts saw curving shards of mirrors poking up from the ruins of a few of the crates. One had cracked apart to show a parabolic panel surviving miraculously whole—till a man jumped down to kick at its unprotected back. A shiver and it became a sparkling curtain collapsing into a heap of uselessness.

A few snags.

One man looked up to where her mounts circled. He pointed at them and the others shaded their eyes and looked too. Mwadi decided to fly the kattar-kattars a bit further off. She wheeled over Rima's dry watercourse; when Rima saw the birds she beckoned for them to land.

Small stones lined the empty streambed. Mwadi reminded her mounts they needed grist for their gizzards and set them pecking.

"Good," said Rima. "I wound up the film and stuck the spool under that rock there. See it? You can carry that back—I'm gonna have a little talk with them saboteurs before I leave."

No. But Mwadi couldn't stop her. Already she was gone. And the princess had promised. Mwadi abandoned two of her mounts and pushed the last toward the crevice Rima had indicated. Dangling the heavy film roll from her gaping beak she launched herself into the pale blue sky. Stubborn woman.

Her bird's neck ached. She should have kept control of the other two kattar-kattars and traded the work off between them. How long could she stand the strain? How long did she have to? Focused on ignoring her pain, she let her mount's ears miss the purring advent of Ilunga's motor. But then she saw the Napier itself, its colors unmistakable, though half-concealed in the dust cloud kicked up by its tires and blown ahead of it. Blown in the direction of the saboteurs and Rima.

SHE SHOULDN'T TURN back. The photographs were precious. Rima would want her to save them, to make the risks she'd taken worthwhile. Mwadi struggled grimly on, flying through air that had somehow become thick as porridge.

BANG! That wasn't Rima—shonguns fired quietly! She dropped the precious film and reversed her mount, going faster without her burden. Reaching the site again she smelled blood and gunpowder. Heard a muffled scream. BANG! Another shot.

She flew higher, out of bullet range she hoped. Below, the three saboteurs made fast feints toward Rima, who knelt on one knee, one long arm hanging loosely at her side, the other aiming the shongun at their faces. Behind the Napier crouched Deveril Scranforth holding a small, gleaming pistol. Of her brother the princess saw no sign. He would never have lent his motor out—not even to his closest friend. Where—

A sudden, dizzying shift in perspective and there he was—lolling head first off the motor car's driver's seat. Bright rivulets trickled across his dark face and dripped to the floor—but he lived. In tentacle-like motions reminiscent of last night's drunken flailing, his arms fought to grab the steering wheel, the gear shift, anything with which to right himself. He kept hitting them and slipping ineffectually off.

Could she help? Where was she? Still riding a kattar-kattar—but a new one? No—a lost one regained. Once more her consciousness was doubled: she found herself both up in the air and perched on the Napier's roof, head tucked down and cocked sideways to peer in at the windscreen. What had triggered the link's resurgence? Proximity? Lack of movement?

The bird's protective coloration blended somewhat with the Napier's dust-covered grey paint. That and the gun battle had kept it from discovery so far. But surely—

Shhk!

A guttural cry burst from a saboteur stumbling, falling, clutching his thigh. The curling edge of the shongun's three-lobed poisoned blade protruded above his red stained fingers. His cry subsided into whimpers and curses.

"Shut up!" commanded Scranforth. "You're not dead yet. I'll kill you myself. You'll tell no tales—"

"My photographs gonna reveal everything! Your whole scheme!"

The white man shot at Rima over the motor's bonnet without aiming and missed. Mwadi's recovered mount "ga-ga-ga'd" and tried to flee. She forced it into the Napier's interior through the passenger-side window. Shhk! Rima's return fire sent the bird screeching and flinging itself at the windscreen, pale gobbets showering from under its tail. The princess tried to calm it but her brother's moans and bloody thrashing wouldn't let her.

From above she saw Rima seize the shongun by her teeth and attempt to crank it one-handed. After every two shots it had to be rewound—but why not use both hands? She must be hurt.

Four blades left—the shongun had been fully loaded when Mwadi checked it last night in her boudoir. If Scranforth didn't have any extra ammunition—or if he'd left it in the Napier, out of immediate reach—Rima and her attacker were evenly matched. But add in the two saboteurs still standing—

Without allowing herself think of the consequences, Rima dove. Claws out like an eagle's she aimed for the face of the man with the gun. Predictably he shot at her. Twice. Fortunately he missed. Pulling out of her unnatural stoop with just inches to spare she felt her mount's wing muscles tearing. Only a little, she hoped. She was able to gain the heights again, the men's voices shrinking beneath her like their foreshortened figures.

Unless she viewed them out of the eyes of her other bird. Drying blood and shit smeared much of the glass, but the open window showed the pair of unwounded saboteurs huddled together. Indistinct murmurs escaped their conference. Then in silence they turned toward Rima and leaned forward, their intent clear: to rush her together.

So close! Mwadi urged the panicking kattar-kattar to exit the window she'd entered by. That would distract or deflect them. She couldn't move! Ilunga's arms wrapped her in a tight embrace. The bird panted, its heart speeding toward death. She should leave it before she died too.

Quickly she twisted her other mount midair and plummeted downward. The saboteurs gave up their charge and ran shrieking for the cover of their truck's cab. A third shot. A nearer miss. The fallen man sobbed something and began crawling toward the truck as well. Much better odds.

"Didi?"

Who had called her? Only Ilunga mangled her name so. Trapped against his heaving chest, her exhausted mount listened to his weakly whispered words with failing ears.

"I know. It's you. In there. Listen. Jealous. Don't be. Like me. You can't. Help."
Alone each phrase made sense, but how to connect them? She couldn't ask him
what he meant. She couldn't let these be his last words.

On her bird's next breath she fled it. Barely in time.

From the sky above she could see Scranforth duck beneath the Napier. He'd
be able to hit Rima from under there, and he'd be safe from her one functional
mount. But with only one bullet left—probably—

BANG! The actress hunched forward, caught herself with her shongun
hand. Where was her wound—

The white man rolled free of the motor's chassis and sprinted toward Rima,
launching himself at her silently like a striped hyena. He bowled her flat. The
shongun shone in the sun just a foot away, but Rima struggled fruitlessly to
retrieve it till Scranforth choked her motionless. Then he raised himself up on
one elbow and stretched across the sand to steal his opponent's weapon.

Mwadi reached it first.

As she flew off with the shongun's trigger guard firmly in her mount's grip,
Rima recovered. The kattar-kattar's last sight of her was of her flipping her scarf
around Scranforth's neck, presumably a preliminary to strangling him as he'd
strangled her.

Mwadi heard the freight truck roar to life. It passed her and turned north
onto the Cairo road, going fast. Following her memory of the map she did the
same, more slowly.

Far heavier than the film roll, the shongun was slippery, too. Her mount's
feet ached when she finally unclenched them to let it plunge safely into the
waterhole where her human body rested. And where she woke it.

Beside her head a brass clock told the time: one and one quarter hours till
noon. Her servants would wonder where she'd gotten. But it could take a day—or
longer—till they traced her here. She sat up carefully and poured a goblet of water
while she considered her plight. And Rima's. And Ilunga's. Should she walk to the
road she'd flown along, flag down assistance from whoever happened to be faring by?

But then the Cadillac appeared on the horizon. Then it came close and
parked and disgorged her love. Stepping into the light, Mwadi greeted Rima's
tired and radiant smile with her own, almost as battered, equally bright. They
exchanged a quick, light hug—not tentative, only cautious, and even so Rima
winced when Mwadi touched, once again, the juncture of hip and thigh.

"Damn fool grazed my side. Ricocheted a rock off my shoulder, too. Sir
Jamison ain't gonna be happy how I spent my vacation.

"But look. Least I got your brother back alive." The actress pointed to Ilunga lying on the motor's rear bench, her cape spread to cover him. A grimace told Mwadi he felt pain. Better than feeling nothing. "What he got to tell us about how he and his 'friend' turned up is worth more even than them photographs I sent you here with. I'll take em anyway, but later."

Princess Mwadi thought she could find the place where she'd let them drop.

"No room for the tent with the prince in there, but we ain't got time to take it down now anyway. Need to get him to a doctor."

You too, Mwadi thought but didn't say. "I'm ready." She climbed in behind the steering wheel.

THE SUN SHALL LIE
ACROSS US LIKE GOLD

BENJANUN SRIDUANKAEW

IN THE CELL there is little light, cast so that any officer or visitor to Madiha's cell would be backlit, indistinct: all the advantages of an interrogator. She listens to the noises of metal and sometimes of flesh on stone. It is a holding facility, not one meant for permanent imprisonment. This is not final. She will not be here forever. She has been here for only half a week, and they have not beaten or bloodied her. This is rare good fortune.

The back of her mouth is dry and sour and her limbs hurt with terrible anticipation, with the paranoia that has turned to prescience then to reality. She'd disembarked from the iron kite with the surety that this is a safe harbor. Now she waits and counts the minutes, to keep precise track of time. Numbers: those are dependable, solid, the parameters with which she delineates her world.

The gate at the far end of her corridor opens, steel on steel. Three figures. She tries to judge from a distance, through murk and shadow and the small window in her door. Her pulse thrums in her fingertips, drumming in her wrists.

She pulls back away from the window. In a moment the visitors are upon her. She knows enough Thai to tell that at least one of them is aristocratic.

The window is lifted all the way up. A face cast in shadow and ringed with the sun, but this much Madiha can tell—"I thought you'd be a man," she says without thinking.

The thin mouth curves. "I hear that a lot." The Siamese woman takes a water-bowl from someone behind her and offers it through the window. "What have they told you that made you think I would be a man?"

Madiha cradles the bowl. It is nielloware, finely hammered, tactile and chilled against the heat. She does not take a sip, not yet. "The *policier* told me," she says slowly, "that I await the mercy of a great personage. And so I thought that perhaps I caught the eye of a lord with freakish tastes who didn't want my face or body ruined. It seemed unlikely, yet was the only cause I could imagine."

They are speaking French, a language Madiha has picked up in her travels. She's learned Thai too in preparation for her voyage here, but she's not fluent. This language between them, each foreign to the other twice over. She tries to peer behind the Siamese and sees two girls, obscured as much by the absence of light as by this woman's presence. Servants or ladies-in-waiting.

"How do you like Bangkok, *mademoiselle* Wahab?"

It seems an odd question to ask, especially when Madiha has seen so little of it between disembarking and detainment. Almost it seems designed to rile her up. "It's large. It's hot. It has a river. In that, I suppose it resembles Cairo."

"Where you were born. Yes, I suppose. Is that why you chose Bangkok?"

Madiha doesn't answer.

"Let me ask differently," the Siamese says. "How many *anglais* did your machines kill before you had to run?"

Her breath quickens. The hinge on which the door swings between punishment and—what? "A garrison's worth." She clenches her hands. "They were soldiers. Those are men prepared to die. Is that not so? For their country and *la reine*, their occupations."

A long moment during which the Siamese studies her. Weighs her on an indefinable scale against a currency Madiha cannot guess at. "I'm Aunrampha Panthapiyot. You're free. Come with me."

THE BATH IS a marvel of luxury, the tub as large and nearly as deep as a pool. Nielloware rather than copper, as complexly made as Aunrampha's water-bowl: images of kinnaree and snake-women in pursuit of one another, forever circular. Full-length mirrors line the wall so that each and every of Madiha's movements is doubled and quadrupled, chasing each other into exponential eternities.

Madiha stands in this vast space, the scent of clean water and jasmines and turmeric filling her lungs, and strips. She keeps her clothes close to hand, so that at the slightest provocation she can run. She tests the taps gingerly—she's seen heating and plumbing before, but her station never warranted her free access—and opts for cool water. Bangkok's heat is not a fraction as punishing as that in the city of her birth, and there is so much vapor in the air, the river's presence as close as a breath on the back of her neck. Close to river, close to sea: the mud and the silt, the spray and the salt. In that, nothing like Cairo at all.

She cleans herself, scrubs off four days' worth of grime and sweat and dirt, dipping her head in. Her belongings have been brought here, the small luggage and the currency, and she's checked it several times to make sure all is in order. Nothing sensitive, only the sentimental. What is sensitive stays in her head, the safest vault of all.

Two girls appear to help her dress. A pearlescent silk blouse, a skirt they call sinh, oxblood fabric threaded in gold. They offer her bangles and a complicated necklace, filigreed and jeweled in sapphires; she refuses both. Gold has a particular weight, carries the luster of obligation. Even if it is in truth plated brass she does not want anything to do with it. The girls do insist on a touch of rouge and powder strategically applied. It's meant for complexions much lighter than Madiha's, and put on with a heavy hand would have made of her an ashen ghost. They put color on her cheeks, line her eyes, and exclaim at her eyelashes, marvel at the sharpness of her bones: how chiseled her jaw, how sculpted her face. Her stomach roils, part nerves, part hunger. There is no blueprint for how to behave in genteel captivity, no formula that'd prepare her for this.

Then they bring her to a veranda.

She's told to seat herself on the floor, before and below the lady whose domain this part of the palace is. In good light she sees that Aunrampha is no shadowy torturer but a woman Madiha's age. Fifty-odd and well-dressed, a glint of silver at the ears, a string of precious stones around her neck. Unremarkable to look at, Madiha would have said, if not for the circumstances. And then there's the automatons, though Madiha makes a studious effort to ignore them.

"I'm glad my clothing fits you," the Siamese lady says. "You're very tall. None of the girls' pha-sinh would have served, unless you're willing to show your knees. Be at ease, Madiha Wahab, no one will offer you harm in Siam."

Madiha copies the serving women's posture, legs folded back, prim. It's not an easy thing to manage and she knows her knees will soon hurt. "It would ease me, *mademoiselle*, to learn what I've done to merit your clemency." She means to be forthright without being obsequious. Something in this woman tells her meek slavishness will not go far. "Clear negotiations and direct terms have never failed to soothe me."

"I appreciate that in a person. I'm interested in your expertise."

Her eyes do stray, then, to the automaton. It stands taller than most people, six feet and a half, with the face of a Siamese drama-mask. A creature of frictionless skin and the clean gleam of ceramic, though she knows their bones are steel underneath, their chassis as strong as armor. The reason she selected Bangkok as her endpoint, when it felt like no other options remained. She could have gone further east, to Peking or Tokyo, but her funds had limited her. The iron kites are faster by far than any seafaring vessel or train, with the price to match. She had needed fast, as fast and as far from Cairo as she could get.

Five years ago, on the brink of a French invasion, Siam unveiled its automaton army. The fulcrum on which Siam's fate pivoted. Farangset gunships to flotsam, its soldiers to gristle and watery blood in the river Chaopraya. Overnight this nation reshaped its place on the map of power, from toothless collaborators of Europeans to a country that must be reckoned with. "Yes," is all Madiha would say.

"Then you know we owe allegiance and friendship to neither *Français* or *Anglais*."

"My pardon, *mademoiselle*, but your *policier* detained me."

"A matter of you being, according to *anglais* dispatch, a fearsome terrorist. Pure slander, I now realize; a gentle temper such as yours couldn't harm a mosquito." Aunrampha makes a helpless gesture. "I must offer you recompense. My girls can give you directions, find you lodgings that might suit."

One of the girls hands Madiha a fold of promissory notes. She is unfamiliar with Siamese currency, but even at a glance it seems an inordinate amount. "Just like this, *mademoiselle?*"

"It hardly suffices. I would've gotten you out sooner, but I was away at the time and could only send back an order to handle you civilly. I hope you can come to think well of us whether you mean to make your home here or merely pass through."

Madiha clutches at the notes. "In this part of the world nowhere repudiates the reach and might of the *colonisateurs* as you do. *Je vous adresse mes plus vifs remerciements, mademoiselle.*"

"It's nothing." When Aunrampha gestures, the sole ring she wears glints. An oddly plain piece, brass set with a faceted black stone. "Before you leave, may I ask what happened to your automatons?"

She takes a breath. Lets it out, sip by sip of air. "I destroyed every last one of them before I departed Cairo. Nothing of them is left—the smallest coupling, the tiniest rivet. The blueprints I consigned to fire, every single copy. There are no more mannequins of my making and there will not be any again."

THE SECOND TIME she meets Khunying Aunrampha is on a hot, shadowed day, the sky blotted not by clouds but by iron kites. Flat and wide, their locomotive engines a distant hum. They fly low. Madiha knows European merchants are still allowed in Bangkok—though not French or British—and this is as much for their benefit as anything else, an unapologetic display of might. *This is strength, this is fire, this is what we have.* On the belly of each kite is carved an eagle-headed man, what the Siamese call khrut, golden and divine. The air is tart-sweet with the smell of mangos and passionfruits, the aroma of glutinous rice on the grill.

She has her neck craned back, her gaze so fastened to kite trajectory that she does not notice Aunrampha until a hand falls lightly on her arm. Madiha jerks her head down, skittish, and forces herself to calm when she sees who it is. Aunrampha has put a spread of chicken kebab down on the wicker table, a cup of yellow-orange sauce next to it. "Chicken satay," the lady says. "Malaya dish. I understand you don't eat pork."

Madiha does not. She is no longer as devout as she should be, has not been for a long time; even her decision to pursue violence has been one against her faith. But some things don't leave easily. What one eats, what one doesn't. The humors and substance that add to and become one's body. "My thanks." She enunciates the words slowly.

"You've been learning Thai! How superbly rare."

"I've been trying since before I left Cairo. Tutors weren't easy to come by." She dips her head. "I apologize if I butcher it terribly, Khunying Aunrampha." She's learned to shape the syllables and, if it is halting, she can now pronounce Aunrampha's name and title with the right tones. The sharp rise on *ying*, the smoothness of *Aunrampha*.

"Not at all, my Farangset is tortured and while my Angrit is decent enough—" Aunrampha laughs, a sound like watery silk. "Those languages never sound right on the tongue. *Anglais, français,* cradle-speech of enemies all."

Aunrampha is dressed in simple cotton today, a pyramidal farmer's hat shielding from the sun. The simple attire does not disguise who she is; three automatons follow her, shadow-close. Madiha measures their proportions, trying to project how fast they really are, how adept they might be with blade or firearms.

"What do you think?" Aunrampha nods to the automatons.

Madiha glances at a dragonfly that has alighted on the far corner of the table. Beautiful and intent and still, reading the world for signifiers of survival. Counting out the dimensions of existence, what is safe and what is not, air currents and heat and human presence. "At a glance I would call them immaculate, eerily so."

The lady turns the ring on her finger. She wears it on her left hand, the place of a wedding band, though as far as Madiha can tell the lady is not married—Madiha asked around the market, out of incipient curiosity. Perhaps in Siam the placement means something else, or nothing at all. "It is said that your machines were a perfect mimesis of the human form. That they couldn't be told apart from flesh and blood."

The dragonfly flutters, wingbeats hypnotic. "I suppose one might say so." Madiha tastes the chicken, pretends that the meat is of the utmost importance, her sole imperative. "It wouldn't be a precise truth. They don't talk, they don't..." But already she's yielded too far, admitted too much.

"That is fair." Aunrampha smiles briefly. "Would you like to see ours in action? Perhaps it'd be of some academic interest to you. No obligations. Besides, I'm known as terribly staid. It would do my reputation good to be seen with a glamorous, exciting far-traveler."

Madiha doubts that, but despite herself she feels a strange frisson. Too long without human contact, too long without anything close to flattery or even kindness. "If you wish."

Aunrampha stands and takes her elbow. "Let's go then."

They travel by canal, crossing the city's breadth on a small steam ferry. Madiha expects to arrive in some garrison of black steel and cold stone. Instead it is an open ground of beaten earth and trimmed grass. A rectangular field, divided by netting down the middle. Around this field, an audience watches and breaks into intermittent applause. Not courtiers or soldiers, but farmers, artisans, the same people she sees at market. She tries to make out the game. A rattan ball is bounced and kicked almost too fast for the human eye to track, passing between two sides of the field. The players are not human.

She pays close attention then. The automatons are sleek and fluid, a far cry from belching European machines that serve as locomotive mounting for artillery. One team is painted white, the other red. They keep the ball constantly airborne, the trajectory effortless, their cabled sinews unburdened by sweat or fatigue. "They're a marvel of invention," she says. Her own were never this sharp, this finely animated. Or, she is tempted to say, this intelligent. "Your engineer must be one of a kind."

"She was." Aunrampha splays her fingers on the riveted fence that separates the game from its audience. "She used to call them the closest she'd have to children. This was her idea—to have mechanics iterate on them, make the automatons stronger and faster, and then put them to competition. A spectacle, something the average citizen can enjoy so the automatons would be more than just instruments of war."

"Does she no long work for you?"

"No. We parted ways more finally than that. An ailment of the lungs." A particular look comes over Aunrampha. In that moment the poise and position falls away. "You might have gotten along with her."

The lady is human after all, luminous in grief. Incredibly, almost despite herself, it strikes Madiha then that Aunrampha is one of the most beautiful creatures she has ever seen.

THE THIRD TIME they meet is in a house on the outskirts of Bangkok, far away from the palace.

It is a small domicile, nothing like the buildings closer to the city's heart where the architecture has received the European influence of brick and slate and marble. Here it is mostly wood, a house with a single story held up by high stilts. Meant for a bygone time where the city was flood-prone, the ground soft, the capital forever sinking inch by inch.

Aunrampha has had her cook prepare food Madiha can eat with a clean conscience, a sour-sweet dish of raw papaya and nuts and dried shrimp, roast chicken seasoned with garlic and oyster sauce, a wealth of glutinous rice. Plainer fare than what is served in the palace, Aunrampha says, where the meals are elaborate and the desserts sculpted—beautiful marzipan creations, but not always to her taste. "I used to eat like this more often," she adds. "Most of my waiting-women have terribly refined palates, and this they see as peasant food."

"Your old engineer?"

"Yes. Ging loved her dishes simple. This house was hers, really; I was merely a guest." Aunrampha's fingers stray to the brass ring, the simple band with its simple stone. "When she passed she said she'd had a full life. That she had few regrets."

Madiha chews on a mouthful of rice, considering her next words. "Are such things... permissible, here in Siam?" Giving Aunrampha the room to assume she means quite something else.

"For women to be wife and wife?" The lady holds up the ring and laughs, a brittle noise. "Of course not. What a world that would be, what a paradise. Such things are at best ignored or thought nonexistent. Still, we had decades together and accomplished great deeds. But that's past now. It is my twilight, and what remains is for me to maintain her legacy. Defend the country for which she died. Does the thought shock you, that two women should live as intimate partners, far more than friends?"

She is more shocked that Aunrampha is so open—though perhaps in the lady's position, little could possibly offer her harm, let alone a foreigner of no means and a terrorist's reputation. "There were—some of us in Cairo. Of course to most it seemed merely women who were very good friends. The *anglais*... the Angrit, they call us perverse and disgusting." Again she says too much, but what has she to lose this far from home?

"I am sorry." Aunrampha's hand falls on Madiha's. "Was it worth it?"

Coming to Siam. Leaving Cairo. Building her machines and sending them forth to do what they did. "No." She glances out the window, at the Bangkok horizon that's slowly turning familiar: the temples with their gilded finials, the high walls of the university with their stained-glass naga, a mosque. The last she has never set foot in. It does not feel right, somehow, not yet. "I'd assassinated a handful of Angrit officers, but that was all. In the end I was only one woman. Those I could trust as compatriots I'd never put in danger. Those I could put in danger I did not trust. And so here I am, exiled, having achieved nothing at all."

Aunrampha's fingers tighten, just the slightest pressure on Madiha's wrist. "I wouldn't say that. You've struck fear in them and you did it alone. When the time came, you successfully retreated. You braved a journey that couldn't be easy, overcame every difficulty in your path. This is not nothing."

Madiha looks at where their hands join, marveling at what it suggests, at what is possible. The sun's radiance across their hands like a ribbon of liquid light. Of course it is primarily what she can do with automatons. But to discover they have *that* as well in common, against such odds. "You're kind." Her voice is tight. Then, more precisely and evenly she says, "In what areas is it that you're looking to improve on your automatons?"

The lady widens her eyes. Slowly—with regret, Madiha likes to think—she lifts her hand away. "That's not the sole matter on my mind."

"You've given a clear impression of what you want from me, that's all. From the start you said it is my expertise which interested you." Madiha takes a little satisfaction as she sips her water, the nielloware icy against her lips, and peers at Aunrampha over its rim. "I cannot rely on your charity forever and must find a living if I'm to make Bangkok my home. I believe in clear negotiations, Khunying Aunrampha."

Aunrampha shakes her head, rueful. "I suppose I deserve it. Very well, we shall be definite on the terms of your employment."

"First my salary," Madiha says. "Then we can proceed to discuss my courtship of you, and whether you would receive it."

The lady blinks, taken aback, and then she laughs. "Of course. In all things we shall have the most direct of terms, the clearest of negotiations. Shall we begin?"

The Word of Menamhotep

I.

It always started like this: in a room with a corpse, the air thick with the iron tang of blood and stale tobacco. Policemen milling about treading valuable evidence underfoot, Bainbridge in a foul temper, and a head thick from the morning's first intake of opium.

Newbury sighed. Perhaps he'd fallen into something of a rut. So far, a cursory glance at the scene had failed to stir even an inkling of enthusiasm. He had no notion why Bainbridge had demanded his presence—the dead man appeared to have been shot, judging by the bloody hole in his chest, and there was little sign of anything of a more esoteric nature, besides a handful of vaguely obscure—and rather dry sounding—volumes of Ancient Egyptian history on one of the bookshelves.

"Well?" said Bainbridge.

"Give me chance, Charles. I've only just arrived."

Bainbridge muttered something unintelligible beneath his breath. Newbury dropped into a crouch beside the body.

The dead man's face was lily white and slack jawed, his eyes open and staring. A thin line of blood had dribbled from the corner of his mouth, stark and obscene, while more had drained from a wound in his chest, staining the front of his shirt and congealing on the oak floorboards beside him. He was lying on his side, as if he'd been attempting to roll over when his heart had finally given out. Newbury estimated he'd been in his mid-fifties, but had lived a reasonably adventurous life, judging by the leathery complexion and deep lines around his eyes. He'd been well travelled, but the loss of so much blood had deprived his cheeks of their earlier colour. "Foulkes tells me this is the third one you've found in similar circumstances this week," he said.

"Did he, now?" Bainbridge's moustache twitched with irritation. Evidently, he'd been expecting to reveal this troubling information to Newbury himself.

Newbury checked inside the lapel of the man's jacket. No wallet. "What did you say his name was?"

"I didn't," said Bainbridge. "He's Matthias Bright, an archaeologist. Quite famous in certain circles, apparently. Wrote some contentious papers challenging the accepted lineage of the ancient kings of Egypt. Caused quite a fuss amongst those concerned with such things."

"I think I recall something of the matter. Old Pyecroft at the museum was greatly put out by it all." Newbury appraised the dead man with new eyes. "How interesting."

"Hmmm," mumbled Bainbridge. "Not half as interesting as how he ended up on his drawing room floor with a quarter inch hole in his chest. It'll be more than a few fusty old professors getting uptight if we don't get to the bottom of this soon. Assuming, of course, that none of *them* are responsible."

Newbury frowned. "It's entirely possible, but in my experience, professional rivalry in academic circles is rarely cause for murder."

"Well, *someone* certainly took a dislike to him," said Bainbridge. "Although I'm damned if I can find any evidence of a third party. The door was locked from the inside."

Newbury glanced at the window. It was shut. So the assassin hadn't taken a shot from outside—not unless one of the policemen had already closed the window. "Any obvious connection to the other victims?"

"Parsons is looking into that now, although it seems reasonably obvious—they were all academics with an interest in antiquities. And Ancient Egypt in particular."

"And they were all shot in the same way?"

Bainbridge nodded.

Newbury studied the body again. "There's no exit wound."

Bainbridge frowned. "Yes, I noticed that. In fact, I was specifically looking for it. There's something strange about the exit wounds on the other bodies."

"How so?"

"The trajectory of the bullets entering the bodies and the angle of the exit wounds don't seem to make sense. It's as if the bullets ricocheted around inside the ribcage before exiting at high velocity."

"Which is a clear impossibility," said Newbury. "Did you recover any of the bullets?"

"No."

Newbury stood, stretching his back. "Anything else?"

Bainbridge reached into his pocket and withdrew a small object, wrapped in a white handkerchief. He held it out to Newbury. "This is why I sent for you. We've found one at the scene of each murder. Practically identical, down to the dusting of white powder around the base."

Interest piqued, Newbury took the object and weighed it in his palm. It was about the size of a pipe bowl, and relatively light for its size. Slowly, he unfolded the handkerchief.

It was a scarab beetle, crudely rendered in plaster. Its carapace had been painted glossy blue. Bizarrely, it had inaccurately been given eight legs instead of six. He turned it over. There was a small, roughly hewn cavity in the unpainted base of the plaster, about the size of a thumb nail. The base was covered in white plaster dust.

"That's it?" he said.

"We found it on his desk," said Bainbridge, nodding. "Same with the other two. Any idea what it means?"

Newbury shrugged. "Nothing that I'm aware of. It seems like one of those cheap souvenirs you'd find in a souk. Only, even they wouldn't make the mistake of giving it eight legs instead of six." He ran the tip of his little finger around the edges of the hole in the base of the thing, frowning. "Can I hold onto this? I'll head home, do a bit of poking around."

"Of course." Bainbridge grinned. "But first…"

Newbury felt his spirits dropping. "No, Charles. Not today. I haven't the patience to face her."

"She's growing tetchy," said Bainbridge. They both knew that was a grave understatement—Newbury hadn't visited the Palace for weeks. "What do you expect me to tell her?"

"Tell her I'm engaged on the case," he said. "Tell her I'm chasing the dragon. Tell her anything you damn want."

"Be it on your own head," said Bainbridge, with a heavy sigh.

Newbury slipped the scarab into his jacket pocket, now neatly folded up in its handkerchief again. "I wouldn't have it any other way," he said.

II.

NEWBURY HAD LEARNED to detest the morgue. The acrid stench of carbolic, the sluices awash with blood and other foetid bodily fluids, the all-pervading aura of death.

It wasn't that he'd developed a sudden aversion to corpses—more that he supposed he'd just spent too much time here in recent months. Although, on reflection, it might simply have been that all the bodies he'd come to examine had proved so disappointingly *ordinary*.

Bainbridge was waiting for him in the foyer, leaning heavily on his cane. He straightened up when he saw Newbury duck inside out of the rain. "You're late," he said.

"Indubitably," said Newbury, brushing droplets from his coat.

Bainbridge shook his head. "The surgeon's waiting for us, down here." He indicated the way with a wave of his cane.

"Did he manage to retrieve the bullet?" asked Newbury, as they walked the length of the tiled corridor.

"Oh, he found something much more interesting than that." Bainbridge stopped before an open doorway, and ushered Newbury inside.

Matthias Bright's corpse was lying exposed on a marble slab inside, the flesh pale and waxy. The eyes were shut, and the chest had been closed with a ladder of thick, black stitches.

The room itself was tiled in the same white and brown porcelain as the corridor, and the accoutrements of the surgeon's art were everywhere to see— untidily scattered upon work surfaces, trolleys and shelves.

A gaunt surgeon was standing beside the slab. He was tall and thin, with a balding pate and long, bony fingers. He was dressed in a bloodied leather smock. He peered at Newbury from beneath heavy, hooded lids.

"Doctor Breal," said Bainbridge, from over Newbury's shoulder. "This is Sir Maurice Newbury. I'd like for you to explain to him precisely what you've just explained to me."

Breal nodded curtly, inhaled so that his nose emitted an alarming whistle, and then spoke. "Contrary to initial appearances, this man was not shot."

"Then what was responsible for the hole in his chest?" said Newbury.

"This," said Breal, taking a kidney shaped dish from the nearest trolley and holding it out to Newbury.

Inside was a small metallic object, about the size of Newbury's thumbnail. It resembled nothing so much as a small insect, with a series of fragile-looking legs extending from a brass carapace. It was presently on its back.

"I found it wedged in one of his ribs," said Breal.

"May I?"

"Be my guest."

Newbury upturned the dish and allowed the little device to tumble out into his palm. He held it up to the light. "It's a scarab," he said. "With eight legs."

"Quite," said Bainbridge.

"And if you'll note the rather vicious mandibles..." said Breal.

Newbury used the tip of his finger to turn the scarab over. "It appears as if they're designed to rotate," he said.

"Indeed," said Breal. "I believe the device used them to burrow into the victim's chest, piercing his heart and causing a slow and rather agonising death. It's quite ingenious."

Newbury returned the scarab to the dish, and glanced at Bainbridge. "I suppose that explains the exit wounds you noted on the other victims. If similar automata killed them, the devices will have exited the victims to avoid detection. They won't have been concerned with trajectory."

Bainbridge nodded. "That was my thinking, too. And it also explains the lack of a third party. They were targeted assassinations. We even have the delivery method."

"The plaster scarabs," said Newbury. "The small cavity in the bases. The automata must have been sealed inside, and dug themselves out when activated or triggered. A seemingly innocuous object suddenly becomes the tool of an ingenious assassination."

"So what are we dealing with?" said Bainbridge. "What's the significance of the scarabs? Did you find anything?"

"I fear not. I can find no mention of an eight-legged scarab in any of my books or files. I'll pay a visit to Aldous this afternoon, see if he can shed any light."

"Very well," said Bainbridge. "And I'll keep digging, see if I can't turn up a more definite connection between the victims. There has to be a reason they're all being targeted." He shook his head. "It's a rum business, Newbury. You think it's one of your lot?"

"My lot?"

"Some godforsaken cult, or some such. You know what I mean."

Newbury grinned. "It remains a distinct possibility."

"And what of Miss Hobbes? Where is she? I presume you'll be engaging her in all of this, too?"

"In time. She has some other business to attend to first."

Bainbridge sighed. "She's turning out to be as darn mysterious as you are, Newbury. I tell you, you're a bad influence on that girl."

Newbury laughed. "I rather think you underestimate Miss Hobbes."

Bainbridge shook his head, and then waved in the direction of the door. "Well, go on then. Go and see what Mr. Renwick can dig up. I'll call on you later at home."

"I'll look forward to it," said Newbury, with a grin.

III.

ALDOUS RENWICK WAS perhaps the most peculiar man that Newbury had the fortune to call a friend. Wild in appearance, with chaotic wisps of stark white hair, nicotine stained fingers and a grizzled, unshaven aspect, his most startling feature was his left eye, or rather, the device that had replaced it—a protruding mechanical lens that had, he claimed, been wired directly into his brain, replacing the original organ. It was a disconcerting object, shifting in its ball socket as if independent of both Renwick and his other, remaining eye; black and glassy save for a pinprick of orange light in its strange, fathomless depths. Newbury believed the device—or at least the surgical work that had been carried out on Renwick's brain during its fitting—to be accountable for the man's somewhat unconventional demeanour.

He was peering at Newbury now, over the top of a jar of the strange, pink brew he drank instead of more traditional beverages. They were sitting in the cluttered back room behind his bookshop, surrounded by the paraphernalia of a lifetime studying the esoteric and occult. "An eight-legged scarab, you say?"

"Yes, that's right." Newbury took the plaster beetle from his pocket and passed it over. He watched Renwick appraise it for a moment, turning it over in the palm of his hand. His mechanical eye whirred. He raised his hand to his nose, and sniffed. "At first I wondered if it was a mistake—a crude error perpetrated by someone trying to approximate the real thing, but then I saw what came out of it, and realised the error was intentional." Newbury had outlined their findings at the morgue upon his arrival at the shop. Renwick had immediately placed the closed sign in the shop window, locked the door, and ushered him through to his lair.

Renwick placed the scarab on his workbench and crossed to one of the bookcases that seemed to line every inch of the wall space in the room. He searched the serried spines, his fingers dancing over the cracked leather bindings. He found what he was looking for and pulled a book down, blew a cloud of dust from the pages, and returned to where he'd been standing beside his workbench. He opened the book and began leafing through.

Newbury waited patiently, a smile tugging at the corners of his mouth. He'd seen this before. Renwick was checking his facts before reciting his conclusions to Newbury.

After a couple of minutes, Renwick looked up from the old tome and peered over at him quizzically, as if he'd forgotten Newbury was there. "Menamhotep," he said. He held the book out, tapping the left-hand page. Newbury took it.

"Menamhotep?" He glanced at the image in the book. It was an engraving of a listing stone pillar, high on a windswept moor. The carving had been eroded through centuries of exposure, but the central image was still largely visible—an eight-legged scarab beetle, surrounded by other, barely visible runes and sigils.

"A lesser known goddess from early-Dynastic Egypt," said Renwick. "She typically took the form of an eight-legged scarab or a spider-headed woman, and was the overseer of fate, responsible for weaving the vast web of causality. No action went unrecorded by Menamhotep, who alone understood the connection between all living things. She had the power to bring lovers together, or steer them apart; to start or end wars; to ensure the long reign of a Pharaoh, or end it suddenly in bloodshed. From the centre of her web in the heavens she witnessed all things, past and future."

"But this engraving shows an English landscape."

"Ah, that's where it gets interesting," said Renwick. "See, Menamhotep was largely forgotten during the earliest days of the Old Kingdom. No idols have ever been found—just fragmentary records, a few passing references in hieroglyphic reliefs. Her cults faded, and she went largely unmentioned for nearly two thousand years. But then the Romans settled in Egypt, and for the briefest of moments—just a few months—her cult was revived, before once again passing into obscurity." Renwick sipped at his strange concoction, and gave a satisfied sigh. "By then, the Romans had settled in Britain, however, and from that briefest window of revival, brought the cult to our shores."

"So the cult flourished here while it died off back in Egypt?"

Renwick nodded. "For a while. It was taken up by the locals, who identified Menamhotep with an ancient pagan spider spirit of the woods. Over time, she became Anglicised. Worship continued into the Saxon period, but was abolished with the establishment of Christianity. By the year 900 she was all but forgotten, save for a handful of old monuments on Dartmoor."

Newbury tapped his finger against his lips, thoughtful. "Yet someone doesn't want to let her sleep." He folded the book shut and placed it on a wavering stack beside his chair, and then got to his feet. "Thank you, Aldous. You've proved as invaluable as ever."

Renwick smiled and inclined his head. "Glad to be of service." He picked up the plaster scarab. "May I?"

Newbury grinned. "Just don't tell Charles," he said, reaching for the door handle.

IV.

"WE'VE ESTABLISHED A clear connection between the victims." Bainbridge stalked into Newbury's drawing room, the bowl of his pipe in his hand as he stabbed pointedly in Newbury's direction with the mouthpiece. Rivulets of rainwater were still running down the back of his overcoat, dripping all over the floorboards. "We need to hurry."

"Charles, you're *wet*. Think of the books."

Bainbridge stopped before the fire and turned on the spot. He regarded Newbury through a wreath of smoke. "Listen, are you coming or not? I have a police carriage waiting outside."

"Coming *where*?" Newbury leaned back into the soft embrace of his sofa. His head was throbbing, and he was beginning to feel a little unsettled. The tainted cigarettes in the wooden box on the side table were calling to him, but the thought of Bainbridge's bombastic objection was enough to stay his hand. He took a swig from his brandy instead.

"To the British Museum. We need to find a man called Oleander Crow."

Newbury drained his glass. "Is this about Menamhotep?"

"Menamo-who?"

"The eight-legged scarabs. They're a reference to an Ancient Egyptian goddess called Menamhotep. An old cult that came to Britain with the Romans."

"Well that would certainly make sense," said Bainbridge. "It seems all the victims were part of an expedition to Egypt last year. They found something in the desert—a particularly noteworthy tomb, mummy and treasure and all that—but apparently there was an antechamber where the walls were covered in ancient hieroglyphs, reciting some previously unknown legends. They took photographs, and they've been working together to study the texts since their return. They were planning to publish shortly, having recently completed the translation work." Bainbridge exhaled a ruffle of smoke from his nostrils. "Crow was the expedition leader, and the only survivor of the four. At this moment he's either our chief suspect, or the next intended victim."

"I've known Crow for years. He's a good man. I can't believe for a minute that he'd set out to harm his colleagues," said Newbury.

"Then we'd best hope we can get to him before they do—whoever *they* are."

"Alright." Newbury pulled himself up out of the pit of the sofa, stretching his weary limbs. "I'll get my coat and meet you at the cab in a moment."

V.

THE BRITISH MUSEUM was shrouded in a veil of mist and rain as the police carriage trundled over the flagstones and pulled to a halt outside the main entrance. It was approaching early evening, and the usual stream of visitors had evidently been dissuaded by the inclement weather—the grounds appeared deserted.

They clambered out of the carriage and, with heads dipped against the rain, sprinted for the cover of the main lobby.

"His office is in the basement, close to mine," said Newbury. He led the way across the marble concourse to the private stairwell that disappeared down into the gloomy belly of the museum. He hadn't visited his office here for some weeks, and knew that he'd have an enormous pile of paperwork to contend with when he did. Veronica, too, had been otherwise engaged with her sister over at Malbury Cross, leaving the running of the office to Miss Coulthard. He assured himself she'd have matters in hand, and resolved not to disturb her. At least, not if he could avoid it.

The passages beneath the museum were a warren, linking offices, study rooms and storage areas, as brimming with treasure as any buried tomb in the Saharan sands. They hurried along the tiled corridors, leaving a trail of dirty rainwater behind them.

"Here," said Newbury, indicating a door. Crow's name was printed in black on a small brass plate affixed to the door. Through the glass pane, he could see that a gas lamp was burning inside. He rapped on the door, and then tried the handle.

"Oleander?"

He stepped in, and Bainbridge bustled in behind him. The room was a small antechamber to Crow's main office, which he'd converted into a reading room, lined with books and scrolls, and with a small table and two chairs. Another door led into the adjoining office, where Crow was sitting hunched over his desk.

"Oleander?" repeated Newbury.

Crow looked up, peered myopically over the top of his spectacles, and then grinned. "Sir Maurice! Haven't seen you around these parts recently, what?"

Newbury crossed into the other room and shook Crow by the hand. He was a short man in his fifties, who'd retained a full head of dark hair that was nevertheless shot through with a startling streak of white, just above the left temple. His skin was tanned and lined, and his grip was firm. He was missing two front teeth, which he delighted in telling everyone had been lost during a fight with a Bedouin during one of his fateful expeditions. No one knew whether it was true, but Newbury had a sense that the truth more than lived up to Crow's telling of it; Crow was a man who'd seen things in his lifetime that most men could only begin to imagine.

"Oleander, this is Sir Charles Bainbridge, of Scotland Yard. We need to talk to you as a matter of urgency."

Crow sighed, removed his spectacles, and rubbed his eyes. "I presume with regard to the recent deaths of two of my colleagues?"

"Three of your colleagues," corrected Bainbridge.

Crow looked suddenly stricken. "Oh, no, not Matthias?"

"I'm afraid so," said Newbury. "He was found this morning. He died in the same way as the others."

"Which was?"

"He was assassinated by a tiny automaton of an eight-legged scarab, hidden inside a plaster decoration."

"An eight-legged scarab..." Crow frowned. He reached down and opened a drawer in his desk, and then took out a small plaster scarab, which he placed on the desk before him. It was identical to the one taken from bright's house that morning. Bainbridge glanced at Newbury.

"Where did you get that, Dr. Crow?" said Bainbridge.

"It arrived in the post this morning. There was no note. I assumed it was a little joke from Matthias—it relates to the work we've been doing, you see…"

"Regarding Menamhotep?" said Newbury.

"Yes, that's right," said Crow. "We've been translating a mythic cycle that we discovered in a tomb last year, during our most recent expedition. It's known as 'The Word of Menamhotep', and it's a creation myth—along with a series of accompanying rituals and incantations—referring back to pre-Dynastic Egypt, and a pantheon of gods that are mostly now forgotten, or later became transmuted into some of the more recognisable deities that you tend to hear about." He waved his hand. "As far as we're aware, the story hasn't been told for nearly four thousand years. It's a fascinating insight. The writings purport to be the recorded words of Menamhotep herself. Menamhotep was a minor deity, with little more than a cult following, really, so to find a text like this after all this time…"

"Where is the translation now?" said Newbury.

"Well, it's all here, collated in this folder." Crow indicated a large manilla file. "It's painstaking work. We've had to do it all by hand, from photographs. I'm in the final stages of collation."

"Bring it with you," said Newbury, getting to his feet. "We're taking you somewhere safe."

"What? Don't be ridiculous," said Crow, looking flustered. "I have work to do. Important work."

"Dr. Crow. Your life is at risk," said Bainbridge. "Consider this: whoever is responsible for the deaths of your colleagues knows where you work. And they've sent you that," Bainbridge pointed at the plaster scarab, "with the clear intention to cause you harm."

"But it's just a plaster decoration, as you said." Crow reached for the scarab and picked it up. As he lifted it, a plume of white dust billowed from the base. Puzzled, Crow turned it over to reveal a small cavity in the base. "What?"

"Up, now!" bellowed Bainbridge, grabbing Crow by the sleeve and hauling him roughly to his feet. Newbury reached over and grabbed the file, tucking it inside his coat. "We're leaving."

Crow flinched, and at first Newbury thought he was responding to Bainbridge's rather forceful grip on his arm, but then he noticed that the man was swatting at something on the back of his hand. "Charles! It's on him!"

Bainbridge twisted, releasing Crow, who stared at Newbury for a moment, clearly terrified, before holding up his right hand. There was a small, bloody hole in the flesh, and Newbury could see something moving beneath the skin.

"What...what...?" he mumbled, confused and pained. He scratched at the wound, trying to prise the scarab out with his fingers.

"Hold him down, Charles." Newbury searched in his pocket for penknife. "I'm sorry, Oleander. This is going to hurt, but there's really no other option. We have to work quickly."

As Bainbridge grappled with Crow, pinning his hand to the table, Newbury moved in, the knife grasped firmly in his fist.

"No, no, no...what are you–" Crow broke off into a shrill scream as Newbury dug the tip of his penknife into the back of the man's hand. Newbury could see the burrowing scarab forcing its way through the man's flesh, digging through muscle as it moved towards the wrist. If it got into his arm, Crow's life was forfeit—there was no way they'd be able to get it out of him before it had finished its work and punctured his heart.

Newbury twisted the handle of the knife, and then, keeping the pressure on, flicked the blade up and out, sending a hunk of bloody flesh—and the scarab— sailing across the room, where they struck the rear wall and slid to the floor. Dark blood welled from the wound, spilling out all over the desktop. Crow looked as if he were about to swoon.

"Hospital, now," said Newbury. "I'll see to the device."

Bainbridge nodded, shepherding Crow from the room, leaving a trail of dripping blood in their wake.

Cautiously, Newbury crept around the desk, his eyes tracking across the tiled floor. The ragged hunk of Crow's flesh—about the size of a postage stamp—was lying against the skirting board, sitting in a small puddle of blood. Beside it, glinting in the warm light of the gas lamp, was the tiny metal scarab. It was on its back, its legs scrabbling at the air as it attempted to right itself.

Newbury glanced at the desk, and his eyes fixed on a heavy glass paperweight, filled with blooming swirls of blue and yellow. He snatched it up and slowly approached the scarab. It remained on its back, still attempting to right itself. Dropping into a low crouch—careful to keep as far back as he could—Newbury raised the paperweight above his head, then brought it crashing down upon the scarab.

The porcelain tile fractured under the force of the blow, and Newbury's arm reverberated painfully, causing him to involuntarily release the paperweight. He rocked back on his haunches, clutching his forearm, while the glass semi-sphere rolled away across the floor.

He looked down. There, on a broken fragment of tile, was the twisted chassis of the scarab, tiny cogs and broken limbs surrounding it like a pool of spilled blood.

VI.

"Just the thought of something that small being so deadly," said Veronica. "It's enough to make you fear opening the post ever again."

She was sitting in the armchair by the fire in Newbury's drawing room, while Bainbridge paced, and Newbury leaned against the windowsill, smoking a cigarette. Elsewhere in the house Newbury's valet was hard at work crafting one of his culinary delights for dinner.

Oleander Crow had been safely installed at Bainbridge's house, under the watchful guard of Parsons, one of Bainbridge's most trusted junior officers. His hand was going to take some time to recover, but at least he was alive.

"It's really quite a clever conceit," said Newbury. "Easy to deliver, difficult to detect. And to build automata that *small*…"

"Really, Newbury. You can't tell me you *admire* the handiwork of these villains," said Bainbridge.

"I admire their methods, if not their actions," said Newbury.

"I must admit to being confounded by them," said Bainbridge. "My men are out there scouring every damn crevice of London, but so far, there's no obvious lead. We can find nothing related to this so-called Menamhotep, and try as we might, we can't establish a motive for anyone else connected to the expedition. There's no reason any of them would want any of the victims dead, and their alibis all seem to hold up. We'll keep going, of course, but it's damn frustrating when the answers fail to present themselves like this."

Newbury stubbed his cigarette out on the windowsill and crossed to the sideboard, from where he retrieved his copy of the evening newspaper. "If you'll forgive me, Charles," he said, unfurling the broadsheet and leafing through the pages, "I took the liberty of interceding. I decided a more direct approach might prove fruitful." He found what he was looking for, folded the newspaper open on the right page, and smoothed it down, tapping a small advert amongst the classifieds.

Veronica and Bainbridge had moved around to stand behind him, peering over his shoulder. The advert read:

TO THOSE WHO SEEK THE WORD OF MENAMHOTEP
WHAT YOU REQUIRE IS IN SAFE HANDS
TOWER BRIDGE, 7PM FRIDAY
SIR MAURICE NEWBURY

"Of all the foolhardy things…" said Bainbridge, trailing off. "Don't you see what you've done? You've made yourself the next target. What if they come after you here, with one of those *things*?"

"Perhaps," said Newbury. "But even so, it would flush them out. And why risk it? If they're after the translated pages, they have no guarantee they're here. Better to chance the meet."

"Surely they'll see it's a trap," said Veronica.

"I imagine so," said Newbury. "But at least we'll get a sense of what we're up against, and how important those translated pages really are to them. As Charles said, it's not as if we have any other leads."

"I don't like it," said Bainbridge. "Not at all." He tugged thoughtfully at the edge of his moustache. "But it's done now. Assuming they see it, of course."

"They'll see it," said Newbury.

"So, tomorrow evening," said Veronica. "We're coming with you, of course."

Newbury glanced at her, and grinned. "I wouldn't have it any other way." He tossed the newspaper back on the sideboard. "We need to make preparations. We have to assume they'll come armed and ready for an ambush."

"Oh, we'll be ready," said Bainbridge. "I'll get word to Foulkes right away. Whoever these murderous devils are, we'll be waiting."

"Like a spider at the centre of a web," said Newbury, with a grin.

VII.

NEWBURY TURNED THE collar of his overcoat up against the pattering rain. A thick mist had settled across the river, shrouding the opposing tower, hugging the road and swirling around their ankles. It softened everything, as if it were somehow dispersing reality itself, leaving Newbury with the odd sensation that he was floating, up there on a bridge between two worlds.

He stood with Veronica and Bainbridge, leaning against the rail, waiting. Bainbridge hadn't stopped checking his pocket watch, despite the fact that bells all across the city had only just finished ringing out the hour.

Newbury peered over the railing. Below, he could see the mast of a ship, jutting rudely from the mist. The river itself was utterly obscured.

"They're here," said Veronica.

Newbury turned to see a figure walking towards them from across the bridge. They were dressed in a thick, black overcoat, rendering them in near silhouette; a moving, shifting, shadow. As they drew nearer, he discerned that the figure belonged to a woman. She was wearing a hat, pinned neatly on the side of her head, atop a neat arrangement of thick, dark hair. She was pretty, with a dark complexion and startling brown eyes. She'd had a harelip as a child, which had been surgically corrected, leaving her with a charming, impish smile. She was carrying an umbrella like a stick, still folded away, despite the weather. "Sir Maurice Newbury?" she said, as she approached.

Newbury pushed himself away from the railing. "And you are?"

The woman extended her hand. Newbury took it. Her fingers were cold to the touch. "Mathilda Bathurst. I saw your advert in *The Times*."

"Quite." He noticed Bainbridge bristling beside him.

"I believe you have something of interest to us."

"Us?" said Newbury.

The woman smiled. She carried herself with a supreme air of confidence. "My associates and I would very much appreciate it if you were to simply hand it over."

"Now look here," said Bainbridge. "I think you misunderstand. Three men are dead, and I have every reason to believe you and your *associates* are behind it. You'll be coming back to Scotland Yard with us to answer some questions."

Bathurst laughed. "Sir Charles, I'd heard you were an amusing man." She held out her hand to Newbury. "Now, the papers."

Newbury reached inside his coat, but withdrew only his battered silver cigarette case. He popped it open and took one, then returned the case to his pocket. He huddled over for a moment while he lit it with a vesper. "First, I want to know what you intend to do with them, and why they are worth the death of three men to obtain. Is it a simple act of suppression? Are you attempting to prevent their publication?"

Bathurst sighed. "Menamhotep wills it, and it shall be done," she said.

"Oh, how dreadfully disappointing," said Newbury. He blew smoke from the corner of his mouth. "For just a moment, I thought you were going to be more than just another inane follower of an obscure cult."

"An obscure cult?" The woman scoffed. "You have no idea of the web we have weaved throughout this city. Of how long we have worked in the shadows, or the lengths we will go to, to see Menamhotep rise. Those papers are just the beginning." She glanced at Bainbridge. "You can take me in, incarcerate me, kill me, but within the hour another will stand in my place. Far better that you hand over what is rightfully ours. I might even allow you to live."

"You might allow *us* to live?" said Bainbridge, incredulous. "Come on, Newbury. Let's get this over with. I'm anxious to get out of the rain."

Bathurst took a step back, and at first Newbury thought she was about to turn and flee, but instead she made a gesture above her head, snapping her fingers. Almost immediately, two figures appeared from the mist behind her, shambling forward on stiff, ungainly legs. Within seconds, another four had appeared in their wake, marching across the bridge with the same stuttering gait.

"Revenants," said Veronica.

"No," said Newbury. "Listen." There was something almost mechanical about the newcomers, and as they moved, he thought he heard the whine of servos.

"These are the saved," said Bathurst. "Their spirits reborn after death. This is the power of Menamhotep."

Two of the figures had now lurched fully into view, and the full horror of the occasion became apparent. They were shambling corpses, their flesh embalmed and dried, smooth and stretched across their decaying bones. Their eyes were missing, their sockets dry and hollow, staring and unseeing. They were wrapped in trailing bandages and adorned with necklaces bearing eight-legged scarabs. They were mummies, either plundered from their resting places in far off sands, or somehow recreated here, on British shores, in a gross parody of the funeral rites of the ancients. Their skeletons had been wired to brass supports, their joints fixed with servos, and they lumbered in a terrible semblance of life, powered by the same technology that had driven the tiny scarab automata.

Bainbridge raised his walking cane. "Stand aside, Miss Hobbes." He twisted the head of the cane and the shaft began to unpack, levering apart to reveal a reinforced glass chamber within. The main shaft began to spin, generating a spitting charge of electricity, which crackled inside the glass chamber, causing the very tip of the cane to spark and crackle. "Foulkes," he bellowed, and Newbury heard running footsteps from behind, as the six policemen came charging in, revolvers loaded and ready.

"You can prevent all of this, Sir Maurice, by surrendering the file," said Bathurst. "What happens here is your responsibility."

"Fire!" bellowed Bainbridge. The police revolvers barked, and four of the shambling mummies seemed to stutter for a moment, before continuing their ponderous, onward march. "Again!" called Bainbridge, and the shots rang out in quick succession, like snapping dogs. Once again, the mummies stumbled, but continued on their way.

Bathurst laughed. Newbury was beginning to wish he'd brought a weapon, rather than relying solely on the police. He cast around for something he could use against the automatons, but there was nothing to hand. He'd have to think on his feet.

The first of the things was nearly on top of them. Bainbridge stepped forward, brandishing his cane. "Call them off, Miss Bathurst," he said, his voice level.

Bathurst said nothing as the mummy took a further step towards Bainbridge, raising its hand as if to take a swipe.

"Have it your way, then." He jabbed at the thing with the tip of his cane, piercing the dry flesh of its gut and causing the electricity in the glass chamber to discharge. Lightning crackled across the mummy's entire frame, arcing between its remaining teeth, causing the servos to spark and the long-dead flesh to ignite with a sudden *whoosh*.

The mummy took two more stuttering steps forward, and then collapsed in a burning heap, its wired joints juddering, raindrops fizzing on its superheated frame. Wretched black smoke curled from the remains of its flesh, causing Newbury to wrinkle his nose in disgust.

The rest of the police had surged forward, and were now concentrating their fire on one automaton at a time, which appeared to be paying dividends, as another of the things went down while Newbury watched, and the police swiftly reloaded and began their assault on a third.

Bainbridge placed his foot on the smoking corpse and wrenched the end of his cane free. He twisted the head again, causing the spinning section to re-engage, and the charge once more began to build inside the chamber.

Newbury glanced at Bathurst, weighing his options. There were still three automata unengaged by the police, and while Bainbridge moved to tackle another of them, Newbury didn't fancy his chances against the others unarmed. He knew they would intercede if he tried to make a move against the woman. Veronica, on the other hand, had begun edging along the railing, evidently with a view to heading Bathurst off if she tried to make a break for it. He decided to remain where he was for now. He had the file, after all, which might prove to be their only leverage if things went awry.

"I'm impressed," said Bathurst. "I can see I'm going to have to engage a little more in the way of persuasion." She rapped the end of her metal-tipped umbrella against the ground three times in quick succession, and then smiled at Newbury mischievously.

Somewhere beneath Newbury's feet, something made a sharp scratching sound. He glanced down, half expecting to see the ground suddenly erupt around him, but all remained still, quiet.

He heard Veronica gasp, and turned to see her falling back from the railing, where an enormous black beetle had begun clambering up over the side of the bridge, its eight mechanical legs stabbing at the ground as it fought for purchase, scratching at the stone. It was about the size of a police carriage, with a fat, bulbous shell of glossy plates, and two twitching mandibles jutting from the front where its mouth should have been. Two men wearing goggles and black robes were strapped to its back in a leather harness, riding it as one might ride a horse. It was monstrous, an engine of destruction, built to the design of the eight-legged scarab so synonymous with Menamhotep.

"Veronica, run!"

Close to where the machine had emerged from under the bridge, Bainbridge was yanking his cane from the ruins of another mummy. He glanced up, just as the scarab dragged its bulk over the edge of the rail and dropped to the ground a few feet from him, its mandibles clacking as it advanced. He twisted, raising the cane, but the charge was spent, and there wasn't time for it to replenish. He backed away, glancing for support from the other policemen. "Foulkes!"

Bullets pinged off the armour plating of the scarab's head, and the man in the front of the saddle slumped suddenly, a fine spray of blood misting into the air where a bullet caught him in the throat. He listed to one side, gurgling, while the man behind him took up the controls, and the machine lurched forward, its mandibles grasping for Bainbridge.

Bainbridge swung his cane like a club, battering at the mechanical proboscis, but the shaft simply rebounded off the brass, and he staggered back, narrowly avoiding the burning mess of the mummy he'd just despatched.

As Newbury watched with a sense of dawning horror, the machine skittered forward—surprisingly agile now that it had cleared the railing—and scooped Bainbridge up in its mandibles, swinging him violently from side to side as he grappled to prise himself free.

Unsure what else he could do, Newbury pulled the file from inside his coat and ran to the edge of the railing. He thrust his hand out, over the sea of mist and the swirling river below. The file fluttered in the breeze, which threatened to wrench it from his fingers.

"Stop!"

The sound of gunfire and ricocheting bullets ceased. The scarab stopped shaking its head. Only the steady advance of the mummies continued, accompanied by the gently whining of their servos. The driver of the scarab looked down at Mathilda Bathurst, who was standing by the vehicle's feet, watching Newbury with a curious expression.

"You realise if you let go of that folder, we'll have no reason not to kill your friend," she said.

Newbury glanced at Veronica out of the corner of his eye. She looked as if she were getting ready to make a play for Bathurst. He shook his head, and, frustrated, she held her ground. "And you realise that if you *do* kill him, I'll destroy the only copy of this file in existence."

"Then it seems we're at something of a stalemate," said Bathurst, with a grin.

"Let him go, and you can have the file," said Newbury. "No tricks. Just a straight exchange. We give you the file, and we all walk out of here."

"How do I know you can be trusted?"

"You have my word."

Bathurst laughed. "I trust you see the irony in that?" She nodded to the scarab driver, and he operated a lever, releasing the mandibles and causing Bainbridge to slump heavily to the ground. He crumpled onto the wet road. "The file," she said, holding out her hand.

"Tell your followers to back off, first."

Bathurst sighed, and with a wave of her hand, dismissed the two remaining mummies. They turned ponderously, and then shambled off into the mist on the other side of the bridge. Newbury waited until they had gone.

"And *that*," he said, nodding his head to indicate the scarab.

"Go," said Bathurst. The driver—still operating the controls over the slumped form of his dead colleague—turned the machine around, and clacked off into the rainswept night. Bathurst lifted her umbrella and pressed the tip against the back of Bainbridge's neck.

Slowly, Newbury lowered his arm and stepped away from the railing. He took two steps forward, and then stooped and laid the file on the ground. Raindrops were pattering upon its surface, staining the card. Soon, the pages inside would be unreadable.

"Back away," said Bathurst.

Newbury took three steps back. "Now let him go, and we'll retreat from the bridge."

"Sir Maurice," said Foulkes from somewhere behind him. "We can't just let her get away."

"We can, and we will, Inspector. I won't forfeit Charles's life for *this*."

"Very wise," said Bathurst. She lifted her umbrella away from Bainbridge's neck and beckoned to Veronica, who came forward, stooping to Bainbridge's side. Slowly, she helped him up, collecting his cane, and together they staggered towards Newbury.

"All right, Foulkes. Tell your men to back away now." Newbury came forward to help Veronica, shouldering some of Bainbridge's weight. He was dazed, and bleeding, but alive.

"You heard him," said Foulkes. The reluctance was plain to hear in his voice.

Together, the six policemen retreated in a line, refusing to take their eyes off Bathurst until the thickening mist had enveloped them.

Newbury watched as Bathurst hurried over and crouched to collect the folder, which she swiftly slid under the protection of her coat. Then, opening her umbrella and resting it nonchalantly on her left shoulder, she turned and walked away.

"Until next time," said Newbury.

She didn't look round.

VIII.

"You shouldn't have allowed her to get away. It's unconscionable."

"I'm pleased to see you're back to your old self, Sir Charles," said Veronica, passing him another brandy. He was slumped in the armchair by the fire at Newbury's house, wearing a brooding expression. The doctor had been and gone, and warned him under no uncertain terms that he needed to rest up for a few days. He'd suffered a few bruises—mostly to his dignity, it seemed—but otherwise he was quite well.

"You allowed her to get away with three counts of murder," Bainbridge continued, his eyes following Newbury as he paced around the room. He looked furious. "And now you're damn well smirking about it, too!"

"I did no such thing," said Newbury.

"Then what do you call allowing her to walk away with the bloody prize, then?" He caught a glimpse of Veronica scowling at him, and softened. "Look, I'm grateful for what you did. Of course I am. But surely Foulkes could have taken steps on the bridge. A well-placed bullet to slow her down and she'd be in custody now. At least then, justice would have been done."

"You heard her, Charles. Her little speech about the cult. We underestimated them, badly. Look at the resources they have. That *machine*…not to mention those walking cadavers. I believe she was telling the truth when she claimed that someone else would be waiting in the wings to take her place if she fell. Bringing her in wouldn't have made the slightest bit of difference. They'd still be out there, and the people who are truly responsible would be free to carry on as if nothing had happened."

"Isn't that true now?"

Newbury shook his head. "No. Because now we have a name, and a face, and a sense of what we're dealing with. Now we can go after the real prize. We can dig them out, drag them into the light, and discover what they're really up to. Then we'll make them pay for the crimes they've committed, too."

Bainbridge nodded. "Alright. I see your point." He smiled. "What was it you said, earlier? 'I'm not sure I agree with your actions, but I admire your method.'"

"Something like that," said Newbury, laughing.

"But what about the file?" said Veronica. "Surely there was more to it than a simple creation myth. There has to be a reason they wanted it so badly and were prepared to kill the men involved in translating it. You mentioned rituals and incantations—do you think they're going to try to use them?"

"It won't do them much good if they do," said Newbury.

"Because it's all poppycock," scoffed Bainbridge.

"No," said Newbury, a little more emphatically than he'd intended. He crossed to one of his bookshelves and took down a leather folio. He opened it and withdrew a sheaf of pages covered in neat, spidery scrawl. "Because I kept a few choice pages back as insurance."

Bainbridge guffawed. "I'd love to see the look on that woman's face when she realises."

"I'm not so certain, Charles. We made an enemy today. She didn't seem the type to let things rest. This is tantamount to a declaration of war."

"Then war it shall be," said Bainbridge.

Veronica crossed the room to stand before him. She put a hand on his arm. "And when the time comes, we'll face it together. This time, we'll be ready."

"Hear, hear," said Bainbridge. "Now get over here and fetch me my pipe, would you, man? It's time you admitted I was right."

Newbury raised an eyebrow. "You were?"

"Yes. About it being one of your lot. A cult. You can't deny it now, can you, eh?"

Newbury sighed. He looked at Veronica. "You know, I think he might have a point."

"I suppose there's a first time for everything," she said, laughing.

Silver Linings

TEE-MORRIS-&-PIP-BALLANTINE

WINTER, 1896
CAIRO, EGYPT

"AH, CAIRO," WELLINGTON sighed as he stood on the ship's gangway for a moment, taking in the impressive desert vista before him. "The cradle of civilization and human innovation."

"Along with the cradle of oppressive heat, barren wastelands, and flies that you could hitch up to a hansom and use as a cheap alternative to camels," grumbled his junior archivist as she disembarked.

Wellington Books looked down at the diminutive Eliza D. Braun, arching an eyebrow at her as she twirled her parasol in annoyance.

"Miss Braun, come along, are you telling me you do not find Egypt tantalizing in its history, its undiscovered mysteries? Why, the foundation of modern language and even the sciences began here."

She bit back, "If I were fond of this kind of heat, I would take holiday in Australia. Hold my parasol." Eliza unwound the veil from around the top of her pith helmet, and then snatched back the parasol.

"And here I thought you were a romantic," he muttered.

"A romantic? Is that why you insisted on taking an airship to the Sudan, and then chuging upriver on this boat?"

"Chug upriver?" Wellington asked, stunned. "It's the *Nile!*"

"Oh for god's sake," she seethed, giving the horsetail swatter a few swings, "let's get this over with!"

Hefting his huge brown case, Wellington lumbered down the gangplank, ignoring Eliza's protestations to leave it for the porters. He had thought the two might extend their stay after their official duties were completed, but it was apparent that his partner was immune to what he had heard described as "Pharaoh Fever" by travel brokers.

Perhaps this would be a brief stay of only a day or two, and then an airship back to London. No need to prolong this little jaunt if he had to share it with one immune to the wonders of Egypt.

"Mr. Books, Miss Braun?" a voice asked.

Wellington and Eliza turned around to see a tanned gentleman, unmistakably English in both his features and in the disdain etched in his face. Whether that expression was for him or for his fellow archivists from headquarters remained a mystery.

"Something I do love about being an archivist for our shadowy Ministry." He looked as if he was about to burst out into bitter laughter. "We do not stand on ceremony or secrecy. After all, how dangerous is our position, really?"

Eliza snorted. "You'd be surprised, mate."

Wellington did not care one jot for the way this man was sizing up both him and his partner. The man removed his pith helmet and casually fanned himself as he approach them.

"Marcus Donohue, Ministry Archivist, Egypt Branch." He motioned around him. "Welcome to Hell."

"Dunno about that," Eliza replied. "Australia's outback in the summer makes this place look positively welcoming."

"And Cairo is a pleasant change from January in London. Dead of winter and all," Wellington added. "This is quite nice."

"Quite," he said, looking around him as if incredibly inconvenienced. "Shall we proceed then?"

Wellington nodded and motioned for Eliza to lead the way. Her scowl assured him that her mind had been made up about their visit to Cairo. Perhaps he would save a lecture on the beauty of Egypt for another trip. Between Eliza's demeanour and the local office's reception, brevity was most certainly in order.

EGYPT HAD NEVER disappointed Eliza. She still remembered her first case here with Harry. While Paris remained a special jewel in previous assignments and the countryside of Beijing offered ancient mysteries that opened her eyes to amazing possibilities, there was something alluring about Egypt. Harry had taken her to the Giza Pyramids shortly after their arrival, a stop that had absolutely nothing to do with the case they were assigned but her partner had insisted. They had watched the sun set behind the ancient monuments, and that was when he imparted the importance of this diversion.

To solve a case, to unlock the mysteries of what we deal with, he began, still looking in the direction of where the sun had disappeared, *you need to understand the world around you. Not the world on a whole, but the culture, the people, and the history you are in now. That is your first step in closing a case.*

Eliza still remembered her response: *True, but a fist full of dynamite is also quite handy in unlocking mysteries. Stone pyramids, too.*

He was right, of course, damn him. Her time along the banks of the Nile had been far too brief. It was quite kind of Wellington to try and "broaden her view" of their assignment to Egypt, but she could not voice to her mentor how disappointed she deeply felt.

The truth of it was that Eliza would have loved Cairo if she had been a field agent. However, that goal appeared further and further away. Especially now, returning to the field officially to collect the records of previous cases.

How. Thrilling.

Miggins Antiquities in Egypt was nestled in one of the many tight alleyways of Cairo, and blended in easily with the surroundings. As in their London office, the main foyer and open room were dedicated to cataloguing and inspection of various Ancient Egyptian artefacts. That common looting of tombs was encouraged by their Ministry's headquarters did not improve her mood.

At the back of the receiving room, a single staircase led up to a modest room of four desks. Two of these desks, Eliza knew from previous stations in the Empire, were reserved for visiting agents. The other two were occupied those agents local to the area. The gentlemen planted there—finely dressed Egyptians—looked her over, and then disappeared back behind their respective newspapers.

Donohue gave a dry laugh as he continued to another stairwell. "Now, now, gents, do extend a courtesy to our colleagues from Old Blighty. I'm sure they will let us on to all that we are failing to notice in our sunny part of the world, yes?"

The second flight opened to an office decorated with fine antiquities, Egyptian rugs, and, against the far wall, a pneumatic messaging system that was Ministry-issue equipment. Eliza's eyes, however, were drawn to the desk, modest in size and construction, and the valuables on it. Small statuettes of Egyptian gods and goddesses. Rings and bracelets of gold. Items that would look nothing less than impressive in one's own private collection.

Eliza felt heat under her skin, and she knew this sudden warmth had nothing to do with the surrounding climate.

"Please," Donohue said, motioning to a pair of chairs in front of the desk.

With a quick look to Wellington, Eliza took a seat.

"Is this your first time in Cairo?"

"No," they both said together.

Eliza could see in the corner of her eye Wellington staring at her. She kept her eyes on Donohue.

"Well, thankfully it will be brief. A shame, really," he added, giving Wellington a rakish wink, "missing out on what Cairo has to offer."

"You seem to be doing quite well," Wellington said, brushing a small film of sand and dust free of a Bastet statue. "Egyptian Alabaster. Very nice."

"Privileges of being posted here," he replied dismissively, "and wearing many hats when working overseas with the Ministry of Peculiar Occurrences."

Eliza nodded. "Archivist *and* Field Director?"

"But that does not mean I fail to heed the call of our magnanimous leader," Donohue said, sliding a paper bearing the Ministry seal across the desk. "A transfer of archived material for cataloguing back at Ministry Headquarters?" He chuckled, sliding the order to one side. "How long do you want this process to take?"

Wellington glanced at Marcus askew. "I beg your pardon?"

"Or will you be reporting this as a 'C.F.' as our predecessors have ?"

Wellington straightened. "Whatever do you mean by that?"

"You know, a C.F.? A 'collating fiasco'? That chap who was here last—Whitby, I believe his name was—he knew the game. Reported back to Sound that things were dreadfully in disrepair and insisted on extending his stay here." He shrugged, shaking his head. "My predecessors assured me it was the way of things. One quick message via æthermail and you buy more time to enjoy a bit of the local culture and cuisine."

"Well, Whitby was a bit of a git, now wasn't he?" Eliza snipped. "Buggered off without a word to anyone one day, left the Archives to seed. You're not going to find we're cut of the same cloth."

She caught more movement in her peripheral vision. Hopefully, it was Wellington, beaming with pride. Eliza allowed herself a slight grin.

The proclamation of their ethics seemed to roll off Donohue like water off a duck's back. "An official trip it is, then? Very well. While you load up a hired cart, I'll look into bookings for airships." He jotted down a few notes on the Ministry communiqué, paused, and looked them over as he did on meeting them. "As you all are Ministry stalwarts, I will assume Third Class seating should suffice, yes?"

Wellington leaned forward. "If this will help your office, Mister Donohue, why don't you just direct us to your Archives? We will not trouble you any longer than—"

"Turn around," he interjected. He was looking at flight schedules now.

They both spun about to find six crates behind them. Eliza thought she and Wellington brought more luggage than this.

"That," she began, turning on Donohue, "is *ten years* of cases from Cairo?"

"Yes," he replied, still reviewing travel options for the two of them. "I know this may come as a shock to you, Agent Braun, but as the home office tends to stick their fat noses into our business, we remain watching from our post. Or," he said, suddenly looking up at her with a rather chilly gaze, "we carry out the preliminary work while other agents step in and take credit."

That was when Eliza suddenly remembered Marcus Donohue. The face and the attitude clicked into place "Now just a minute, mate, Harry and I stepped in only because you lot were dragging your feet!"

Donohue sat up, his grin hardly pleasant or jovial. "Expected, coming from the Ministry elite. But now look at us." He gave a snort. "Two peas, aren't we?"

"Well then," Wellington piped up, shattering the palpable tension, "perhaps we should just collect these cases and head back to London as quickly as possible, yes?"

A sudden metallic *crack* made all three of them jump with a start. Wisps of steam were seeping from one of the "Incoming" tubes. Donohue crossed the room and opened the cylinder.

"Well, it would seem that my day with you, Agent Braun, has been cut short. My presence is needed at police headquarters." He waved the paper in his hand. "Marked 'Urgent' so it must be serious." Donohue grabbed his pith helmet and motioned to the modest archives. "If you are the last ones out, please lock up behind you."

Wellington and Eliza both looked at each other, quite stunned at how this branch could still be in operation in light of Donohue's leadership. From the bottom of the stairwell they heard Donohue call out, "Agent Rateb, grab a memo pad. You're with me."

"Charming fellow," Wellington quipped. Her partner removed his coat and unbuttoned his vest. "Well then, let's get cracking. We should try and at least get an idea of how 'well maintained' this collection of cases is..."

WORKING WITH MISS Eliza D. Braun when she wanted to be anywhere else was not for the faint of heart. She had quite the grasp on chilly silences marked with exasperated sighs. Rather than respond, Wellington removed his glasses and pressed two fingers on either side of his nose.

Outside the call to prayer was ringing out, and as if on cue his stomach began to rumble. As he glanced across the top of the boxes, he wondered if now was the best time to suggest a beak for a meal. They had been at this for a good portion of the day, so much so that it was now the evening and they were they only two souls in the office.

However, the expression on Eliza's face as she rummaged through the box he'd assigned her, hinted it was not a good time to suggest anything unless he wanted to feel the wrath of New Zealand. She was muttering to herself under her breath—another bad sign. He caught 'Donohue', 'self-important moron', and other words that would not have been out of place in the mouth of a sailor.

He was just about to take his chances, when steps thundered up the stair-well. An Egyptian, possessing a finely styled beard, sharply-cut cream suit, and a smart boater-style hat common for the region, burst into the office, panting wildly. Wellington observed Eliza's eyes widen and the hint of a dangerous smile pulled at her lips. She was quite ready to escape the mundane, and it was this readiness of hers that often led him directly into the mouth of madness.

"Where is Director Donahue?" the agent blurted out.

"He is still out, answering an emergency call," Eliza said, before Wellington could get a word in.

He looked at them both, then to the desk, and tossed the legal pad across the office. Wellington's grasp of the man's dialect was a bit rusty, but he knew it well enough to recognise it as similar words to what Eliza had used earlier concerning Director Donohue.

The agent took a breath, turning his dark gaze to Donohue's desk. "Bastard said he was going to meet me here!"

"We saw you earlier. One of our local agents here in Egypt. We're Agents Eliza Braun, and Wellington Books on assignment from London—"

"—sent to collect your archives for proper cataloguing back at headquarters," Wellington interjected, hoping to disarm the situation.

Well, *he* thought it was a valiant effort. "Perhaps we can help?" Eliza asked, undeterred by Wellington.

The man was not totally foolish, because he raised a brow in response to this. "The matter is of the utmost urgency and involves the Queen's Own Camel Brigade and Lord Alton Rutland himself."

At the mention of military men and the heir to a duchy, Wellington snapped to attention, his gaze narrowing. "Identify yourself then, and let's be about it."

The man straightened immediately in a similar manner. "Agent Khaled Rateb, currently assigned to Lord Alton Rutland's protection."

Wellington was reaching for his coat before he even realised it. "Explain that while we go."

He dimly heard Eliza race up behind them. "The Camel brigade?"

Agent Rateb shot her a glance. "Yes. The Imperial Camel Brigade is a small, experimental force, designed to move fast and silently in the desert. Part of my assignment calls for embedding myself within the troops."

They secured the office and began to head into the city itself, the chill of the evening already setting in. Offering his arm to Eliza, the two of them shadowed Rateb as he explained his assignment.

"This experiment is the brainchild of Lord Alton and he is getting quite excellent results," Rateb said. "I was assigned to not only investigate any possible incidents but also protect Lord Alton."

"Lord Alton," Eliza continued to press the man, "the Duke of Rutland's only heir, right?"

"Indeed, the very one." Rateb peered around another corner before leading them on towards the far less savoury outskirts of Cairo. "He's a very fine young man, with large responsibilities. This brigade of his is also a testament of his innovation."

"Camels, though." Eliza shuddered. "I would think they'd be dreadful animals if you came under fire."

Rateb shared a look with Wellington before replying. "Actually they take it much better, and are less prone to running off."

He led them down a series of narrow alleyways, the closeness of the buildings making Wellington tighten his grip on his cane.

"Donohue and I were called by the Duke himself to keep an eye on his heir. There was some concern that his life was in danger."

"That would explain Director Donohue's reaction to the pneumatic tube," Wellington said to Eliza. "He seemed quite inconvenienced by the message."

Rateb shook his head, appearing to bite back an opinion. He paused, then spoke his words, struggling for control. "After we had met with the Duke of Rutland—"

"Wait," Eliza interrupted, "the Duke was here? In Cairo?"

"Yes," Rateb replied.

"Then his concerns for his son were sincere," Wellington added.

"Exactly. Donohue told me to volunteer for watch tonight with the brigade, even though there were no exercises today or tomorrow. He told me he would be in the office this evening, if needed. By dinner, I thought this threat, even though it had demanded the attention of the Duke of Rutland, may have been unwarranted until..." The agent shook his head slowly. "You will have to see it to believe it."

They reached the barracks of the Imperial Camel Brigade, located on the edge of Cairo's sprawl. Rateb took them up to the postern gate, removed a lozenge-shaped mechanical device from around his neck and pressed it into a matching symbol in the wall. The gate clicked open.

Wellington was duly impressed. "Security has changed dramatically since my days as a solider."

They slipped into the compound, and immediately Wellington grew suspicious, not of what he heard, but of what was notably *absent*. Even in the evening, there were usually lots of noises to be heard in a military encampment, and so it had been when they passed by the barracks of the enlisted soldiers. He had heard the expected cacophony of carousing, music, and laughter. Once they entered this section of the camp—a sequestered area Wellington knew would be "Officers Only" on account of its specialised operations—other than the low *whu-whu* of a pharaoh eagle owl in the distance, a heavy silence lingered around the archivist and his companions. Perhaps security had changed since Wellington was in the military, but soldiers most certainly would have not.

Eliza must have felt something off too, for she had her hand inside her jacket, undoubtedly ready to pull out one of her *ponamu* pistols. With the skin on his back feeling as though it were trying to crawl off his body, and a tumbling knot in the centre of his stomach making him feel rather nauseous, Wellington was for once not going to dissuade her. Working for the Ministry usually led to indescribable strangeness, and this felt decidedly otherworldly.

Agent Rateb paused for a moment, as if he too did not want to go any further. He licked his lips. "Lord Alton and the men loved to gamble in the evenings, but as always I was excused at sundown, and I went to prayers. When I left, the barracks had all been locked up for the night. There was nothing extraordinary. I'd gone every evening in the same way..." His voice trailed off as if examining his routine was dreadfully painful. "Except just before I left, Lord Alton's cousin, Seth Taylor, had surprised him with a visit."

"Seth Taylor?" Eliza asked. "Are you certain it was Seth Taylor?"

"Most certain. Lord Alton identified the man. Mister Taylor was quite affable, mentioned that he was on an archeological dig in Akeldama, and decided to surprise his cousin and those who serve with bottles of wine. When I left, Taylor was at the card table with the rest of the officers playing, drinking, laughing..."

Wellington and Eliza shared a glance, and he knew she had also noticed the silence. Wrapping his fingers more tightly about his cane, the archivist jerked his head towards the door. "Show us."

Eliza went in first, but when she came to a sudden stop behind the second door, Wellington almost collided with her...until he saw what had made her halt.

The bodies of ten or so men filled the room, splayed at ungainly angles. Already the whole space was buzzing with flies, even though the blood was fresh. A large, round card table had been tipped over and a soldier, still in his uniform, hanged from the rafters above it. His shiny boots were swinging back and forth to the accompaniment of a creaking rope.

"Bloody hell," Eliza whispered, stepping over the body of another man who had taken a shot to the head.

The three of them circled the room, and Wellington was able to make a count: two hangings, a slit throat, five shootings, and two who were disembowelled. He glanced over at Rateb, and wordlessly the agent pointed out a young man lying under the card table, a sword still protruding out of his belly. Lord Alton had been discovered.

Eliza bent and touched the neck of the nearest body. "Still warm, so it wasn't long ago. But the angle of the hilt and blade —"

"Agent Braun!" Wellington on bending to examine the bodies a little closer saw the problem immediately. He eyed the pistol still in one of the soldier's grips. "This man's head-wound—"

"They all committed suicide," Eliza came to the same conclusion only a beat behind him. She was examining a man with a knife still in his hands and a slit throat. "This poor lad here did himself in...like that."

"So they are all self-inflicted." Wellington stared around the room, which up until very recently ago must have been similar to the barracks he'd been used to when he'd been in the military. "I've never seen anything like it." He turned to

Rateb who was standing at the door, his hands tucked behind his back, and his face stern. "Was Lord Alton in poor spirits?"

Rateb shook his head slowly. "No, not at all. When I left he was laughing and joking along with the rest."

Wellington slowly wandered around the carnage, studying the final moments of the officers. "It is not unheard of for men to go mad, from the sun and heat, or isolation. But none of those were a factor here. And for a madness such as this to affect all of them at once…"

Eliza looked up at the man hanging above the card table. "Could it have been some kind of suicide agreement that you weren't aware of?"

Now Rateb looked more than a little angry. "We are not heathens here, Agent Braun! The Brigade was in good form. At least it was before this happened to our officers…"

"And this cousin of Lord Alton's," Wellington asked, carefully getting down on his knees to examine the chaos of cards and blood on the floor, "is he among the dead?"

Rateb stepped carefully around the room, checking. "No, these are all brigade officers."

Wellington cast a glace around the collected dead, and then bowed his head to whisper a brief prayer. His thoughts scattered, though, when something gleaming caught his gaze. He went to reach for it, but thought better and pulled out a pencil from his top pocket. "Agent Braun," he said, pushing the stained cards aside. "Look at this."

She bent down next to him, inclining her head to one side. "It looks like a coin, but what kind of currency is that?"

When she went to reach for it, he grabbed her arm, and yanked it back. "Let's err on the side of caution, Agent Braun, at least when it comes to handling mysterious objects?" Eliza's brow furrowed. "Do I need remind you of your last assignment in Paris with Agent Thorne?"

"But in that situation, Welly, we *knew* what the artefact was."

"Yes, but did you ever wonder about my predecessor? I've always nursed a lingering suspicion that he had not been so diligent, so look more closely, but don't touch it." Wellington could feel the thrill of discovery course through his veins. "This currency is neither British, nor Egyptian. I believe…" He nudged the coin with his pencil into a handkerchief, and held it up closer to her. "Yes, an Antochan stater. See there—it has the head of the Emperor Augustus on it. It dates back to the Roman occupation of Palestine."

"Very odd thing for a bunch of officers to be wagering with," Eliza commented.

"Yes indeed." He turned to Rateb. "Did you say Lord Alton's cousin had been at a dig in Akeldama?"

The Egyptian agent nodded, his eyes remaining fixed on the gleaming coin.

Wellington couldn't help smiling just a fraction. Could it be that he was actually holding a piece of ancient history in his hand? Something that his friends at the British museum would turn green with envy over?

"Welly!" Eliza snapped, "stop smiling like an idiot and tell us what you know!"

As he poked around the currency, he reminded himself that as amazing as this find could possibly be, this was still the site of an atrocity. "Silver coins, Miss Braun. From an ancient site very near Jerusalem." He gave a soft *"Ah"* as he spied three more coins just like the one in the kerchief. "What—has time in the field erased your memories of Sunday morning church?"

She gave a dry laugh. "My father was a publican. We would be getting the pub ready for the congregation's after church fellowship while the vicar held court."

"Akeldama. The Field of Blood." It was Agent Rateb. His voice sounded hollow, haunted. "This is where Judas Iscariot met his fate betraying the prophet."

"Wait, hold on, mate—you're talking about the Judas Iscariot, as in he who betrayed Jesus Christ?"

"Indeed, and he was paid with thirty pieces of silver." Rateb pointed just in front of him. "There is another coin here."

Wellington pushed the coin into the kerchief. For currency thousands of years old, they gleamed as if minted yesterday. "According to Matthew 27, Judas hanged himself out of guilt. Since those thirty pieces of silver was considered blood money, they refused to return it to the temple's treasury. They instead used the money to purchase a patch of land commonly known as the Potter's Field."

"That's according to Matthew, Welly," Eliza offered. "Acts says that Judas himself used the silver to buy Potter's Field himself, where he then committed suicide." She looked at both men and shrugged. "I said we prepared the pub on Sunday morning. Didn't mean we never cracked open a Bible."

"Scriptures tend to differ on what happened to the thirty pieces," Rateb said, staring at the silver. "Other accounts claim it was melted down. Still more claim the silver was buried with Judas." His breath suddenly caught in his throat. "Gloves."

"Come again?" she asked.

"Taylor. I remember when he was introduced, he was wearing gloves. When I left for prayers, I happened to notice he was still wearing them. I recall thinking how warm his hands must have been."

"So you're saying, and yes, gents, this is for my clarification," Eliza asked as Wellington bunched up the ends of the kerchief and tied them securely, "these five coins are from the thirty Judas Iscariot was paid with for betraying Jesus? That's..."

He raised one finger. "Before you say 'that's impossible' think of the other objects the Ministry has collected over the years."

"But these are only five pieces," Rateb interrupted. "Where's the rest?"

Eliza glanced over the dead soldiers once, then twice. "The one survivor of tonight's card game—Seth Taylor. I didn't realise he was related to the Alton bloodline." She shook her head, looking at the card in her hand. "I've dealt with him before, once in Barcelona, another time in Lisbon. Both times, confrontations involving the House of Usher. We had nothing on him in Spain, but he left quite a trail of evidence in Portugal. Whispers from the House of Lords were hinting that Taylor's uncle was less-than-happy about his nephew's shenanigans."

"And with Lord Alton here dead at his own hand, nothing stands between him and the title." Wellington said, his eyes falling on the gutted aristocrat on the floor. "It's obviously suicide so there's no blood on his hands."

"But there is," Rateb said, his hands clenching into fists. "Lord Alton was a fine young man. He cared about the people of Egypt, he really did, and now..." The agent gestured to the bedlam around them.

"He should pay," Eliza agreed, "And he will."

No sooner were the words out of her mouth, when a hideous commotion broke out in the compound. The wet roars of camels filled the air, and Wellington knew that something had to be terrifying the beasts. Eliza must have come to the same conclusion. She darted out of the room ahead of him.

Wellington managed to grab Eliza just before in front of a camel bolting for the main gate. Astride it was a lean young man, working the skirmish saddlebags with both hands. Gatling guns on each side of the camel twirled and snarled at the gate. The wood surrendered to the assault; and when the doors collapsed to the sand with a groan, the camel and its rider galloped out into the night. Without so much as a "thank you" she dashed for the camel enclosure, swearing loudly. Apparently her disdain for the ships of the desert was not feigned. Wellington and Rateb ran after her.

"Those coins are deadly," Eliza said, grabbing hold of the bridle of the nearest, outraged camel. "Imagine what the House of Usher could do with them!"

Rateb tapped Wellington on the soldier. "Give me the coins you found.

Showing them to Donohue might inspire him to rouse Agent Noujaim and the local authorities."

"Donohue can find us using the ETS rings," he said, handing the cinched kerchief to Rateb.

It took Wellington a moment to remember how; but with the right manipulation of the bridle, he managed to get his chosen mount to flop down on its knees. The skirmish harness each of the brigade camels wore was kept fastened on five camels just in case of raids from the desert tribes. It made the camels harder to handle than usual though.

Eliza let out a little yell as the camel lurched up. "Finishing school never really prepared me for this sort of sport," she said, running her hands over the controls of the saddle's guns. It was a poor joke, since he'd studied her record and Finishing schools had been spared the delight of educating Agent Braun.

"You're never too old for new experiences," Wellington quipped as he mounted the camel and ascended upward.

"I'm liking this side of you, Books, you know that?"

"Yes, and that scares me a bit," and with a cry, Wellington drove his camel into the night with Eliza right behind him.

ELIZA WAS PREPARED for neither the stride of the camel, nor the exhilaration she experienced upon riding it. The warm Egyptian wind caressing her face as she and Wellington closed in on Taylor and, under the full moon's glow, she took everything back she ever considered derogatory about camels.

Cutting through the darkness ahead were an array of torches surrounding the ancient pyramids. It was a safe assumption, based on Taylor's urging of his mount forward, it was not because he wanted to clock in some very late sightseeing.

"Look there!" Wellington shouted above the noise of the camels, pointing just to the right of the pyramid.

Eliza squinted, and could just make out running lights of an airship emerging from the star-filled sky. "It has to be the House of Usher picking up their recruit."

"We can't allow him to reach them!" Wellington shouted, his camel now matching hers.

"Right then," Eliza said, shoving her hands inside the levers of the skirmish saddlebags, "let's see what we have here..."

Wellington's warning was lost in the concussive explosion that shot out from the right saddle compartment.

"Found the rocket launcher!"

Two small explosions briefly overpowered the moon's grey-white luminance. Neither Eliza's nor Taylor's mounts seemed bothered by the ordinance.

"Eliza!"

"Change of strategy!" she shouted just before firing another projectile.

This time, the ordinance exploded in front of Taylor. Much like a horse, the camel concluded that forward was not a wise direction in which to continue, so it stopped abruptly, dropping to its knees in the sand. From the way his arms and legs flailed as he soared into the darkness, it appeared Taylor was not prepared for that.

Wellington and Eliza had brought their own camels to a halt and returned to ground just as Seth Taylor found his footing again. He was now at a dead run, making his way towards the nearest pyramid.

Eliza drew her ponamu pistols and made chase. She had lost him in Portugal. *Not here*, she thought. *Not tonight.*

Above her, the drone of the Usher airship grew louder. Eliza could still make out Taylor in front of her, climbing higher and higher up along the face of the pyramid. She replaced one of her pistols and started her own ascent, but paused on hearing a *clickity-clickity-click-clack* higher up.

The airship was running out a rope ladder and dragging it along the pyramid. She would have to take her stand now.

Eliza stopped, pulled the hammer back on her pistol, and watched the man scrambling just above her. She fired and the shot hit something because she heard Taylor scream and some loose rock roll down the pyramid face. She climbed up another pair of stones, but stopped when a grunt came from Taylor's position. Eliza could just make out the rope ladder in the moonlight, swinging back and forth. On its third pass, Taylor gave a sharp cry and the slack ladder went taught.

"Go on," she whispered as the airship's engines revved.

More loose rock tumbled down the pyramid as the Usher airship lifted Taylor into the night. He swung wide, struggling to hold on to the rung above his head, one leg dangling useless underneath him.

Eliza waited for Taylor to swing back before she fired. He lurched, slipped free of the rope ladder, and slammed into the jagged pyramid face. He rolled down several shelves before coming to a stop, one arm dangling underneath him.

"Bloody good shot, Eliza," Wellington called from underneath her.

Eliza holstered the pistol then looked over shoulder. "Not really, just lucky."

"A lucky shot in the dark?"

"No," she chuckled, "lucky that white is a fashionable colour here in Egypt."

ELIZA ADJUSTED HER sun-spectacles as she watched the gangplank of the *Ra* being pushed out. While her features had been less than affable on their arrival, she seemed a bit regretful to be leaving Cairo. She picked up her cup and saucer and took a contemplative sip of tea.

"There's still so much we could do, Wellington," she said suddenly.

"Agent Braun," Wellington said, setting down his own cup. "Are we going to have this conversation again?"

"Maybe," she said, grinning wryly.

"This is a dangerous game you're playing, Eliza, sneaking in field assignments while we're supposed to be fulfilling archival duties."

"Oh come on, Welly, you are starting to enjoy yourself when we break the rules." Wellington gasped. "I am not!"

Eliza leaned in, pointing an accusatory finger. "Are you going to tell me you did not feel a thrill when you held in your hand the very silver paid to Judas Iscariot?"

He opened his mouth to protest but his throat seized up. Damnable woman. It was just terrible when she was right. "Perhaps," he admitted begrudgingly. "A bit."

"*Ha!* I knew it," she proclaimed, taking a sip of her own tea.

The waiter placed a third setting at their table, and Agent Khaled Rateb joined then, his smile mirroring that of the Egyptian sunshine. Wellington almost failed to recognise him with his cheerful disposition.

"Mr. Rateb," Eliza said, smiling wide, "you're looking considerably happier."

"This is my normal state of affairs," he responded, kissing her offered hand. "I'm afraid you caught me at an inopportune moment." He cleared his throat and shrugged.

"No matter," Wellington responded, toasting him with his teacup. "I'm pleased we happened to be present—" and he stopped to return a stare Eliza was giving him, her accompanying smile far too wicked, "—to assist you."

"As am I." Khaled handed Wellington a polished wooden box that fit neatly in his hand. Carved in it was the Ministry coat of arms. "Here you are. The Cursed Silver of Judas Iscariot."

"Excellent," Wellington said, looking the box over. "It will find a safe and secure home in the Archives."

"I have no doubt."

"You will make sure to keep our involvement to a minimum in your official report?" Wellington asked.

He ignored the soft groan from Eliza.

"I have a few more details to add, but in my preliminary report I made certain that your names appear only as logistical support for the Egyptian office. Have no fear."

"Excellent."

A horn blared from the *Ra*, making their heads turn in that direction.

"There you are. Your voyage home." Khaled pulled out Eliza's chair, then motioned to the airship. "As a token of appreciation, you will be flying First Class."

"Oh, that was not necessary—"

"But we will accept it graciously," Eliza blurted.

"And eagerly, it would seem," Wellington said with his eyebrow quirking.

"Mister Books, Miss Braun," and with a tip of his hat, Khaled took up his tea and departed.

"So where to next?" Eliza asked. "Please say the Bahamas. I can honestly say I have not investigated *any* cases peculiar or otherwise there, so it truly would be a warm getaway." She held up a hand. "But with serious Ministry responsibilities our priority, of course."

"Sadly, no." Wellington pulled out the schedule he and Eliza had left England with. Several offices had been already checked off, and now they were due to head to... "Scotland. Edinburgh offices." He gave a smile and whispered. "Yes, the Edinburgh Express."

Eliza raised a single eyebrow. "Welly?"

"What?"

"You have a look in your eye."

"Oh no," he replied quickly, "No-no-no-no, not at all. It's just..." He looked at the schedule again and nodded. "Eliza, have you ever travelled by hypersteam?"

KHALED RATEB STOPPED in the street to look up. Through the opening between the row housing of Cairo, against a cerulean blue expanse, the *Ra* climbed to its cruising altitude. He was duly impressed with the two archivists, certainly not the idiots that Donohue had initially described to Noujaim and himself.

Then again, this was Donohue. Hardly a man of honesty. Or ethics.

He continued his way through the streets to Miggins Antiquities, up the first staircase to the four desks of the agents' receiving area. Zeyad Noujiam was at his desk, hidden behind the paper. Khaled felt a tightness well in his throat on reading the headline concerning Lord Alton's death. A tragic suicide, and a blow to the spirits of both Egypt and England.

Khaled took in a deep breath and asked in his mother tongue, *"Is he here?"*

His fellow agent glanced over the top of his paper. *"Upstairs,"* he replied before snapping it back up.

He climbed the staircase to enter the proverbial lion's den that was the director's office. The six crates that had held the past decade of cases, more precisely the ones that had captured the interest of Donohue and his predecessor, were now en route to London with Agents Books and Braun.

"I assume you have a reason to be up here, Rateb?"

Marcus Donohue was looking at what appeared to be a gold statue of an Egyptian queen, his latest acquisition from one of the many excavations happening outside of city limits. Fascinating how the British called what they do "archaeology." He thought of those kind of digs as "grave robbing."

"Agents Books and Braun are en route to London, Director."

"I deduced as much on account of the absence of archives." He narrowed his eyes on the inscription etched in the base of the statuette, the magnifying glass seemingly revealing the secrets of its glyphs.

Seconds ticked by. Khaled remained where he was.

"I take it there is something else?" he asked. Khaled noticed the always-present annoyance in his voice sounded more pronounced now.

"Where were you last night?"

That grabbed his attention. "I'm sorry, Agent Rateb, but did you just ask of my whereabouts?"

"Yes, sir. I did."

"And you are asking this because?"

"Yesterday we were on assignment. You assured me last night that you would remain on watch at least until tonight in order to keep watch over Lord Alton."

"Yes, I know," he said, his eyes still on the statuette, not Khaled, "and that didn't work out so well for Alton, now did it?"

"Sir, when you were needed—"

"No, Rateb, no, when *you* were needed," he said matter-of-factly, "you buggered off to pray."

"Director Donohue," Khaled snapped, struggling to keep his composure, "I was given your word that you would be on call. Had it not been for the archivists, I would have been working alone in keeping a dangerous talisman falling in the hands of the House of Usher."

"Yes, I read your report. Had it not been for the archivists, it would have been a lone Egyptian against—now let me see, what was it, ah yes—a lone agent from the House of Usher. Surely you could have handled that." He sat back in his desk, interlocking his fingers together as he considered Khaled. "Or perhaps not. It's as I've always said: throw a monkey in a suit and it's still a monkey." He stood, crossed around his desk, and stood toe-to-toe with Khaled. "Allow me to remind you, Rateb, that if it weren't for the British Empire and our technology you would not be wearing these fine clothes whilst working for the betterment of Her Majesty but rather begging for scraps covered in your own shit!"

Khaled continued to stare forward into space. He did not expect Donohue to raise his voice in such a fashion. Most uncharacteristic of him. Hopefully Zeyad heard that.

"Never question my intent or actions. Ever."

"Yes, sir," Khaled muttered.

Donohue stepped back. "I believe you're done here."

"Actually, sir, before they left, the archivists did inform me that Ministry Headquarters are expecting increased occurrences on account of recent archaeological digs."

The director laughed bitterly. "Is that so? How melodramatic."

"This is why," and Khaled pulled out from his coat pocket Wellington Books' cinched kerchief, "Ministry Headquarters has seen it to to raise your pay. This is an advance."

Donohue froze. "Really?"

"Yes, sir."

Donohue took the kerchief from Khaled's hand, and loosened the knot. "Good Lord!" he gasped, eagerly taking one of the silver coins and holding it underneath the magnifying glass. "This is legitimate currency?"

"Quite."

He chuckled. "I suppose they *are* expecting us to be busy, aren't they?"

"I'll be downstairs if you need me, sir."

As Khaled descended the stairs, he glanced at the director's desk. He silently reminded himself to make certain he got a hold of Agent Book's handkerchief before the investigation launched.

FROM THE PEN OF
MATTHEW DRIGHT

ANTONIA

CLEOPATRA

ANTONIA AND CLEOPATRA

THE PLACE: THE Sahara desert, endless, arid, parched. The time: a little after midday, the merciless sun directly overhead. Somewhere like this, water can be more precious than gold, a drop of moisture worth more than all the riches one can imagine. It was this biological imperative that propelled the mosquito to land on the perspiring forehead of one Corporal Frederick Algernon Hooch, and the very same imperative that drove it to sup eagerly at the rivulet of sweat that tracked down the peaks and troughs of his sunburnt face, past the flick of his moustache, and down to his chin. Corporal Hooch slapped distractedly at his face. Failing to dislodge the insect with brute force, he exhaled heavily in its direction, seeking to dislodge it from its perch. This proved equally ineffective; instead, his moustache simply shivered comically, and he was forced to slap again, with increased force. The mosquito departed unperturbed, buzzing away far from Hooch's reach, where it taunted him with a lazy loop around feet of the sphinxes followed by an unhurried barrel roll around the pillars and a gentle landing upon the weathered nose-stub of the Pharaoh.

"Corporal?"

Hooch scratched his forehead where the mosquito had been, sighed, and turned to squint at the approaching figure. The Lieutenant was barely more than a lad, his face burnt and peeling. He clutched his canteen as if it were the most precious object he'd ever touched. He executed a salute so lazy it bordered on mutinous.

"What is it, lad?" asked the Corporal, though the answer was perfectly clear.

"The men, sir... they were hoping that perhaps we could... stand down?"

"Stand down?" The Corporal huffed and puffed. If there had been enough moisture left in his body, his ears might have steamed. "Stand down! What pultroonery! Need I remind you, Lieutenant, that we are on the hunt for a vagabond at large! A master criminal, Lieutenant Smythe! Shameless scoundrel of the sands..."

"Yes, Corporal, sir," said Lieutenant Smythe wearily.

"We must be alert, and ready! Poised to intercept her unsalubrious exit...!"

The rest of the soldiers all studiously avoided looking in the direction of the conversation, standing rigid to attention with the exaggerated indifference of eavesdroppers. They stood ringed around what might have appeared, to an unstudied viewer, little more than a dip in the ground, punctured in its centre by a half-submerged sandstone block the size and height of a man. The soldiers' rifles pointed in its direction, the bayonets gleaming in the relentless sun.

"Understood, Corporal," said Lieutenant Smythe. "It just... it's been seven hours."

The soldiers continued to, very obviously, exhibit no reactions.

"Absolutely not," said Corporal Hooch firmly. "She could appear at any time!"

For a few moments, not a great deal happened. The sun continued to burn, the sand continued to be sand, the temple ruins continued to be temple ruins. Then, with the air of a man no longer able to contain a sneeze at a funeral, one of the soldiers slapped himself firmly on the cheek, and there was one less mosquito in the world.

The Corporal's shoulders sagged. "Very well, Lieutenant Smythe," he said. "At ease, company."

Amidst a chorus of relieved sighs, the platoon relaxed. The bristling ring of blades dipped, some even boldly laid aside. Lieutenant Smythe bobbed a hurried, thankful salute, and retreated to his men, who slapped him heartily on the back and proffered water tankards, which he declined with a saintly expression on his face.

Corporal Hooch shuffled a little away from the pack. Their youthful bonhomie always made him uncomfortable, made him aware of the creak in his bones, hear the Oxford pedigree in his syllables. "Scoundrel of the sands," he muttered to himself. "That's a good one. The desert desperado. The scallywag of the souks! The Nile—"

He paused.

Beneath his feet, he fancied he felt a faint trembling, as if a herd of animals were stampeding under the sand. He opened his mouth to call to Lieutenant Smythe and the rest of the men, but none of them seemed to have noticed the vibrations. They were all slumped now in the vestiges of shade they could find. Two were even playing cards. He shut his mouth again.

Seconds later, he could ignore the growing shaking no more. "Lieutenant!" he called out, but it was too late.

The sandstone slab they had been guarding so diligently not five minutes before exploded outwards in a rain of shale and billowing sand. The soldiers dived for their rifles, spluttering and half-blind. Triggers were fumbled. There was the sound of bullets ricocheting and panicked shouts.

From out of the maelstrom, a creature leapt. It emerged from the sand, bearing down on Corporal Hooch, who fell back, his hands raised against its onslaught. It's powerful, mechanical legs were a churn of pistons; its jaws champed, levers pumping in its burnished cheeks; its eyes burned with fire from within a bronze skull. On its back, two bronze mountains—no, *humps*—jettisoned steam.

Gadzooks, thought Corporal Hooch as he fell beneath its galloping metal hooves, *it's a bloody camel*.

The Corporal's men made a shambolic attempt at pursuit, but they were outstripped in seconds. Somewhere, Lieutenant Smythe was shouting: *Kneel! Fire!* The platoon fell to their knees in ragged formation, raising their rifles and taking aim, but the bullets merely pinged off the animal's metal exterior, rebounding into the desert wastelands.

Atop the mechanical creature, a small figure was perched between the humps. The figure was female, diminutive, and clad in a strange mix of colonial military jacket and corseted bustle. Against the barrage of bullets, she clutched a dented pith helmet to her head. A mass of wild black hair streamed from beneath it as she galloped away from them on her steed.

Faintly, she could be heard, in a smoky, joyful voice, shouting, "Geronim-*whoooooaaaaa!*" as the mechanical camel bucked.

"After her!" screamed the Colonel, dragging himself up from his undignified position on the floor. "Post haste! Make chase! The fiendish floozy!" The soldiers continued to fire, and he stomped out in front. "I said *after* her! Don't you know who she is! Antonia Jones, plunderer of the pyramids, pilferer of the pharoahs! *Apprehend her at once!*"

"Pursue her, men!" ordered Lieutenant Smythe, and at his word, the soldiers made for the corral of horses, galloping after her.

"That woman!" Corporal Hooch muttered, dusting himself down. "I have never encountered such a *larcenous* woman! Such a..." He cast around for words.

Beneath Hooch and Smythe the ground was continuing to shake. "Corporal," Lieutenant Hooch said, shaking his superior by the arm. "Corporal!"

"Such a... *what* is the word?"

From the shadowed hole through which Miss Jones had torn free of the sands, there came a sound: a skittering, hopping sound, the sound of many things moving in the dark at once.

"Such a... a..." Corporal Hooch continued to stare at after the departed fugitive.

"*Corporal!*"

A single, lone figure emerged from the hole. A statue, cast from clay, the size of a short man. Its face was painted in the simple, Egyptian style that adorned a thousand artefacts in a thousand museums across the world. Its mouth opened, wider than seemed entirely human, splitting at its painted lips, and what lay within was most definitely not of clay: sharp, canine teeth chittered in the rotten, festered mouth of a corpse long-dead.

It hopped forward, bouncing on legs that had been formed together by some ancient artisan. Lieutenant Smythe raised his rifle in shaking hands, but the strange-statue creature didn't flinch. Instead, it opened its dead man's mouth, and emitted a high-pitched, keening scream.

Behind it, from deep beneath the Egyptian sands, called up from the catacombs and burial chambers that lay beneath the temple, more of them came, teeming from the gloom to stand rank behind their horrifying leader.

"...a *magnificent* woman," Corporal Hooch said, turning. "That's it. *Magnificent*—oh my sainted aunt!"

He was thrust aside by the first statue-creature, and then barged and flung out of the way by a succession of them as they streamed between Hooch and Smythe. Their mouths opened in unison, screeching their chilling cry to the empty skies, hopping implacably towards the horizon, the direction in which Miss Jones, perched gloriously atop her dromedary automaton, was dashing herself.

THE PLACE: THE Wagh El-Birket district, Cairo. The time: the purpling dusk.

Night settled over the Nile, the darkness creeping up the warren of narrow streets into the district, swallowing up the dancing girls who turned and swayed, the lairy soldiers who drank and whistled, the pantalooned men who watched and scorned. In the gloom the streets came alive with a new energy, like a caged animal prowling behind bars. On the surface there was warmth and light: the lanterns of the brothels warm and tempting, the drunken babble in a myriad of languages, the mingled aroma of roasting meat and hashish. Underneath it, unspoken and menacing, an undercurrent of silk-wrapped, shadowy secrecy, held in the dark hollows of the alleyway girls' eyes, in the cudgelled, jealous glances between the locals and the uniformed British, in the rustle of robes pulled up in discrete doorways, the clink of exchanged coin. This, *this* was why people came to Wagh El-Birket.

Where the banks of the river and the city met was a rickety dockland, strung with red lanterns. The incline of the streets and the narrow jetty conspired to point the stumbling footsteps of the needy in the direction of what lay floating atop the waters: the Elysium Parlour. But of course, you've heard of the Elysium Parlour haven't you? The boat, in a ragtag collection of shapes and colours. You heard tell of its bizarre and long-forgotten origins: beginning life as a Chinese junk, or a Spanish galleon perhaps, though who can tell anymore? It's a patchwork boat, built from the body parts of other boats, stitched together with lanterns and blind hope. You've heard about its cabins piled on top of galleys, walkways piled on top of gantries until it resembles a teetering castle, complete with spires and gambrel roofs. You've heard about the silks fluttering at its door, enticing.

At the edge of the dock, a figure, short but feminine in shape, shrouded in a cloak both too thick and too dark for the humid heat, lurked, watching. With an air of concealment, it looked once left, once right, then scurried to enter.

Inside, hookahs breathed sweet smoky clouds into the air; women bound in silks and little else lounged on fine throws and cushions. Men, of all shapes and sizes, were attending to the women: intimately entangled, subservient or looming dominant depending on the size of their evening's pay or their particular speciality. In one corner, a gimlet-eyed Turk juggled bottles, poured the contents into a row of silver glasses, and set their tops alight in one theatrical flourish. Facing him across the sea of sensuous bodies, a small stage was lit by rheumy footlights, upon which a woman, naked but for the layers of gold paint, clutched a live, writhing snake to her breasts and recited petrarchan sonnets.

And if you've heard about the rest of the Elysium Parlour, of course you already know what else lurks within: beneath all of this saturnalia, below the feet of the patrons and the girls, below the hookahs and the cushions, the floor was glass. The murky green of the Nile curdled underfoot and, under the ample buttocks of a lady spread beneath the ministrations of a turbanned Arab, a crocodile blinked bewildered at the strange scene above him.

The Madame of the house swept forward, statuesque, leatherclad, a whip coiled at her waist.

"*Welcome* to the Elysium Parlour," she said, well-rehearsed intimations of depravity flavouring each syllable. "The jewel of the Nile, the Sultan's spicy secret, the answer to your heart's wanton cry. *I* am the famous Madame Cleopatra Bonny." She traced a finger along the whip lazily. "You may have heard me referred to as the Iron Mistress. The *ashikret al-hadikh,* also."

"Really, my dear," said the cloaked figure, "you *must* get a real job." She pulled back her cloak, revealing her face.

"Ah," said the Iron Mistress. "Good evening, mother."

THUS IT WAS that the two most infamous ladies in Egypt sat down to tea and cucumber sandwiches.

The first, the lady Antonia Jones, renowned relic-thief and intrepid defiler of tombs, pyramids and necropolises, wanted in sixteen countries of Africa (as well as Tibet, Japan and Wales.)

The second, her daughter Cleopatra Bonny, possessing of both her mother's bosom and beauty, but rising a foot in height above the maternal curls of Antonia. The Iron Mistress, the madame of the Elysium Parlour, purveyor of peoples of pecuniary persuadability into passionate pacts, who had sailed her glass-bottomed brothel around half the world or more, before fetching up here, on the shrouded banks of the Nile, in Cairo.

"What *is* it?" asked Cleopatra, tilting her head.

Between them, a clay pot sat on the table amongst the tea-things. Its head was carved into the shape of a pharaoh, outlined in faded, red paint. In the hollows of its eyes, something gleamed. It was, in Cleopatra's considered opinion, singularly unremarkable.

"It's rather less than impressive, isn't it?" Antonia said, sipping her tea daintily. Held in her callused hands and against her sand-blasted, filthy face, it looked like an absurd, fripperous trinket.

"All that way—risking all sorts of danger for... *this?*"

"I was given very specific instructions," Antonia said. "Drawings. Descriptions. It's not even made of gold, but apparently its very valuable. The client was quite firm on the matter."

Cleopatra unhooked her whip and laid it beside the teapot. "Who's the client?"

"I have no idea," said Antonia. "We never met face to face." She set down her teacup and looked around the anteroom. "You really must have a tidy up around here," she said, tartly. "It's all a bit... bohemian, wouldn't you say?"

"Mother," said Cleopatra, refilling her teacup firmly, "I'm a brothel madam. We're hardly in the market for stuffiness and starch. Why, for Cairo, we're the very *lap* of luxury. Stop avoiding my questions. Mysterious client. Elaborate."

Antonia wrinkled her nose. "Brothel madam," she sighed. "So common."

"Internationally wanted thief," Cleopatra rejoindered. "So *criminal*."

"Perhaps," Antonia said, "but never *common*."

There was a knock at the door, followed by the tousled head of a young boy. "Missus said you wanted me, ma'am?"

Cleopatra waved towards her mother. "Thank you, Aziz. This poor down-on-her-luck beggar from the street requires some errands to be run."

Antonia rummaged in her pack, producing a clutch of folded parchments and a handful of an odd, shiny material.

"Is that *steel wool?*" said Cleopatra.

"Yes," Antonia said. "Aziz, take this to wherever you've stabled Barnabus and feed this to him. He gets hungry about this time. This should do it. His furnace will need stoking, too."

"Yes'm," said Aziz.

Antonia handed him the letters and a handful of paistres. "Deliver these to their addresses," she told him. "The blank one goes to The Eyes of the Sky. I'm sure you'll know how to pass a message." Aziz retreated.

Cleopatra arched an eyebrow. "The Eyes of the Sky?" she said. "He's... not a man to be trifled with, shall we say. Is he your client? I thought you didn't know..."

"I don't," Antonia said. "But if anyone knows the competitive value of things in this city, it's him."

"Dangerous game, mother," Cleopatra said.

"Perhaps," Antonia said, "but so is running a house of ill repute in the heartland of syphilis."

"It'll probably turn out to be worthless," Cleopatra said. "Wild goose chase—I'd put money on it. The Eyes of the Sky won't give you a handful of coin, and your mysterious client will have vanished. If he was a client at all. He could have been sending you into a trap, trying to catch the ignominious Lady Thief of the Deserts."

Of course, if they packaged it up and sent it off to London it'd would probably still fetch a decent price, where the populace grew ever more giddy at the faintest whiff of Egyptian history, fuelled by penny-dreadfuls and the lurid tales of expats. Even the status of her mother, the elusive master thief who shamelessly robbed her homeland of its treasures, would likely add a frisson to such a sale. But Cleopatra kept quiet about that.

"There *were* a good deal of soldiers camped out waiting for me," Antonia mused. "I didn't pay much attention to them. I was too busy with more... *interesting* encounters."

"Spare me the details," Cleopatra said.

"Oh, my dear, not *that* kind of encounter. No—something darker and more monstrous I fear, lurking amidst the cobwebs of the tomb. But no matter—I evaded them. Thanks to good old Barnabus."

Cleopatra leaned closer to the curio. "Shall we... take a look inside?"

"Tamper with the goods?" Antonia said, aghast. Then, after a moment's consideration: "Oh, go on then."

They cleared the table, setting the delicate tea-things aside and removing the white lace cloth. Antonia produced a set of delicate instruments in a leather case from her seemingly bottomless bag; Cleopatra fetched a gaslamp from the cupboard and opened its flame. They had just bent to their task when they were interrupted by a knock at the door, and a stifled, nervous voice announced, "Madame Bonny! The donkey is in the stable."

"It's a camel," Antonia said. "And we know. We sent Aziz down not two—"

"That's not what she means," Cleopatra said, sweeping the statuette off the table and seizing her whip.

"Well, what in heaven's name does it mean, then?"

Cleopatra pursed her lips. "It means, oh miscreant-mother-mine, that the *law* is here."

CORPORAL HOOCH FIXED his eyes firmly on Cleopatra's nose. Her eyes burnt too fiercely for him to quite dare meet her eye to eye, and to look elsewhere—be it further south on her body, or in any direction about the Parlour—was altogether too dangerous to risk. Thus, he addressed her nostrils: "We are in search of a fugitive, ma'am. We have reason to believe you can help us with your enquiries."

Madame Bonny shifted, rolling her hips and tutting her lips theatrically. "A fugitive, sir? Oh, how thrilling. But no, no, nothing of that sort here."

Hooch dared to swivel his eyes a hairsbreadth to the left. Undulating bosoms swung into view, and he quickly looked back. "We have... information," he said, the words tripping over his tongue, "that suggests we are likely to find her in your... establishment."

Madame Bonny's lips formed a little O of shock, which she held a fraction too long. "Oh my! Sir, you shock me. No—not hide nor hair of a woman, fugitive or otherwise. Pray tell, who exactly is this person you seek?"

"She's... well... I don't quite know how to describe her. She's—somewhat short. Although, not in the way of a, er, gremlin, or such. Really quite—um—handsome. She is—well—"

Clearing his throat, Lieutenant Smythe stepped forward, interrupting his superior. "Perhaps this will help," he said, and produced a parchment on which was sketched a charcoal likeness of Antonia. The word 'magnificent' went unheard, mumbled into Hooch's moustache.

"That woman?" Cleopatra spat on the floor; it pooled above a submerged lilypad. "That *qahbaa!*"

"You know her?"

"Know her?" Cleopatra was practically apoplectic, waving her whip around above her head. "She's a filthy beggar from the district. Used to daily entreat me to come work at my fine establishment. I would tell her *no* and throw her out immediately. Why, she's ancient enough to be someone's mother. We would never have one so *old* or *common* here!"

From somewhere distant to the chamber, there was the pointed sound of something smashing.

Lieutenant Smythe possessed none of Hooch's shyness, and boldly stared around the room; the girls quailed beneath his gaze, as did those men sober enough to fathom the situation. "Is that so?" he said. "Work here, is that it? And this establishment is of course a—"

"—temple of religious worship," Cleopatra supplied. "The men come to consult my gurus on the matters of spirituality. Quite legally."

"Gurus," said Lieutenant Smythe.

"I promise you," Cleopatra said, "a visit to the Elysium Parlour is a *heavenly* experience. Isn't it—Private Lopjollop?"

Behind Smythe and Hooch, a soldier did his best to become very small and inconspicuous.

"Well," Lieutenant Smythe said, smiling sweetly, "if this woman should appear again, seeking employment... as a guru... please do inform the authorities immediately."

Hooch piped up, feeling it was time to take control of the situation. "Yes, quite right, little lady," he said. "This terrible, nefarious, beautiful woman *must* be brought to justice at once. I must get my hands on her!"

Cleopatra bobbed a curtsey. "But of course," she said. "I will immediately inform yourselves, good sirs, have no fear! The very moment I see her, that common fishwife."

The sound of the soldiers shuffling awkwardly back down the gangplank covered the sound of a second something smashing on the other side of the wall.

"Of course they would have been watching," Cleopatra told her mother, as they wound their way through the night streets. Music and singing, and the stamp of hundreds of feet, could be heard a few streets away, but here in the warren, following the lines on the scrap of parchment in her hand, there was no-one to be seen—as if they knew to avoid these streets in particular.

"No doubt," said Antonia. "Though they would have to have been particularly dedicated to have observed our passing tonight. And much sharper than I believe our Colonel Hooch is capable of."

Cleopatra craned her neck. "Hooch? Is that his name?"

"I know," said Antonia. "Ridiculous name for a ridiculous man."

The soldiers posted along the dock hadn't been particularly subtle. Despite their best efforts at appearing undercover, a white face stood out a mile in Wagh El-Birket, no matter how assiduously it was draped in robes. Aziz had returned, bringing with him reports of the watchers on the dock, and a note for Antonia.

"The Eyes of the Sky wants to see us," she said. "He's left us a map to find him."

Aziz pointed out the window. "But—the men!"

Cleopatra ruffled his hair. "I suppose we'll have to go the wetter way," she said. And they had—over the edge of the deck at the rear of the boat, swimming silently along the darkened Nile until they could alight from the river downstream, away from the watchful gaze of the soldiers.

And now they were here, in an area of the city where even Cleopatra felt a tingle of nervousness, deep in her belly, warning her. No matter how hard she tried, she couldn't shake the feeling of being watched.

"I'm quite lost," she told her mother. "We're going to have to follow the map back, otherwise we might never make it out of this warren."

"Nonsense," Antonia said. She thrust the bag containing the statuette into Cleopatra's arms, and snatched the parchment. The map was leading them deeper, to a point marked with a round, black spot. The music and singing was fading. "Just a few more turns."

"I'm warning you, mother," Cleopatra said. "I've never met the Eyes of the Skies—but I've heard plenty about him."

"If you think this is the first slumlord ruffian I've ever encountered," Antonia said, "then it's high time I told you some bedtime stories, my dear."

The music and singing was gone from earshot—which was when Cleopatra realised that one sound had not faded. The stamp of feet.

"Mother—"

The wall to their left disintegrated into a hail of adobe chips and billowing stone dust. From out of the cloud marched—no, *hopped*—a creature the like of which Cleopatra had never seen, the size of a man, but made of clay or stone, it's mouth open and screaming.

It wasn't alone.

"Run!" Cleopatra and Antonia screeched to each other at the same time.

They hurtled away, the map and their destination forgotten, taking turns at random, with the legion stamp of the statue creatures in pursuit. The tight-knit twist of streets would have been easy to lose a human pursuer in—a quick turn down a forking alley, a duck into shadow—but misdirection or subterfuge was useless; the statue squadron tore through anything it its path. Awnings, trees, carts: all were shredded in their implacable hopping path, marching furiously with their festered mouths opening and closing in sinister shrieks.

"Ready!" called a man's voice from somewhere nearby. Then, more panicked: "Aim! *Fire!*"

A parade of bullets slewed into the front ranks of the statue creatures. Where they found their target, shards blossomed like fireworks, but it slowed their progress not a jot. They bounded onwards with jagged holes in their torsos, limbs hanging askew. A second round of bullets rallied against them—and it seemed as if their salvation was coming from nowhere until Cleopatra's brain caught up and she recognised the voice.

"Fire!" hollered Lieutenant Smythe, and quieter, a fraction behind, a "Yes, fire!" from a flustered, red-faced Corporal Hooch.

The soldiers were emerging from the side alleys, rifles blasting in their hands against the charging army of monsters. It seemed to finally halt their progress—or at least divert their attention. As one, the statue creatures turned to advance upon the soldiers, the two forces ranged against each other across the the narrow street, the ground littering with rubble and bullet casings.

"Mother!" screeched Cleopatra. "Are these...things...what you encountered'?"

Antonia daintily adjusted her hat. "Yes, dear," she said.

"I'm thinking..."

"Run?"

"Run."

"Oi there!" shouted Colonel Hooch, lurking behind his men. "You're not going anywhere!" His words fell on deaf ears—or deaf backs; Cleopatra and Antonia were already madly dashing away from the melee. "Stop right there!" And with that, he abandoned his platoon and took off, huffing and puffing, in his own pursuit, calling after them almost pleadingly.

He caught up with his quarries in a blind alley.

"Hold up right there," he said, between breaths, brandishing his revolver. "You *fine* ladies are under arrest."

Antonia and Cleopatra caught each others eyes as they turned from the blank wall.

"Now really, Corporal," Antonia said, stepping closer. "Is that quite necessary? I'm sure you could turn a blind eye. Just for tonight. I could... *reward* you." She draped a hand around the Corporal's neck. His huffing and puffing redoubled. "My daughter here has a fine establishment where we can be alone. I mean... it's a bit bohemian for my tastes, but—nevermind, I'm sure you'd ·be *quite* comfortable..."

Corporal Hooch spluttered. "Well—that's a fine offer—and you're a fine woman—but—*duty*, you see—"

"I quite understand," Antonia said. "An upstanding man like you, that just *thrills* me. I wonder... are you quite as *upstanding*... in the boudoir?" She leaned close.

"Well—I—er—I must confess, you've quite unmanned me, miss..."

"Indeed, it seems I have," Antonia said, stepping away, the Corporal's pistol twirling elegantly on one finger. "I suggest you turn around, Corporal, and forget you ever saw us."

"Oh," he whispered, almost to himself. "I could *never* do that."

"Put the gun down!"

Over Hooch's shoulder, Lieutenant Smythe advanced, his rifle aimed squarely at Antonia. She sighed, and let the pistol fall, stepping back towards Cleopatra. "Oh fine. What do they say in the penny dreadfuls? It's a fair cop, guv'nor."

More soldiers were assembling behind Smythe, uniforms ripped, some nursing bloodied faces. They too aimed their rifles.

The stamp could still be heard, drawing quickly nearer.

"I suspect," said Antonia, "you should arrest us with all due haste. I don't think you've held off our mutual friends for very long."

"Kneel down," Lieutenant Smythe ordered.

"Poor you, dear," Antonia said to Cleopatra. "Always a bus-man's holiday."

"Mother," said Cleopatra, enunciating carefully. "Hold my hand."

"Hold your hand? Don't be silly, my dear. They're not going to execute us. How mawkish of you. I raised you better than that."

"Mother," Cleopatra repeated. At the length of the street, the statue creatures had reappeared, bounding towards them with savage glee. "Hold. My. Hand."

And, with that, they were fifty feet above the city.

One second she was mired in their blind alley, the next Antonia was soaring upwards, into the warm night air, whipping up through the clouds. The city receded below, her feet scudding over the domed rooftops. She was above the battleground, a ranged fight as the soldiers and the statue widened, the chaos becoming bloodier.

For a moment, she thought that perhaps, at the most fortuitious of moments, she had sprouted wings and taken flight, but then she gathered her wits enough to look upwards. Cleopatra was splayed in mid-air, the arm pointing downwards clutching Antonia's wrist, the other upwards to a dangling rope. Following this lifeline, it vanished into the belly of an airship that loomed above them, though at this angle, and partially obscured by cloud, there was little more visible than a mossy keel and the suggestion of the huge balloon from which is hung.

The hull of the ship was carved and shaped into the visage of Horus, its round angry eyes glaring down at the rooftops of Cairo.

"Tremendous!" she hollered against the wind. "We found our destination! The Eyes of the Skies has found us!"

"*Ladies!* You—are—under—arrest!"

Antonia glanced back down, momentarily dizzied by the fast-receding skyline, then swore richly. Clutched to her ankle was an unexpected passenger.

"Under arrest, I tell you!" shouted Colonel Hooch.

Antonia waggled her foot, attempting to dislodge him, then—gauging the potentially fatal distance to the ground below—thought better of it. Instead, she opted for appealing to Hooch's better instincts.

"Oh, lay off, you buffoon," she shouted down.

"How dare you! I am a member of Her Majesty's finest!"

"Mother!" Cleopatra's call was frantic, drawing Antonia's attention—but too late. Spreadeagled as she was, with both arms fully occupied, Cleopatra could do nothing to intervene. The bag strung over her shoulder—the unremarkable artifact at the heart of their current travails tucked neatly inside—was falling open.

The pharaoh head of the statuette emerged from the bag, like a curious cat, and then—painfully slowly, inevitably—it tumbled out.

Antonia snatched with her spare hand, but it bounced through her fingers, plummeting downwards towards the vanishing city.

"And I am certainly no buffoon!" Hooch cried upwards, which was all he managed before the statuette struck him squarely on the temple. It shattered, bathing him in a fine, diaphanous sand. His head lolled, unconscious and his fingers opened around Antonia's ankle. She swung wildly to grab him; the corpulent Corporal might be intent on arresting her, but letting him plummet to his death wasn't all that attractive a prospect either.

"Well," she shouted up to Cleopatra, "at least that's shut him up."

For a moment it looked as if the airship above them was descending, and then her brain realigned and as she realised that, no, *they* were being drawn up, wound into the belly of the ship, under the savage beak of the eagle.

"IT WERE," REMARKED the Eyes of the Sky, "tremendous valuable. I woulda been prepared to offer ye a deal more than yer client. If ye hadn't gone'n beaned this poor bloke on t'head and lost it."

He was sat cross-legged in what was most accurately described as a throne, swathed in purple velvet robes that would have seemed ostentatious—even ridiculous—in a person of less poise and threat. With each word he spoke, there was a glimpse of teeth, filed to points. The top half of his face was hidden by a silver mask, fashioned into the visage of Horus. A cruel beak overshadowed most of his lower face, and the eyes of the mask, unmoving and dead, pinned them unblinkingly.

"Perhaps," said Antonia. "It is a great loss to be sure, though one feels that if you had arranged a more traditional transit to your abode, we might not have been in the position to disperse the goods over *the whole of bloody Cairo*."

The Eyes of the Sky chuckled, licking his teeth. "Ye talk pretty," he said. "And you talk clever." He ran a finger up the delicate carved inlay of his throne, rough yellow fingernails counting out the notches. "I like pretty," he said, each syllable as sharp as his teeth. "I don't like clever."

"Since we're here," Antonia said, "perhaps you could illuminate my daughter and I. We were curious you see—quite a few people seem to be have gone to some lengths to retrieve our poor deceased artefact. It was very well protected." She peeked over the boom to the city below. "Still is."

The Eyes of the Sky leaned forward; Horus, despite its fixed expression, looked affronted. "Ladies, what t'hell do you fink I am? Does this *look* like a library."

Alexandria had to admit that the poop deck of the airship did not, in point of fact, look like a library. It was a little heavy on armed pirates for that.

"I'm not a bloody curator," the Eyes of the Sky continued. "Do you know who I *am*?"

It was hard not to know who he was, not in Cairo. It was whispered that he owned most of the dignitaries in town—Egyptian, British, French, it didn't matter—and half the army majors too. And that was the tip of the iceberg. Stories abounded. Men scooped up from the street by the ghostly airship, found days later killed in horrific, though inventive, ways. The philandering sheik dissolved in a bathtub of leeches. The swindling oil trader, force-fed hunks of bread containing scorpions. The crooked consulate, left mummified alive in the baking sun on the steps of the Consulate.

"No," said Alexandria, "I can't say as I do really."

"But," said Cleopatra, "we know you were interested in what we were selling, which means you know *why* it's valuable. And since I've been attacked by statues and swung through the sky all for nothing—the least I'd like is an explanation."

The Eyes of the Sky rose, and walked to the edge of the deck, a king surveying his kingdom. "A *khat nejena*. A soul prison."

"A soul prison?" Cleopatra asked.

"It was only fer the greatest men of Egypt," the Eyes of the Sky said. "The Heka, they had t'power—to preserve the soul, in a vessel. Went against all the laws of the gods, but it could be done. So's it could be returned to 'em at a later time in history. To claim their glorious reward, presumably. Course, it meant they were kept out of the claws of Anubis. Suspended between life and death. Anubis wouldnae like things like that. They'd be damned when they finally made it to t'Underworld."

"But it's just a clay statue. One myth is as good as another. The ancient gods aren't real, they're just another paper pantheon. They died out."

The Eyes of the Skies' teeth glinted in the moonlight as he smiled. "Mayhap," he said.

"So what—drag these soul prisons out somewhere down the line, pop the soul back into another body, off they toddle?" Antonia asked. "Bit of a kerfuffle, given they'll end up with eternal damnation."

"That's why it was for only the greatest, bravest of pharaohs," the Eyes of the Sky said. "Or craziest. They were buried deep, protected by their *shabtis*— the statues built to defend them against harm and evil."

"The hoppy creatures," Cleopatra said.

"Yes. *Shabtis.* Implacable, inhuman, and unlikely to stop until they've recovered the *khat nejena* in their care. Or the soul is restored to a body."

"Well that's just spiffing," said Antonia. "Seeing as I don't have it."

Cleopatra peered over the rail. "They seem quiet enough now," she said.

"Yes," said the Eyes of the Sky. "Funny, that. Vanishes just at the convenient time, don't it, your precious cargo?"

"I can assure you it's most certainly *not* convenient," Antonia said.

The Eyes of the Sky stalked toward her. Around, the casually alert crew stiffened, and reached for their weapons. He cupped her cheek. "Perhaps, m'dear. Perhaps. You know—I'd pay a great deal to have a soul trap. 'N if I thought someone was hiding it from me—"

"I assure you," Cleopatra told him, seeking to distract him from her mother, "it's definitely gone. Smashed open on the good Colonel's head. Nowt but dust and shrapnel by now."

The teeth clacked together smartly. "Prove it," he said.

On the deck, the previously comatose body of Colonel Hooch sat bolt upright, as if awoken from a dream. "𓂀𓏏𓅱𓆣𓏤𓈖" he announced. "𓂋𓏤𓂀𓇳"

"That should do it," said Antonia.

"You don't understand, we need to see Sephiroth *right now*," Cleopatra said.

The girl squinted at her through the narrow crack in the door.

"Right now!" Cleopatra repeated.

"You will meet a dark and bloody death," the girl said.

"Bull!" Cleopatra retorted. "I know exactly who you are, Tawaret. You weren't a mouthpiece of the spirits last I checked. Though you were promising that you were the best in the Sahara at giving b—"

"But stranger, you will find many fortunes before your untimely demise at the hands of the cruel desert and the merciless sun!"

"Tawaret, you know exactly who I am. I'm the Iron—"

The door slammed, then reopened a second later. The girl curtseyed them inside. "I predict many mysteries and pleasures for you," she said.

"𓀀𓅱𓂀𓆓𓇳" said Colonel Hooch.

"What on earth's he jabbering about now?" asked Antonia.

The Eyes of the Skies, his blade resting against the base of Hooch's spine, just above his bound hands, snickered coldly. "Not for your pretty ears to hear," he said.

"The language is old," Antonia said.

"Well 'course. It ain't tripped off t'tongue in centuries."

Cleopatra advanced on the girl. "Now—I know this operation. I am not looking for trinkets. I am not looking for fortunes. I do not need to know I will meet a tall handsome stranger, because I employ plenty of my own. I need the *real* service—understand?"

Tawaret cringed. "The spirits grant us many wisdoms."

"I *need*," Cleopatra said, "to see Sephiroth. Now"

"I see... I see... I see a man who was wandered many leagues from his home."

"Don't give me that!" Cleopatra said.

"A man who cannot linger long in his domain at the behest of his burning loins!"

Cleopatra sighed, and fingered her whip. "Tawaret, let me explain a few things to you. It's been a long night. I'm here with my dodgy mother, an even dodgier gangster, and what is—if things are really to be believed—the disembodied soul of Khufu I in the body of a rather hairy British officer. I'm in need of a Heka, and there aren't many around these parts any more. Show me to Sephiroth, or I'll show myself. Through you."

The face of Horus interjected itself over Cleopatra's shoulder. "I have a chest full of ravenous scarabs in the cart, if that helps?" it inquired helpfully.

Tawaret stamped her foot, glaring. "I see *a man who is not here*."

"Well then," Cleopatra demanded, "where is he?"

"It's a small world," Antonia said.

"Not so much as you'd suppose," Cleopatra said. "He's here more nights than not. He's a big fan of Nyssa. She does things that—well—"

The Eyes of the Sky flourished his knife. "Can we get on," he said. "Things to do, people to exorcise."

"⸢𓀀𓏤𓇋𓆓𓈖𓂋𓏤⸣" spat Hooch.

"Not since I were a lad," the Eyes of the Sky said.

Blasting into the Parlour, Cleopatra lay about her with alacrity, puncturing the languid malaise of the late evening's work. "Fetch Nyssa and Sephiroth!" she demanded. The girls scattered, leaving a confused heap of addled men beached on the floors, blinking at their hookahs and squeezing their empty pockets. Cleopatra strode across the room, not bothering to step over the bodies where she encountered them, eliciting pained squeaks from those unlucky enough not to roll away quickly enough. In the doorway leading into the heart of the Parlour, she hollered after the scurrying feet: "And quickly!"

"Madame Bonny," Sephiroth said, when he had been fetched, half-clothed, red-faced and still tying his robe.

"Sephiroth," she said, snapping her fingers. "Time to unsaddle the powders and chantings. Unleash the unctions and bones. I've got a job for you."

"Uh—" he stumbled for words, and Cleopatra cracked her whip.

"Oh, for crying out loud, Sephiroth. I know Nyssa's good, but she can't have knocked your senses clean out." She pointed at Hooch. "Soul trap. Statue go boom, Hooch go pharaoh."

Sephiroth threw himself down at Hooch's feet, bowing and scraping.

"Oh for crying out loud," Cleopatra said, poking him with the toe of her boot.

"𓏏𓏏𓏏 𓃭𓇌𓈖𓏤!" Hooch said, pleased.

"You need to get it out of him," Cleopatra said.

"No! No!" Sephiroth looked aghast, as if Cleopatra had desecrated his home in front of him. "Sacred!"

"Yes, probably," Cleopatra said. "Sacred pharaoh, I get it. But do you really want the sacred spirit of a pharaoh... in *that* body?"

"THEY'RE ON THE docks," Aziz said, peering into the door. Sephiroth was circling the room, chanting words Cleopatra had never heard spoken before, his eyes half-lidded, his concentration total. He had chalked hieroglyphics onto the floor in a circle, in the centre of which sat an engraved statuette of Anubis. (At first no-one had been quite sure how to get hold of that, but it was surprising what sort of trinkets could be found at short notice in Wagh El-Birket.)

"The *shabtis* or the soldiers?" Antonia asked. She was pacing by the door, turning her pith helmet over and over in her hands.

"Both," Aziz said. "On either side."

The Eyes of the Skies frowned. His knife was still held warningly against Hooch, who was now seated in an armchair, muttering happily to himself in an unintelligible language. "And they're not... doing anything?"

"No," said Aziz, peeking out of the window.

"Why are they not tearing each other apart?" said Cleopatra.

"They're waiting," Antonia said. "The *shabtis* for their pharaoh, the soldiers for them to make the first move."

"Be that as it may," Cleopatra said, "but they *will* move."

"Yes," said Antonia. "I imagine so."

"Right then," Cleopatra said, and stalked out.

In the main chamber of the Elysium Parlour, Cleopatra took the stage. "Ladies!" she called. "Attend!" and waited as the girls gathered from every twisted intestine of the boat. The threat of danger had spread through the Parlour quickly; they were restless and wild-eyed.

"Something is coming," Cleopatra said. "Thanks to the ministrations of my mother—a woman capable of getting into just as fine a mess as myself on occasion—we will shortly be called up on to fight for our lives against two forces. One, horrifying monsters from the margins of history. The other, British soldiers. I shall leave it up to your discretion to decide which to be more afraid of." She paused. "I'm fairly clear, myself."

She rested a boot on the footlight, spread her arms wide, a warrior princess addressing her tribe.

"Girls," she said, "we will take up arms, and we will fight them! We will not be alone. The Eyes of the Skies' minions shall rain down fiery tears upon our attackers. And here—in our home—we shall make our stand! Take up anything you can consider a weapon." Conspiratorially, she added: "I have discovered in my time that a hatpin in certain sensitive areas is quite effective."

Antonia bobbed her head in. "Not to interrupt the rousing speech," she said, "but Sephiroth is ready."

"Very well," Cleopatra said. "Ladies—do me proud."

They raised a cheer for her—a weak one, though perhaps in the circumstances it could be excused—and she stepped down amongst them, directing them towards the accoutrements of the Parlour that could be turned to violence.

From the anteroom, chanting began.

"He's started," said Antonia.

IT WAS A bloodbath.

The second the chanting began, Hooch's eyes flew wide. He stood straight up and screamed, "𓃀𓃀𓃀𓃀𓃀𓃀𓃀"

Attack.

On the dock, *shabtis* took up an excited hopping and hurtled forward as one towards—not the boat—but the platoon. The soldiers raised their rifles, their shots proving as ineffective as in their last encounter. Lieutenant Smythe— gibbering in terror at the head of his troops—led a ragtag retreat to the doors of the Parlour, only to be met by a bristling array of makeshift weapons. Curling tongs, fire irons, flails and pleasure implements, all brandished with ferocity, trapping the soldiers between the women and the *shabtis*.

From above, a rain of fire—arrows poured down upon the *shabtis* from the airship that swept in above, the vast beak of Horus plummeting in from the thermals. Some of the *shabtis* shattered, some burst into flame, hurling themselves into the Nile where they extinguished with a potent sizzle.

The destruction of its front flanks did nothing to discourage the rest though: still the *shabtis* advanced up the jetty, towards the soldiers—only now they they had a new target, and rather than ripping into the remains of the platoon, they hurled themselves at the Elysium Parlour, bursting in through windows and ceilings, making short work of the matchstick walls.

No longer being ripped apart at the hands of stone teeth, the soldiers rallied, striking out to rescue their Colonel. The entry chamber of the Elysium Parlour descended into a maelstrom of fighting, the three forces meeting in a flurry of action: a trio of girls shattered a *shabti* between their flourished brands; the Eyes of the Sky leapt falcon-like through the air, his knife flashing, his teeth ripping at the throats of soldiers; Aziz vanished beneath the gnashing jaws of a *shabti*; Lieutenant Smythe grappled with a stone warrior, emptying his last round into its temple, wriggling free from the grip of its still-moving torso where it pinned him beneath its weight.

In the centre, Cleopatra wielded her whip like a conductor in the grip of an overture, sending soldiers flying back from the door to the anteroom with weals rising on their faces, shattering *shabtis* at the neck and stamping on their remains.

And then, beneath their feet, the glass floor cracked, and the Nile rose amongst them. For a moment, everyone was equalised, spluttering for purchase and breath, and then the fighting resumed, frantic amidst spumes of bloody spray.

Cleopatra retreated to the anteroom, bounding across the heads of sinking *shabtis* like stepping stones in a graceful one-two-three dash.

Hooch was thrashing in his chair, spitting obscenities in his ancient tongue. Sephiroth was still chanting, the words echoing with a depth and vibration the walls of the room could not have created, his eyes vacant and unseeing.

"Daughter!" Antonia proclaimed, hugging her tight.

"Mother," Cleopatra said, extricating herself.

"The battle rages?"

"The battle rages."

"Then I have a friend I must rescue. Attend to the ritual."

And with that, Antonia vanished through the door, into the rising river water.

"A friend?" Cleopatra mused to herself. "Surely she can't mean...?"

But that was precisely what Antonia meant.

And so it was that, as Sephiroth completed his ritual and slumped in a faint to the deck, and as Hooch's eyes reopened once more lit by the tea-stained soul of a British Colonel, the first sight to greet his rheumy eyes was Antonia Jones perched atop her dromedary automaton, pounding through the water towards him, swinging a cutlass at the enemy hordes around her and shrieking, at the top of her majestic lungs, "*Geronimooooooooooo!*"

"What a magnificent woman," he said to himself, and lapsed back into unconsciousness.

"SUCH A HELPFUL man, The Eyes of the Skies," Cleopatra remarked.

"Quite so," Antonia said. "Remarkable really, how you've wrapped him around your little finger."

"Not so much," Cleopatra explained. "It was those teeth, you see—filed to points. Quite memorable. At least, that's what Fabian thought."

"And who," inquired Antonia, "is Fabian?"

Cleopatra smiled benignly. "Oh mother," she said. "You think the Parlour only has girls?"

"Ah," said Antonia, then, after a moment, "I see! A most potent secret, in these times."

"Indeed," said Cleopatra. "Of course, he's still got his soul trap. And you've got a very nice price. I'm not a cold-hearted blackmailer. Just—calling in a favour or so."

"Quite right," Antonia said.

"Mind you," Cleopatra said, leaning close to her mother, "it was quite a mess in there during that ritual. One couldn't be completely sure that bounder Khufu's soul ended up in the Anubis statuette. It could have been anything. Anything close to hand."

She produced a bottle from her pack—a dusty, battered whiskey bottle.

"A present. To your health, mother," said Cleopatra, passing it to her. "Until next time."

Antonia kissed her daughter on the cheek. "Until next time," she said. "I shall keep an eye out. Where are you planning on going?"

"Oh," said Cleopatra, "we'll see how far he'll fly me. I was thinking... Japan? I'll learn the dance of the seven veils, become the Silken Mistress."

Cleopatra Bonny rose up, borne away on the winds, proud at the entrance of her Elysium Parlour, the dilapidated boat festooned in ropes and strung below the Eyes of the Skies' airship. She raised a hand in farewell, soaring up and away from her mother, into the skies.

"Well, that's that," said Antonia. She tucked the flask away and turned to face the horizon.

"Are we ready?" said her companion, shuffling up to her, sweating and red-faced.

Antonia kissed him on his perspiring forehead. "We are, my lovely Colonel Hooch. Come along, Barnabus."

Into the desert sand they strode, the great relic thief Antonia Jones swaying aback her trusty steed, her companion following behind, clinging nervously to the back of his own. Into the sunset, towards tomorrow.

"Geronimo," she said.

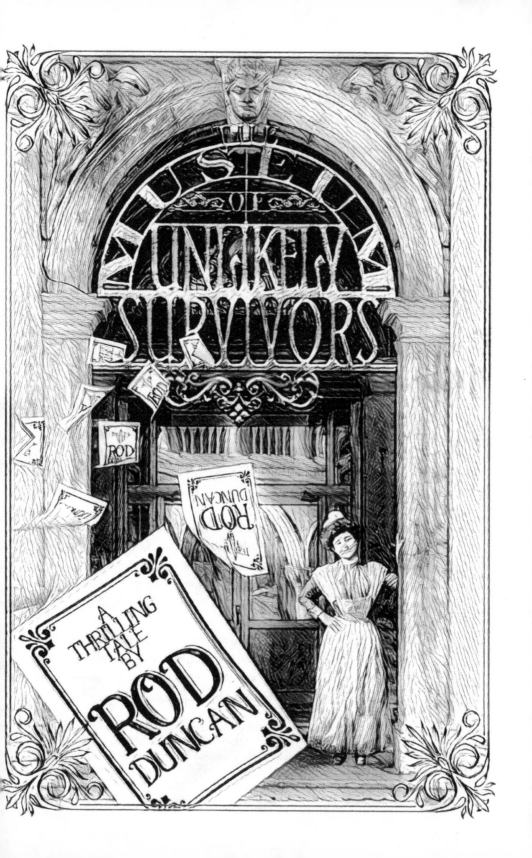

The Museum of Unlikely Survivors

*In which a marvellous automaton tests the laws of probability,
a valuable antiquity is stolen and the good qualities of a
cleaner are recognised.*

Rosa knew it as the Museum of Unlikely Survivors. But then, she was only the cleaner. It was more properly referred to as the Drummond-Johnson Bequest. Comprising a disparate assortment of objects acquired by Drummond-Johnson the 3rd, it represented not so much any theme other than his own mercurial enthusiasms. [1]

Serious antiquarians were unimpressed. They saw no reason why the only known specimen of an extinct stag beetle should be displayed behind the same glass as an undamaged example of Byzantine brittleware, a poster of the Great Banzzini from a time when no one knew he was going to be great and a uniquely carved Egyptian emerald. Whether catalogued chronologically, alphabetically, or geographically the collection made no sense.

The general public, however, being too ignorant to know better, took to the Drummond-Johnson Bequest with ardour, flocking to the wing of the Museum where it was housed. This further annoyed the academic community. The opening of the collection had been attended by a scattering of London's wealthy

---

[1] Just as Drummond-Johnson the First had had the knack of earning money—through the nutmeg trade—so Drummond-Johnson the Third had the knack of spending it. The second Drummond-Johnson contributed to a moderate increase to the value of the estate. He often remarked that his main goal was to instruct his son in the ways of frugality and moderation. By the time Drummond Johnson the Fourth inherited, the family had been reduced to a semi-detached residence in Frome.

philanthropists. But as the weeks passed others began to seek it out. The curator was distressed to see men wearing loud check jackets strolling between the cabinets, and to hear them, for such men invariably talked in voices that could be heard from the next gallery. The odours of cheap hair oil, sweat and even gin began to mix with the more wholesome smells of bees wax polish and camphor.

Such was the state of things on Rosa's first day at work. She had been assigned to the Drummond-Johnson because of its unpopularity among the other staff, and because being the most recently employed she had the least say. But she liked it well enough, discovering that she could talk to its visitors in a way the curator could not.

"They will insist on smoking," he told her. "I can't abide tobacco. But what can one do? And the mud they bring with them!"

She was soon to discover that they left property as well as mud behind them. And in unusual quantities.

"What do I do with this?" she asked on her third day.

She held out an engagement ring for the curator to inspect. It had been lying on the floor below the Mummy of an Unknown Priest circa 2000BC. The ring was gold, in colour at least, though the stone was certainly glass.

"My goodness," he said. "You must take it to the back of the Fellows' Tea Room. You'll find a cupboard marked Lost Property. Write out a label for it and then hurry back to work."

"What will happen to it?" she asked, concerned for whoever had lost such a precious item.

"It will be sold if it's not claimed in twenty-eight days," he said. "Though I doubt such a piece of tin would raise three shillings."

The ring was reclaimed the following Friday, as it happened, by a young man with an earnest expression. Rosa was glad to be the one to place it in his hand, though in the meantime, she'd been obliged to make two further visits to the tea room, once with a pack of playing cards and once with a baby's shoe. So frequent did her comings and goings become over the following weeks that the Fellows complained and lost property had to be transferred to a room in the basement. Thus it came to be presided over by the boiler engineer, who seemed more than pleased by Rosa's company.

"Have you seen this?" she asked the curator one day, when she'd been working at the museum for three months. "A full set of horseshoes. Who brings horseshoes to a museum?"

The curator glanced down at them over his spectacles. His thick eyebrows arched, as if to indicate regret at her naivety. "There is no reason," he said. "The people who visit the Drummond-Johnson Bequest have no reason for anything. One may as well ask why a goldfish swims counter-clockwise in its bowl."

Rosa had long since detected a pattern in the contents of the lost property room; every item was of a type that an ordinary man or woman might wish to be blessed with luck. The curator and the fellows were not ordinary men, however, and she knew well enough not to try to present a theory of her own. Great men needed to believe that they'd discovered things for themselves.

"Last week I found a dice," she said, trying again to lead his thinking.

"That is the plural," he explained. "The singular is die. Now, can't a chap find peace in pursuance of his studies? Bring me a pot of tea, won't you. And a biscuit."

In the lost property room she found the boiler engineer taking a moment of rest. He was himself old enough to be mistaken for an exhibit.

Placing the horseshoes on the shelf, she took the pencil on its string and wrote out a label. *Four horseshoes. Hardly worn.* Then she printed the date. For a moment she thought about appending a note that the discovery came just two weeks prior to the Cheltenham racing festival.[2] But then the boiler engineer awoke.

"More from the Drummond-Johnson?" he asked.

"Wouldn't you know it," she said.

"Where in the room?"

"Same as always," she said. "Under the mummy. He's such a fright, you might think he was going to reach out and grab you."

THE MUMMY WAS one of the most popular exhibits in the entire collection; which is to say, one of the most popular exhibits in the Museum. Why the people of London had taken to it, the curators couldn't fathom, for it represented everything they disliked, being a piece on its own, with no context and no documentation of substance.

The label on the exhibit described it as the mummy of an unknown priest, but even that was supposition. It came from a tomb near Karnak. Having been robbed in antiquity, the tomb contained nothing but the remains of mummies. Hidden under a collapsed wall, the 'priest' was the only one to have survived intact; the others had been unwound, so to speak, by treasure seekers.

---

[2] Before coming to the museum cleaning business, Rosa had worked in the household of Mr H__, a financier from Bayswater, whose wife had objected to her looks. It was in pursuance of a greater understanding of money that Mr H__ invested time visiting the racetracks of the home counties. Thus Rosa had acquired some familiarity with the racing calendar, since she'd often been obliged to accompany him, on the grounds that "Luck smiles on a pretty face."

The priest was sold initially to one of Napoleon's doctors during the Egyptian campaign. He intended to use it for medicine, ground mummy being much the fashion at the time, and considered something of a panacea. Half of the mummy's left foot had thus been consumed before the owner died. Who it passed to after that is unclear, but having miraculously survived the wreck of a steamer in the Mediterranean, it came to Europe, where it was purchased by P. T. Barnam and transported to America.

The great showman constructed for it a sarcophagus, modelled on the kind of sensational illustration that accompanied news of the discovery of any Egyptian antiquity. Whenever a visitor stood on the pressure pad before it, silent clockwork would open the sarcophagus, as if by the magical power of the mummy within. It was inauthentic in every sense, but was everything the nickel-dropping public loved to see. Having earned a small fortune with it in America, he decided to try his luck in the capitals of Europe, sending it back on the ill-fated steam ship *Ville du Havre*.

The ship sank in the middle of the North Atlantic with the loss of two-hundred-and-twenty-six souls. But through a quirk of fate the sarcophagus dropped free when the hull broke open, floating for three weeks (for it proved marvellously watertight), before making landfall on a beach near Galway.

THE FIRE HAPPENED when Rosa had been working at the museum for almost a year. It was fortunate, the curator said, that it began away from walls and cabinets. The only damage was to an eighteen-inch section of the gallery's wood block flooring.

On the following day, she found herself approached by many of the visitors, who wanted to know if she thought the mummy itself had been the cause, it being the closest exhibit. She told them that she did not. When they pressed her for more information, she found herself relating something of its history, particularly the *Ville du Havre* episode. They must have known the story already, it being the cause of much of the mummy's celebrity, but all seemed pleased to have it from the woman who cleaned the very glass behind which it now rested. Their eyes would widen. They'd say how brave they thought she was, considering the curse.[3] And then, perhaps, they'd press a coin into her palm as an expression of gratitude.

---

[3] In the aftermath of the *Ville du Havre* disaster, a tabloid newspaper of low repute quoted an unnamed antiquarian as having said that a hieroglyphic inscription had been found in the mummy's tomb. Rendered into English, it read: Death crawls on blooded knees to any who

By the middle of the afternoon a joiner had replaced the section of charred flooring and the only sign of the museum's near disaster was a lingering acrid smell, which is the aftermath of any fire being doused. Rosa, whose purse had yet a little room for more pennies and farthings, was thinking of dusting under the priest yet again, but was interrupted by a bookish man wearing blue tinted spectacles, accompanied by a woman carrying a document case.

"We're looking for the curator," said the woman.

"Yes ma'am. Who should I say is calling?"

The woman produced a visiting card.

Rosa read it aloud: "Professor Inklayer. Statististical Safety Consultant."

"And his secretary," said the woman, offering a gloved hand.

"Professor of what?" the curator asked, once they'd been introduced.

"Professor of mnemonic statistics," said the secretary.

"Oh?" said the curator, as if he suspected he was being tested in some way.

"I'm here about the fire," said the professor, whose accent was exotically continental. "They tell me there was no clear cause."

"We thought a cigarette might have done it," said the curator. "But that would hardly catch on a wooden floor. There really is no accounting for it."

"Professor Inklayer is here to do just that," said his secretary. "All accidents may be accounted for through the study of statistics, once one has discarded the notion that chance has no memory."[4]

"I don't understand," said the curator.

"Yours is a collection of unlikely survivors," she explained. "And the mummy is the most unlikely of all. Have you not wondered why the public leave trinkets around it? They hope the luck will rub off. But once the equations are balanced,

---

disturb my bones. The *London Times* carried an article questioning the veracity of the curse story. This approach was echoed in other respectable papers, which were thus able to spread the wildest speculation without losing their journalistic integrity. Whatever the truth, the Mummy of the Unknown Priest had achieved in death a fame that multiplied with each unlikely survival.

[4] Classical statistics holds that no matter how many times a coin has turned up heads, the chances of it doing so again will remain 1 in 2. Some find this counterintuitive, reasoning that if ninety-nine throws have come up heads, the hundredth will also, since it is almost certainly a gimmick coin with heads on both sides.

Professor Inklayer's theory of Mnemonic Statistics offers a third interpretation. It posits the existence of a Universal Probability Field, which can be distorted locally by extremely unlikely events. Thus chance does indeed have a memory and after a run of good luck, the probability of bad things happening will measurably increase.

It is interesting to note that the general public were capable of simultaneously believing the mummy of the unknown priest to be cursed and regarding its proximity as lucky. How this was possible no statistician has yet been able to explain.

we see that the very reverse is true."

"Indeed?" said the curator, whose brow had pinpricked with sweat at the mention of equations.

"Indeed," said the secretary. "The professor has calculated that, given the extraordinarily low probability of any of these objects surviving, and given also their close proximity to each other, an aura of bad luck will have been generated sufficient to cause spontaneous low probability accidental disaster events. He calls them SLADEs."

"He means to say the fire had a cause after all?"

"The professor means to say that the fire, or some disaster like it, was inevitable. The night watchmen getting to it in time was another lucky escape, which merely intensifies your problem."

It was a strange kind of conversation, Rosa thought. The secretary giving the explanation, the curator looking to the professor all the while, and the professor himself nodding, sagely. Rosa pretended not to notice, which was easy enough because no one properly looked at her, except perhaps for the secretary, whose occasional glance seemed more than perceptive.

"What can be done?" the curator asked.

"It must be studied," the secretary said.

"But do you mean to say we might be in danger?"

"Professor Inklayer means to say that, if his fears are proved correct, the collection may need to be dispersed."

The curator blinked rapidly, like a man who tastes a steak and kidney pudding only to discover that it has been fashioned out of marzipan. Then the corners of his mouth began to curve upwards. The smile spread until it illumined his entire face.

"I must tell the Director the bad news," he said. "Rosa, see to it that this gentleman gets all he needs."

WHAT WITH ALL the arrangements that needed to be made, Rosa had been quite forgotten, except by Professor Inklayer, who required fresh pots of tea from time to time, and once a packet of throat pastels when the museum's dry air began to irritate him. The upshot of it was that no one had dismissed her. She would have liked to know if there would be payment for all the extra hours, but it never seemed the right moment to ask.

The half-hour warning was called. The visitors drifted away. The museum fell quiet. In the far distance she could hear doors slamming and bolts being slid.

The secretary gave her the professor's coat to carry, and the leather document case. These she held, standing just outside the circle of fellows, who had been assembled in the atrium to stand witness.

"A museum—any museum—is a repository of unlikely survivors," the secretary told them. "But the Drummond-Johnson Bequest unusually so. Whether he knew it or not, Drummond Johnson the 3rd was attracted to objects that had come close to extinction but still survived."

The professor nodded. The fellows frowned in concentration.

"You are assembled here in the place furthest from any of your collections. By this, the professor wishes to determine a baseline measurement." And then, to Rosa she said: "The document case if you please."

Rosa passed it to the Professor, who extracted a clutch of dice. Having shown them around the circle, he invited the Director to cast them onto the floor. They rattled and spun and came to rest showing a jumble of different numbers. The curator was next to try, and then some of the fellows took a turn. Each throw resulted in a different scatter. In short, the dice did just what they were supposed to.

When everyone had been satisfied, the secretary scooped up the dice and led the way up the wide marble stairs to the wing that held the Drummond Johnson Bequest. Rosa followed on at the back, trying to keep her footfalls quiet. The party stopped next to the Mummy of the Unknown Priest,

"Cast them again," the secretary said, passing the dice back to the Director.

He threw and they clattered. The fellows crowded forwards for a better look. Hearing them gasp in surprise, Rosa went up on tiptoe to see for herself. Every dice had thrown a one.

IT WAS A strong indication, the secretary said, but not yet proof. For that, they would need to repeat the experiment in a controlled environment, removing anything that might interfere with the aura.

"There can be no one present," she explained.

"I should certainly be there," said the Director.

"Would it be lucky or unlucky for you if the Drummond-Johnson Bequest was dispersed?" she asked.

The Director's non-answer was answer enough.

"Every person nearby adds to the risk of contamination. Is the throw of a six lucky or unlucky? The answer will be different depending on your perspective. When the day comes, even Professor Inklayer will need to keep well clear."

"Then who is to throw the dice?"

"The test," she said, "shall be conducted by a marvellous automaton."

IN TRUTH, IT was an object the like of which the curator had never seen. Nor the Director, nor any of the fellows. Four men in brown overalls arrived on the Monday morning and hauled it into the gallery, placing it directly over the spot where the fire had broken out.

Its outstanding feature was a mechanical arm of brass poles and articulating joints, which, on the turning of a handle, would cast any dice held in its mechanical hand. These fell into a glass receptacle not unlike a fishbowl. The next revolution of the handle operated the camera shutter to record the result. With the revolution after that, the bowl tipped the dice back into the grip of the mechanical hand.

The delivery men complained it was heavier than they'd been told, and wouldn't leave until they'd been well tipped. According to the professor's explanatory note, a tightly wound spring was housed in the plinth on which it rested, and an escapement by which means the arm would be triggered into motion every half hour through the night.

Having cleared the gallery, the curator pressed the button, as directed in the professor's instructions. A faint whirring noise was heard from within.

"The world is changing so fast," he observed sadly, then ushered Rosa out and closed the doors, leaving the machine to conduct the experiment undisturbed.

Rosa was back first thing in the morning to see the doors opened and the men in brown overalls carry the automaton away. They left a letter from Professor Inklayer, who said he would send his report just as soon as the photographic plates had been developed and the equations calculated.

AND SO IT came to be that the Drummond-Johnson Bequest was dispersed.[5] Where the unlikely survivors had once been displayed, a collection of cuneiform tablets were put on show, arranged in date order to the great satisfaction of the curator. Visitor numbers dwindled. The scents of beeswax and camphor drifted undisturbed in the air of the quiet museum.

Rosa was the only one saddened by the change. Life seemed less exciting

---

[5] Most of the exhibits were sent for storage accompanied by warning notes that no one item from the Drummond-Johnson Bequest be placed in proximity to any other. For safety's sake, and according to the recommendation of Professor Inklayer, the mummy of the unknown priest was repatriated to a museum in Egypt.

than it had been, and with little property being lost she had to find excuses to visit the basement and share a cup of tea with the boiler engineer.

"I know the visitors were noisy," she said to him. "But I liked them well enough. They had hope in their eyes. I do admire people with hope."

"We had a lucky escape if you ask me," he said. "The ice was thin under our skates. And that's a true fact."

"I'm not sure I agree," said Rosa, but did not elaborate. It didn't seem her place to say more.

SHE WAS TO have one more encounter with Professor Inklayer, sighting him at a variety performance in Western's Music Hall. She'd had to borrow a pair of opera glasses to be certain. His hair was rather browner than it had been when he was calling himself a professor. The blue tinted spectacles had been replaced by a monocle. But it was the self-same man, sure enough. This time he was playing alongside a comedian and a performing dog. His part of the act was mainly running away.

She insisted on being let in through the stage door, by which means she talked herself into the dressing room corridor. It was there that she confronted him.

It had not been his idea, he said, which Rosa found easy enough to believe. He'd been chosen because he could affect an Austrian accent, which the woman said was close enough to Bohemian that few in London would know the difference. When Rosa suggested the constabulary might like to hear about what he'd done, the professor who was not a professor went down on his knees and begged for mercy. She asked for the address and he gave it all in a rush, though he couldn't give the woman's name, for he didn't know it himself.

IT WAS A pleasant villa, though small, with bay windows at the front and a tidy garden of paths and rose beds.

"You?" said the woman who was not a secretary.

"Yes," said Rosa.

"How did you find me?"

"I'll tell you if you let me come in."

The house was sparsely furnished, but arranged with a good eye. There being no maid, the woman herself went to fetch the tea things. As Rosa waited, she stepped around the drawing room. The woodwork had a tolerable polish, but when she ran a finger over the mantelpiece, it came away with a smear of dust.

"I expect you'll want to ask what it was all about," the woman said, once they were seated and the tea had been poured.

"I do know what it was about," said Rosa.

The woman tilted her head, as if curious.

"You made up that thing of mathematics for the professor to say.[6] Then you did the trick with the weighted dice. That got you to have the machine put in the museum at night. And the watchmen locked out too. You were hiding in the base of it, I reckon. It had to be you 'coz the professor was too big to fit. Once it was quiet, you climbed out and had the run of the place. That's when you stole the carved emerald. In the morning you got back inside and they carried you away."

"Has an emerald been stolen?" the woman asked. "I didn't read about it in the papers."

"Papers don't know it," said Rosa. "Nor the curator, nor the Director, nor the fellows. Only me. I'd cleaned that cabinet twice a day since I started. You put it in too straight, ma'am, if you don't mind me saying. The real emerald was off by a fraction. That made me look twice. The colour was too green. It was much alike, but I'd seen the real thing too many times to be taken in.

"The only bit I don't get is the fire. How did you start the fire?"

The woman took a sip of tea as if biding her time to consider before making an answer. "If I had wanted to start such a fire, it would have been easy enough. I could have dropped something that looked like a cigarette, just before closing time. It would have had a delay built in and a few drops of kerosene inside. Just enough to scorch the floor. Not enough to do any real harm. But tell me this: if you're so certain in your theory, why haven't you told the authorities?"

In truth, Rosa wasn't exactly sure why she'd kept it to herself. In part it was the habit of not speaking out of turn, in part because it would have made everyone so unhappy to know it. But there was something else: an admiration for the woman, the secretary who controlled a professor, who outwitted the curator and the Director and all the fellows.

"I wanted to know why you stole it," she said.

"Did I steal it? I may have taken it, but did it really belong to the museum in the first place?"

---

[6] The woman did not, in fact, devise the theory of Mnemonic Statistics. The real professor Inklayer published it in 1893 in the Journal of the Statistical Society of Bohemia, vol. 4, pp. 23-31. It did not revolutionise the study of statistics, as he had hoped. Neither did it ruin his standing in academic circles, since the Journal of the Statistical Society of Bohemia ran for only five years and had a circulation limited to a handful of universities. Included in the paper were plans for a machine capable of repeatedly casting dice and photographing the result without an operator being present.

"Mr Drummond gave it them," said Rosa.

"He did," said the woman. "Before that, he bought it from a collector in Chelsea, who bought it from the cousin of the governor of Egypt, who bought it from an American army captain, who robbed it from a tomb in the Valley of the Kings. If it belongs to anyone, surely it belongs to the people of that land. And if they now have it back, has any harm been done?"

"Do they have it back?"

"Yes. Or, rather, one of them does."

"Did you sell it to them?"

"I'll admit that I was paid for my work. But so is a lawyer and a curator. And a cleaner for that matter. Do you really think that what I did was theft?"

"I do," said Rosa. "But I don't blame you for it."

"You'll forgive my asking," said the woman, "but do you plan to tell anyone?"

"I do not," said Rosa. "I just wanted to know. That's all."

"Thank you," said the woman. "But it seems I'll be moving on again anyway. If our Professor Inklayer has talked to you, he'll surely talk to others. A new address is needed. And a new name. It's all such a nuisance for a woman working on her own." She regarded Rosa over the rim of her teacup. "I don't suppose *you* would be in the market for employment?"

"As a maid?" Rosa asked.

"That would be a waste of your talents. I need an assistant who notices things that other people miss. You couldn't be holding them back though. It would be very much your place to speak."

And Rosa, who'd long since discovered that she hadn't the soul for dusting cabinets of cuneiform, said: "I'd like that very much."

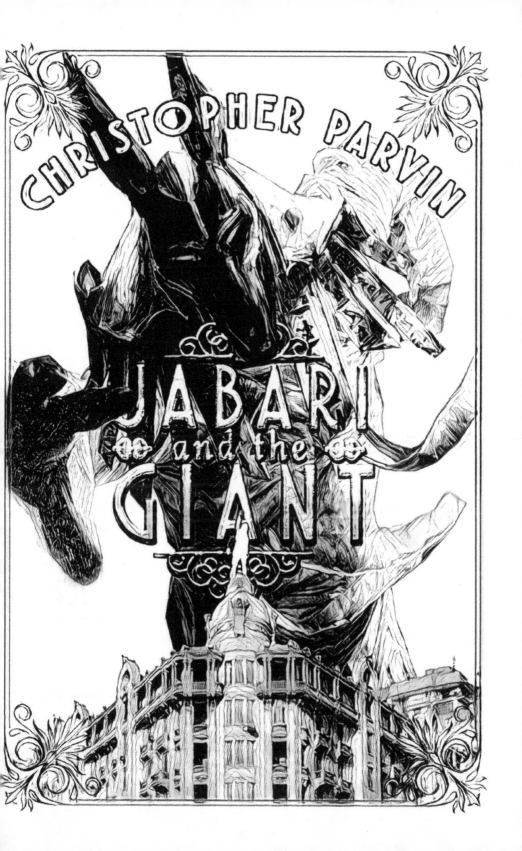

Jabari and the Giant

THE PRIESTS WORK single file with just enough room for a tourist to slip past the hefty canisters on their backs. Tiny lamps flash in the reflection of their goggles, dark sweating skin burnished as they work on the tunnel walls.

Acolyte Jabari stands in an alcove in traditional white kilt and gold collar, an ornamental guard as much a fixture as the signs for public toilets. The flying stone dust makes his bald scalp itch and the noise of compressed air drilling through rock hisses in his skull. As chores go it's not the worst but far from the best.

Whispering and shuffling, a new batch of tourists wander past with their guide. Like all the others, the guide is a young girl with a black wool wig hanging low over her brow, malachite eyeshadow almost melting from her face. Jabari doesn't envy her. In these new pyramids the passages are wider than normal—the priests with frowning over their measuring sticks as they begrudgingly give way for commerciality—but they are still not much more than low shafts of windowless stone. He watches them leave, her voice fading as it plods through her speech with all the expression of someone already dead and buried in the pyramid.

As one the priests step back from their work and holster their nozzles. Before them a full mural of Isis has been carved, her rainbow wings spread wide and surrounded by nonsense hieroglyphs. Commerciality. With a muttered prayer they set the image glowing with soft green blue light, stretch their arms and walk from the tunnel.

After so much noise the hush rushes in until Jabari feels weightless. Discreetly he checks a pocket watch tucked under his kilt, wondering why his replacement is so late. Amis lives by punctuality; his personality won't allow anything else. Yet with the people he's been keeping company with of late... Jabari buries the thought. The Isis Faction might be secretive but they're charitable; who could begrudge them a bit of play-acting and mystery?

An hour passes and the growl of his stomach echoes so loud it's almost obscene. A quick look outside won't hurt, Jabari reasons. Just to see if Amis is on his way. With the awkward step of the guiltily nervous, Jabari abandons his post.

Stylised arrows are hidden among the wall's cartouche to help visitors find their way but really they are unnecessary in these small builds, each one never more than five passageways from the surface. More and more of these smaller pyramids are popping up like weeds in the sands to feed the growing influx of tourists, all identical but for whichever deity is pandered to on their walls.

Avoiding the main entrance and its official guards—the emotionless expression must be as much a part of the uniform as their matching black skirts, Jabari thinks—he goes left to the cleaner's access, presses his palm against the thick sandstone door and enacts the only spell he's managed to master in over a year of training. Harsh white light eats a rectangle from the gloom and Jabari steps out blinking in the sun.

Far to the east the Nile runs its course through Hapi's great purification plants where the god sits under domes of blue and green glass, charging the coils that cleanse the waters that pass his thighs and posing for photos. In the mid-day sun it blazes, a thread of liquid silver visible as a train departs. Closer, a squat grid of clay and pig iron boxes, the homes of priests and students, offer a little space devoid of humanity's press. Small clockwork dogs stand sentinel at the compound entrances like tiny bronze Anubises.

Jabari stands feeling the sweat pop on his flesh. There is no one making their way towards to pyramids from the small academic village, no sign of the stocky form of Amis. As he turns back to the door, resigned to hunger, the Chariot of Ra pulls in to the nearby station with a chug of steam. A single passenger disembarks, pale even by western standards, and starts towards Jabari and the pyramid.

The passenger is waving with unnerving enthusiasm.

"Helloooo there!"

The woman is slim and tiny, dressed in blinding white linen and a large floppy black hat. She carries a small clutch in one white gloved hand, the other stabbing the sand with a swagger stick. Jabari doesn't call back. He watches the woman stride towards him, unsure what he is supposed to do.

"Hot here isn't it?" the woman bellows again.

Leaving the loose sand for the limestone path, her heels click merrily and she makes better progress. Up close she barely reaches Jabari's chest, skin stretched across her cheek bones like fine canvas, her eyes a dark twinkle. Her accent is English, one of the Pan-Atlantic counties, and she holds herself as if ready to strike, though her smile appears genuine.

"Amelia, Amelia Grace. Do you work here by chance?"

"Tours are by arrangement only," Jabari intones, the foreign language thick in his throat. He nods back the way she has marched; lingering tourists mingle some way away, frantically buying cheap papyrus parasols from bearded merchants. They look like nothing more than a flock of confused flannel geese.

"Oh there's no need for that my dear! We're all friends here, after all. So be a good chap and show me round, yes?" She takes his arm with a tough grip. "Through here? It's all jolly thrilling isn't it? Magic and such. Are you a priest?"

"No, wait…" Trying to keep track of the woman's questions, Jabari plants his feet at the pyramid's entrance and almost succeeds in pulling the woman off hers.

"Bloody hell. Problems, my dear boy?"

Out from the glare of the sun he can see the woman is really quite old. Her hair under the hat is drawn back in a steel grey page boy.

"Of course," she suddenly exclaims, "payment. I mustn't forget. Now, I find this money so confusing. Here, that's enough yes?" She pushes a small fortune of hedj coins into his palm and beams up at him.

"That is far too much…."

"Nonsense. Shall we go in? You wouldn't want a old woman like myself to overheat out here would you? I'd positively cook."

Allowing himself to be lead, he re-enters the passage, reasoning there is nothing much to do until Amis arrives to replace him anyway, and none of this is really his fault at all.

THE TRIP IS slow going. Jabari dredges up all the teachings he can remember from school. Fortunately the newest builds only offer a few dummy traps to entertain, the story-covered walls showing only the most famous or easily depicted.

Here is Creation; the primordial waters of chaos silently slosh back and forth as the magic activates. His impromptu guest marvels at it all, prodding at the fresh plaster and sending up blue green flakes of energy that dissipate around her face like dying fireflies.

Here Geb has been carved directly across the tunnel flagstones, the bright shining stars of his sister Nut glowing from the ceiling. Jabari talks about their forbidden love without shame, even as Amelia guffaws into her glove.

In the next tunnel an oversized mural of Shu fills the wall. When the magic is triggered, a cool breeze stirs sand from the floor and chills the sweat on their skin. In his gut Jabari smothers a pang of jealousy. A bit of clockwork and a few spells, the mark of a second year acolyte—journeymen work, yet so much more accomplished than anything Jabari could create.

"How divine," Amelia comments, completely missing her own joke. "Such marvels in these tunnels. I begin to understand why so many of my fellows are flocking to your county. Just marvellous. How far down do these tunnels go?"

"Not much further," Jabari's replies shortly. Occasionally he glances behind, expecting a priest to appear any second and demand to know why he had forsaken his post.

"Come now don't be bashful. We've all heard the stories—hidden passages, mummified old chaps wandering the halls killing virgins and the like."

"I'm sorry, there are no secret passages in the new builds." He struggles for words, watching the woman's expression harden. "Those practices," he continues uneasily, "have long since past. Not since our gods returned to the world."

"I see. How unfortunate."

"Unfortunate?"

"Well, it'd make a wonderful aside, wouldn't it dear? You can't tell me you've never thought about it? You're a young man, full of spunk and ideas. Where would you put a secret tunnel if you wanted one?"

Jabari doesn't answer, instead watching with amusement as Amelia's attempts to coax secrets from the walls with jabs of her stick. As they continue her interest in his stories visibly wanes, her frustration building, until she stops short.

"What's this one?"

"That is Set," Jabari answers, crooking his fingers in a ward against evil. The mural is plain by temple standards: no colour, no magic, a simple rendering in black and white showing the casting down of the mad god by Horus.

"Not a very inviting picture is it?" She pokes at the black paint and Jabari has to hold himself back from snatching her stick. "These figures along the bottom—people, is it?"

"His victims. Thousands killed. We need to move on."

Reluctantly, Amelia follows, still chatting.

"He's not in the guide books is he? I'd love to see him—sounds thrilling."

"He's dead," Jabari says with feeling. "Praise be to Ra."

It's an old story, how Set killed Osiris and Isis resurrected him to conceive Horus. How Horus, outraged and young, fought Set on every front to avenge his father. When the gods returned to earth after their long absence, they bought their old animosities with them, and the final battle of Horus and Set saw old kingdom crusade against new. The hawk-headed god finally won, feeding Set's body to Sobek so he could never raise again.

Time moves on.

This seems to quieten the woman for a while, and Jabari leads her on. They cross an intersection that contains one of Jabari's favourite murals, a floor-to-ceiling depiction of Hapi in hippo form. The magic activates before they've even close, an invisible wave of good feeling and purification that washes away his negative thoughts.

"We're almost at the end," he smiles. This old woman is nothing but a harmless curiosity, he has decided. Amis is just late, and everything will be fine.

Amelia grips his arm, her grin matching his. "I do hope you're not holding out on me," she says. "Cheating me and so forth. If I haven't paid enough for the *full* tour you only need say, my dear. I've got plenty more."

The wave of Hapi's goodwill fades quickly and suddenly Jabari isn't as sure that those twinkling eyes of hers are as friendly as they seem. They remind him—he realises—of an asp, about to bite.

"Perhaps we should return to the surface," he stammers. "I've never really given a tour before. One of the qualified guides will know if I'm missing anything."

Amelia slips a hand into her clutch and pulls free a pistol. It's a strange contraption, the barrel oddly wide and a mesh cage of copper wire where the hammer should be. Jabari is appalled to see a chunk of sandstone within, carved with the name of Sekhmet the warrior and pulsing with hot golden light. It's an abomination, a sin against the gods, that a weapon imbued by their power should be wielded by a foreigner.

Outrage nearly overwhelms his fear, but then she is shaking the bag and he thinks: what other abhorrent secrets could she be concealing?

"You're a bright boy." The playfulness is still in her voice, but colder now, more teasing. "So I want you to think really hard. Where are the deeper tunnels?"

Perplexed the whiplash change in situation, Jabari panics quietly. A melting sensation is soaking through his bones. He stares around the small chamber, feeling his chest tighten. The guilds travel slower than he does; they are taught to take their time, turn the tour into theatre so their charges won't see the shabby plaster and undressed stone behind the magic. Would there be a party nearby to hear him shout?

The woman—this Amelia creature—doesn't rush him. She doesn't move like an old woman any more; her hand is steady, and she even appears taller, as if the act of threatening strangers invigorates her. The regular lighting down here is too dim for anything but mood, a few crystals connected by wire and strung across the passage's ceiling; might she miss even at point blank range?

The lights.

"A power room," he blurts. "You haven't seen that. But it's just—"

"Excellent. I had great faith. Do you know where it is?"

Relief is just as intoxicating as fear. Jabari can feel his limbs lightening as he tries to recall the basic construction of the pyramid. It would only be an additional chamber, hidden away behind some panel in the last reaches of the tunnels, but perhaps that is all she needs.

They walk for five minutes. Enough time for Jabari to regain his composure. He questions his guard but to no avail. They pass through familiar tunnels, magics activating around them.

Some way short of their destination, Jabari stops short. Amelia almost collides with him, jabbing him painfully in the back with her blasphemous gun.

"Careful dearie," she hisses.

Jabari stares at the ground. A bracelet, just a simple bronze token on a string, but one that Amis often wore lies on the flagstones. Jabari forgets his fear, forgets his questioning of the woman, and thinks only of Amis. He starts to wonder if there is a reason he has not considered for his friend's late arrival.

He picks up the bracelet.

"What do you have there?"

"Have you seen it before?" he asks, voice flat and suddenly unafraid.

"What? Some trinket. Means something to *you*, though. Belong to a friend?"

A corkscrew of hot anger works through his jaw.

"Did you do...?"

"I assure you I've harmed no one...yet. Continue."

Unsteady, Jabari starts walking again. The Isis Faction—could they be involved in this? Why hadn't he paid more attention? If anything has happened to Amis, if he's dead....

He stops again, and this time Amelia collides fully with him. She curses, and prods him with the gun again.

"What in the world! Really child you're quite comely, but it's nothing a gaping hole in your back won't cure. Start. Walking."

The power room is hidden behind an unimaginative depiction of Ra in his chariot, and they reach its door without finding the corpse Jabari has been expecting since he found the bracelet. Feeling a little hysterical, Jabari depresses the tiny sun disk above the god's head and the door swings open with a hiss of pneumatics. A wave of boiling air hits them in the face and despite his earlier assertions that the traps of ancient days are long gone, Jabari leaps back, remembering stories of pressurized acid.

"Well…" Amelia arches her eyebrow and pushes the door wide with the pointed toe of her boot. Inside, an obsidian obelisk is connected to a boiler and several copper pylons. Spools of wire spider web through the chamber's upper reaches before lacing through cut channels in the walls. Amelia steps inside.

Briefly, Jabari considers pushing the door closed behind her. Instead he raises his hands in what he hopes is a placating gesture. "Please, that's all there is. There aren't any more tunnels—it isn't the old ages."

Amelia smiles broadly. "Oh I think this is more than enough. You're a good soul. For your sake, I hope I meet with success." With that cryptic message, she slips around the obelisk with a devilish grin.

There is a flash of orange light, a screech, and then her head re-appears. "You," she says. "Come here."

Rounding the obelisk, he sees she has been brought up short by a sheet of dark orange light—security magic. She looks up at it, tapping her foot impatiently. "Hell's teeth." She rounds on Jabari. "Open this."

"I don't…."

The gun spits out a marble of light. It strikes by Jabari's head and corrodes through as if the stone were nothing more than butter.

"I realise I've been terribly rum with you, my dear boy, but this simply won't do. If I had as many summers left as you I'd happily sit down and explain all the intricate workings of espionage, but I simply can't spare the time. So stop playing silly buggers and take down this…." She waves at the wall of light blocking her progress.

Jabari steps forward. He watches his hand raise, dislocated from his own actions. Something in the woman's tone has propelled him, and he thinks that he would be doing this even if she didn't have a gun trained at him. He tries the only spell he knows. The wall of light blinks out.

"Oh, rather well done. Right..." The woman seems ruffled. She looks at Jabari with an unexpectedly soft expression. "Success and all that. Ta-ta!" She disappears from view, the merry click of her heels fading.

Bewildered Jabari peers around the stone. He brushing its surface with his hand and pulls away, the skin from his knuckles scorched.

"*Ibn el-Kalb*," he hisses. Behind the security magic, thick cables run away down a severely sloping tunnel. He hesitates; his stomach rumbles again; he glances back at the open doorway. Then he sets off after the madwoman who apparently knows more about his pyramid than he does.

INSTEAD OF LESSENING, the deeper he travels the more the heat increases. The lights end without warning and Jabari stumbles along in the dark, cursing the small stones that catch in his sandals. Of the old woman there is no sign.

When Jabari was a child he visited the Giza Plateau with his parents. They took the Apophis Express, its gleaming emerald sides still fresh from the factory. They weren't alone; hundreds of people took the pilgrimage from far across the United Egyptian Kingdom.

The earliest automatons were a gift from Thoth. Here, these gleaming bronze-plate miracles with Ibis heads that towered over the populace offered water to the strange pale-skinned people from the northern colonies. Men in long embroidered robes like birds of paradise sold beer and clockwork scarabs with lapis chip eyes. Priests with thick kohl and glittering metal amulets stood guard by the turnstiles so the area didn't overcrowd. It was a pantomime, rich with hundreds or years of religious iconography and played with the festival air of a jubilee. The gods were back. Long live the gods.

They waited for hours under the hot sun, Jabari's excitement growing. He had filled his stomach with fried fish from the hissing vats of oil, and sweet barley pancakes crispy at the edges and doughy in the centre. All the while the crowds thickened. It should have been claustrophobic but a shared sense of purpose held them all up. One woman fainted in rapture. A man fell to his knees babbling in a dialect not heard since Khafu sat on the throne, and was plucked from the crush by a Thoth automaton. Jabari could feel it, the spirit of the place, this cradle of life.

He was disappointed.

The plateau is a sheet of blasted glass several feet thick and clouded with half molten sand. Where the gods landed. a black star marks the bedrock. Of the old great pyramids there is nothing left on the surface, but under the melted dunes tunnel mouths can still be seen descending into unknown depths. Jabari remembered his father, stood head and shoulders above the rest of the people, his feet directly over one such opening. A quirk of fate had left the glass only slightly opaque in this spot and the tunnel's shaft gapped hungrily beneath his feet.

Jabari had refused to stand with him. The great man had laughed and teased, his mother had laughed and cajoled. Jabari hadn't moved.

Now those memories are fresh in his mind. They haunt him as he feels his way along the pitch-black tunnel: that same feeling of a maw swallowing him up. His ears are starting to feel muffled, as if he is sinking beyond the reach of sound. Who is Amelia? Why are there power cables running so deep under this pyramid—this gloried toy built for the tourist trade?

When his eyes start to ache from straining to see he instead looks at his feet, can almost trick himself into thinking he can see their movement. Then, gradually, he can.

A rich red light blooms ahead. Amelia is crouched by a cut rectangle opening and backlit in scarlet. She does not seem surprised that he has followed.

"My dear boy, how old are you? You move like an adolescent calf."

Embarrassed despite himself, Jabari squats down by the woman.

"By the sun god, who are you?" he demands, putting all twenty one years of authority in his voice.

"Never mind that. You have bigger problems."

And she's right.

Beyond the tunnel an immense cavern has been hollowed out of the bedrock. Man sized scarabs scuttle over the stone, clipping away with metal mandibles, their uncased workings clicking and spinning. Huge columns of the automatons have linked limbs like a giant insect jigsaw to stabilise the roof, and even more move like ants through adjoining passages, spiriting away rubble to who knew where. In the centre, large bronze vats of water steam and boil under a reinforced lattice of pig iron. Priests calmly stroll along walkways without railings, hands behind their bare backs as if lecturing in front of a class. In fact, Jabari recognises several of his old teachers.

They are building.

"What...?" At first the scale defeats his imagination, but slowly he begins to turn the shapes into a form he can recognise.

"It's a foot," Amelia mutters.

He can see it clearly now, a great big toe, ugly with patchwork and rivets, a monster of mixed metals, the solid curve of an ankle, the shin disappearing off through a hole in the distance wall, a monster laying on its back.

"It's not going to be here." Amelia is talking to herself, ignoring Jabari gawping beside her. "I need the head maybe. No. Mummification. Boy, the chest is most important yes?" She doesn't wait for an answer, neatly shucking her linen jacket and trousers to reveal a black cat suit clinging to her skinny old frame. Jabari stares, scandalised.

"For a boy who can chat so candidly about incest, you're easily embarrassed. You better go back now."

"Please," Jabari begs, "what is this?"

Amelia sighs, squats back down beside him.

"I don't have time for this. But let me put it this way and maybe you can work out the rest on your own: some people aren't happy we have peace. There are many men on my side who would welcome the return of the profit they were making from war, and some on your side that think concession of any kind is shameful. This is their answer."

"But...."

"Enough. I'm not getting any younger, my dear."

He watches her sling one bony leg over the ledge and find the rung of a ladder, and then she is gone. Alone on the shelf with nothing but the foot to stare at, Jabari wishes she'd come back. Magic crawls across the beaten metal of the gargantuan thing, a sick corruption pulsing red, spitting out questing black tendrils that burn Jabari's vision if he looks at them too directly.

More than Amelia's gun, more than anything he's heard of in training, this magic revolts him. As acolytes they all pass before Ra and are gifted with the ability to use magic. It's a seed; nothing more. Some, with training, become full priests; others like Jabari never do more than dream of it. And some, it seems, some use it for blasphemies such as...*this*.

Whatever it is, it simply shouldn't be.

It's too much. He races back up the passage and out into the ignorance of fading day.

AMELIA'S WORDS LINGER in his head.

The world is at peace. The Egyptian Empire and the Pan-Atlantic Confederacy have signed a treaty. The war is over. Yet there was so much death. There was outrage when the vice-pharaoh under Ra announced the news: the gods had returned, nothing should stand in Egypt's way. But the gods were ambivalent about war, beings beyond the comprehension of men. In short they couldn't be relied on. Forefront to the debate were the priests who saw it a sin to capitulate, to not force the Egyptian pantheon on every inch of the world's soil. Their voice was small but always present in the market places, in government, an echo through daily life like the wind in the palms.

Jabari walks from the temple to the train station. Indecision runs in hot waves through his chest. Months, maybe years it would take to build such a thing. Nothing bad has happened yet, he reasons, and if it did an automaton, even one that would dwarf the pyramids of old, would still be easily destroyed—if not by the Pan-Atlantic's weapons then on the whim of a passing god. There must be more to it but he can't grasp what.

Amelia; she knows so much more than him. *Leave it to the professionals.* He repeats that as the last train pulls in. He decides to visit his parents, though he is not sure where the decision arises from; perhaps a longing for the security of childhood.

Leave it to the professionals.

The carriage is almost empty and night's cold breath has gripped the desert; only the habitual warmth of a large city keeps his teeth from chattering. New Cairo is a sprawl of honey coloured apartments and punctuating obelisks. The train races over raised rails, flashing past the overflowing verdant green of roof gardens, its slipstream ruffling the head of palms. To the west where there is still space to expand out into the desert the skyline is a jagged tooth of construction—new hotels fighting each other for greater height and views—but to the east the oldest parts of the city are visible, entrenched heavy stone and the soaring stained glass canopies of great souks.

Jabari gets off at Cleopatra Station. He pauses by the fountain to wash his face and gaze at the fixed stone gaze of Cleopatra defeating the Roman. Her hand gushes water over the legions' chiselled shields. Everything is normal. Students from New Cairo University congregate by the milk bar; a few titter at Jabari's costume. Builders walk home in sullen clumps and administrators chat with varying states of energy. Laughter, arguments, the tinny sound of music from crystal sets, the bubble of household boilers and the hiss of escaping steam issuing high about the buildings from verdigris corroded pipes.

Yet out there under the cooling sand....

A little street cleaner clatters past on six double jointed legs. It is an older model, panelled sides dented and nibbled at by rust. An outsized hippo head opens its mouth and its sides concertina as a hidden vacuum sucks up the litter clogging the gutters. Feeling sick Jabari continues on.

At night the gods rest, their manifestations fading like desert mirages, only to return at sun up. Ra withdraws to fight his endless battle through the underworld and the cities magics are put on reserve to compensate. The seascape atmosphere of blue green light that has become the hallmark of the kingdoms international face is replaced with the softer saffron glow of gas lamps. The queer light has a curious effect. Above the street, twenty-foot billboards carry desert-desiccated advertisements for the latest metal servants, announcing the newest, longer-lasting, sweeter scented Re-Animator with its smiling Pharaoh Mummy; in the gloaming the paintings turn seductive in the half-light. The familiar ever-present glow of an emergency Re-Animator store is a balm. The Re-Animators are a relatively new invention, a concoction of Isis's gift to mankind and embalming fluids that can keep the dead walking and talking with a semblance of the family member's candour. It has become a staple of Egypt's life.

Cairo is never a city sleeping, but a city changing track.

It all serves to sooth Jabari's nerves. So what if they are building something under the sands? He's never had any doubts about his teachers, and so he has no reason to suspect it isn't some new marvel to stun the world, another rivet in their dominance. He pushes the memory of the scarlet light out of his mind.

The smell of cooking is rich as he enters the residential district. He can almost taste the salt and goat on his tongue, the vegetables yellowed with spice and sharp with aniseed. These streets are home: comforting, familiar. Yet outside his parent's apartment he stops. It is a home like a hundred others. A blocky building of sandstone with heavily plastered sides. The thick walls and deep windows that have served Egypt for centuries are now offset against wide open balconies, glass sheeting, lime green plants in azure glazed pots slipping over the harsh squared lines. He already knows what he'll find inside; his father cooking in the kitchen waving a knife as he chops, talking animatedly while the steam slicks his dark face in sweat. His mother will be sitting by the balcony with her small army of clockwork frogs to defeat the flies, enjoying the cool sage winds of the desert night and painting postcards to sell on her stall.

Jabari can't bring himself to cross the doorstep, to bring what he's seen into his parent's house. The decision strengthens him. He lingers in the empty street listening to the sound of people's lives dislocated by walls and almost lost under his own breath, and feels something inexplicable drop away inside him. He turns and wanders back into the warren, realising it isn't his parents he has come looking for.

Amis has family in the city. He turns east.

Before long the streets widen, the buildings growing more spacious. He walks past the VI Luna Temple Library and its tall statue of Thoth. Is that what they are making? But no; Thoth is impressive but still only twenty five foot high; the thing he saw would rival the old pyramids in scale, and for what purpose? A war machine? Impractical. You cannot simply pour magic into an inanimate object and make it live for more than an hour at most, and something that size would require endless winding clockwork, and at least steam to drive it's pistons in a boiler, bigger than the thing itself. Even then it'd have no authority. From the Anubis headed police patrolling the streets to the little outdated Hippo collecting trash, they all operate under the iron fist of punch cards and programming.

He silently offers a prayer to Thoth's impassive Ibis head, begging for wisdom.

Who is Amelia Grace? he wonders again...

He freezes in shock.

...and why is she crawling from the temple library's window?

"Shai be damned," Jabari curses as the library's alarms start to wail.

"Well, fate has a limited repertoire," the old woman says, dusting down her catsuit with one hand. In the other she is gripping a book. Behind her, a stocky youth is following her from the window, turning back to help a wiry little girl down from the ledge. He recognises her, Jabari realises, and as he squints he realises that he also knows—

"You've ruined everything you lunatic!" As soon as the girl's feet touch the floor she storms at Amelia.

"Must we deal in hysterics?" Amelia drawls. The girl, a guild of thirteen years old at most and still wearing her woollen wig, looks ready to kill.

"Shut up," Jabari snaps. The newcomers turn to him in surprise.

"Jabari?" Amis whispers.

"Amis," says Jabari flatly.

Amelia has no patience for their reunion. "Jabari, darling, be a love and tell these fools we don't have time for idiocy."

As if summoned by her words, the sound of an Anubis guard interjects itself between them, not yet visible but drawn by the noise of alarms, its claws clicking on the stone.

"Hold this, dear." Amelia shoves the book into Jabari's hands and starts to run. The other sprint after her and, stunned, Jabari follows.

The girl still finds breath to rant. "Whelp of a jackal! We could have stopped the rite!"

"My dear girl," Amelia snaps back, putting all her emphasis on the word *girl*, "it was already far too advanced for that. I did the only thing I could."

They round a corner and hurtle down a sloping street lined with palms. A few curious eyes watch them pass but no one leaves their doorways.

"And what good have you done besides piss the priests off?"

Jabari marvels at this tiny young girl with the mouth of a labourer.

"Satiya, enough," Amis hisses. The girl fumes. The name helps Jabari finally place her: Satiya, Amis's little sister.

"Will someone explain what is going on?" Jabari shouts after them. The book is heavy, and he is panting hard. The earth rumbles; the others exchanges fearful looks but don't speak.

They run until the library's sirens fade, replaced by the sounds of oblivious laughter and the quiet hiss of gaslamps. They've entered a new residential district, more than a few houses freshly complete and still empty. "Through here." Amelia points to a dark recess and, lungs burning, Jabari gladly follows her into a courtyard. Disused and cool, the little space is half-filled by a half finished fountain. A sandstone Isis stands in the dry base, all sharp angles and chisel marks. In one corner a narrow stair leads upwards to the rooftop.

For a second time the earth rumbles, this time more violently. Jabari slumps against the wall and slides to the flagstones.

"Give me the book," Satiya demands. Jabari holds it out to her, but nimble as a goat Amelia snatches it from his fingers.

"Now now, I don't think that's going to happen. We have our own plans for this mouldy old thing." Her gun is back in her hand, Jabari realises—and Amis and Satiya seem no more comfortable with this than he does.

"I don't understand," Jabari whispers. "What is—what were—what…" He trails off.

Amis takes pity on his friend. He kneels beside him, one eye on the gun in Amelia's hand. "The priests aren't happy about having peace. They see any world that doesn't bow to the gods as a sin. They want to continue the war, rule the world whether the world likes it or not."

"But the gods want peace—Hathor even tours!"

"Which means—as far as the priests are concerned—that they're not worth worship," Satiya replies softly. Her eyes are heavy with sorrow even in the dark. "And if they're not worthy, then the priesthood will find one that is. And by worthy, they mean a god that that won't be against bringing the whole world to heel."

"The monster they are building?"

Amelia is twirling her gun. "They've raised Set, sweetheart. But I in my humble efforts have given you a chance, if you know how to sieze it."

Jabari's head reels, horror climbing his throat. Set. The mad god. Destruction itself.

"*You've* given us a chance?" Satiya rounds on the woman, apparently unconcerned about the gun. "You bust into the rite shooting like a drunken vulture and snatch the book of the dead just as *we're* about to start a counter spell—and you think *you've* helped! If we hadn't gone after you then you'd still be wandering the tunnel shooting *xara* out of the walls and looking for sunlight."

"Thanks to me, Set isn't bound to his new body. It's more than *you* two managed. Now I enjoy talking to *children* as much as I enjoy travelling by boat, by which I mean I both of them make me feel nauseous, so it's really time I was going."

"Now hold on a minute—"

"Enough!" Jabari's shout startles them all, even him. Amelia fumbles the trigger, firing a shot that catches Isis in the stone face.

"Oh bugger."

"Blasphemy!" Satiya roars.

Jabari feels like stamping his foot. "Will someone just explain. Who *are* you?"

Amelia smiles, curtseys. "Amelia Grace, Pan-Atlantic spy, grandmother, Libra and currently your saviour. Sort of, but not entirely, at your service."

"Saviour! You're a thief." Satiya takes a step towards Amelia.

"And, uh, we're Isis Faction," Amis adds weakly. "We've been working against the more extreme priests for a while."

"Ah, yes," Amelia snaps. "Isis Faction. You've been doing such a *wonderful* job."

"Why aren't you working together?" Jabari tries to keep track. "Set is...." his throat closes at the thought and another wave ripples through the flagstones.

"You're a very sweet boy, but you're far too naive for this story. My patrons don't especially want a new war, but they're really far more interested in the chance to read *this*." Amelia hefts the book of the dead. "Now—I really should be going."

A second shot takes off the tip of Isis's wing and Amelia dives for the stairs, Satiya on her heels. The boys jump to follow her. On the flat rooftop Satiya lunges, her sandaled foot catching Amelia behind the ankle. The old woman stumbles but rights herself and then it is as if she has suddenly taken flight. Comically, the three Nubians look upwards as Amelia ascends away from them—and it is only after a moment's attention they see the rope that has descended to her from a pitch-black hot-air balloon that hovers above.

"Give me the book!" Satiya shouts futilely after her. With a smile, Amelia stuffs the ancient text down the front of her cat suit and begins to haul herself up the rope like a geriatric circus act.

Jabari watches her go and just before she passes from the corona of the city's glow they match gazes. "Here," she suddenly calls, throwing the gun down. It arcs through the air into Jabari's hand and misfires, sending a beam of Sekhmet's borrowed power out into the sky. Jabari is knocked off his feet, landing in an undignified heap. "Don't say Aunty Amelia never gave you anything. Cheerio my dears. It's been too divine."

High above their heads hands reach out of a thickly painted basket and none-too-gently pull her inside. Tiny thrusters belch smoke and push the balloon on its way out over the desert, leaving New Cairo far behind.

"I'd like to skin that woman," Satiya mutters. She turns to her brother. "What are we going to do now?"

Something about Amis's expression stirs Jabari. He struggles to his feet, buy is almost knocked back to the ground as the strongest quake yet ripples through the city. Somewhere pots topple and smash the minuscule tinkle of broken pottery a relatively calm vanguard to the abrupt sound of wrenching stone and dirt.

Satiya is the first to see it, the outline of a fist against the stars, just beyond the city limits. Veins of scarlet light thread their way up its metal carapace as Set wakes in his new body.

A dust cloud engulfs the sky as the mad god pushes his riveted shoulders from the desert floor. Three miles away and still Jabari is forced to close his eyes and spit grit. His magic is palpable even from this distance; the sensation of Set's hellish glow is like hot grease on the skin. The priest's colossus unfolds itself, stands fifty feet high and stretches, cracks in his armour spilling scarlet light like blood.

"He is not locked into his new body," Satiya is saying, though she doesn't sound very certain. "The resurrection isn't complete, he can be expelled..."

"We have to go," Amis urges.

"What? We can't just leave, we have a duty to help protect..." Satiya protests.

Jabari looks down at the gun in his hand, looks over at Amis, his face fearful. He feels something unlock inside his ribcage. *He is not bound to his new body.* The monster shakes sand from its joints, turns turning crimson eyes on the city.

War. Death. The shocks of the day are nothing compared to this.

"I was just hungry," he whispers, a fleeting echo of the scents outside his home playing across his senses. His mother; is she still sitting on the balcony paints forgotten, watching death rise from the desert? Has the paring knife fallen from his father's hand in fear? His resolve hardens.

"I have an idea," he says, surprised his voice doesn't shake.

THEY WAIT FOR Satiya on the city's main thoroughfare. Tons of dressed stone line the road, bisecting the city neatly from the steps of the pharaoh's palace to the outer slums. Chaos rules. People from all walks of life flood the palace's approach; crowds demand to know what is happening, why the gods have abandoned them.

But of course, the answer is simple. It is night, and as Ra sails through the underworld the gods sleep waiting for the new day. Hours away, lifetimes in terms of the damage Set could do before the sun god returns with hot-headed Horus beside him.

Amid the pandemonium, Jabari feels oddly calm.

"I thought you were dead or hurt," he mutters.

"What?" Amis keeps checking the roads. Restless, his muscled arms flex and he bounces on his heels. Jabari reaches under his kilt and retrieves the bracelet he found that morning. Silently he hands it back.

"Oh."

"I thought you were dead," he repeats. Gently Amis clasps Jabari's shoulder. The heat of his palm could sear to the bone.

"Well, I'm not."

"Found one," Satiya shrills, rounding the corner at speed in the back of a camel car. The ugly contraption is roofless, gold painted flanks flaking with rust, three wheels each side and a double hump of boilers spouting steam down its centre.

"Where did she learn to drive—she's thirteen years old!" Jabari marvels, as if, after everything else he has seen from Satiya that night, it is driving that stretches the bounds of incredulity.

"How did she convince our mother to let her be a guide at the pyramids instead of going to school? She has her ways."

Jabari looks sidelong at him. "Can you do this?"

Amis swallows, nods. "I never made it to full priesthood. Next year perhaps I would.... never mind. I can do this. But first we need the Re-Animator."

"Way ahead of you," Satiya shouts, revving the engine of her stolen vehicle for emphasis. "Now let's go." Gingerly the two men climb into the car's open back and Satiya slams on the speed, sending them careering down the boulevard.

In the distance Set can be tracked as a red stream demolishing the outer toy pyramids with tempestuous rage. The tiny constructs, these little power houses so key in his resurrection, fold like papyrus under his metal heels.

It is clear, Satiya remarks, that the Priests are not in control. Jabari wonders how much of that is Amelia's doing.

"How were you going to stop the rite?" he shouts over Satiya's jubilant screaming. The grin plastered to her face is far the most unnerving thing he's seen all night.

"A counter spell, almost an amendment to their invocations. He would still rise but delayed by a hundred years," Amis explains. "It wasn't perfect, but..."

"Would it have worked?"

Amis sheepishly shrugs.

"The elders thought so. It's what all my training was leading to. I was chosen for this."

"You didn't think to inform the Pharaoh?"

"And say what? His Demi-Priest is among them!"

Jabari glances at Satiya hunched over the wheel, and the fast approaching wall.

"Satiya...turn."

"Not a chance."

"Satiya!"

The camel car mounts the pavement, reduces the wall to rumble and spills its passengers into the room beyond. Jabari swallows blood and almost throws up as his mouth fills with thick salt. His shoulder feels bloated, an ache in his left leg pulsing in time with his heart.

"What were you thinking?" he snaps, then clamps his mouth shut as he feels a tooth wobble.

Satiya crawls from the car grinning, and gestures around her. As the dust settles Jabari can make out counters and glass, refined crystal lighting with hidden copper wires adding delicate white glows to countless display cases.

"It's a shop," he says, confused.

"You're a genius!" Amis breaks open the closest case and loads his arms with bottles from within. Jabari realises the sweet musk cloying at his nostrils is coming from the bottles already crushed under the car's wheels.

"Re-Animator..."

"How much do we need?" Satiya is like a spider scuttling from case to case, heaving a plaster case of Orisis to smash the glass displays. They fill the car's back seats with bottles—some in the shape of sarcophagi, others the oddly tactile shape of mummies with the atomiser in place of a head—and back the car out of the wreckage.

Three Anubis guards squat in the street, their doglike bodies shining pure gold. Witnessing an act of looting, their pre-programmed synapses snap to life and they trot in pursuit.

"That's just what we need," Amis sighs as the car picks up pace. "Go for it Satiya!"

His sister yells something formless and pushes the boilers to their maximum speed. They blast away, leaving the Anubis guards lolloping uselessly in distant pursuit. They hurtle around corners, barely missing lamp posts, and only demolishing two cartouche benches. At first the streets are empty, abandoned, but other cars appear on the roads as they approach the residential district, each one laded with belongings and confused children as families try to escape the city. A diminutive old man in a loin cloth sits atop a cart scarab hitting the poor automaton with a back scratcher in a futile attempt to make it walk faster; some couples have taken to the streets on foot, the most affluent spraying stiff jointed mummies with their choice of re-animator so ancient uncle Baba and great grandmother Halima don't perish left in the family crypts. Amongst them are more Anubis guards, but bewildered by the sheer amount of transgression they fall back, skittering backwards and forwards racked with incision. If they had been real dogs Jabari wouldn't have been surprised to see their tails sink between their legs.

"Turn left here," he directs, and the car skids to oblige. The fountain of Cleopatra comes into sight. The train station beyond it is clogged with terrified people. "There," Jabari points, and they pull up under the pig iron struts of a giant billboard advertising Horus Air Travel. He turns to Amis. "You *can* do this?"

Amis nods solemnly and stands up. Satiya ties his hands to the support rail between the car's boilers, then heaves their stolen hoard from the backboard. Jabari and Satiya smash the bottles at the billboard's foot.

The Re-Animator finds a few dead weeds and lives. There is a brief spurt of green life, but nothing more.

Amis starts to chant; the magic is beyond anything Jabari can fathom, but he understands what the spell is doing, directing the Re-Animator liquid towards the inanimate. It fights him, but Amis persists.

You can't simply pour magic into an inorganic object and make it live...but for a while you can give it the semblance of life.

High above, plywood creaks and paint cracks. With painful slowness, the gilt and varnish face of Horus blinks and peels away from its backing.

Amis's eyes have rolled back in his head, words spill in a garble from his lips.

"It won't last long," Jabari warns, herding Satiya back behind the wheel. "Now—to get his attention."

A lot more people watch them as they speed through the city this time, what with Horus swooping above them like a gaudy kite.

They drive east toward the river and the pedestrian embankment. It is deserted and that sight alone bites at Jabari's confidence. The Nile embankment is always busy, the great souk that runs its length studded with restaurants, shops and ornaments. Devoid of patronage it is shabby and pallid. He feels as if he's already failed.

"Stop here," he orders. "Amis, you need to fly it higher."

A slim trail of blood snakes from Amis's nostril but the jagged circle of Horus's stupidly blinking head floats out above the flat rooftops.

They wait; it doesn't take long.

Underlit by the city's gas lamps, the whitewash of the hawk's cheeks flashes brilliant: a beacon in the night. From the desert there is a roar both animal and mechanical, the screech of ancient loathing and stressed copper cables. The mad god has seen them and his stride is immense.

The flagstones jump at interval and Jabari realises it is because Set is running.

"Go!" he shouts, and Satiya takes off along the deserted street.

The colossus don't take long to catch up but their mad young driver begins to sway, sending Horus's mask swinging through the air to avoid Set's grasping fingers. The metal giant is already looking worse for wear. Unbound, his power breaches the carapace in gouts of twisted scarlet light. However, it is still the power of a god that glows like lava below its cast iron ribs, and with each new rupture another seals over. As much as his metal body struggles to contain the power within, contain it it does. It would take the power of another god to defeat him, and they are all out of gods eight long hours before dawn.

In eight hours Set could conquer the world. In eight hours his strength could have grown exponentially; he could appear in any capitol in the world, laughing insanely; he could burn the Great Karnak in Russia until the buildings melt with the snow, crush the half mile high statue of Bastet in Delhi and use the rumble to block the Ganges.

Ahead, a domed bulk sits across the river, a purification plant. The rushing sound of water escalates as hidden currents hit against a blockage. Satiya is forced to slow and with a scream of success, Set snatches their impromptu puppet from the air. He pauses. If his giant face could form expression Jabari imagines it'd be puzzlement.

He laughs and that laughter frees him from despair

"Can...can you untie me?" Amis groans. Blood plasters his lips and chin.

Satiya takes a knife to the knots and Jabari doesn't want to think about where she got it.

"Come on, we have to get inside before he comes to his senses."

Between them they drag Amis through a side door and into the gloom of the building's interior.

"You have to say here," Jabari insists.

Amis grips his hand and presses a bracelet from his wrist into his palm. "I want you to have it, for luck."

"Thank you. Satiya, stay with your..." he looks around for the girl and sees her already running across the vestibule. There is a tour guide amplifier clutched in her hand. "Satiya!"

Outside, Set roars in rage realising he's been tricked. With a last look at Amis, Jabari races after Satiya's bobbing wig.

Set's red glow shines down through the stained glass domes in the ceiling, turning the world a watery purple. Walkways of grated metal lattice the river, channelled through the great halls to pass between Hapi's golden coils like the mouth of a canyon. Together the young guide and the hapless usher race across platforms spanning the swift waters. They need to be on the other side.

Set isn't one for patience—or doors. His fist smashes through the skylights, littering the air with blue-green flakes, a deadly glass monsoon. The falling shards cut ribbons from Jabari's bare arms and chest. Satiya fares a little a better, protected by the thick bleached canvas of her dress but she too is painted crimson by the time they pass the immense copper coils and stand hand in hand over the river beyond.

To their right an etched cartouche sign asks them to queue quietly.

"What if this doesn't work?" Satiya asks under her breath.

"We die."

"Just wanted to be sure." She inhales, filling her lungs until her chest balloons against the fabric and cracks the handle of her sleek brass amplifier. "Set, you son of a worm! Defeated weakling! *Xara*-eating beetle unfit to wipe my buttocks!" she bellows.

The monsters face peers in through the broken glass and rivets pop from his forehead in anger.

"Scum! Insect! Imagine losing to a hawk…! Sonless beast. *Tozz fiik wa filli abuuk!*" Jabari adds.

Set kicks through the walls. Plaster, brick and painted murals cascad into the Nile.

"Did we over do it?" Jabari backs away, shuffling until he feels the safety rail pressed icy cold in the small of his back.

"Overdo it?" Satiya looks at him with such condescension that Jabari feels his face turn hot. Shaking her head, Satiya lifts the amplified back to her and lets loose with such a stream of curses in so many languages that Jabari feels blasphemous just standing near her.

Set clearly understand every word. He storms though the plant's crumbling facades, his enormous feet planting themselves into the waters.

Jabari screws up his eyes and regrets every moment since abandoning his post that morning. Amis's bracelet digs into the soft flesh of his hand and he offers up one final prayer. Raising Amelia's gun, he points into the churning water above Set's foot. Set is reaching for him, the heat the metal fingers making Jabari's his skin prick then burn before the machine has even reached him. He cries in pain, and fires blind, then throws himself backwards from the bridge. Air rushes past his scorched body as he plummets into the river.

Set stumbles into the gap between coils.

Steam obscures Jabari's fall, but that monstrous reaching hand never touches him. Instead, the diffuse red glow of the newly born god contorts like a fly in a web. The purification coils blaze golden, releasing Hapi's stored power in a flood from the reserves, the waves of purity sweeping away the the sudden influx of contaminant that has dared to pass through it.

The light winks out. Jabari hits the water and a moment later is followed by the peeling segments of Set's empty case.

RA RIDES THROUGH the sky at a languid pace, wondering at the unusual torrent of worship from the city below this morning. Such strange creatures these humans are.

On the un-dammed banks of the Nile, miles down the desert from New Cairo's urban sprawl, Jabari feels the sun drying mud on his cheeks and blinks. The sky is clear, a cloudless periwinkle at the edges and a deep hot blue in the centre.

"Well, you're alive. But you stink."

Satiya's scowling face blocks out the sun for a moment, and then she wanders away. Jabari stares after her. She's lost her wig in the river, revealing a shaven head below. Amis is sitting in the mud by his side, looking back toward the city and its thin trails of smoke.

"What do we do now?" Jabari asks, then winces as the burnt skin of his face stretches below the mud.

"Leave the mud on. It'll help with the burns until we can get to a healer."

"That's not what I meant."

"I know."

They sit in silence, each with their own thoughts.

"Will they come after us?"

Amis snorts, plucking a bulrush from the river bank and stripping its brown fur with his thumb nail.

"A priest in training, an usher and a thirteen year old guide spoils the plans of the most powerful people in Egypt. What do *you* think?"

Jabari has nothing to say to that.

Above the day moves on. Ra sails across the sky, oblivious to the complications of the people below him. In Cairo, the Anubis guards are being repurposed, tasked with clearing the rubble. On the edge of the Nile, three weary youths wonder which direction they should go, and to the far north, where the desert becomes the sea, a black balloon can just be seen, hovering in the sky.

To Kill A God

The sky is overcast,
The stars are darkened,
The celestial expanses quiver,
The bones of the earth-gods tremble,
The planets are stilled,
For they have seen the King appearing in power
As a god who lives on his fathers
And feeds on his mothers
—*The Pyramid Text*

The Prophet (peace be upon him) said: Let him who hears
of the Dajjal go far from him for I swear by Allah that a
man will come to him thinking he is a believer and follow
him because of confused ideas roused in him by him.
—Imran ibn Husayn, *Book of Battles*

As the airship clipped across the Mediterranean my dreams were plagued
by queer visitations. Between Algiers and Tunis dim shadows devolved into
vague glimpses of mutilated geometries and degenerate glyphs; maggot-infested

stacks of parchment rotting before dead, hemorrhaging eyes; agonized figures with anatomy closely resembling men ululating perverse prayers into cold and indifferent heavens; mad cackling from within unfathomable clockwork machinery.

I, for my part, was not accustomed to nocturnal visions such as these, the likes of which I could not dwell upon when awoken for fear of returning to those disturbing scenes. I would wake in a cold sweat and it was all I could do to keep myself from retching, although I took care to compose myself lest one of my porters hear and send word of any disturbances on to my patron. In the face of the incredible work before me I could tolerate the odd nightmare.

I believed I could tolerate most anything, for I was young and invincible, a keen intellect, a self-styled polymath, as if such vanity insulated me from what I was to face.

I had recently completed my graduate studies in the languages department out of a great, old university in New England. My *Treatise on Primordial Ciphers* had scandalized Essex County's intelligentsia with its agnostic rhetoric. My academic work on arcane history and supernal symbolism was decidedly controversial, and those in my social circle were lauded as iconoclasts or lambasted as degenerate dandies depending upon whom you spoke to. Good Christian families contested my courses as satanic, and preachers castigated the university for supporting my work, the usual bothersome, empty quarrels of the faithful. My colleagues and I reveled in the notoriety.

However, I'd tired of the clockwork intrigues and dullard politics of academic life as of late, so I was all too ready to accept a sabbatical, tantalized by promises of ancient texts not even my university's sizable archives of arcane literature housed. My patron's proposition included mention of a related matter he hoped I'd look into *quid pro quo*. To boast of being flown to "the city of the Conquering Star" for such a request was the little temptation I needed.

After a nauseating cross-Atlantic steamship voyage I spent a week recovering, speaking at salons and visiting sympathetic colleagues at Oxford before boarding a new passenger airship, the *Indomitable*, flown exclusively by Quigley Airships. Quarters were cramped, and most of my fellow passengers were boorish English bureaucrats and their families, en route to clean house in Lower Egypt's metropolis, or wealthy Muslims returning from their dealings in the West. Weather favoured us, a dry wind blowing steadily from the south, but we were still scheduled for stops in Tripoli, Benghazi, and Alexandria before following the winding skein of turquoise, the western Rasheed offshoot, south to the capitol; miles of green stretching out on either side of the river before terminating abruptly into yellow-gold Egyptian desert. It was aboard the airship that the dark visions began their nightly assault on my mind.

Aside from my bout of nightmares, a single, disturbing incident marred the journey into the ancient Egyptian city; a Muslim man we had lifted in Benghazi, my adjacent cabin neighbour, took ill above the Nile Delta soon after departing Alexandria, and was confined to his room by captain and crew. They locked his door from without, and what began as weak cries from within turned quickly to feverish sobbing, and then terrible silence. There were whispers of a fresh plague wreaking havoc on the Mediterranean, not helped at all by powerful winds from the south. Despite being a man of a cold, rational, scientific mind, I, like my fellow passengers, averted my eyes from his cabin door as if even looking upon it was a contaminant, and packed to be off the airship as soon as we landed, for the smell was terrible.

LOCALS CALLED THE winds *el-khamáseen*. The oppressive heat and dry breeze out of the south that so favoured airships did little for my suit, for I was soaked with sweat before stepping off the *Indomitable*. I was jealous of locals working in the airship yards for their loose fitting robes, although some of the poorer sun-baked labourers wore less, and I didn't want to imagine the effect such sickening heat would have on their temperaments or minds.

The dry air made it difficult to breath, and the only benefit I could see in clinging to the land was the verdancy of the Nile, much improved by local progress in irrigation technologies. Otherwise any sane person would have abandoned the land, despite the history and harsh beauty of the Delta.

I was unceremoniously packed into an open carriage with three sweating, complaining British families, our luggage heaped onto the backs of a phalanx of asses. We started south from the Quigley Airship fields and traversed over the canal, passing the old sandy stonewalls into the city proper.

The streets were mostly unpaved and narrow, breaking off one another at astounding irregularity. How anyone navigated this mad old city I could not fathom. We took a great thoroughfare hemmed by rows of shops on each side of us. The buildings loomed higher above the street than they should, no sense of unifying design, with odd, latticed windows angling down at the street, hiding any number of observers from above. Minarets reached up from the jumble of rooftop terraces and lopsided stone structures at odd intervals, and the ancient Citadel of Salah al-Din sat grand, oppressive and watchful on the side of the

Mukattam. Out of the squalor and chaos of the city opulent palaces would rise without warning, like reveries of twisted, decadent kings.

A long-winded British diplomat, who seemed weary of his squawking children, explained to me this section of the city was considered the European quarter. The old Khedive had been obsessed with creating a "Paris on the Nile," boulevards lined with palaces, punctuated with gardens and squares. British control in the region centred around the Midan Tahrir. The people of Maṣr became entirely stranger as we turned into this garden district at the south of the city, near the otherworldly blue river to the west. Here the smarter set of European expats mingled freely with oddly garbed Muslims, meek, cowed women entirely swathed in dark cloth while colourful robes flapped off their flamboyant men in the breeze, like the difference between peahens and peacocks among the black crows of England businessmen and their swanning, preening wives. I watched as a woman in a voluminous Parisian dress fainted dead away, and was carried off by European men who looked ready to follow her suit. Overexertion? Or this new plague? Well, one hoped the former.

When our queer train stopped before a grand hotel, aping something straight out of Montmartre, the man pointed out the headquarters of the British Army of Occupation, a former palace of the khedive's army. The jocular, sweating, reeking diplomat claimed I could seek refuge from the madness of the barbaric, superstitious locals there should I ever need, despite the fact that I was a Yankee.

I was expected there, and while wiping my brow with a soaked handkerchief an Arab approached me, who I took to be the manservant of my patron. He was little more than a boy, dark brown skin and obsidian black hair, a patchy beard barely growing upon his jawline, his dress modest. The boy was generous with his grins but frugal with his aid as I gathered my valises.

"Hello," I intoned, nodding to him as he lifted a small chest containing some of my work off the ass and immediately plopped it into the dirt. He turned and gave me a bashful grin. "Do you speak English?"

The boy grinned his response. My Arabic was barely functional at best, but I attempted what I could, "Betetkallem 'engelīzi?" The idiot shrugged and motioned for me to follow, not making any effort to help me with my bags.

I grumbled some English curses at him, discarding my soiled coat and hefting the chest over my shoulder.

After we crossed the boulevard called Kasr et Ali I was relieved to find the idiot had the sense to hire a mule for my things, though I wasn't afforded the luxury of a coach. He led the beast from the swath of European styled buildings eastwards, into the thick of the winding, claustrophobic lanes, and I could do little but follow. Less and less I saw the influence of western civilization in the shadowed corridors of the city. Despite the press of the buildings and their inconsistent designs I took this to be an enclave for wealthier Arabs, for gone were the squealing, half naked urchins I had seen on my way into the city. Many of the ornate doorways were inscribed with the bizarre, beautiful Arabic script that lauded "the Great Creator, the Everlasting," I recognized, in white or black characters.

We crossed a narrower boulevard on our travel into the city and I saw a crowd gathered ahead, listening to a ragged street preacher of some kind. As we neared, my porter clearing a path for the animal, I was close enough to see that his eyes were swollen—perhaps an untreated case of ophthalmia? I could garner little from his hoarse cries, but I took it that he was lambasting some doctor, or scientist? I felt oddly self-conscious as I passed beneath the sightless gaze of the man, for he fell silent as we cleared the crowd, and a number of men and women turned to look. I was eager to be away from the preacher for reasons I couldn't say. I realized that the touch of progress at the extremities of the city had barely penetrated the persistent, superstitious, old ways. Airships may cloud the sky above Maṣr, and roaring steam-powered engines may pump the very waters of the Nile to give the city life, but no technology could change the heart of man.

Finally, my simpleton porter pulled the mule through a gate, unlocked with an enormous, clunky wood-block key, into an unpaved courtyard. I moved to remove my baggage, but he shook his head and waved for me to follow him.

We entered an ornate, whitewashed antechamber just inside of the house. The room was blessedly cool, lit only by high windows that defused the light from the courtyard. Within the first room, a few inches lower than the rest of furnishings, was a small, tiled fountain decorated in white, black and intricate red shapes creating stars and suns. Unashamed of my rudeness or ignorance before the useless porter, or for the cleanliness of the water, I dove to the side of the pool, cupping my hands and drinking deeply before splashing my face. I looked up to see the young man standing beside me, grinning, holding out a cup he had retrieved. I thanked him, for whatever reason, and spent a moment drinking to satiation.

The idiot removed his shoes, modest slippers, and I followed, glad to feel cool tile beneath my feet. He motioned for me to follow him up some stairs, and we climbed into a second room, similarly decorated save the fountain. Up into the highest apartment of the house, a richly decorated comfort room. Within was a large, lofty recess furnished with two plush mattresses, one across from the other with a mat between them. On the smaller mattress, bathed in the dim light that made its way through the latticed windows, sat a woman in plain but comely robes.

She glanced up, closing the book in her lap. Her large brown eyes were ringed in kohl, but the makeup could not hide the effects of age, perhaps twice my twenty-two years or more. Her face was the pale brown of an Arab woman not much out of doors, and her dark brown hair done up beneath a gold-hemmed Muslim kerchief, showed some ashen colour at the temples. Her keen eyes studied me a moment.

"Mr. Crosswhite, 'salāmu-`alēkum," she intoned.

I raised an eyebrow. It had been my understanding that the Muslim female was not allowed to talk to men other than their family or husbands, some such nonsense that made our own societies of chaperones and polite co-ed functions appear liberal. "I hope I am not intruding, madam. Am I to await your husband here?"

She chuckled politely, "You would be waiting some time, sir. My husband is in Exeter on business." She motioned for me to take the divan across from her. Her English was fluent, the Arabic accent I was familiar with intermingling with a British one. "I am Surayya Al Serafy, your host and patron in our city."

I was aghast, cursing myself inwardly. My patron had only communicated with me through painstaking word-of-mouth, a series of visitations by the portly, enigmatic Arabic scholar at my university over the past year on behalf of the "great household of Al Serafy." Now I knew why I had learned so very little of whom I was to be working for.

"Madam," the young man standing next to me said, stepping forth. "You have much to discuss, I will take Mr. Crosswhite's bags to his apartment."

She nodded, "Šokràn, Abd Al-Latif." He gave a respectful bow and then turned to leave. He flashed a grin at me and I could barely contain a scowl. Within a matter of seconds both my patron and porter had revealed a double helping of deception. I felt the complete fool.

"Please," she motioned again at the divan opposite and I accepted her invitation, fuming. "I apologize for the untruth, but should it get out that I am conversing with an intellect from America, there would be awkward questions."

I gave an exaggerated shrug. She, again, seemed to be appraising me, a small smile playing at her lips. "I found your dissertation of utmost interest."

I goggled at the statement, "How on Earth did you get a hold of it?"

She patted the book in her lap, "My husband and I may be Muslim, but he is a modern man. He, unlike most of his countrymen, welcomes the British. He encourages my intellectual projects if I am discreet. Another way he differs from his fellow Egyptians, I suppose."

I nodded, "I don't mean to sound blunt, Madam Al Serafy, but I have traveled a long way to a strange city. Why am I here?"

"I have a project," she said. "The first portion of which is the translation of an old Egyptian text."

Surayya Al Serafy laid out the details of the project in as efficient a fashion as I needed to finally feel some comfort in the matter. I asked questions where I needed, but soon felt confident in the initial work she outlined. I would have access to the text and some of the more useful apocryphal works secured in the vaults of Al-Azhar University, where I would work as a visiting languages scholar in the employ of her husband. She promised my studies in ancient languages, and my cipher, would be of the utmost importance in the work, hence why I had been selected. Other translations had been attempted, but could only glean the meanest understandings of the tract. I saw the work before me, the translation of an ancient, arcane text unread since before the Common Era. The prospect was intoxicating.

"THE KING OF the hungering star," was the closest I could come to a translation of the text's title, or perhaps "Silence of the dark god," depending on the syntax. The tract, written by a Ptolemaic scholar named Naukratius of Alexandria, who was also a tutor of a crown prince, was impossibly well-preserved and written in a mixture of Demotic Egyptian and Koine Greek. The former was not a specialty of mine, but workable. The early pages were concerned with a retelling, or perhaps a reinterpretation of the death and resurrection of Ousiri.

The silence of the dark god, however, referred to the familiar, old Egyptian god as something equating "the Conquering Chaos," although who's to say if that was a perfect translation; a king of madness and a dark prophet of the world of whispering shadows, or the entropic infinite beyond the stars. The story inverted the myth, presenting a kind of hero or primal spellbinder in the form of Sēt, and detailed his monstrous transformation before killing the dark, mad king. A sort of ironic examination of ancient myth, an allegory, I quickly surmised, for the sake of a prince considering the treatment of power.

As the week and my work progressed, so did the little Arabic I have return to me, and was much improved by Al-Azhar's lead archivist, the venerable and patient Sheyk Halim Abdel-Dayem. The wizened old man's grasp of languages and esoteric knowledge was astounding, and he even referred me to several helpful texts within the university's vaults, chiefly an old but intelligible translation of the text written by the Mad Arab of Yemen, an unbound parcel of papers within a mundane cracked leather cover kept aside from much of the other works in the archives, under lock and key.

Several references within on glyphs pertaining to queer, primordial gods of the East proved useful in sections I couldn't otherwise understand. However, the chronology of *The silence of the dark god* and the Mad Arab's writings, with centuries between them, eluded me. Had the Mad Arab read Naukratius' work? Or heard of it? Or did they simply share some esoteric mythology. I found these questions vaguely unsettling for reasons I couldn't put into words, and I leafed through the mad pages of the eldritch text sparingly.

"How do you have this?" I asked as Halim brought me the dark, old tome, once again, later in the week. Of late the university had begun to attend more to secular leanings, but it was first and foremost a Muslim theological institution. I would have thought this heretical work lost in one of the university's purges, or purposefully destroyed by a man of faith, I explained.

The man gave his aged, rotten smile to that, "There are those of us who keep the old knowledge, praise be to God!"

With the steady improvement of my Arabic, not to mention a change of dress into the more appropriate and cool drawers and long, loose, full-sleeved shirt of the local style, I could walk the grounds of the school with some anonymity. Despite the fact that I kept clean-shaven unlike the majority of Muslim men, I was swarthy and dark of hair, and so could mostly remain unobtrusive if left alone.

In the southeastern inner courtyard of Al-Azhar, facing Mekkeh, was a spacious, intricately designed portico reserved for a place of prayer. I found myself fascinated with the *saláh* and would often break when I heard the *muëddins* of Al-Azhar—for it had been a mosque far longer than a university— intone the call to prayer. Five times a day the entire city would ring with the sonorous voices of the men atop the minarets, an ethereal chant which sent a chill up my spine despite not being of the faith.

I would sit in an alcove nearby and listen to the droning ritual ablutions, chanting and supplication of the men, for there were no women at Al-Azhar. After a portion of private prayers the *khaṭeeb*, a learned man, would intone teachings of Islam in the form of a sermon. I would practice my language by translating snippets, and found the ideas beautiful, if foreign to my own agnostic understanding of the world:

"Know that the present world is a transitory abode, and that the world to come is a lasting kingdom," the preacher would intone, his high, singsong voice ringing through the courtyard. "Make provision, therefore, in your transitory state for your lasting state, and prepare for your reckoning and stand before your Lord: for know that ye shall to-morrow be placed before God, and reckoned with according to your deeds; and before the Lord of Might ye shall be present, 'and those who have acted unjustly shall know with what an overthrowal they shall be overthrown.'"

I mused that this was not a sermon out of place amongst religions of the Western world. If anything there was more poetry and elegance to Muslim worship. For all their backwardness, it was no more or less than the petty superstitions and mad theology of their Christian counterparts of New England, or any other religion that had come before.

To my annoyance Madam Al Serafy's servant, Abd Al-Latif Aboul-Enein, made regular visits to me at Al-Azhar, grinning away his useless life. He would rifle through the early pages of my translation and question me about its contents. Why a mere servant would take such an interest in an old Egyptian fable was beyond me.

Beyond the servant and the archivist, my only companionship was a small, half-blind mouser I took to calling Cleopatra before I discovered she was a he. The one-eyed cat would appear in the dark of the night, a single amber eye glowing out of the dark. He would accept table scraps and a few moments of affection before dashing off into the shadows about whatever nocturnal business the little monster had.

"Tell me what you think of the work so far." I was again in the great house of Al Serafy, seated on the larger divan across from the lonely matriarch. She had read through my writings thus far, in my presence, and now placed the papers before her and looked to me.

"Well, the mythology is snarled. The author makes no distinction between Thōth and Ousiri, and this business to do with the heroism of the evil god... And this Naukratius seems fixated on the manner of Ousiri's incarceration, and the breaking of the god into fourteen pieces," I replied, nudging through the papers, pointing to the termination of my past week's work. "The scholar seems obsessed with the dimensions of some device, or machine, the likes of which I scarcely dare describe before my work continues. The properties, the materials, the glyphs or text associated with it..."

"Good," she handed me the stack of papers. "You are making excellent progress, Mr. Crosswhite, and your attention to detail is superb. I hope you will continue in this manner."

I gathered my things to depart back to my apartment for the night, though I dreaded another evening of nightmares and restless sleep in my oven of a dwelling. Every night my terrible dreams seemed to mount in intensity so that I would wake in the heat of the heavy evening air gasping. I dreamed of my university in New England, only the locale had that odd, shadowed dream quality of being not quite what it was meant to represent. I was scrambling through the darkness, fumbling my way towards my office but for what? Safety? To find something? Light barely penetrated the windows even though I knew it should during daylight hours. The sun was eclipsed, and would be eclipsed, for someone had told me it would never naturally shine on us again. I tripped over something and fell, and when I felt for what it was something weakly grabbed at my ankle. I fought it, caught a glimpse of two eye sockets, hollowed and bloody, and crawled away, sobbing, down the darkened hall. Dreadfully, this was typical of what I saw as I slept. I saw places I knew but were hellish and perverted. Creatures, or perhaps victims of the mad dream logic writhed and chittered just out of sight. Was I searching for something as I plunged through the lost world of my night?

More disturbing even than these; after awakening from these visions my sleepless hours seemed punctuated with tortured screams ringing through the city, a growing problem, it was rumoured. I put it down to plague festering just out of sight, and my own exhaustion, though others whispered superstitious nonsense I had come to expect of the Maṣree, talk of curses and dark spirits.

As our business concluded and we made plans to have me report my progress again in a week's time, Madam Al Serafy rang for the damnable porter. I stood to leave but saw her, again, appraising me with a critical eye. "By the Prophet, you look so much like your mother," she murmured.

I couldn't begin to form a thought to question what she meant, so taken aback by her statement was I. By the time I had regained any senses, the damnable, grinning servant had arrived and my patron had turned back to her book.

SOMEHOW THE CITY seemed to preoccupy itself from that which walked openly in the streets of Maṣr. While I kept close to my apartment when not at Al-Azhar, as advised, I was not spared sight of the terrible disease. I had glimpsed figures in alleyways, writhing in puddles of red-brown, crying out for water, or family, or God's mercy in weak voices, clouds of flies the only answer to their pleas.

If the stench and flies weren't enough, groups of men and women would gather around unholy preachers in the streets. The city was rife with these madmen, and the Muslims perversely called them saints. The worst of the sort was a man not unlike the one my porter and I had passed on the way into the city; perhaps the same man, though his condition seemed to be degenerating rapidly. It was a miracle he could stand upright, for he seemed little more than pale, grey flesh stretched over skin and bones. He appeared to rot from the inside, dried red-brown leakage down his leg advertising the disease, staining the rags that he wore.

Words barely escaped from his cracked, bloody lips, but I could now understand the diseased street preacher with my improved Arabic. He offered praise up to Allah, the only God, for protection against the infidel Munir Alnnajm-Al'aswad and his evil arts. I recognized the name as one whispered as a warning between scholars at the universities, always with an invocation to God to protect them.

I was more disturbed to see that when the diseased madman collapsed, a number of the crowd rushed forward to give him water from bowls and cups prepared seemingly just for him. Like others of his kind, the Muslims whispered that he was a saint. If a saint, the only thing he would bless them with was a swift transmission of the mortal illness. Shifty looking merchants waited nearby, claiming themselves magicians, and sold scraps of cloth and paper with Kur-ánic verses inscribed, which customers placed on their persons like a charm.

I questioned my archivist friend when I arrived at Al-Azhar. He explained the water was specially prepared with verses of the holy text written on the receptacles, washed into the water, and then drank. A cure, or so the vulgar believed. Much like the charms of the charlatans I had seen passed out. Holy protections.

"We are a superstitious people, by the Prophet!" he exclaimed, giving a dramatic shrug. "The recent years have not been kind to the learned of our beleaguered country."

I asked him about this Munir Alnnajm-Al'aswad and the man blanched. His affable nature evaporated and he became very nervous and subdued. He lead me deeper into the archives, away from where other scholars worked, toward the section where he kept secluded the text of the Mad Arab of Yemen I had consulted so often.

"Don't fail to see Dr. Munir Alnnajm-Al'aswad when he returns to Maṣr," the archivist whispered. "By the Prophet! His knowledge is terrible... I dare not speak of it... and wonderful, I attest. My mind cannot escape that which he showed."

His much-darkened manner piqued my curiosity. He gave me a name of a man who would know a man who would know where I could observe the great and terrible demonstration of this controversial figure for myself, if I wished, but he warned me not to speak of it to anyone. He said that the experience changed men, even the rational.

Abd Al-Latif, my patron's servant, tailed me more closely in the proceeding week and regularly read over my translation, to my great annoyance. He made notes to himself, specifically concerning the various materials I translated out of *The silence of the dark god*: the central fixture, a large, long chest made of cedar, ebony, ivory, silver and gold; the stone encasement, the various primordial gears and cogs, the strangely anachronistic mechanics; the blades, each marked with cryptic hieroglyphs.

At the end of the week, I mentioned my plan for a diversion to the quarter of Old Maṣr that night, for he had taken to walking me to and from my nearby apartment, excitedly discussing Naukratius' bizarre supernal machine. His signature grin vanished and he snapped to attention, questioning why I was going so out of my way to the southern extremity of the city. Foolishly, I explained that I wished to see the demonstration of Dr. Alnnajm-Al'aswad.

He seemed stricken with fear. "I cannot let you do that."

I rankled at being commanded by a servant who had taken pains to irritate me. I stated that he could attempt to stop me, but nothing in my agreement with Madam Al Serafy had forbidden me from seeing the city and amusing myself. Abd Al-Latif agonized over this, pleading with me periodically throughout the rest of the day not to go. I ignored the boy.

As I locked my writings away, he confronted me, his face pale. "If you will do this thing, I will go with you." If he meant to protect me from whatever imagined, the quaver in his voice and the trembling of his hands inspired little confidence.

WE FOUND OURSELVES below the Hanging Church just after the *maghrib* call to prayer, as the sun dipped over Giza to the west. The sonorous voices of the city's *muëddins* had just faded away when we spotted a plump man in strange black robes, a brass cross hanging from his neck.

Sheyk Halim Abdel-Dayem's man had been a woman; a whore, I took it, for her mode of dress, her residence in a degenerate bathhouse near a British Army barracks and the showings of pox about her person. She seemed disappointed by our lack of interest in her commerce, but was more open to discussion when I parted with a generous amount of piastres.

She directed us to the priest of the Hanging Church, a curious Coptic Orthodox church suspended above a gatehouse with whitewashed twin bell towers that seemed to mock neighboring minarets for their foreign design. The priest seemed skittish and hesitant to speak to me, but when I mentioned the Doctor, he bowed and bid me follow. Up a flight of steps we went and into the intricately decorated, gold-gilded ancient edifice. The priest brought us to an alcove decorated with an icon of a gold faced, dark winged angel, corpses lying about his feet. The angel's eyes were ivory white, as if blinded by cataracts, and a lion-faced serpent hung about his shoulders.

"Seekers of knowledge, yes?" the priest whispered as he stooped over and lifted a tile beneath the feet of the angel, his cross clanking quietly against the floor. "Read this, then burn it," he said, handing me a paper. Before I could say a word he disappeared into the ancient church.

"By the Prophet, Mr. Crosswhite! I beg you!" my uninvited companion pleaded as we neared our destination. "If we are spotted amongst this sort we could be arrested and killed!"

I said he was welcome to turn back, I could make my own way into the night, but he relented and followed me, brooding. I was pleased to get such a reaction out of him after two weeks of idiotic grinning.

I followed the directions and we found ourselves near the waters of the Nile in Old Maṣr. Down a quiet, clean alley we found two dark-robed men of indeterminate race, perhaps Nubian? Or out of India? Whether they served as disciples or guards I could not tell, for we passed them quietly and ascended an impossibly high, rickety set of stairs into the Doctor's apartment. I soon lost track of whether we were on the third floor of the building... the fourth? I didn't think it went as high as the fifth floor but we climbed for a minute straight before we entered the incense-choked room.

A few dozen men and even a few women were seated on small mattresses about the room. There were Muslims, French, Africans; an English couple, a man of middling age and a beautiful young woman murmured to each other, dressed in finery as if attending a night at the opera.

I disbelieved this was a temporary residence, so full was the dark, cavernous room of strange devices of alien design. Among them, I spotted what looked like a telescope, but affixed to a mighty, slumbering steam engine and adjusted

with intricately cogged machinery alongside a panel with countless dials. A brass
globe sat nearby, but I did not recognize any of the continents it predicted, and
the planet seemed to be mechanically orbited by an excess of alien moons. There
was also a tank of brackish water, serviced by devices that pumped water into
it and seemed to monitor the conditions within through lights and a display
panel in a language I could not place. Something stirred within; I shuddered
and turned away, disturbed by the twitching, shadowed, reptilian, fetal shape I
had glimpsed.

Through the low hanging, sickly sweet smoke a beam of light shone from a
strange device, seemingly clockwork in design. A lantern sat within, projecting
yellowish light through a semi-transparent screen or glass slide that was
routinely, automatically changed, perhaps by some internal mechanism that
timed out each display, for no assistant attended the machine. When we entered
the light from the queer machine was perversely displaying a Kur-ánic verse
that explained: "He grants wisdom to whom He pleases, and whoever is granted
wisdom, he indeed is given a great good and none but men of understanding
mind." A little on the nose, I thought to myself as we took a seat near the front.

As if on cue, the projecting machine snapped off with a mechanical whir,
and several of the dark robed figures moved about the room to dim the oil
lanterns. From amongst the gloom and clockwork pandemonium of the room
stepped an enormous stone slab of a man.

Dr. Munir Alnnajm-Al'aswad—for it was clear this was he by his regal
posture, his very presence—was more effigy than man. He was nearly seven feet
tall and walked with a slow, ponderous gravity. A welcoming smile was set in his
face as if carved to withstand the eons.

A single eye sparkled brightly out of his dark skinned, angular, thin and long
bearded face. And it was indeed a single eye, for the entire half of his upper, right
face was masked in bronze, seemingly set permanently with enormous bolts that,
given the position, affixed into his skull. Fixed in place of an eye was a lens, or
aperture, that glowed as if lit by a candle within, and whirred and spun in tandem
with his flesh eye with an intricacy beyond anything I'd believed possible.

"Out of the blackness of a millennium of ignorance, I come with a message
of knowledge and science, of our sole salvation." He spoke with a deep, guttural
voice that boomed through the space in an accented Arabic. Thus began the
demonstration of the depraved doctor.

The light-projecting machine whirred to life without the attention of the
Doctor or any of his dark robed disciples, although I saw them moving about the

room lighting fresh incense. I feared we were all to asphyxiate in the smoky air before this otherworldly man, and I have to believe now that his demonstration was little more than some daemonic hallucination induced by the fumes, for if what we saw was true...

Dr. Alnnajm-Al'aswad began to systematically dissect the previous ages of the world in a far ranging sermon that spun circles around scripture and pulled random details from the pages of mythology. He painted a picture of vermin scattered about the world, destined to rot from within, dismembering each other for sport and feasting on worm-chewed corpses. Each new slide depicted some atrocity committed in the name of kings, or holy men, or out of superstition, or fear. Holy men raping women, or children, or each other; messiahs dissecting the unborn to understand the workings of unlife; wounded soldiers bleeding out in apocalyptic charnel landscapes. I couldn't believe he spoke about humans, but he seemed to name my deepest shames, the shames of my people, every eon of them that had come before.

The Doctor extrapolated on this, inducing the future through blasphemous psychological texts and a perverse algorithm that seemed to unfurl the very minds of men to a mathematical standard. Taking these things to a logical conclusion, he took us forward a hundred years into the future, two hundred, three, a millennia. He showed us impossible technologies that would interlink the world and enable the enslavement of minds through insidious civil control. He showed us the concentration of wealth and power to an increasingly small, decadent class of subhumans while plebeians starved, stripping the planet of every last iota of natural resources. He showed us a tyrant rising to power and somehow massacring an entire portion of the world, and then this playing out over and over again with successive generations, in profane rapidity. He showed us cancers turned on their heads and engineered as sentient cures and weapons. He showed us the air clouded with great metal crafts that poisoned out of existence the very beings they shepherded through the sky. He showed us mechanical beings so small as to barely exist rending the very fabric of space and time. He showed us oceans boiling with acid, foliage crumbling into ash, air thick and impossible to breathe, men feasting on their children with little other option for food. He showed us the last gasps of human existence as we transformed into something so terrible as to be beyond imagination. He revealed the cure of all plague and misfortune, a cure that would only cost the very destruction of every last holy book and place of worship that we stupid humans clung to.

It was at a juncture of his terrible, interminable demonstration, as Dr.

Alnnajm-Al'aswad was explaining schematics for self-replicating clockwork machines in the depths of space feeding off the energy of stars, that I realized the elderly Muslim man sitting next to me was cackling madly—had been cackling madly from the start, a sound which I mistook for my own, droning horror. I watched now as two dark, robed disciples came forward and dragged the broken, howling Muslim forward to a rough wooden table at the front of the room. We looked on as Dr. Alnnajm-Al'aswad began to vivisect the aged Muslim before our eyes, showing us crimsons and purples and yellows and terrible bilious greens. None made a move to stop him, not even myself.

"By the Prophet! Is it getting hot in here?" my companion's empty voice murmured from my side, pulling at his robes as the Doctor lifted a still beating heart from the neatly separated rib cages. The heat was unbearable, maddening. My stomach churned and my brain seceded all reason.

The doctor volunteered the English woman for a demonstration, and the enraptured lady began to tear her clothing. The doctor produced a steam-powered machine, a contraption that seemed to cross an obelisk with a blasphemous medical tool. The English woman's chaperone looked on unmoving as the doctor's disciples enacted unspeakable things upon her; the aged Brit began to sob and plead, and at that point he was dragged away, screaming for help, lost to the darkness. The lady looked on to the abduction of her companion and merely laughed and shrieked, muttered unintelligible gratitude, and it was at that moment that I watched flesh wrench apart to reveal impossible clockwork machinery within and I realized that I had become a madman amongst my kind, for none who would abide these blasphemous technologies could be called sane. No, I had lost my mind from that first, terrible image of a dissected child who was more amphibian than mammalian. That it was a photograph, and recent, made it all the worse. Who could look on such a thing and not have faith that we were little more than some failed cosmic experiment?

"I'm so hot, by God, so very, very hot." A pawing hand that was not my own tore at my robes, and I let it for hope that it was coming to take my life. It was then that the Doctor drove us all out into the hot, damp streets. I shrieked that I was not afraid, and the others echoed my cries to the emerald-yellowed moon, though through deluded courage or genuine rapture I could not say. We came upon a ragged, frightened patrol of guards and fell on them, tearing and raping and feasting and spitting mad verse in incomprehensible tongues. We noticed that there were no lights in the world and that many of buildings were crumbling to the ground or burnt out or had doors painted to warn of plague rot within and the tombs we passed were desecrated and the holy centres abandoned and toppled and we knew this was the case throughout the world. There were more of us now than there had been but this did not bother us for why shouldn't there be and we fell into file without words and separated with a number heading wordlessly upwards towards the great Citadel that sat upon the mountain, the only structure in the land that blazed from within and showed terrible naked inhuman figures dancing on its parapets and committing unholy acts on what had once been the last bastion of faith in an entropic world, our way heralded by nightmarish shrieking in the dark not unlike those that had plagued the city during my time there so long ago. My group, including my half-naked, deranged, grinning companion and myself, capered across the last remnants of a bridge and out into the terrible, bone choked expanse of desert before we came to the great monuments to the dead that now teemed with twisted life and terrible unlife. We filed down within the shadowed crypts where worshipping dead hands reached out for us and we watched as the primordial technology of these great resurrection machines worked to awaken those of the old faith, the old knowledge, those who had brought their entire courts with them to the dark abysses of the afterlife and returned with knowledge that would ruin the very vestiges of humanity thousands of slaves had been worked to death and constructed to preserve and we looked upon a glittering, intricately mechanical throne the colour of the emptiest expanse of space and it was unoccupied but from it emanated a mad cackling and yes, I realized at last that the Doctor had pulled the very skeins of madness from my dreams with his unfathomable, dark algorithm for this was the hellish stuff of my nightmares incarnate. For now we could see the place where stars had once been that only revealed the entropic expanses that reigned supreme cocooning the blind, idiot mad god trembling and trumpeting his disgusting fleshy melody, a world of unearthly tissue and appendages more massive than any star writhed at the centre of all, the very graveyard of galaxies and energy and the mad Doctor was there and he had been there all along and his mechanical eye fell on me and I understood that it was great and terrible and I could understand why the mad, diseased saints raved against him as they rotted in the streets and it was looking upon this that I finally found the final, terminating release.

THE MELANCHOLY WAIL of the *muëddins* drew me forth from my darkness. I was not alone when they woke me, naked, beneath the last glistening of stars. The dark night sky was beginning to pale in the east. Before I could open my eyes my body ached, and my mind grasped at the last corrupting tendrils of nightmare that had plagued my sleep; for they had to be yet more of those nightly dark visions, I told myself, hallucinations wrought by the fumes of the charlatan doctor's apartment. No man could commit the heinous acts I'd witnessed in the blackness of my sleep and claim he had a soul.

As I forced my eyes open I saw Cleo was there, his cat's eye watching me in purring judgment, sitting on the edge of the building. Stirring at my side was Abd Al-Latif, naked as I, our robes spread beneath us as an impromptu mattress. His eyes fluttered and he grinned sheepishly at me; he stretched and groaned. Muscles rippled beneath his dark brown skin, and there was a smattering of hair about his chest. He wiped at some long-dried discharge between his thighs, then stood and walked to the side of the building, pissing off into an alleyway below. Aghast, Cleo bounded away into the morning.

The second repetition of the *adán* drew my attention to the minaret that gazed over the city nearby, within sight, and I scrambled to cover myself with our discarded robes. "Don't bother," he muttered, finishing his natural business. "The mosques mostly employ blind men as *muëddins*, so that they won't be tempted toward sinful voyeurism of the hareems and terraces of houses the *mád'neh* look over."

When the *adán* had finished I watched for some time as Abd Al-Latif went about his devotions with perfect poise and timing, facing Mekkeh, naked body bathed in the light of the rising sun. When he returned to my side, my companion ran a hand over my chest and then down, and I shuddered at the touch. "Personally," he continued, "I've always believed this doesn't stop the *muëddins* from their own secretive fantasies. The unseen is always much more tempting for its mystery."

I considered this a moment, "Did we...?"

"Yes."

And we did again. And we did not speak of the crazed aberrations we had imagined or shared from the demonstrations of Dr. Munir Alnnajm-Al'aswad, if indeed they'd even happened, for it was better to forget, or try.

THAT AFTERNOON, AFTER letting slip where he was to go after our morning's exertions, Abd Al-Latif—who it turns out was not at all a servant but an accomplished, young engineer—showed me the thing upon which we had collaborated, unbeknownst to me. We boarded a small, personal airship used to transport cargo short distances. As we flew I marveled at the stark beauty of the land just beyond the green valley of the Nile.

Within a repurposed mastaba some distance out of the city, he had created a workshop where large quantities of exotic materials had been delivered. The tomb had been stripped of the treasures of its ancient owners and was now mostly a dusty, dark, manmade stone cavern. Ebony, ivory, silver and gold, large planks of cedar, slabs of stone. Cogs, gears, a durable, modern differential steam engine, and the composite building materials; saws, industrial cutters, small cranes, levers, pulleys, needed to put the thing together. He seemed to be building a long, factory-like device that would deliver whatever it was meant to convey from the initial "chapel" above, down through the earth into the room that must have once contained a sarcophagus. In this room rested instead a newer stone and wood coffin, about a foot taller and wider than one built for a normal human. It was inlaid with various locking devices and contained within a system of retractable blades, powered from the steam engine without. Abd Al-Atif demonstrated this section of the machine; this was the section he had most recently completed, based on my translation of the arcane text at Al-Azhar. Anything within would be bisected twice into fourteen pieces and then deposited in a lower container of specially constructed cedar boxes.

It was a steam powered, clockwork, modernized version of the Ptolemaic scholar Naukratius' ancient machine theorized to kill a god.

I WAS INCENSED, and insisted on being delivered to Surayya Al Serafy's apartment. I demanded to know why I had been hired to fulfill some silly fantasy to reconstruct the rambling designs of a pompous, Greco-Egyptian fabulist.

"I had intended to show you," she said, calm and unperturbed by my stomping into her home unannounced. She had been at afternoon prayer, but had torn herself away without hesitation. "I had intended for you to help complete it."

I swore at her and said I would take no further part in the farce. If it ever got out that I had been hired to construct a mythological machine for superstitious Muslims I would be shamed and laughed out of my faculty.

"What if I told you that we aren't building this as some empty project?" she asked cautiously.

"Then you're mad. You assume that a god is real and walks among us, and will somehow stumble into this machine."

She considered me a moment with those appraising eyes, then said, "Your mother believed she was a djin."

This silenced me. I demanded to know how she knew my mother, and what she had to do with this. My mother, I stated, was some Italian or Greek prostitute who had tempted my father at an impressionable age. She had professed her love and devotion, then left him used and defiled. She had deposited me without a word on my father's college doorsteps, shaming him enough to flee Oxford and seek a new life, inspiring him to devote himself to a new, faithful life in New England. She was the reason my father had become been a spiteful, brimstone-breathing Baptist lunatic.

Madam Al Serafy's eyes grew cold at the mention of my father. "I knew them both. We were all at Oxford at the same time—or, rather, your mother and I were receiving private tutelage while your father was at Oxford. He taught us Christian theology, and he pressed himself on your mother."

I was dumbstruck. She took my silence as consent to continue. "Your mother's name was Asra Al Manawy. She and I had been friends for as long as I can remember. She was a beautiful woman, of great learning and faith, but she was always of a…delicate nature. Doctors said she was given to a neurotic disorder, but she believed she was followed—or perhaps possessed—by a djin, an evil spirit that whispered to her and made her do evil things.

"I knew when your father appeared in our lives it would lead to naught," Madam Al Serafy whispered. "He was a slick man, charismatic, and of even greater delusions than your mother. He believed his faith was god-sent and could turn her, and she believed submitting to a holy man would drive the djin out. Yes, he fled Oxford, but only when he was accused of taking liberties with several of his tutelage students, including your mother. This was after she had given birth to you. When you were born she claimed the voices had ceased, that the djin had left her, before she bled out from within. She named you Abdul Haq. Your father claimed you before fleeing to America. I thought it was only to drown you and rid the world of the physical manifestation of his sins."

I felt nauseous as she related her story. I wanted not to believe her, but at the same time I cursed my hated father, the hypocrite Reverend Crosswhite.

"Faith can be an incredible power," she continued after a moment's silence. "I don't mean only the faith of Muslims, or Christians, or Jews. There are certain esoteric teachings that say faith, or belief, or worship manifests itself on an unknown plane, bleeding into this world. The collection of energies that no man or woman has been able to describe. Some attribute the prevalence of spirits, demons and ghosts throughout time to this phenomenon. Others believe it's this inaccessible power that once allowed spellbinders to work their dark magicks. The same scholars say this is why the God of Christians—or that of Jews, or the

Allah of Muslims—is so cold, and distant, and schizophrenic. It is easier to have a multitude of gods who represent every facet of the world, or human psyche. To put all our faith into a singular deity, attributes of utmost compassion and ceaseless wrath, is enough to allow that energy to gather and drive what arises mad. I am a woman of faith, but I know there are also dark powers from out of time that existed long before we did and will go on existing when we are gone. I retain my faith because I prefer to give power to a single God of terror and beauty over a multitude of gods too terrible to imagine."

"Gods do not walk among us," I stated, although in the second I spoke something in my mind aligned all of the glyphs and archetypes of *The silence of the dark god*, and the dread text of the Mad Arab of Yemen, and my own studies into languages and their connection to the arcane. I saw the fish-headed Mother and Father of the Sea; the Dead Priest or Dread Hierophant; the Black Satyr of the Primal Woods. My mind reeled as I remembered mentions of the Lost Gate God, the Demon Sultan of Entropy, and the Black Pharoah, the Messenger, the Conquering Chaos. I shuddered and pushed away these thoughts, too awful to dwell upon. These were things of degenerate cults and cannibal backwoods savages. They were not of the civilized world.

Perhaps my patron noticed my reaction, or a change in my countenance. Perhaps she'd received word of where I'd been the previous night. "They do, and their works are great and terrible, and you have looked on them."

I SOON AFTER completed my translation of *The silence of the dark god* and relocated my work from Al-Azhar to Abd Al-Latif's workshop outside of Maṣr. This was partially to begin my new work, drawing out the requisite hieroglyphs on the machine parts where they were required. I wouldn't admit to even my closest friends that I had dabbled with minor glyphs and wards, only exchanging the least of offerings for lesser thaumaturgies. The power of alchemy and spellbinding had long left the world, as any who studied arcane history knew, and the little power that remained was so small and mundane as to be pointless. Even so, I had never brought those kinds of studies into the classroom—even some of my more liberal friends would rankle at the idea of spellbinding in their midst, however subtle and contained.

What Naukratius' primordial prison machine required, however, was blood sacrifice, the demands of which greatly disturbed even an agnostic like myself. Daily, Madame Al Serafy would have goats, sheep and calves delivered to me to fuel the spellbinding I was to attempt. Abd Al-Latif would make himself scarce when the animals arrived. I tried to go about my task with scientific objectivity, but the screams and twitchings of my materials turned my stomach, and the dark powers they enabled terrified me.

The second reason for my relocation was the proximity to Abd Al-Latif. Our dalliances beneath the starlight continued on a nightly basis. He had explained to me that many citizens kept a *malkaf*, a sort of small, rooftop shed open to northern breezes, protected from bugs with netting, where they slept during unbearable heat. We set up an impromptu *malkaf* with some leftover materials, open to the stars and the hundred holy songs of the city's *muëddins*, and slept naked beneath the night sky after our exertions, with cyclopean Cleo always gazing on in confusion or disgust at human rutting. The stone-cooled air of the workshop was a welcome relief from the hellish heat in the city, and we pursued our diversions there as well—I had even begun to delude myself that when we were in the heat of the moment, the runes I had been painting in the alchemical solution glowed a faint green or blue as a sort of electricity crackled in the air, but I put those imaginings down to adrenaline and nerves.

I had dallied before amongst my decadent friends at the university, even participating in a few bouts of blasphemous group activity on nights celebrated but unspoken of, among certain circles at the old university, but there had been nothing lasting in the same way as Abd Al-Latif. We could not go an evening apart. For me it was a physical need, to possess someone and experience the comfort of soft breathing in the empty expanse of night in a mad, alien city like this one, with screams of nightmares ringing out through the dark, a chorus to which I added my own as I slept, I was told. However, I recognized for Abd Al-Latif it meant something more. He had a wife and children somewhere— he'd been married off at a young age—and seemed affectionate enough when he spoke on them, but to me he seemed emotionally demonstrative bordering on loving after intercourse. He listened raptly as I spoke about the history of sodomitical love—the pairings of knights and samurai, Greeks and native braves, the passions of Sappho, of Queen Christina of Denmark. He seemed especially keen on poetically inclined stories from his own culture: Abu Nuwas, and the sultan Mahmud of Ghazni and his slave boy Malik Ayaz. He had known many men who indulged, and had even done so himself on occasion, but he never imagined a continuity of lovers. These stories helped him reconcile the guilt he felt for however many of his sins were enumerated in the ponderous Kur-án, for he still prayed whenever he could get away from work to purify himself and participate in the *saláh*.

Of our task he seemed entirely sure of its purpose and success. If the alternative was the degeneration of our world into unfathomable perversion and dark knowledge, there was no choice in the matter but to make his machine work, however thankless the job would be. He had shown me the rough manner of the workings before I started my task of binding spells to the necessary parts of the machine, for once primed the spells could only be used once, or so I believed from my studies. The target would be made unconscious in the initial room and placed on a steam-powered conveyor. A series of hieroglyphs would be activated, which the Ptolemaic scholar Naukratius theorized would immobilize and weaken the supernatural victim, and prepare it for the blades to cut into the supernal material it was made of. Eventually it would be deposited within the coffin, stood upright, constructed to contain it. The bladed clockwork machine would be imbued with divine power to rend the thing into fourteen pieces, placed in protected cedar boxes and scattered, never to be brought back together again. I was reminded of Egyptologists' claims that pyramids and assorted funerary monuments were created as resurrection machines, with spells functioning to revive the properly prepared. I mused that perhaps what the pharaohs had lacked was a little clockwork machinery to put things in motion, or perhaps the ritual removal of the major organs didn't help.

In the great, terrible city of Maṣr we could display affection as many men did, but never to the degree that we wished. In the cold crypt where we put the ancient mechanized trap together we were two indulgent boys play-acting as scholars and arcanists. While we carried on, plague-ridden corpses were piled onto wagons and transported out of the city where they were burned en masse. To be away from the permeating stench of burning human flesh and excrement was a relief.

My dreams worsened as we completed the project, not helped as I'd hoped by the distance from the city. At night I watched a parade of aberrations through the streets of distant Boston, Portland or Manhattan, an exodus into the ocean with a scaly being of unfathomable size looking on from a rocky reef throne, men and women clawing their eyes out for fear of glimpsing what came from out of time, disgusting rites performed in inhuman tongues and the sacrifices they made in the names of lost gods. I slept little, and my work and attentions to Abd Al-Latif became feverish. Without rest fantastical horrors and the bizarre, awful project began to bleed together.

MADAME AL SERAFY only inspected the work she had sunk enumerable amounts of her absent husband's resources into once, and this was to deposit the last piece of workings.

It was strange to see the progressive Muslim woman out of her apartment, wrapped in the full veil of her contemporaries. She arrived on a small, private airship and departed on the same after a cursory glance at the machine, handing a small chest to Abd Al-Latif. It was little bigger than a breadbox but incredibly ancient and ornate in its arcane decorations. The machine she examined began just inside the initial room, with a closed conveyer belt that terminated with a drop into the waiting modern sarcophagus below, complete with intricate blades. She did not comment on them but I could swear that where I'd binded glyphs throughout the machine using the lifeblood of the sacrifices the symbols gave a faint glow. Perhaps proof that the binding had worked, or my own crazed imagination in face of this mad project.

"Place this in the lower level and open it only when you are ready. It could show up immediately or wait a few days, but it intends to leave the city for the East soon so I do not think it will take long. I will have fresh supplies brought regularly until the deed is done." She nodded at both of us. "Let us pray to God for the power to protect the world from evil."

I REFUSED TO return to the city with Madame Al Serafy, claiming that I preferred to be here when we activated the machine. When she had left and we were alone at the old mastaba again, we joined together once more in the fading light of the day. To Abd Al-Latif's knowledge, the machine was optimal. That morning, I had completed my spellbinding with the nauseating sacrifice of a final, wretched lamb. The sooner we activated it the better, for the machine was primed and the power as potent as it could be. Again, even in the midst of our joining, more fervent and desperate than any of the other nights we had spent together, I could swear the runes splayed across the room and machine reacted with a marvelous cerulean glow.

Madam Al Serafy had left us a rifle and a pistol in the event that our target brought disciples, and both armed—although I doubted Abd Al-Latif was much better with a pistol than myself—we shared an embrace before he clambered down the side of the chute into the lower tomb. He called up that he was opening the chest, and for me to take shelter until he could return.

I could swear I heard a thrum, or perhaps a disturbing buzzing, like a swarm of flies larger than it was healthy to imagine in the distance. As I crouched behind a discarded packing crate and listened to Abd Al-Latif climb the ladder back to the main room, I saw the doorway darken seconds after the mysterious chest had been opened.

It filled most of the doorway, nearly seven feet tall. A horrible dread welled up inside me when I saw the glint of brass, the empty shimmer of the ersatz right eye. As it stepped into the doorway I could swear the eye was fixed on me, but then I heard that thrum again as the figure went rigid, then collapsed to the ground with a sickening thud.

"By the Prophet! You've done it!" Abd Al-Latif hissed as he clambered out of the hole, barely daring to approach the figure. He continued to exclaim to his Prophet as we cautiously crept forward. The thing was quite paralyzed; I could not even see the telltale sign of life of a chest rising with breath.

"P-please…" it croaked as we began to lift it, limbs twitching as the paralysis began to wear off, "I—am—but—a—simple…d-doc…"

A terrible fantasy entered my mind as we lifted the body on the conveyor, one where Madam Al Serafy had some grudge against this man, perhaps one shared by her fellow superstitious, backwards Muslims for the Doctor's marvelous, terrifying grasp of satanic sciences. One where I, an idiot, foreign youth with a fascination for the arcane, was used as a scapegoat for the gruesome murder of a prominent but controversial Egyptian doctor. Everything she told me could have been a lie, even what she had stated about my mother. Abd Al-Latif would be in on this plot, his seduction merely cementing the partnership.

Then I saw the terrible, glowing eye, glinting with some intelligence independent of the human one. I hefted its shoulders onto the conveyor belt. It seemed to be recovering from the paralysis faster than we had anticipated, so as soon as we had its head in Abd Al-Latif slammed the compartment shut, sealing the thing within. He ran over and pulled a lever down, and the great dynamo buried beneath the mastaba roared to life, belching steam that quickly filled the space. My companion swore; the lever was not catching as designed and so he had to hold it down or else energy would be cut to the machine.

As the mechanisms began to spin into action we heard an awful shrieking, not quite human and not quite animal, and a great pounding from the initial shaft that led to the final, executing, spellblade coffin-device. Mighty blows from somewhere within the steam rent the night, but Abd Al-Latif's machine held together, and with each successive thrum I knew the hieroglyphic spells were weakening the impossible supernal insanity within.

However, we listened as the thing caught halfway down the chute at a mechanical aperture meant to apply a series of spells that directed the final blades within before dropping it down to the final resting place. After a moment of silence, we heard a terrible crashing and the screeching of metal from that section. Abd Al-Latif swore again and said he would have to climb down and activate it manually. He told me to hold the conveyor lever to keep energy flowing into his machine. Clutching the lever with two trembling hands, I watched as he dashed off into the mist and disappeared.

Soon the terrible pounding and wrenching of metal faded away and I was left alone amongst the steady whirring and clanking of the great supernal machine. I did not pray, for after all I had seen I could not believe in a god that would listen, but I hoped the relative silence from our victim meant our machine had achieved success.

At that moment there was the worst screech of bending metal, and Abd Al-Latif began to scream in mortal terror from below, diffused through the steam and mechanical workings. I could not leave the lever, but I could not ignore that his leg was pinned and he cried out that he could not reach the release to terminate this horrible business.

"Do you truly think you can hold me?"

An awful, steady *clunk clunk clunk* told me that the thing within had managed to crawl up the chute of the machine. There were too many limbs at work within; I could not bear to think about it. It had reached the drop and climbed over and I could hear it now working its way backwards along the conveyor, struggling but unerringly advancing towards me from within. The deep, cold voice echoed, vibrating through the entire machine, harmonizing with the machine workings. The thump of the multitude of limbs…

"These spells are amusing. They may have even held me for a time, but you can't truly believe that this wind-up toy would contain me."

There was a slam beside my head as it reached the initial compartment, and then a purring. The sounds of the excess of limbs thumping against the metal sides, I could not bear it. It spoke to me through metal, but it's words came as within my very mind, punctuated by Abd Al-Latif's pained screams of help from deep in the tomb.

It whispered of the work it had planned for the world. We would finally allow the pretender gods to fade away forgotten, and out of the crumbling edifices of their believers' works would rise a new era of science and reason. Mad reason, but to understand the universe in all its infinity was mad, and to understand the terrible beginnings and inevitable end of our kind to come was mad. To understand that something dead dreamed at the bottom of the ocean awaiting a return to unlife…

but no. I cannot think about what dwells below.

The thing said it brought the old knowledge, but because linear time was but a fantasy of beasts scrabbling in their own fecal matter this old knowledge would be new, and would allow great work to begin. We had attempted with our eons of petty worship and superstitious incantations to hold the knowledge off, but finally that would be allowed to rot away, for it was inevitable.

It had come and allowed itself to walk into our silly trap because that too was inevitable, and it had been incomplete for so long. The fourteenth piece would allow it to go forth with its message of dark knowledge and whisperings of the audient voice. If the great arcanist Naukratius could not overcome the crawling chaos, nor the holy men of Egypt before him, what made me think that I could do so with my scribblings? All I had to do, it whispered, was release the lever and lift the seal, for it would have its fourteenth piece and it would have the world partake in its knowledge of which I had merely seen a sliver. I had known all along this endeavor would fail, it whispered. I had known what none would admit: that a god is a more terrible and incomprehensible thing than any human would ever despair enough to speak of.

Why did I release the lever and lift the seal and allow the thing out? There were too many limbs and perhaps I had known all along we were but playing with toys the way men are wont to. I had submitted readily enough that terrible night I had marched the streets of the fallen city and looked up at the too-close moon and seen the empty throne of the universe. If I'd been given a choice, if choice existed, I'd chosen the power of dark oblivion. My eyes squeezed shut so I could not see, I heard it scramble out and away into the mist of the mastaba, the patter of its many legs sounding more amphibian or reptilian than human. After one terrible, sobbing, ululating shriek, Abd Al-Latif's cries for help were silenced. I stood awaiting my inevitable end, as the steam caressed my face and the terrible silence of the dead machine filled my ears. I heard it step before me, and it asked if I would look upon what had drawn it there. I opened my eyes and looked into the ancient chest and could see that unfathomable nothingness stared back at me.

*

PROFESSOR SEXSMITH:

I am attaching the narrative, at your request. I understand the university is keen for closure on this case, but I would let the matter drop given what my inquiries have turned up. I will of course attach a full report, but I shall outline my misgivings here.

On the matter of Virgil Crosswhite, there was no trace of him in Cairo save these unsigned papers left in a basement apartment in a southern Cairene slum where last he was traced. A professor at Al-Azhar mentioned the man had appeared feverish and disturbed in his last days at the university before disappearing into the desert. The city is only now beginning to recover from a terrible plague that took a third of its population, so I assume he took fatally ill and was burned or buried in one of the mass graves that dot the countryside.

As for his association with Surayya Al Serafy I cannot attest, for she was consumed in an unrelated fire that began in a mosque and took her home, as well as much of a city block. Her widower husband knows nothing of the project, but admits she was given to such superstitious intellectual fancies. If such a project existed perhaps it was lost in the fire, for no other copy or original of the supposed text exists.

On Abd Al-Latif Aboul-Enein my report will relate a great deal more, for I spoke with him at length. The feverish text suggests that he was trapped or murdered within a desecrated Egyptian tomb, but the man was quite alive and teaching at the university. As for the degenerate claims of their relationship within the narrative, the man admits he'd been requested by Al Serafy, an acquaintance, to escort her guest between the university and his lodgings, but little more. The man seems healthy and wholly masculine. He has a newly pregnant wife and a child, I met them and spoke with them for the little English they understood. His children and wife appear meek and cowed next to the man, and there is something off about his grin—but there's little point in dwelling on such inane details.

As for this Dr. Munir Alnnajm-Al'aswad, from what I've heard the man is a traveling charlatan. He left Egypt some days after Crosswhite was last seen, but this is little more than a coincidence. He's touring now in Malaysia with a contingent of attendants, or so I'm lead to understand, although those who spoke to the man claim he had designs for America eventually, so perhaps you'll have the chance to see him for yourself. There's little to the narrative's supernatural claims, for the city was in the throes of an epidemic, so any truth in horrors and visions rests in that. Although it is true, from my inquiries, that wherever he goes a queer faith in science arises—Cairo, southern India, the Indochinese peninsula, all have seen a rise in agnostic cults. Aboul-Enein admits he was much changed by the doctor's demonstration, and has brought the teachings and his subsequent research to the university. In my unsolicited opinion the people of Egypt will benefit greatly from it. Perhaps he will haul these backwards people into a new era of rationality and material science.

I should also mention this detail of a false eye mechanism is bunk, according to those I've interviewed. None make mention of such a specific detail, and a recent photo I obtained from a British correspondent out of New Delhi shows the man whole. I don't need to add that technology has brought us far, but such an intricate piece of machinery as to serve as a replacement eye or limb is centuries away, perhaps impossible.

I say drop the matter, as I don't want to waste your money further, for my enquiries have led to little that suggest more than an academic given to neuroses who became the unfortunate casualty of a plague in an unhygienic foreign city. There's little good that can be learned from the ramblings of madmen.

Yours truly,
H.P.L.
Private Investigator,
66 College Street,
Arkham, Massachusetts

The Infernal

ANNE-JENSEN

The first few weeks were okay. Or maybe not okay. Bearable. When not in class or in bed, I sat on the steps leading down to the front gardens, the Corinthian columns flanking me like privates minding a general. My fellow students moved like shoaling fish, or flocking birds: back and forth, up and down the stone stairs, individuals indistinguishable from one another but, as a body, radiating purpose. Great theories must behave like this, when developed within the mind of a masterful thinker: tiny point after tiny logical point (each point cast as a student, in my metaphor) following one another, with constant pressure from behind to reach a complete and logical conclusion. Such were my notions then, and I was almost at ease—and if I wasn't exactly behaving like a young man during his first year at university, at least I was thinking like one.

The third week was harder. The weather deteriorated: sharp, violent gusts and chafing sands, barbed promises of the full-blown *khamaseen* to come. I was forced to retreat, up into the refectory. All around me, my peers gesticulated, laughed, yelled, debated, lived. The isolation I felt was a physical thing, like a funeral shroud. I did have a mobile phone, but who could I have called? The farm had—has—no landline and anyway, what would I have said? *You were right, mother. I don't belong here.*

No. Never.

Looking out through my dust-covered dorm windows, the suburb of Giza presented itself in ghostly lines, the browns, the reds and the yellows of the whirling sands blurring out the hard lines of the city. To the south, Menkaure, Khafre and Khufu were just visible, white and pale triangular faces in the angry winds. They seemed to me like tools rather than tombs: mythological cogs that might be activated by the right knowledge or touch and, like a scene out of an action film, raise the past from under the sand. A *hijaab* falling away from the base matter of things, revealing a truer Egypt.

As you can see, I had not given up on philosophical daydreaming.

In the fourth week, I saw it. Down by the palm trees, the familiar spiky protrusions standing out—grotesque, offensive—against the soft, curved architecture of the landscaped gardens. I ran down as fast as I could, out of breath, raising my arm to protect my face from the chafing sands. But by the time I had descended the steps, it had gone, of course. I had never caught up to it before, why should it be any different now?

THE FOLLOWING DAY, the weather cleared and Nasser came to sit with me.

I CAN OCCASIONALLY—rarely, and only when *in extremis*—ask for something, and then simply be given it. By whom, you ask? I don't know. I have theories, although I am loath to give them any credence. They are not scientific. Not even philosophical. No, not at all. But it is not the fiend's doing, I am sure of that. (I am sure of that now.)

That evening, after seeing it again, I was in low, low spirits. It had followed me from the farm, there was no denying it. And if it was able to show itself here—where next? I was low—*in extremis*, as I said—and that was when Nasser introduced himself to me. My desperate wish for company had seemingly been granted.

HE HAD A habit of pacing ahead, sideways, crab-like, slashing at the air with his arms and hands as he spoke. His demeanour and address were refined. Opulent even, at times.

"But seriously, my friend. What will you do?" he said.

He was to become a doctor of medicine.

"Philosophy has many uses," I said, simply for something to say, my hands deep in my pockets, as they often were at that time. I started to flex my fingers. Relaxing, making fists, relaxing. Nasser laughed, his angular face close to mine, goading me: "And what do your parents say to this?"

My father's creased face and weary body blinked into existence in my mind's eye, tired, kind, cotton pollen and the chemical stink of pesticides clinging to his tunic. My grandfather, a shrivelled facsimile. Both had died years ago, from the toil.

And my mother...

"I have their blessing," I said.

Or thought I said. When I came to—Nasser on his knees next to me, repeating my name again and again, wafting a piece of paper close to my face to revive me—I realised that the fiend was not the only thing that had followed me all the way from the farm to the city.

WE LOOKED OUT over Giza from my room. Menkaure, Khafre, Khufu. I told him all that you now also know: my 'attacks'; the fiend; the occasional granting of wishes. The winds had finally died down and the stillness allowed the noise from the street to carry through: throaty back-fires from clapped-out engines, shrieking horns, catcalls, insults.

"Well," said Nasser. "You see things that I don't." He looked at me benignly. We had skipped classes, me for the first time. "You have consulted with physicians?"

"Yes," I said. As a child, my mother had had me examined. As a teenager, I had seen some old practitioner, more *mufti* than clinician. And I had done so reluctantly. Here, with my new friend, I found myself asking if he might have an opinion, professionally speaking.

He watched me closely and, after a pause, said: "It would be dangerous for me to pass judgement, as I am yet in training. But you should meet an acquaintance of mine. He shares, well...My interests. I think he could be of help to you."

Remember the things I have told you: Nasser was to become a doctor, and he had been sent to me as a wish granted. For many years, I had hoped for nothing more than to be rid of the fiend, and to cease having these embarrassing episodes of fainting. What could I have said, then, other than, immediately and without hesitation: "Yes. I will go with you." I even added a 'thank you' at the end.

I WATCHED, WORRIED, as Nasser knocked, hard, insistent, on the shuttered door, hand and arm acting as a mallet against the woodwork.

"We should go back," I said, flexing my fingers in my pockets.

Nasser grinned. "Mr Kabbani is home. Just wait." And the door did open then, held ajar by a small, round man. He peered at us through the gap, his eyes odd, white globes of judgement, and I saw myself reflected in his vision: young, gaunt, haunted. I knew then that I could not go through with it—seek help from a stranger like that—and I took a step back, about to return to the dorm with no excuse or explanation. But then, good God: out of the corner of my eye, there it was again, creeping along the street, from doorway to doorway, its yellow-slatted eyes on me, then off me, then on, like neon bulbs in a dark corridor, flickering. I felt the thump of my heartbeat, in my chest, in my ears—would they, *could* they, see it? And I lifted my arm, ready to point. But then, of course, the black surged and my knees caved in.

Impeccable timing.

NASSER'S HANDS WERE on my shoulders, gently rocking me to and fro; Mr Kabbani entered into my field of vision, also. His large eyes *were* strange (but I would say that now, of course) and fleshy-looking, as if malleable within their sockets. Full mouth, ruddy cheeks. A wispy mop of dark-black hair. His voice was high-pitched, almost piping.

"Sit up slowly," he said, and I obeyed.

The flat was opulent. What is that word? My grandfather used to use it. *Kitsch.* Large woven carpets, huge, ornate hangings depicting stylised hieroglyphs, gods, animals, pharaohs. The corners of the fabrics gently lifted away from the walls, drifting in the breeze generated from the body of Mr Kabbani moving to and fro, fetching cups, preparing tea.

"You are here because you need help?" he eventually said, seating himself. "With your condition?"

"Yes," I said. Nasser was perched on a sofa-like structure, massive russet-coloured cushions all around. Cushions on my chair too. The tea was black. Grainy. A deep, sweet taste of molasses, with a kick at the back, and a hint of something…what? Cinnamon?

"And you are a philosopher?"

"No." I struggled up from my own chair. "No, you mustn't think that." I felt my cheeks burn. The audacity of it.

"A thinker, then. Someone who wonders at life's mysteries." In Mr Kabbani's tinny voice, 'wonders' sounded like 'wanders'.

"As we all are," said Nasser, quickly, noticing my discomfort. Coming to my aid. Or so I thought.

"Indeed. As we all are," said Mr Kabbani.

Outside, a woman called for her husband or son. "*Habib, Habib!*" With each mouthful, my tea became grainier and sweeter. The furniture, the cushions, the walls seemed to move ever so slightly, as if losing, then regaining, their hold on the world.

"I would like to conduct a little experiment," said Mr Kabbani, leaning forwards. "With your permission, of course." He shifted in his seat, getting comfortable. He was right in front of me, settled on an expensive-looking chair Nasser had brought from the kitchen. His head was large. Luminous.

"You believe me? What I see?"

"Perhaps. Can we try? I will need to touch you."

As an answer, I leant forwards too, meeting him halfway across the empty space between us. Closed my eyes.

"I shall just place my hand... here... and here..."

Each finger was a separate contact point on my forehead, surprisingly soft, like the wings of a passing moth. Tendrils of cold spread through my mind, ice cracks under a heavy weight, and then:

COLDER STILL. QUIET. *No, not quiet. Silent. Like holding one's breath, or crouching under an oncoming blow. Everything waited. One beat. Two. Three.*

Then reason caught up with my eyes and I opened them.

The street was wide. Street, I say. Lane or path is better. But wide, like a dry river bed. Only it didn't feel dry underfoot. Not exactly squelchy, but...I lifted my left leg, watched as a perfect outline of my footprint in the dust held its shape for a moment before slowly evaporating.

I looked up, startled. Movement? Yes, further down the lane. A man? He walked in an elegant, almost gliding manner, advancing towards me. I was relieved; I did not want to be alone. He looked as if he would reach me within a minute or so. No doubt he would be able to tell me where I was.

And where was that? I craned my neck. There was a structure to my right, a building, gun-metal grey, protrusions extending along its width, like balconies on an apartment block. But these were not balconies. They were, what...moving?

I became aware, abruptly, of a deep thruump thruump *vibrating through the, what.. wherever I was...and I looked up. What seemed like sails—weathered, mealy—billowed far above me and, beyond, something membranous pulsed to the beat of the* thruump. *Caused it? And just visible, high, high up into the void was a speck of luminescence, you could call it a planet maybe, yet not as bright. Or brighter, in some ways? And, of course, I was not outside, looking up at heavenly objects, I was—*

The man brushed past me, our hands almost touched, and I saw he was walking something on a leash. An animal? Small, round, blurred edges, a bundle of fluff, with

no neck from what I could see, so what could the collar be attached to? Yet the cord
swung as they moved—not leather, a chain? And the links clanked against the small,
furry animal that loped, bounded, strained—

No. My mind could not take it.

Another building, further ahead. Steel-like material gleamed and clicked; long
thin arms, like scissors, extended from it. Krrr-tock. Krrr-tock. Whistling and
thudding. A pipe, running alongside the path, vented mist-red steam.

No!

How do I get out?

Back, back, I pushed back against the spot I had first emerged from, something
soft, like fraying cloth, a taste of sourness in my mouth, acrid bile surged up through
throat and nose and:

BOLT UPRIGHT IN the chair, fighting the embrace of both cushions and Mr
Kabbani. "I need to be sick," I said, and then I was sick, leaning over the armrest.
Dark, brown, sweet-smelling liquid spewed from me—the remains of the tea—
and sloshed noisily onto the floor.

I was helped, stumbling weakly between Mr Kabbani and Nasser, out
into the bathroom. Floral patterns, shiny faucets, lukewarm water. Afterwards,
whilst I washed myself down, Nasser disappeared. Moments later I heard wet,
sopping sounds: my friend, my granted wish, cleaning up after me.

WE HAD LUNCH together, Mr Kabbani, Nasser and I. The very next day. In a
little roadside *Hookah* café (chosen by Nasser of course) near the Museum of
Egyptian Antiquities. How ordinary. (I thought so then, and I am thinking it
now.) The winds had died down completely and the sun was out, pale, an off-
white disk above the Cairo skyline. Nasser was declaiming to us on some subject
or other, arms in the air, torso and head rocking back and forth, like an oversized
metronome, keeping time with his own utterances. I did not pay attention to any
of it, and after a while Mr Kabbani gave a short nod, like a signalman greeting a
train on time. "Let us talk to our friend a little," he said.

Nasser smiled. "Of course."

Mr Kabbani speared a date with his fork. Lifted it from his plate. Studied
it. Studied me. "Reading philosophy. You inquire into the affairs of the spirit?"

I shook my head. "I am more interested in the scientific workings of creation. In
the material. Corporeal. The Afghan scholar, Faizani, you may have heard of him—"

Mr Kabbani cut into my sentence with a gesture. "The thing you see. The creature."

"Fiend," I said. Winced.

"You think he is simply an abstract?"

I looked away, I had to. Bit my lip. "No."

"Well, neither do I. Even though I cannot see him myself. Nasser here has not seen him. Even as the fiend is chasing you down, causing you to faint. Not exactly, hmm...corporeal? And nor is what you witnessed yesterday, I think."

What could I say? Nasser's left hand came to rest on my wrist, a firm, supportive squeeze.

"But fear not," said Mr Kabbani. 'This shall all make perfect sense to you shortly.' He raised the fork to his mouth and the date disappeared behind fleshy lips.

Nasser removed his hand, smiled a gentle smile at me.

"So how did you..." I cleared my throat. Started again. "How did you become, ah, interested in such matters as these...interested in hypnotism?" I looked at Nasser as I spoke, but it was Mr Kabbani who answered.

"I have seen that place myself. Where you went. Once. Though we do not travel there via...*hypnotism*." He pronounced the word distastefully.

The steam, the hissing pipes, the straining of the animals, the *machinery*. I shivered at the memories.

"What did you make of it?" I said.

"Mr Kabbani didn't stay there long, his system couldn't—" Nasser said, before Mr Kabbani stopped him with an outstretched hand. "Enough. Akil need not hear about our failures."

I looked at Nasser. Mr Kabbani. History here, clearly. But I was too fearful to pursue it. Instead, I said: "You think it has some...has a...well, connection with it. The fiend?"

Mr Kabbani chewed loudly, and small specks of date ejected from his mouth as he spoke. "Here, in this world, what you call the fiend is a mark. Your mark: like the shadow of a creature cast from *that* world. A shadow that reaches out to you from time to time. And it is that shadow that has persuaded me that I would be able to help you."

"I see."

I didn't. But I wanted to.

So I WENT again, with the aid of the tea (I wasn't completely blind to their methods) and Mr Kabbani's doughy hands. And this time he gave me a bucket to sit with. "Be vigilant for a dome-like construction," he whispered to me at the last second, his fingers rested cool against my forehead. "It will likely be high up. If you see it, make that your destination."

I TOOK A *few steps down the lane. Or river bed. The man and his dog-like shape were there, patrolling the same area, and then there were more of them (perhaps they had been there all the time). A hulking big figure loomed by the second tower. Yes, I know: I should have recognised it immediately. But it took me a second before the dreadful truth sunk in.*

The fiend seemed perfectly at home, its ebony spikes matching the growths of the structures behind. Watching me, the head cocked like that of a vulture contemplating its dying prey. Expectant, I realised; my presence had been awaited.

My first instincts have always been to chase it; here I took a step back. And another one. Its head straightened and those eyes… I raised my hands, as if to ward off an oncoming blow. Looked around me. A bit further ahead, the lane divided up into several paths, like a junction, with what looked like pipelines joining from above. There, I thought, and I hurried towards that junction spot, not daring to take my eye from the fiend. It stood ominously still. Following my progress. A hiss of steam escaped from a joint in the pipework, and the krrr-tock sounded louder. Something trembled—me, I realised. I reached the junction and saw that it operated almost like a staircase, step-like structures leading both up and down. On this level, paths ran from this central column in all directions, with pipework alongside.

What should I do? Up, down…? The tower shivered. No, quaked. Rattling descended down those stairs, a bone-xylophone played by a madman, and something shrieked then, the infernal sound several octaves above all the clattering, booming and thudding. I looked up. The fiend was at full pelt, loping towards me and I ran. I ran, I ran, I ran, scrabbling at the cloth that held me back, back, out, out, out, waving my hands wildly, finding the spot and I had to beat at it this time, as if something was blocking me from the other side, ripping it, tearing it and:

NASSER HANDED ME a cup of tepid tea. I drained it in one, without thought, I was that thirsty.

"You arrived," Mr Kabbani said, blinking slowly. How I stared at those egg-white orbs, struggling to piece things together.

"Yes," I said.

"The same place? The street?"

"Yes," I said. "Well, like a path. Or a walkway."

"There are inhabitants?"

"Of a kind."

"I knew it," said Mr Kabbani, collapsing back against the wooden lattice of his chair, the crack as loud in the room. Somewhere, a tap drip-dripped. I flexed my fingers.

"What is in the dome. Why did you want me to go there?" I asked, but Mr Kabbani ignored me.

They did not want you to return. Did the fiend say that? I glanced around. Nothing.

"Describe the building," said Nasser.

"It is like a giant tower," I said. "With structures inside. There are walkways. Humanoid shapes move along with odd appliances. As if walking them. Like pets. It is very different. To here. Yet…" I hesitated.

"Yes?" said Mr Kabbani. Moved closer.

But I shook my head. I could not say it.

"You must go back," said Mr Kabbani.

I fumbled for the arm rests, pushed myself up and away from the chair. "Another time," I lied. I knew I would never go back voluntarily. "I need to rest." And that much was true: I felt immensely drained, as if recovering from illness.

"But this is your opportunity," said Mr Kabbani. "Your chance to confront that thing that has been haunting you since your childhood." I turned towards the kitchen door, felt myself sway. I put out a hand against the doorway, steadying myself. Took another step, aiming for the entrance.

"Stop him," said Mr Kabbani.

Nasser's arm around my shoulder and I felt, for that brief moment, gratitude—before, that is, he used his strength to swivel me on my feet, about-turning me to face again that gaudy room and Mr Kabbani.

"This time, block off the passageway properly," I heard Nasser say and the last thing I saw before light faded from my eyes was a wall hanging depicting the snake-god Apophis fighting Ma'at, the goddess of truth, fiery colours of orange, reds and ice whites swirling around them. But there is something wrong with it, I thought, and then I was gone.

A WOMAN'S VOICE, muffled. "Please, Mr Said. No need to remove your shoes."

"Madame, I wouldn't dream of entering your home in footwear."

A scuffling sound; nervous laughter. The creak of a door. Footsteps.

"Akil, *ya danaya*—look who has come to visit you."

Silence. Then: "He looks… at peace."

"Yes, always like this. Always. Even his hands, he usually moved his fingers just so, but now..." A soft touch, a butterfly brushing against one's cheek, and then a wet, choking sound, something halfway between a breathy sigh and a smoker clearing her throat. She is crying.

"Madame Essa, I am so sorry."

"No, no. Please don't. There, see. I am fine."

"You must find all this very straining."

"Yes. But it helps to know that my son has friends like yourself in this world."

"To be perfectly honest, Mrs Essa, I didn't know him that well. Akil kept himself to himself. Didn't, you know...socialise...with other students."

A sniff. "He always was a loner. His fainting illness made him so, right from an early age."

Another silence, longer this time.

"What do the doctors say?"

"Something to do with a locked-in syndicate. Or a version of it."

"Syndrome. Locked-in syndrome."

"Yes, of course, you are a medical student. You must know." She sniffs again, then cloth being rubbed, and a trumpet blast: she is blowing her nose. "They suggested that he might have taken something. A drug, or...there's a snake venom, they say. He was depressed. And whatever he took left him like this."

"Is he able to speak? Has he, you know... said anything?"

"Not to begin with. But now, sometimes. He sees, too. Look, he blinks if you do this."

A dark shadow swipes across the membrane.

"So he has spoken to you?"

"He makes some kind of drumming sound. And something like a ticking clock. Gibberish. Oh and a name, sometimes. 'Kabbani'. Whoever that might be. But listen to me prattling on. Without offering you any refreshments."

"A glass of water would be welcome."

"No coffee? Or I could cook you a—"

"No."

And she shuffles away, no doubt disappointed. She loves feeding people.

Silence. In his world, anyway. Not in mine.

"Akil?" says Nasser then, softly. I see the outline of his nose and jaw as if drawn in crude charcoal. Light and dark, very little definition. Closer and closer. "Akil? Can you hear me? Mr Kabbani said to tell you. Go up. Enter the dome. It's your only way out now."

I REALISE YOU will think I have invented both Nasser and Mr Kabbani. To justify my failings, perhaps. I did not study philosophy, not properly. I have no friends—clearly—and am lying prone in my childhood home, my mother nursing me. What better way to negate all these failings than to simply leave the miserable life, and body, behind? 'Check out,' as my once fellow peers would no doubt have termed it?

It was not Apophis and Ma'at on that wall hanging, but a depiction of the human digestive system. Intestines. Liver. Gallbladder. I know that now, because I recognised it: the exact position I arrived at when I was deposited here, shut in for good. Just above the intestinal tract. My lungs billowed above, and my heart, a tiny orb from where I stood, laboured at optimum capacity. Thrump-thrump-thrump-thrump-thrump. The beat of fear and panic literally coursing through my veins.

Since then, my body has calmed. I have made it to somewhere just below the inferior and superior colliculi—the optic and auditory nerve centres. I learned a little about the human body, you see, as Mr Kabbani and Nasser bundled me out of Mr Kabbani's apartment and back to my dorm room ("he has just had too much to drink"). Before the poison shut me off from the world completely, I heard them discuss all the pathways I might be able to take to reach the dome. The dome: that luminous speck I saw when I first got pushed in here. Cerebrum. Brain, to you and I.

Nasser asked: "Would you have taken the journey yourself, had it not been for the accident?"

It took a while before Mr Kabbani answered. Or perhaps it was just my perception of time, skewered like everything else. "No. This will be more interesting. You will visit him occasionally, once he returns to the mother's farm. Track his progress. And when—if—he gains control…"

"We won't find an easier test subject, that's for sure." Nasser's voice sounded echoey; hushed. And then there was no voice for a long, long time.

What is a day in here? A week, a year?

If—when—I gain control, I imagine I shall emerge as something monstrous.

My placement is now such that I have regained my hearing, and I can even see a little, which is a vast improvement. I have also reclaimed most of my memory, which is how I have been able to recount the tale of my internal banishment. What I can't remember, though, is when I started speaking to you.

But you are always present now, close enough for those barbs to stand out in their fine, sheer brilliance. We had to make peace in the end, didn't we? And I see, on your body, how one of your protrusions might in fact be more of a leash than a spike. If I reach out and take it, we could become connected, just like the other pairs in here. Master and commander. Man and dog. Spirit and fiend. Perhaps you were originally sent me as a wish granted, all those years back, foreshadowing this infernal trap. Although, as you might imagine, I am now slightly suspicious of things seemingly 'going my way'.

Above, a soft light pulses across the dome's surface. Steam from the pipes hiss and spit and the machinery thuds and stomps. You are across the walkway, at your usual spot. How long will it take us to get all the way up there? I am suddenly reminded of a book we read in class, back in my first week at university. An introduction to philosophy, a chapter on Thales: "The most difficult thing in life is to know yourself."

I am surprised, shocked even, that I remember it. And I will have a few things to say about the subject of knowing oneself, if I do ever manage to get out of here. I won't need to study philosophy. I have become the embodiment of it.

A GHOSTLY TOUCH, a caress against my lips, my cheek. My mother wiping my mouth clean, no doubt, after having fed me. She hums a few bars, tunelessly. She has me now, completely—I am going nowhere. Perhaps we all get what we wish for, in the end.

I TAKE A step away from the auditory nerve path, almost bumping into one of the blood cells trailing their proteins. Clink, clank. They ignore me, and I ignore them. My journey towards the dome above has begun. I have to try, don't I? The central stairs are the obvious solution. Or perhaps I should attempt to climb the outer shell, circumventing the cortex—that way, I won't get scolded by the steam, and I might also avoid those scissor-like projections that seem to be everywhere. I stand, indecisive. You watch me keenly. You won't be able to scramble up the outer webbing easily, not with your spines. Okay, the staircase it is. Come along then, fiend. Let us go see what the dome looks like from within.

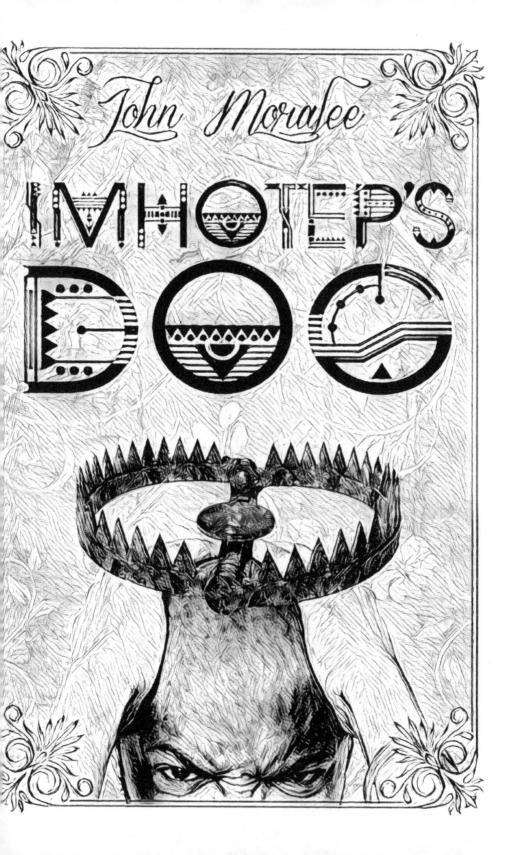

Imhotep's Dog

"Dog!" my master called out from his bath. "I have it! I have it! Get in here, you wretch!"

I hurried into his room, where Imhotep was soaking his frail body in a huge stone bathtub filled with steamy water. That morning his naked flesh was bright pink from the heat. I really hoped he did not want me to scrub his back; a thousand years had turned the skin leathery and pungent. "Yes, master?"

"I've just thought of a great new weapon," he said. "Write down my idea before I forget."

I grabbed a quill and some papyrus. "I'm ready, master."

"It's called The Acid Bath Murder Machine. It consists of a bath filled to the brim with acid. A cage suspends above it containing my victim. The victim is slowly lowered into the bath and the acid dissolves them little by little, causing the most exquisite agony. The acid kills them slowly. Once they are dead, I shall simply pour the contents of the bath into the sea, leaving no trace of what I did. What do you think?"

I thought Imhotep was an evil madman, and his invention diabolical, but I had to admit the intelligence in its design. That was Imhotep: clever enough to have designed the Great Pyramid and created the first clockwork heart, clever enough to turn the complex machinery inside his chest to the job of immortality.

And though the rest of his body had decayed like any other mortal around the scarab-like device that kept it moving, his mind, keen and cruel as ever, had continued inventing the machines that secured his power in Egypt, second only to the pharaoh.

And now here he was, flailing in a bath as I sloughed away his decaying skin, and listened to his latest macabre invention. I might have thought Imhotep was an evil madman, he was my master, so I grinned and lied. "It is a brilliant concept, master. You've done it again."

"It's not as good as Pythagorus' *Death By Triangles*—but I only spent a couple of hours working on it."

"It shows," I said.

"Pardon?" he said.

"It shows how clever you are, master, that you think so quickly."

Imhotep dismissed me with a wave and I returned to my quarters. They were quite large for a slave and they had been mine since he bought me at the slave market when I was ten. I had been one of a dozen young boys brought to his home, into his library, where he tested our intelligence with a game of shells. He placed a small green olive under one of three shells on a table, then he shifted the shells around, moving the ball between them, slowly increasing the speed of his hands until they were almost a blur. He asked each boy in turn to point at the shell hiding the olive. Every boy studied his movements carefully before choosing—incorrectly. They were taken away to be sold to someone else. When it was my turn, I watched as closely as the other boys, following the ball from shell to shell until I figured out the trick. After Imhotep had stopped moving the shells, I did not point at the one I had last seen the ball beneath. I pointed at Imhotep's hand, because he had palmed the ball, leaving the shells empty. He smiled, impressed.

"I will keep this one," he told the slave trader. "He shows a modicum of intelligence, which I shall need in my new assistant."

After choosing me, Imhotep fitted my neck with one of his newest inventions: the death collar. It sat tight around the neck, fastened with a clockwork device that required winding up every day by a special key he kept locked in an iron safe in his library. If the collar wasn't wound up, it would tighten until it choked me and cut off my head. He demonstrated what would happen to me if he did not wind it every day by showing me another collar decapitate a prisoner of war, and then he had locked the key in the safe, making sure I had seen it locked away far from my reach. Over the years I had inspected the safe in snatched moments; it had a six-digit code only known to Inhotep that he typed into a numbered pad connected to a series of complex levers and pulleys. The order of the six numbers triggered the lock mechanism. I had no hope of discovering these numbers, and though there was occasionally an opportunity where the key was left, if only for a moment, unguarded, Imhotep had thought of that too. There were seven keys inside the safe, all marked with the days of the week. They had to be used in order or the mechanism would be sprung. The collar could only be removed if all seven keys were used together, so there was no point in stealing just one of them.

If the collar wasn't wound each day, it would tighten around my neck until it cut through my throat. The image of the prisoner of war had lived in my dreams for months after, his face red and asphyxiated, blood vessels bursting in the whites of his eyes in the moments before the collar had tightened fully and the musculature of his neck had crumpled in on itself as insubstantial as a scythe through reeds. "So, boy, don't ever think of betraying me or running away," Imhotep said. "For my device will kill you within a day."

And so I became his personal slave, his reluctant apprentice in his theoretical scientific work…and in his sadistic practical experiments on prisoners of war. Imhotep loved testing his weapons on live humans, proving his machines were effective at killing. I had witnessed hundreds of his sickening experiments since I passed his intelligence test, dutifully inscribing the results for my master on scrolls now stored in his great library. I had always wondered if my life would have been better or worse if I had failed his test.

That intelligence test had been many summers ago.

Imhotep had invented hundreds of such devices since, which he sold to torturers and weapon masters so he could live in a palatial house on the shore of Al-Iskandariyah. I'd been wearing the collar for over twenty years. I hated it and Imhotep—but my life was not too bad for a man in my position. I had been allowed to marry another of his slaves. Her name was Vara. She was a strong and beautiful Thracian. My wife was also fitted with a death collar. She cooked and cleaned the house and tended to our master's roof garden. That day she was in our room, resting on the straw mattress because her belly was swollen with our first child. She was crying, which was not like her. She rarely shed tears.

"What is wrong?" I asked.

"Nothing," she lied.

"I'm your husband," I said. "Please tell me, Vara. Why do you cry?"

"Husband, I do not want our son to be born a slave," she said. She was convinced her unborn child would be a boy because he kicked her so hard.

"He will not be," I said. "He will be born a freeman."

"He will be a slave if he lives in this house—with that madman. Imhotep will fit our child with a death collar, making him just like us."

I touched the collar around my neck. It felt as if it had just tightened. "There is nothing we can do about that. Without the combination to his safe ..."

"I have been thinking about that," my wife said. She spoke very quietly, her dark eyes narrowing. "We could torture the old man into telling us the code."

"Torture?" I had never heard my wife speak of such things, but I could see she was deadly serious. Vara was a kind and gentle woman incapable of killing a spider. For her to consider torture as a solution to our problem revealed to me the depth of her despair and desperation. "Imhotep is a stubborn man, Vara. His heart would stop long before he told us his code. And then, without the keys, we would die of decapitation."

Vara sighed. "You are right. It was foolish thinking. Imhotep is too clever. We will never open his safe. Our son will never be free."

I sat on the edge of our bed, stroking my wife's long silky black hair, lowering my voice to a whisper. "We'll think of a way to be free. I promise you our child shall not be born a slave, my love."

Vara turned and kissed me passionately, her lips tasting like juicy grapes, sweet and ripe. "I want you, my husband. I need you now."

I was eager to please my wife—but a creaky whiny voice from the master's bathroom killed my ardour.

"Dog!" Imhotep called out. He had named me that as a joke because he treated his slaves like animals. My real name, the name I clung onto as my free name, was spoken in a different tongue. I could hear Imhotep splashing water on the floor in a pathetic attempt to get himself out of the bath. "Dog, get me out of here! Dog! *Dog!*"

"I'd love to let him drown," I said to my wife. I stood up wearily. "I'm coming, master!"

Imhotep was glowering when I returned. "I called for you many times, you oaf! Do you want your neck screws tightening?"

"No, master. I was resting, master. I do apologise."

"Just get me out of here, you cretin," he said. "I shall have to invent a device for elevating myself out of my bath. Write a note about that when you have dried me."

"Yes, master."

I could so easily have drowned him then, a thought I had had on many a day before, but the seven keys stayed my hand. Instead I lifted his weak old body out of the bath and dried his wrinkled sagging flesh. I helped him dress in a white tunic and sandals.

"Prepare my horse," he said. "I have an important meeting today with the Pharaoh."

"Yes, master," I said.

That morning I travelled with Imhotep through the beautiful streets of Al-Iskandariyah, passing the Temple of Isis, walking beside my master as he rode on a white horse up a hill toward the Castle of Horus, which was a fortress protecting the city. It was a hot sunny day and the air smelled of the sea. My legs were aching when I got to the castle gates—but I enjoyed the view of the harbour below filled with Egyptian fishing boats, their sails gleaming in the golden sunlight. The castle was an impressive sight, with its walls of solid stone.

"Halt!" a guard ordered.

We stopped at the gate.

"Let me in!" Imhotep demanded. "I am Imhotep!"

The guards recognised Imhotep. They hurried to open the gates for us to pass into the courtyard, where soldiers were practising combat with swords and spears. We were greeted by the royal guards. I helped Imhotep off his horse. He thanked me by belching something foul in my face.

Normally slaves were not allowed inside the castle, but I was permitted to remain with Imhotep because I was also his scribe. We entered a large marble hall where the Pharaoh was sitting on a bejewelled throne, flanked by several rows of guards and minions. The Pharaoh wore a magnificent gold crown and shimmering golden armour.

"Ah! My great scientist!" the Pharaoh said in a booming voice that echoed throughout the great hall. "Today is a wonderful day! We must speak of war and weapons!"

"Always my favourite subject, Your Majesty," Imhotep said. "How may I assist you?"

The Pharaoh did not answer immediately. Instead he dismissed his entourage so only the three of us were in the room. The men began to talk like old friends; I was invisible to them, unworthy of note.

"I have learnt something grave," the Pharaoh said. "The Romans led by Marcus Claudius Marcellus intend to invade Egypt. They intend to attack this city, as it is the gateway to The Nile. I need a new weapon to destroy them before they reach our shores. Can you devise something before they arrive?"

"Of course! They do not call me a genius for nothing. I shall invent the most fiendish of weapons to destroy our enemies. How long do I have to devise it?"

The Pharaoh sighed. "I need it within days. The airships are already on their way."

"That is not much time to build a weapon." Imhotep rubbed his chin in deep malevolent thought. "Yes! I have something! It is so brilliant and simple only a genius could think of it!"

"What is it?" the Pharaoh asked.

"I shall invent a deadly Heat Ray!"

The Pharaoh clapped his hands gleefully. "What will it do?"

"It will use the power of the sun to burn the enemy airships to cinders. The Roman legions will die in absolute agony, roasting on the decks like pigs at a feast."

The Pharaoh looked worried. "You can build this Heat Ray in mere days?"

"No—I can *build* it in hours. But first I must perfect the design." He turned to me. "Dog, we must go back to my home. I have much work to do if I am to destroy the Romans."

We returned to his library, where he began drawing plans on a papyrus scroll. He caught me looking wistfully at my wife when she brought him some lunch, which was always the same, a slice of freshly-cooked goat pie stuffed with olives and spices, garnished with bay leaves. "Are you drooling at the sight of your pregnant wife or my piece of pie?" he said, chuckling darkly. "Either way, you should be concentrating on helping me! You can drool over her or it later, when you are not supposed to be working."

"Sorry, master."

"Bring me my table of equations and constants," he said.

"Yes, master."

I hurried to obtain the scroll from its alcove. Meanwhile Imhotep was drawing large circles on his plan, which seemed to involve over a score of mirrors focussed on a single point. He drew circles within circles and connected them with straight lines and curves. His design was like a work of art—beautiful - and yet its purpose was dark and dangerous. The way his arthritic hands moved so swiftly reminded me of the shell game so long ago. He was older, but he had not lost his dexterity or mind. Imhotep stopped only to stuff his mouth with my wife's pie. "Hmm. A piece of pie makes the creative juices flow! A piece of pie makes them die! I am a poet! They all know it! I am the man with the plan!" He hummed a little tune to himself as he continued drawing his new death machine.

I swept the crumbs of pie off the table and ate them when he was not looking. My wife's pie tasted delicious.

Imhotep completed his design for the new death machine—The Imhotep Heat Ray—by the time the sun was low. He would have taken it to the castle himself—but he yawned. "Here. I am tired and need rest. You take this to the castle now. See to it the Pharaoh receives my design tonight, Dog. Not a moment can be wasted."

"Yes, master," I said. "I shall ride like the wind."

"You are not using *my* horse," he snapped. "You could fall off and lose my design. Walk. You have two legs. Use them."

"Yes, master."

I rolled up the scroll and headed for the courtyard—but on my way there I stopped in the hallway to have a curious look at my master's plans. His weapon used an array of seventy very polished bronze or copper shields as mirrors reflecting the sunlight into a powerful beam. His calculations showed the concentrated heat of the sun would ignite wood in the blink of an eye. The weapon could be easily aimed at the enemy's airships, destroying an entire fleet, saving Al-Iskandariyah. Imhotep had invented his most lethal weapon—but I did not want it to succeed. I wanted to stop him making more death machines. If his new weapon failed, the Pharaoh would lose faith in Imhotep.

By making a few subtle alterations to the plan, I reduced the power of the Heat Ray by a factor of a hundred. The beam would now be no warmer than a lick of a candle. I would be executed if my alterations were discovered, but it was worth the risk to see my master fail.

That night I delivered the faulty plans to the Pharaoh. I thought my wife would be pleased when I told her what I had done—but she kicked me out of our bed. "You fool. They'll know you did something when they test it."

"They won't have time to test it properly. It will *seem* to work. Just not at the power expected. Imagine the Pharaoh's reaction when Imhotep fails. He will be furious. If I point out the errors, the Pharaoh might make me his new inventor, freeing me from this cursed collar."

"That will never happen," my wife said. "You've doomed us both, my husband. If the test fails, we will be executed for helping the Romans the very moment Imhotep discovers what you did to his plans."

Such foolish action! I had not thought of the consequences—but there was nothing I could do now. It was too late. I could not tell Imhotep about my alterations.

"You had better pray to the gods tonight for a miracle," Vara said. "Only they can save us from your impulsive act."

I did pray. I prayed the gods would intervene.

The next day seventy shields were set up on the battlements of the Castle of Horus. Each shield was made of shining copper and held by a soldier directing the light in a parabolic reflector. That afternoon they tested the power on an old ship in the middle of the harbour—but the beam was too weak. It merely dazzled onlookers down on the shore. The Pharaoh was not impressed.

"It will work best in the morning," Imhotep explained. "Then the fire of the sun will be a furnace upon our enemies."

At dawn, two days later, the Roman airships were spotted coming towards the city. Each was elevated by a large gas balloon above the main deck, lifting the mighty ships into the air. I was with Imhotep in the Castle of Horus when the airships came within the expected range of the Heat Ray. The Romans had successfully destroyed our airships with cannons and now nothing except the Heat Ray stood between them and the city. I watched as the mirrored shields aligned, reflecting the morning light, unleashing a heat ray on the nearest Roman airship. A bright dot appeared on the airship's gas balloon. There was smoke—but not the explosive conflagration everyone else expected. I was the only person unsurprised.

"Why is it not burning them to cinders?" the Pharaoh cried out. He had the Heat Ray scroll unfurled in his hands. "Is the design wrong? Check it!"

Imhotep looked perplexed as he took the scroll. I prayed to the gods he would not spot my changes. Luckily, Imhotep was flustered by the Pharaoh. He answered with haste. "No, sire. It must be the sun. It is not high enough in the sky. Target the support ropes attached to the gas balloons. They will burn easier." He absent-mindedly threw me the scroll to keep. "Aim the weapon at the ropes!"

Imhotep was correct about the ropes being easier to ignite. The heat beam set the hemp alight in moments. As the burning ropes snapped, the airship became unstable, veering off course, the deck listing to one side, throwing soldiers into the sea. The Romans fell to their deaths far below. The remaining ropes stretched and snapped one by one. The gas balloon broke away, rising into the sky, dropping the rest of the airship into the harbour. The Romans jumping off the sinking vessel drowned in their armour.

"There! It works."

The Pharaoh grinned. "Do the others."

The Heat Ray targeted the next airship—but the captain had already seen the fate of the other vessel. He had ordered his crew to wet the ropes so they would not burn. The airship was also at a greater distance, making the Heat

Ray even weaker. It practically had no effect, except, perhaps, blinding some crew members. More airships were speeding into view. The Pharaoh ordered the Heat Ray to burn them—but then something happened beyond prediction. A cloud passed in front of the sun. The Heat Ray faltered instantly. Nothing could stop the Romans making it to the city. I could feel the panic around me as the Egyptians realised their weapon was useless in cloudy weather.

"No, no!" Imhotep said. "We need sunlight! Gods, hear me!"

The gods did not hear him.

The airships reached the city outside the walls of the castle.

"Defend the city!" the Pharaoh commanded. "We are under siege!"

The Egyptian soldiers tried to make the Heat Ray torch the Romans as they landed their airships, but the Romans just reflected the light back on their own shields, blinding the men on the battlements. And in all of this, Imhotep was so distracted by the Pharaoh's anger that he did not notice when I tossed the scroll into a brazier. Later my master asked me about it and I told him it must have been lost in the chaos. He was angry—but not as angry as he would have been if he had known the full extent of my betrayal. He only used one of his minor torture devices upon me, rendering me mute for a week.

That day saw the start of the Roman's seige. They would have breached the castle walls in days if Imhotep had not used other war machines against them. And that day lasted for two more years; the Romans attacked Al-Iskandariyah while Imhotep employed a number of new weapons against them, ground gained and lost in a constant war of attrition that we somehow kept at bay. By then, my son had been born and had grown into a handsome child with the beautiful eyes of his mother. My wife and I grew more anxious with every day, watching our child growing. The day he had learnt to walk should have been a day to rejoice— but to us it was just a reminder that he was getting older and bigger. He was no longer a helpless baby.

"Soon our son will be old enough to be fitted with a death collar," she told me in our quarters many times. "And then he will be forever a slave of Imhotep."

"I know," I said, sighing, and thought desperately of those seven keys behind their locked door.

The problem had been on my mind for decades. If only there was a way to spy over Imhotep's shoulder when he was putting his code into the safe— but he only unlocked the safe after locking the door of the library, ensuring he was alone. The library had no windows and the walls were made of thick hard stone—so it would be impossible to spy on him from outside. And there was nowhere to hide inside the library unless you were the size of a mouse. The next morning I felt my collar ticking away as the fiendish internal mechanisms approached the time of rewinding. I stood dutifully outside the library with my wife while our master went inside, locking the door. He opened the door two minutes later, brandishing the key for the day. He used it to wind our collars back a day—then he went back into his library to return it to the safe.

"I wish I had an eye on a stalk," I said to Vira. "Then I could peer through the keyhole."

Imhotep called me into the library to assist him. He was working on a new weapon called the Death Cloud. It used noxious gases, which he would form by mixing acids and metals in huge vats, forming a deadly cloud of unbreathable poison. The genius of his idea was to make breathing masks for everyone inside the castle, so it would kill the Romans while leaving us alive.

"Master, will that not risk killing thousands of our own people below in the city?" I had many friends living in the city. I did not want them to be harmed.

"A few unimportant lives do not matter," he said. "My Death Cloud will finish the Romans. They shall be slaughtered where they stand. In a few days I will have produced enough gas to annihilate them."

He worked on the chemical formula all morning, stopping only to feast on my wife's delicious pie. Her hands were dusty with flour when she brought the pie to the library, giving me an exciting idea.

Later that day, when Imhotep was bathing, I slipped into his library and dusted the safe with flour. My eyes could see it—but Imhotep had long sight. He would not know it was there.

The next day I examined the safe to see which buttons had been touched by my master. The numbers were 1, 3, 4, 5 and 9. There were six numbers in the code—but only five buttons had been touched. That meant one number had been used twice. What possible combination could have been used? It would have to be something my master considered important. An important six-digit number?

There was only one number that I could think of that he valued—but it was not six digits. Pi. It was a special number—but the first six digits were just a piece of it. A piece of pi.

I tried entering the numbers: 3,1,4,1,5,9.

And then I turned the handle.

The safe opened.

And I saw the seven keys.

I unlocked myself, hands trembling. As the final one twisted in the keyhole, I heard a louder click and felt the collar release. For the first time I removed it and felt the sore skin underneath. My shoulders felt unnaturally naked, unburdened of the weight of the collar. I wasted no time locating my wife and releasing her, directing her to fetch our son.

"I have something to do," I said.

Imhotep had his eyes closed as he relaxed in the bath. He did not even open his eyes until he heard the click of the collar going around his neck. Then they widened in alarm.

"Dog, what are you doing?"

"I'm freeing myself from you," I told him. "And I'm taking the seven keys with me—so if you want them back you had better pray to the gods."

I heard him screaming and swearing as I left—but nobody would answer him. The walls of his house were too thick for the noise to escape outside. I doubted he could even make it out of the bath on his own; I had never made a note, and so he had never built the machine he had planned to help him.

The walls of the castle were well defended—but I knew a place where we could climb down without being detected. I used a rope to lower my wife and son to the ground below, following down above them. Our escape had been observed by Roman soldiers but I had already planned for that. I showed I was unarmed and asked them to take me to General Marcus Claudius Marcellus. He was in his tent at some distance from the castle, surrounded by legions of his soldiers.

"You escaped from the castle?"

"Yes, sir," I said. "I was Imhotep's slave, sir. He kept me imprisoned with a collar around my neck which would kill me if I did not obey him." I explained the collar's function. "Today, I finally escaped it because I was desperate to get out of the city. Imhotep has been making a new lethal weapon. A Death Cloud that will kill thousands of people. You must stop him, sir. I can help you break into the castle because I know its weak points. All I ask if that you let me and my family go free."

"Very well," he said. "You have my word. Help me break into the castle and I shall let you go. But you must give me the seven keys to the collar so I can use Imhotep as my own weapon master."

I gave him everything he asked, and soon—with cruel, terrifying swiftness— it was all over.

He began ordering his soldiers to prepare for a new attack. He kept me and my family as prisoners until the attack began. His army was soon inside the castle walls, taking control. The general issued orders for Imhotep to be taken alive—but one of his soldiers encountered a crazy old naked man in the street, ranting about something that sounded like "the circle of death". Thinking the old man was mad, the soldier killed him with his sword.

After Al-Iskandariyah had fallen, General Marcellus released me despite the loss of Imhotep. He did not blame me for the actions of his own soldier. We were given a horse and cart, and some money to start our lives as Roman citizens. Then we were allowed to leave. As we rode away from Al-Iskandariyah, I began to smile and laugh because my old life as a slave was over.

It was a good day. Imhotep was gone, we were free, and I would never again be called Imhotep's dog.

But For The Pieces He Left Behind

❖-❖-E.-CATHERINE-TOBLER-❖-❖

A SMALL FLEET of airships both ponderous and petite anchored over Cairo's flourishing Ezbekieh Gardens, a grand bouquet of balloons clutched in the outstretched hand of the Khedivial Opera House. The landing platforms of copper and cedar, the copper having run with the green and chocolate of an ages old patina, spread like the various mouths of the Nile from the opera house's elegant roof, a lotus crafted across the bustling thoroughfare that divided park from opera.

The scene was serenity itself , the stars twinkling in the blue-black sky as we opera goers—having just indulged in the beauty and grandeur that was *Aida* performed in the very land it heralded—left the opera house for our airships. Serenity—but for the band of fierce turbaned and scarfed pirates hauling me with sabers and pistols across the metal and wood lotus into their own airship.

I had arrived on the *Jackal* but it seemed I would be leaving via the *Argo*, an airship neither ponderous nor petite, but built for speed. She was a sleek vessel, with a sharp nose and a slim backside, a ship that brooked no argument when it came to sky domination. The other airships seemed to part way for *Argo*, captains and passengers unwilling to risk a confrontation no matter how I, flung over the shoulder of one pirate, shrieked for help.

This, my mother would have said, was the peril of a woman attending the opera alone.

This, I thought, had nothing to do with attending the opera alone. I had been everywhere alone: I had climbed Mauna Kea, had ridden to the bottom of Grand Canyon upon a donkey. I regularly did the most outlandish things alone, without being captured by rogues of any kind. Granted, my late husband J.J. was a rogue of another sort, however in my day to day wanderings, rarely did one find oneself captive. Oh, I had fallen from the sky in failing airships, and had found myself chased across Antarctic landscapes by vicious lizards that meant to eat me—but captured? By pirates? It wasn't done.

I had come to Egypt following a trail I'd first picked up in Florence, Italy, amid a collection of da Vinci's mechanicals. There, I found a sliver of J.J.'s own genius, and following the related thread within his notebooks, had discovered a trail toward Egypt. Impossibly vague! My foolish widow's heart hoped the trail would lead to an as yet undiscovered invention of J.J.'s, specifically one he and I had dreamed of together, in pencil upon pages, in hammock-shared whispers— though never built. But within the da Vinci items, I had found the dust shadow of a machine I recognized from J.J.'s notebooks, three disks turning one into another.

The wheels of past, present, and future— Foolish Muriel.

In the grand scheme of things, I was but a widow who enjoyed the distant operas of the world. An explorer, an adventurer. But now, flung over the shoulder of a pirate, my ribs jostled with every jolting stride, I had to believe that the pirates had learned of J.J.'s device—and had tracked me as I tracked it. I had to believe that the pirates, like me, believed the device existed, a device said to be capable of altering the course of the heavens.

With furious fists, I beat upon the back of the pirate who carried me onto the *Argo*, for I would not be taken.

"Put me down!"

The pirate did not listen and in fact tightened his hold upon me, his hand closing over my head so the back of it did not bump upon the portal's lintel when we entered the *Argo*.

What kind of pirate—?

He dropped me to the floor as if to answer that very question. As the *Argo* abruptly bucked from its berth, I slid across the polished wood floor, until my movement was arrested by a low table beneath which I found myself wedged helplessly. The pirates left me there, having a raucous discussion as to something happening outside. I wondered if rescue had shown itself at last, and glanced to the entry in case it had not.

We remained close to the platform. I toyed with the notion of stealing the golden pashmina draped over the nearest chair, and parachuting my escape from the door. I had done worse, leaping from the *Rocha* above Buenos Aires as she plunged to earth, spewing golden caskets and bodies alike. But *Argo*'s door remained well guarded, two bodies posted across its locked face. I could see only the dark eyes of the pirates, the rest hidden by turbans, scarves, and neatly striped loose trousers. They glared at me, arms crossed over their chests, swords gleaming from their waist sashes.

"Did you at least see *Aida?*" I asked from beneath the table.

I thought of the temples built for the stage, and it still took my breath away. I had not come to Cairo to see the opera, but in the end I'd been unable to resist. It had been my dearest hope to see some of the temples and pyramids as I followed J.J.'s cryptic notes, a dahabieh for hire scheduled to take me down the Nile the following morning. But now, a detour.

No matter how I kicked or punched, the pirates hauled me from beneath the table, and carted me toward a figure dressed with slightly more panache. A blue coat draped his shoulders, tapering down to a slim, red pashmina-wrapped waist. Gold stripped trousers vanished into leather boots that had seen a scuffle or two. This figure stood tall at the wheel of the *Argo*, directing another band of pirates outside. I peered out the row of portholes running along the airship's side to see that the pirates had captured the *Jackal.*

I snarled. "You have no right. You can't just—"

The pirate turned on me, the scarf that draped his head swinging loose to reveal a glory of ebon hair beaded with hammered metal and Murano glass. The dark eyes that met my own were not those of a man, but of a brown-skinned woman, heavily lined with kohl, drawn to a careful and precise point at both the inner and outer corners.

"I *can* just," she said, and nodded to the two pirates holding me.

They carried me to a wide, armless chair that was one of four in a round arrangement. A low table in the center held a hooka and the sight of a plate of fresh fruit made my stomach rumble.

"If you're hungry, please. I realize we've compromised your evening, which— if it's anything like a night at the opera for me—would have involved drinks afterward. I fear we have also changed your tour of the Nile."

I slid back into the chair, until I was wedged against its blue velvet back. It gave me the feeling that at least one side of me was guarded, that no one might sneak up behind me and carry me where they wished me. My captors sat on either side, their captain taking the chair directly across from me.

"It will be there, should you change your mind." She drew the scarf from her head, allowing its blue length to hang around her neck with an assortment of charms on chains. "You may call me Mestra. I welcome you aboard *Argo*, Muriel Brennan."

Fury churned in my belly. "Welcome? You captu—" I broke off, staring at this Mestra. She knew my name and also my schedule, having found me at the opera. "This is no coincidence then." I refused to reveal all my cards—it was too early and she was too crafty. Instead, I demanded she reveal her hand. "Out with it then. You will surely know that J.J. is dead—that I buried him on the ice. That—"

Against my better intentions, my voice broke, that nerve still too raw. It was hard to imagine J.J. dead, no longer a living, breathing part of this world he loved so well. In part, it was his fault I'd become a traveler, meaning to see the world since he no longer could.

"Dead, yes," Mestra said, and I wondered if I imagined the way her own voice wavered when she said it. Had she known J.J.? But she sat straight after that little waver, her dark eyes pinning me where I sat. "But not gone, not out of this world, given all that he created."

Mestra snapped her fingers and another of her robed pirates came forward, carrying a wooden case which they placed beside the hooka. This case was bound in brass, twice around its girth, and I would have known it from that alone, had the wood also not spoken to me. There was no question: the case was one of J.J.'s making. He had often ordered olivewood from Italy and carved the cases himself, to enclose his best ideas, his ideas that were inspired, he said, by me.

Mestra opened the brass latches and I wanted nothing more than to throw myself across the case, to forbid her to open it, but she already had—the latches were not locked, already bore the scratches of an illicit entry.

"Your late husband," Mestra said, "was a remarkable man. He had a way of seeing the world that no other had—or does. Not only did he dream these machines, he *made* them." Mestra opened the final latch and turned the case, allowing everyone around the table to see what it held as she swung the lid open.

To the untrained eye, it didn't look like anything, but Mestra carefully opened hidden latches in each side of the wooden case until the box lay flat, exposing the object inside. It looked like another case, gleaming olivewood trimmed with copper, brass, silver, and gold. Every face displayed a different metal, and was marked with countless images. The longer I looked, the more I saw: small moons, stars, horizons, and poles. Unfamiliar languages etched the metal plates, strange landscapes unfolding beneath unknown stars.

The top of the interior case had been made to fit three round objects—the disks I had seen in dust-shadow in Italy, the disks I found drawn in J.J.'s notebook. The cogs and gears on which they would sit were dark with disuse and age, but J.J. Brennan had crafted this case and it would work for centuries to come. I stroked the edges of the cogs and they were not sharp as if unused. They were smooth, as though the gears had already worked a lifetime. The very thing I was looking for. It was too easy, but I was unable to take my eyes from the case. I could not help but touch it, to feel the smooth, finished wood beneath my fingers, to know that J.J.'s own hands had crafted every edge and curve. I could picture him so easily, head bent to the task, eyes narrowed because they had always been failing him in one way or another. But he never let his vision, or lack thereof, govern what he set his hands to.

"You know it as I do," Mestra said. "This is the Brennan Device."

The very thing I was searching for...so it could not be.

Yet, I did not argue with her. It might be—and what then?

"How did it come to be in pieces? I saw..." I trailed off, meeting Mestra's eyes. They were steady on me, her expression eager. "In Italy, I believe the disks were in Italy, among da Vinci's own designs." J.J. was never not inspired by da Vinci—*the Vitruvian Man stands upon a square foundation, but also within a disk that might move forward and back, do you see Murrie?*

"Brennan himself left it in pieces and hid them away from the world," Mestra said, and took a small piece of paper from her gathered robes. She spread this on the table before me, and there—J.J.'s own handwriting. It caught me off guard, that she would have something on her person that he had written, something he had once held.

"He meant for you to—" At my glare, Mestra went silent, but only for a heartbeat. "Forgive me, Muriel, but our time grows short. J.J. wanted to bring you to Egypt, to give you this adventure, but when his heart began to fail, he had to find another way. My crew is that way, but now there is a threat. Ciphut Sinan has learned of the device and would make it his own."

The room was quiet but for the airship's tireless engines, and it was only Mestra's eyes I met when I at last looked up from the case between us. I shook my head, the motion scattering tears down my cheeks. Foolish to cry over such a thing—to want an impossible thing. I had buried J.J. and he was gone, no longer of this world but for the pieces he had left behind. I could not use this to see him again, could I?

"It's not the Brennan Device," I told Mestra.

"It is," Mestra said. "Our time grows short and we must fly—unfold the inner leaves and you will see."

She and her pirates left me with J.J.'s box. And I, curious to the end, did as she bid, discovering that each piece of the box unfolded further; each bore hidden hinges that unfolded twice and thrice more, showing a map when it was fully unfurled. A map was burned into the wood, in J.J.'s unmistakable style. But it was a map without a legend, a map that showed a thousand enigmatic marks. It seemed to be Egypt, but the Nile was not marked, nor the pyramids, or any other recognizable thing.

I knelt before the box, at the bottom edge of the map—but no. It was the top. I turned the box around, and where the burned lines spread in a black chaos, I placed my hand. My fingers became the mouths of the Nile, and in this way my arm became the Nile herself. Down every stretch of my arm, the map revealed a mark in places I slowly began to understand. The bump at my wrist was surely Giza, and if I turned my arm over, the veins in my arm beneath my pale skin ran like a river all their own.

Had Mestra arrived at the same conclusion? I did not ask her, too shaken by what lay before me. It was too easy, too neat a conclusion to my search. But J.J. had made this box, of that there could be no question. Did that mean he had also made his time machine? That he had found the missing piece after all, the piece that would open this time to every other that had come before?

How many nights had we talked about being able to step back through our own lifetimes and experience them all over again, to be, in this way, undying and eternal? While bundled in sleeping bags on Kilimanjaro, while watching the stars from the roof of Hill Fort Kesroli, we had mused about how it could change the world—for better and worse both. J.J. said it was perhaps a thing a person should not do—but in the end, he'd felt it was a thing no person *could* do. There was no way that he could see, to walk backwards upon the course humanity had been set upon.

And yet, this box.

I thought to play along—hadn't Mestra said J.J. had meant to give me an adventure? Who was I to refuse adventure when it swept me from the opera house in a pirate's fine airship?

"Mestra," I called, and she entered the room as if she had been waiting in the corridor all along. She said nothing, only stood waiting for me to continue. "You're looking for the disks. You mean to make this machine work again." I ran my fingers along the smooth edges of the gears once more; I was certain, so certain it had constantly spun itself sometime in the past.

"I mean to prevent anyone else from doing so," she said.

Ah yes—the *other* band of pirates, those now presumably chasing us to gain possession of the fabled time machine. *What if?* my heart whispered. I told it to hush.

"Let us go, then," I said, and Mestra's mouth split in a broad smile.

Mestra guided me onto *Argo's* upper deck, and it was with tired eyes I looked on the Nile beneath us. At this elevation, it was like nothing I had seen before, its waters dark yet reflecting the rising sun. The water divided the land into east and west, as if an ancient god had indeed run a finger down the whole of Egypt. The waters flowed north; it gave me a start to see this, as if for a moment the world had turned backwards, but of course it flowed north, ever toward the mouths which opened into the Mediterranean.

Mestra's crew were all women, a group who believed as fervently as she did that J.J.'s machine had worked and would work again—that only they could prevent Ciphut Sinan from learning its secrets and reshaping the world. As adventures went, it was a good one.

I pictured myself turning the gears as perhaps he once had, sorting the symbols until they aligned into a perfect date—not the day I had met J.J., not the day we had been married, but somewhere between. A quiet day, I thought, a day that we had each spent alone. I would find him in his workroom, his head bent, and I would stride out of whatever portal the device opened, grinning at him, and he would stare at me in wonder, because some part of him would know. He would know that he'd been alone, and now I was there—looking older and sadder because he'd left my present life, but brimming with new stories to tell him. I would tell him about the ice lizards of the Antarctic, and about the floating opera of Buenos Aires. I would tell him about the pirates abducting me from the Cairo opera house, and of our long flight down a darkened Nile.

"The problem," Mestra said as Io guided me to her side, "is that your husband was crafty. In hiding the disks for his machine, he used nothing so common as the temples that draw in tourists—no. His map makes use of wastelands, as surely you saw. Marks where nothing should exist, and yet—" Mestra extended a hand toward the barren desert where I saw a smudge of a shadow. We were far south of the Red Pyramid already, where there should have been nothing but sand and rock, and yet it was not.

In the middle of the waste stood a small temple—or, perhaps "temple" was generous. The closer we came, it seemed little more than a place for an airship to anchor, though to what end was unclear, given there was nothing close. Even the Nile retreated as we veered west. Wind had blown sand into the small structure, leaving little more than a small porch visible. The *Argo* crew made to anchor, and I looked at Mestra, still uncertain what she meant to do.

"You believe there is a disk here?" I asked. I tried to give in to adventure—I did—but I was angry that Mestra presumed to know things she shouldn't. "Further, you believe that J.J. built this machine and then scattered the working pieces of it across Egypt? J.J. and I never travelled to Egypt. If you have studied his works, you know this. Our journeys are well documented." My nose wrinkled; the press did love a good adventure story.

"Indeed," Mestra said, and then looked at me a little sadly in the warm, rising sunlight. "You and J.J. never travelled to Egypt. This does not preclude him having travelled to Egypt on his own."

Mestra moved from my side, to watch Electra lower the anchor over *Argo*'s side. I could only stare, slightly dumbfounded. She was right, of course. J.J. and I had not spent every moment together. We had talked of seeing Egypt together, but it did not mean he had never come on his own. This felt like a barb in my heart, sudden and sharp, and I followed Mestra to the ship's side, where she grinned at me like a jackal in possession of too many teeth.

"Down with you then, Muriel. If the disk is there, only your hands can retrieve it."

"That's—"

Angry about the idea that J.J. had come to Egypt on his own, I wanted very much to argue. It didn't matter what Mestra said, I would argue it. It didn't matter that again she unfolded the piece of paper with J.J.'s handwriting upon it.

"When the first disk you see, tiny you must be," it read.

I wanted to argue that J.J. would never write such a ridiculous thing, but in fact, he would have. He had never insulted my stature, but had come to joke about how he quite liked my size because it allowed us to gain entry to places we might not otherwise. He knew I was a curiosity to the world, and knew this had never pained me. People never looked at a person and saw the truth of them, be they tall, fat, or squat like myself. J.J. could always see to the truth of me, said he liked my tininess because no one would ever know me the way he did—no one would ever take the time.

But if he had written those words...

I couldn't finish the thought.

"All right," I said quietly, and climbed over the edge of the *Argo*, onto the ladder Helen had unfurled.

The ladder of rope and wood slats trembled in the air, but whether from my steps or the slight wind, I could not say. My legs were shaking so badly on the descent, I was convinced I would land on my back in the sand before all was said and done. Standing beside the *Argo*'s mighty anchor, I had never felt so small, and the structure before me only enhanced that feeling. It was not a temple, unless the majority of it had been covered by sand, but what it was I could not say. It stood taller than me, but had no formal doorway. Two columns flanked a very small empty space, into which I knew I could step. With a grunt, I did.

The small space inside was hot and sweat beaded on my skin. I stood in the warm dark, still in my dress from the opera, allowing my eyes to adjust and when they did, what confronted me was another portal, but one I could not fit through. My hand would, though.

A thousand awful things might be inside that hole, but I only allowed myself to list a portion of them: spiders, snakes, beetles, scorpions. Steeling myself, I slid my hand into the slot, discovering a shelf covered in sand. There seemed little else, so I dug as best I could until I felt warm metal against my fingers. The disk was not much larger than my hand and with care, I pulled it free from its confinement.

Outside, in the sunlight, the disk showed itself to be copper. It was covered with symbols I did not understand, and the holes punched through the disk threw a design onto the sand around me. Would they likewise illuminate the case, throwing patterns upon J.J.'s map? If this was the first of three disks, what might they make together?

My heart leapt at the idea and tears stung my eyes as I walked back to *Argo*'s ladder. I tucked the disk into my dress's deepest pocket and climbed my way up, noting with some alarm a dark speck emerging from the threads of fleeting morning clouds. Against the golden light, the object seemed a drop of ink, only revealing its true size when the light shifted. It was an airship, ochre and black, bearing toward us at an alarming speed. I became aware of a shouting above me, the women drawing the ladder up faster than I could climb.

"Muriel!"

I stopped climbing altogether, finding it quicker to let the women haul me up. My gaze remained rooted on the looming airship, a profusion of fabulous red flags and sashes streaming from its sleek sides. It looked like a hyena cutting through the sky, shining metal teeth snapping through a wave of blood.

She was so fast, upon us as I clattered to the deck. Mestra and her crew were swift, but the encroaching ship was quicker; a few well-aimed shots sent the *Jackal* plummeting, and then metal grappling hooks were piercing the *Argo's* heaving side. Black smoke clouded the sky as the *Jackal* sailed down and down. Metal bit into the *Argo's* wooden deck, the deck shrieking as it came apart under the assault. The *Argo* was hauled backward, into the ship's gleaming teeth. Down the metal lines streamed pirates, men who smelled of rum, sugar, and smoke.

Their approach was like a strange aerial ballet, the men moving among Mestra's twirling crew. As I had been with Mestra, I was their chief target, and was soon swept from my feet, hoisted over a crossbeam where they stared at me, squirming in the ropes they'd tied me with. Blood rushed to my head and I found myself laughing at the notion that J.J. and Mestra had planned this adventure. I could not doubt J.J. would have been proud of his collaborator, was maybe smiling down on her even now. An airship assault in mid-air by pirates foul? J.J. knew my heart.

The captain was a marvel, striding onto *Argo's* broken deck like he owned it. He was clad in black from head to toe, though gold shone at his ears and teeth both. His smile for me was golden and fanged, his beard trembling when he chortled. His face was painted with kohl, giving him the sharp look of a hyena, cheeks and eyelids dotted with gold. My heart leapt anew—one did not meet a legend every day.

"Sinan," I whispered.

"Ladies," he said with a sweeping bow. "I am Ciphut Sinan, and given that you have eluded us for a fortnight, I am sure you know we have come to liberate Brennan's Device. We shall not be forestalled or forsaken in our glorious endeavor. You shall provide us with the device or we shall see magnificent *Argo* burned to ash."

"Never!" I cried, playing along as best I could, for Sinan was infamous for destroying every ship he encountered. He had no care for ships beyond his own, saying it would rule the skies at the end of time. I wriggled, but had been bound tighter than strictly necessary; I could not move my hands and had no hope whatsoever of escape.

Mestra and her crew kneeled on the broken decking. Helen spat in Sinan's face when he approached, and Io kicked him in the knee when he thought to touch the strands of amber that encircled her throat. I wanted to cheer them all on. Mestra raised her chin and met Sinan's gaze. She too spat in his face when he made to touch her in a far too familiar fashion.

"Sinan, here."

One of his men emerged with a box—a box that was a fairly competent replica of the one Mestra had shown me. But would it fool a legendary pirate? It did not have J.J.'s flare—there was no brass to bind the box shut, and no latches to keep it secure, but it unfolded to show Sinan a map, one he stroked with his filthy fingers.

Sinan's head came up and he pinned Mestra with his black eyes. "You think to deceive me, Mestra? J.J. Brennan was a careful man, he would not build something so clumsy. These hinges..."

The box swung open, clumsy enough to cause Sinan's man to nearly drop the entire case. The box revealed a secondary compartment, this one bound in fine brass fittings. Though it looked nothing like his later work, it was one of his earliest pieces and I knew precisely what it had been made to do.

This was no mere adventure. This was a true story, the story of a time machine my late husband had actually built, wrapped in a thousand misleading myths.

Oh, J.J.

"Close your eyes!" I cried, and hoped that Mestra and her crew listened before the world exploded in brightness.

When the flash and bang had passed, I opened my eyes to watch Mestra and her crew overtake the stunned men in the smoke laden air. They bound Sinan and his men in their own grappling hooks and launched them overboard; they thudded, trussed and helpless, against the side of the *Black Hyena*.

Argo was worse for the encounter, her decking buckled and torn, but she remained sleek and fast. Electra and Io untied me from my ropes and as the *Argo* fled across the desert sky, there was no sign of pursuit from Sinan. I did not know what to think, for the women were shaken. It did not look pretend, nor was the damage that had left great gouts and breaks in *Argo*'s deck. The *Jackal* smoked in a black ruin on the ground.

"It's real?" I asked Mestra, and she—lady pirate and conqueror of the skies—laughed. Threw back her head and laughed, which set the beads and bands in her hair to jingling.

"All of it," she said. "The adventure and the impending threat. Your J.J. saved us from Sinan after hiding the disks—this is how Sinan came to hear of the machine. J.J. wanted only to bring you back, show you Egypt from the sky, but grew ill before he ever could. The second disk is...well, you will see." Her smile was genuine and warm and she looked like she might envy me.

"And Sinan?" I did not think the *Argo* would survive another encounter with him, to say nothing of the world should he possess J.J.'s device. Did it work? Was it possible?

"Will hopefully not follow before we succeed."

Hope was a thin thread to balance the world on, but we did. *Argo* sailed into the azure sky, high and higher still. At the lush Faiyum Oasis, Mestra charted a course straight up into the clear blue. I could not imagine what awaited us in that sky, but soon found out.

Above the oasis, lost in the shimmer between the sun and Qarun Lake far below, lay a second oasis, this one hidden from the world. In the blue sky hung a blue lake, and within the blue lake stood an island. Everywhere, palm trees flourished, and all manner of birds flocked, sneaking respites from their journeys elsewhere. The air smelled of fruit and salt, and something about it broke my heart. I wished J.J. were here, though took comfort in the idea that he had once been.

Unlike the Valley of Sky which hung above Buenos Aires, this oasis was wholly natural, obscured from the ground below by the way the light coming up from the lake bent, refracted, *something*. It was maddening and I had no time to understand the science of it before Mestra sent me on my way.

"Courageous you must be," Mestra read from J.J's letter, but I saw the third clue written beneath it—*Murrie you must be, trust me.*

Once again, they lowered me by ladder, this time onto the small island that sat in the lake's center. As I descended, clouds seemed obscure the sunlight and for one terrifying moment, all was darkness. Within the dark, I heard breathing and felt the passage of a dozen large creatures. For a second, I believed I was pressed between their large, dark bodies, wet noses snuffling at me in the blackness.

When the sunlight streamed down upon the island again, I was alone. I tried not to notice how the sand around my feet was imprinted with catlike footprints, but it became impossible when the golden bodies swam from the lake, a siege of clockwork sphinx. Some had wings, others did not, but each one appeared bejeweled, lake water sparkling on feathers and fur until I could not tell water from gem. One sphinx approached me, its broad mouth plucking at my gown's sleeve, as if it meant to pull me into the water.

"No," I said, and its ears flicked. I had no hope it could understand, for it pushed at me with its soft nose, herding me toward the lake. The beast would not be distracted. I tried to step around it, and it bowed its broad head and pushed me straight into the cool lake. I spluttered, but could not regain my feet before another of the beasts pulled me down.

All was darkness and I could not breathe. I kicked and pummeled as best I could, and my one scream was ill-timed, for all it did was cost me air. When at last I broke free, I swam my way to the surface, breaking through with an anguished shriek. I clawed at the shore, pulling myself out of the water, but it was not a sky I found myself looking at. I had emerged into a cavern. Beneath the island?

I sat myself up for there was little else to do. The cavern was a hollow of sandstone, a puddle of water. I could see no light from the water, nothing to show me the way out, but I looked around again, trying to determine if there were a disk here. Across the pool, wedged into a crack in the stone, I spied the edge of a disk.

It blended into the rock so well, it might have been rock itself. When at last I pulled it free from the crack in the stone, I found that it was wood, its backside carved with a shape I knew would fit into the machine's gears. Its surface had a piercing of holes the way the metal disk did, but when I wrestled the wet metal from my pocket, I still could not determine how they might fit together. Not until I saw the marking on the edge of the wood disk.

No one else would have known that it matched the marking within the circle of my wedding band. I set the disks down, and pulled my ring free and peered at its interior edge. There, J.J. had etched the shape of his clockwork heart, because he said it belonged with me.

The disks fit together with my ring between them, and once together, thin supports extended outward from the metal disk, linking it to the wood, making a sort of zoetrope structure. I presumed it needed light to illuminate the piercings, and I had no candle, but there in the dark, my ring began to glow.

I dropped the machine for fear that it would burn me. It spun and continued to glow, brighter and brighter, as if the desert sun had flooded into the cavern. The walls of the cavern sparked with shapes, the light drawing a ragged line up the stone, the outline of mountains and then the clouds above them and then the birds above even them. Maybe it was the oasis, maybe it was Kilimanjaro I had climbed with J.J. at my side.

Somewhere high above, explosions rocked the oasis and the cavern trembled. I lunged for the disks, thinking Sinan had found us, but when my fingers bisected the light, the brightness swallowed me whole. The cavern and its small pool vanished. The light changed, deepened, and the piercings on the disks resolved themselves into something wholly familiar: J.J. Brennan stood before me in the dark, a pillar of gold.

Around him, the light still spun, crafting images from the life we had shared together, taking me from apex to abyss and back again. When the light spun past

J.J., he vanished in the dark, while still ahead, mountains were drawn in gold, amber, and copper along the cavern walls. River valleys, shell beaches, oil-black swamps, a thousand stars wheeling overhead. A time machine, but not the kind anyone else would understand.

I took the disks in hand as the cavern cracked open. The stone over my head parted, Sinan's metal-fingered hooks prising it apart. There was nowhere for me to go, the small cavern turned inside out. The sphinx that had taken to the lake fled in panic, shrieking into the sky as the metal hooks caught me up. Sinan hauled me into the sky, the Brennan Device spinning furiously.

Its weight changed in my hands and the metal claw that hauled me from the cavern sagged. The device spun as though it would come apart, the glow of my ring in its center magnified by the sunlight pouring down. The device pulled more and more of the sunlight into its center, as if the light were taffy and we were spinning it into a river, a river that snapped out to encircle the *Black Hyena* and *Argo* both.

The claw hauled me toward the *Hyena*'s maw, into the red flags and sashes that rippled around me like an airborne sea of blood. I saw *Argo* plain as day every time the sashes flapped open, but I could not reach her. Could only watch as the burning bright river of the Brennan Device pulled more tightly around the ship and started to pull us all out of the sky.

Sinan's ship was drawn under and into the light and into it, the way I had been in the cavern. The claw that held me bucked in the fluttering sashes, then finally lodged in the ship's mouth, against a guardrail of golden teeth and spikes. I tumbled to the ground and in my hands, the device stuttered. I saw in that moment how the river of light shot out, how I could control its path by shifting the wheels and gears. The machine responded to me like it knew me.

I picked myself out of the claw and standing at the edge of the *Black Hyena*'s gleaming mouth, I hauled the river away from *Argo* as if I were winding a fishing rod with both hands. The device spun furiously between my hands, sparks like fireflies filling the air around me. And those sparks, as they had in the cave, assembled themselves into J.J.'s familiar shape.

"Murrie—let us go then, you and I."

I swore I heard him speak, and his glowing hand extended toward me. It was not easy, the machine pulling on me as I pulled on it. I knew if I stopped reeling, all would be lost, the *Black Hyena* and *Argo* both, but what did they matter in the face of J.J. before me? I slowed my reeling and J.J. burned brighter, his features solidifying in the darkness between the sparks. There his eyes and there his mouth, slanting in a smile. I slowed my reeling ever more and allowed the golden river to sweep over both ships. I let in the tidal wave that broke the ships across the heavens. *Mestra*, I thought, *oh gods Mestra what have I done?* and for a while, everything was heat and light and I was blind.

IN THE AFTERMATH, everything was an afterimage. The *Black Hyena* was gone and so too the *Argo*, shattered debris raking a distant sky like falling stars. They were all gone—Mestra and Io, Electra and Helen. The legendary Sinan. Dust across the sky I'd left behind.

I stood on a narrow street in Cairo, but Cairo was painted in sepia tones, buildings melting into the street as if they were made of water. The sun should have shone, but it was a black hole in the sky above me—everything that should have been bright was dark, and every shadow burned white. Until I moved.

I stepped forward, halting and unsure, and the world came into focus around me, a photographic negative developing. The buildings stopped melting and the ground was as whole at it had ever been. In my hands, the disks of the device were motionless, but hot, and I dropped them to my feet, where they hissed and steamed and cracked apart as if doused with ice water.

"Murrie."

From behind me, J.J.'s voice.

J.J. and me in Cairo—at long last. I had broken everything to stand here.

I didn't want to turn and look, didn't want to see him run in negative colors and dissolve into the air. But he said my name again and I was helpless against that magic, so turned and found him as whole and living as ever. He looked at me and at the broken device at my feet and he laughed—he laughed and he ran toward me and he scooped me up and it was like breathing for the first time in years.

"Where have you been?" he asked.

"Everywhere," I said. "Everywhere."

The Copper Scarab

K. Tempest Bradford

THE HERD OF chariots that carried Amatashteret and her entourage away from the capital toward the grand pyramids towering on the horizon departed just as the Kheper-dawn lit the sky enough to travel safely at speed. Behind them, a cloud of sand obscured the buildings falling under the horizon and, after a short time, they all stopped looking back wondering if they'd be followed. Amatashteret was sure Yacob-Hur wouldn't bother coming after her even if she hadn't asked permission to take this trip as she should have done.

There were many more important shoulds weighing on her heart. How the members of the High House should have been celebrating the Feast of Iset, but weren't. How Yacob-Hur should have been preparing to take his place in the Netjer House and petition Hathor to slow the sun's journey across the sky on this, the shortest day of the year, but wasn't. How the Nile should have flooded her banks six months ago, but hadn't. For the third year in a row.

All of these shoulds were more important than anything else at the moment, even incurring the Chieftain's displeasure. She'd weathered it before.

A little over a shade after leaving, they were close enough to see the buildings beyond the pyramids that surrounded the Great Lioness: the Library of the Horizon. Amatashteret hadn't seen this place since she'd been sent to Canaan. It looked the same, yet different. Diminished. There were no people swarming the pyramids, their gleaming limestone facades devoid of scholars, and few people on the avenues between buildings. At least those were still intact. After the invasion, many cities were attacked and nearly destroyed. Not here.

Amatashteret turned to watch her daughters' faces as they passed between the Pyramid of the Heart and of the Spirit. They stared with wide eyes and mouths at the artificial mountains. She asked the charioteers to slow down so they could properly see the words written on the limestone. The dense symbol-script of the Khemetans started at the base of each side and went all the way up to the top. The knowledge of millennia preserved on the greatest engineering achievements in the world. She wanted them to see and to want to see more. She was doing this all for them. For all the daughters. For Khemet.

When they rolled up to the Library's administrative building, a woman stood alone on the steps. She was a full-blooded Egyptian with rich, dark brown skin and short, tight curls crowning her head. From the jewelry at her neck and the tattoos on her arms, Amatashteret could tell she was the Superior librarian. She was much younger than the woman who'd been Superior when Amatashteret studied here. She wondered if the older woman had retired or died during the war. And how many Supreme librarians under her must have died or left for a woman barely thirty inundations to rise to this position. Young or not, the expression she wore spoke of a formidable woman who took her duties seriously. Foremost, protecting the library from the invaders. From her.

Amatashteret brushed the sand from her robes and approached the steps.

"Superior, I am Amatashteret, daughter of Meritiset, and a Sister of Seshet." She paused to allow the woman to take in that information. "I'm here to solicit your counsel. May my daughters and I enter?"

The Superior's mouth turned down and her eyes narrowed just for a beat.

"Why does an Amorite princess need the counsel of an Khemetan inferior?"

"I *am* Khemetan."

The Superior nodded to the Chariots, then looked back to her. "Amorite transportation. Amorite drivers. Coming from the seat of Amorite control in this region."

"My mother was Khemetan, and I was educated *here*. These men are my father's kin."

Many beats passed and the Superior did not move or change her expression. Amatashteret took one more step forward and said, "I'm here to beg your help in restoring ma'at—balance—to Khemet. Something we both want, yes?"

The Superior made her wait another moment before bowing her head. "I am

Kemanut. It would be my honor to break my fast with you and your daughters before you continue on."

Not the welcome she hoped for. Still, the woman hadn't turned them away. One step closer to the copper scarab.

WHEN AMATASHTERET HAD last been in the Superior's receiving room the cubbies that lined the walls were filled with papyrus scrolls and there were always dozens of scholars around the many low tables scattered throughout the large, open space. Now the room was nearly empty of everything familiar. The only things left were the images of Seshet, Djehuti, and Piteh looking down on them from the walls. She felt again a sense of not quite rightness—a feeling that had come upon her again and again since she returned to Khemet. A part of her wanted to come back here and find it the same as when she left. An oasis of rightness when everything else was so wrong. It made no sense to hope for that given everything that happened. She could let it make her angry or make her despair, or she could accomplish what she came here to do.

After they observed the formalities—food and beer offered and accepted and imbibed—Kemanut sat across from her and waited with an expectant and skeptical expression.

Amatashteret considered how to begin.

"First, a question. Is the copper scarab still here?"

"The...scarab?" Kemanut's surprise at the query was clear, as was her reluctance to admit she knew about the machine's existence.

"The last year I was here, the engineers were working on recreating the copper scarabs the Ancients used when they built the pyramids of the Heart, Spirit, and Word. We had the frame, and when I left they had worked out how to create the tubes that would carry the steam it ran on. Did they finish?"

"Why do you want to know?"

"After my husband, a Khemetan, went to the West, my father asked me to go to the land of his fathers to be a bridge between our cultures. I did, not realizing the true intention of his request. He knew the Amorite Patriarchs intended to take advantage of the instability of the High House. He wanted my daughters and I away from harm. When we arrived, his kin kept us in Canaan until after the fighting ended. Even after Yacob-Hur established control, my uncles wouldn't allow me to return."

"Wouldn't *allow*?"

"Amorites believe women should be controlled by men. With my husband dead and no sons, I was meant to be ruled by my father's relatives until he sent for me." Kemanut's face reflected the disgust she felt at the situation. "He died before that happened. But then Yacob-Hur struggled to make Khemet thrive. I, through one of my cousins also raised here, convinced the Patriarchs to send me back to give him insight into Khemet and her people. I thought I could make a difference. He won't listen."

Amatashteret took a deep breath to calm herself. Flashes of the last conversation she had with the chieftain threatened to bring her back to the rage and frustration she'd felt at his words.

You weren't sent here to advise me, woman. You were sent to tell me something useful. As it is, all you're good for is showing them a Khemetan face looking down from the High House.

"I tried to explain that in order to rule he must bring balance. To be a leader in Khemet he must adopt Khemetan ways. And that means reinstating the kins-women."

"Which he will never do," Kemanut said. "If the Amorites cannot let their women control their own lives, how would they let them administer all of Khemet, as is our way?"

"You understand my dilemma."

"Why do you want the copper scarab? To use as a weapon against him?"

"Not in the way you mean. Yacob-Hur, like most brute force warriors, only understands power and strength. I've shown him text after text detailing how each aspect of administration is meant to work. He doesn't care. Walk that machine down the capital's avenues and let him see the reaction of the people. That he'll understand."

For several beats Kemanut kept their gazes locked as if she was searching for something in a Amatashteret's eyes. "No. It won't work. All it will do is hand him one more piece of Khemet to destroy or exploit. And I cannot—"

"You think that you can wait them out." Amatashteret had been studying her as well. "You think that as long as Khemetans continue to resist, and chaos reigns without being checked by balance, that eventually he will abandon the land."

The Superior said nothing. Her silence was answer enough.

"You don't understand them. Yacob-Hur doesn't need the rich soil or good harvests to make the Patriarchs happy. There are enough precious metals and jewels in this valley to satisfy them for generations. Only once Khemet has been stripped of anything of value—including the limestone off the pyramids—will they leave. You— Khemet will not outlast them. Let me help you save her."

Again, eyes locked, the two women considered and challenged each other's convictions. A long time passed before Kemanut stood and gestured toward an inner door.

"It's not finished, still. But I'll take you to it."

THE MACHINE WAS farther along than when she'd last seen it. Even incomplete, it was impressive beyond Amatashteret's recollection and now more resembled the insect it was based on. The copper scarab was wider than two wide elephants, filling the subterranean workshop where the Sisters stored it. As she walked around the machine she could see all the tubes running through it, just like the plans she remembered. The head and thorax, which housed the control mechanisms, were done and covered, but the rest of the carapace and wings weren't on yet. Though it had been many years, the copper was still the yellow-red of the sunset sky, which told her someone had been watching over it all this time. Meaning the Sisterhood of Engineers must still exist in some form. Good. She would need them.

"Mama," her oldest whispered as they circled around to the back, "what does it do?"

"Many things, according to the ancient writings. The Khemetans of the Time Before used them to move stone from quarries far up and down the Nile here to build the pyramids. The texts say they lifted the blocks into the air once they were shaped and placed them just so.

"How?"

"That's what we had hoped to find out once we were done."

The scarab's six legs were complete, yet unattached. She wondered how they would move through the sand.

"The outer wings are designed to capture the heat and light of the sun, channeling it here where there's a reservoir of water." Amatashteret smiled at the light in her daughter's eyes as she explored the inner workings. "Heat and pressure builds until it becomes steam, which travels through the tubes to the legs and other parts. That's how it moves."

"Can you make it work?"

She squeezed her daughter's hand. "With help."

She turned to Kemanut, who had been observing and quiet since they came in. "We had enough copper stored to make two of these. Is the rest also here?"

"The Superior Engineer hid it inside a chamber below the Lioness of the Horizon when the attacks started."

Nodding, Amatashteret could imagine how it happened. This workshop was well concealed within the labyrinth of underground tunnels that ran throughout the plateau. Still, this space might have been found by a determined looter. But the path into the giant stone Lion was only known by the Supremes and Superiors of the Library and far more difficult to locate. Those rooms held more than copper.

"We'll need it all. Kemanut, if we can complete the work, get this running, we have a hope of forcing Yacob-Hur's hand. I can't do this alone. I know many of the engineers and metalsmiths and masons are gone. I saw the empty streets. But they aren't dead, just hiding—am I right?"

The distrust still lingered in Kemanut's eyes. "You want them to come back here. You'd have them risk their lives for this."

"I don't—"

"He came here, your chieftain, after he'd already secured his victory, still intent on razing every city within his reach to the ground. The only reason we escaped that fate is because we did not fight. That and one of his generals convinced him that the Library was more valuable intact. So, the buildings still stand. The people..."

The pain of it, the anger, the fear, held tight inside but as clear on her face as it was fresh in her heart. Her voice getting tighter and higher and more raw as she continued.

"Soldiers came for the scholars, the Sisters, the Brothers. First just a few individuals, then whole groups who never returned. Everyone else escaped, hid. The rest of us are all that's left, as far as Yacob-Hur knows."

"I know. I heard that story. The general you mentioned? He was my father." A shard of the wall separating them broke off when Kemanut heard those words. "I was told he was less than diligent about keeping track of who left. Yacob-Hur called it carelessness. I suspect it was a deliberate choice."

"It was." The Superior touched her for the first time, stepping forward to take her hand and squeeze it. "We keep his name in a small shrine in the tunnels under the western Netjer House. I'll take you there tonight."

"Thank you." Amatashteret hadn't expected to find a fresh flower of grief growing within her, and yet here it was. Just as she had many times in the past nine years, she pushed it behind her to focus on the present. "If you know where the engineers, smiths, and masons who escaped all are, please ask them to return. Have them arrive in secret, in small groups. Enter the tunnels on the far western side so no one connects them to what we're doing here. When they arrive, I'll tell them what I'm telling you. I will not have my daughters living in a world ruled by chaos and ignorance anymore. More than anyone, I'm doing this for them."

"It will take time."

"We have time."

"How much? Won't he come for you?"

Amatashteret nodded. "If he does, I know what to do."

MEN CAME FROM the capital three days later. Amatashteret watched chariots emerge from a cloud of sand. When their riders arrived at the administration building with questions and demands, she stood in the shadow of the doorway dressed as a laborer and listened as her cousin played his part.

"Where are Amatashteret and her daughters?"

"We brought her here. She stayed one day, then the chariots went on to the harbor."

"Why aren't you with her?"

"I didn't want to go back to Canaan."

Much cursing followed. She smiled seeing the men leave in the direction of the river. Let them chase the rumor of her all the way back to the Jordan. It would give her the time she needed.

THE ENGINEERS WERE the first to return. They came in groups of two or three, arriving in the tunnels under the plateau without ever being seen in town. The sisters that remembered her vouched her to the ones who didn't. They, in turn, vouched for her to the metalsmiths, who came skeptical but eager to work with copper once more. The smiths vouched her to the masons, who came once the work was underway and the scarab's carapace started to take shape. They lent their skills to lifting the large panels and wings into place, the last pieces needed to make the scarab look complete. Over the weeks of work the tunnels transformed into a small village, everyone sharing knowledge and stories and their hopes for change. It almost approached what Amatashteret remembered.

She tried to only focus on the tasks immediately before them and not on the final goal. At first this helped her not to panic about finding the last component they needed to make the machine move: a ba-spirit.

All the material for building and operating the copper scarabs showed that a ba—the spirit that remained behind when life left the body—was necessary to operating the controls. She remembered helping to assemble the pomegranate-sized nest of minute levers and carnelian buttons where it would sit. She didn't know how they would go about placing a ba there or teaching it how the mechanism worked. With the project moving closer to completion, she could no longer put off solving this last problem.

The day after the left wing had been fitted into place, Kemanut came to the curl of tunnel Amatashteret used as a makeshift office. She brought a small jug of beer with her. Without speaking, she poured some into a pair of mugs and they each drank a while in silence.

"This past week you've been tense," Kemanut said. When she got no more than an unvoiced agreement, she continued. "Do you intend to share the reason with any of us?"

"It's just a problem I need to solve and haven't yet."

Over the weeks the two of them had built a mutual respect, though Amatashteret wouldn't call their relationship a trusting one. She didn't want to give her any reason to doubt the outcome of their work. As much as the others respected her, they would follow the Superior's word over hers without hesitating.

"I see what's in your heart better than you think I do." Kemanut waited for her to meet her eyes. "I watch you with the Sisters and the smiths, careful to guide them without seeming to lead. You say you want to achieve ma'at, to bring back the kinswomen, to restore some of what was. Do you think any of us doubt that means you intend to take the role of Great Mother and Queen?"

Amatashteret had to stop herself from looking away. "I don't want anyone to think I take it for granted that I will."

"You have a strong claim to it. Your mother's mother was a kinswoman."

"That's not enough."

"No, it's not."

Her heart thudded hard against her chest. Was Kemanut going to speak against her if she tried?

"If this is what you want, you need to show you're worthy of it. You need to start acting like a Great Mother."

"I don't understand—"

"No one woman can be every aspect of the netjeret all the time. Hathor depends on Sekhmet who depends on Iset who depends on Nebthet. A queen needs *all* her kinswomen."

Ever since she lost control of her life Amatashteret had kept so much inside of her heart, only allowing the smallest pebbles of her thoughts and plans to drop into the world. To protect herself. And her daughters.

"I've spent so much time working on how to outmaneuver Amorites I'm starting to think like them."

"Thank you," she said after a long pause. And then she went to gather the others.

THE CLOSEST PLACE all of them could fit at one time was a chamber underneath the Netjer House of Djehuti where many of the papyrus scrolls the librarians hid from Yacob-Hur were stored. Once she could see that all the smiths, engineers, and masons were assembled, she held up one of the scrolls.

"Sisters," she called out, making a point to make eye contact with the smiths as well as the engineers, "brother masons, we have one last problem to solve before we can bring the scarab into the sunlight and test it. The mechanism requires a ba-spirit as well as a living pilot to operate. And I have no idea how we can make that happen."

"How did the Ancients do it?" one of the smiths asked.

An engineer standing in the front answered. "There's an incantation in the records. We think it's meant to compel a ba-spirit to do the work. But it's written in the old tongue." The language they spoke evolved out of that, but few scholars knew it completely enough to translate even back before the invasion.

"It compels them? Why not ask?" another engineer said.

"What ba-spirit would remain in this world disembodied for longer than they needed to? Ba take up another life or they pass through the Door of the West with the Osiris," Kemanut said.

"It's been more than a generation since we've had a king that properly transitioned," one of the masons said. "There must be many lost ba waiting."

"There are."

The voice came from the middle of the room and was quiet enough that Amatashteret didn't hear it, all she saw was the turn of a dozen heads in the speaker's direction. It was a young man she'd seen working with the masons, but from the look of him he wasn't old enough to be a full member of the brotherhood. He also didn't look like he could deal with pressure of so many eyes on him.

"Say again, Neferu. Speak loud," the Supreme mason commanded.

"There are many spirits here, waiting, hoping for the king to open the Door for them."

"Here as in Khemet or here as in this room?" Amatashteret asked.

"Both, auntie. More here at the Library then upriver where we came from.

They gather here because of the Great Lion, I think."

The boy was clearly a ba adept, a person gifted with the ability to see and communicate with the spirits. If things ran as they were supposed to, the Superiors of the Netjer Houses would have found him years ago and trained him.

"So we can find them," the Supreme mason said. "How do we get them to understand how the machine works?"

"Neferu, were any of the spirits here engineers?" Amatashteret asked.

The boy's eyes turned gold—a sign he was communicating with the ba around them. "Yes. Many. One says to tell you her name is Aneski."

Most of the other engineers reacted just as Amatashteret did, hands automatically touching the space over their hearts in remembrance.

"The last Superior Engineer of the High House," Kemanut explained to the younger people. "Building the copper scarab was her idea."

Amatashteret cut through the crowd to take Neferu's hand—"Ask her to follow us, please."—and led him back through the tunnels to the giant scarab. She had him stand on a stool so he could see inside the ba-spirit nest.

"Can she get there? Or..." Did it require the spell? She wasn't sure.

"She is there. She says..." he looked to the Supreme mason. "We have to make it in harmony with her?"

No one looked as if they understood what that meant. Her stomach clenched, braced against defeat. They were so close!

"I think she means we have to create a resonance in the copper the same way the Brothers of Anpu create one in the stone when they consecrate the Door in a tomb." Kemanut stepped up to the machine and placed her palm on the head. After a few breaths she began to hum, modulating up and down until the copper vibrated in kind. "Before, I was a musician in the Netjeret House of Iset. I know of the technique, but I don't know the exact resonance. And metal is different from stone."

"We can work with you to discover it," the Supreme mason said. "And with Neferu's help, the ba will be able to guide us."

Elated and hopeful again, Amatashteret crossed her hands over her heart. "Let's begin."

IN THE DARKNESS before dawn on the equinox, Khemetans who came from across the delta and White Fortress region gathered around the base of the Great Lioness. Their voices quiet, reverent; their bodies newly wet with water from the still anemic Nile; they sat with eyes trained on the eastern horizon.

Like the giant stone Lioness of the Horizon, their faces would greet the dawn directly on the day marking the beginning of the harvest season. Most of them tried not to think about how poor that harvest would be this year, just as last year, and possibly all the years to come. Instead, they waited for the life-giving rays of the sun to warm their skin and remind them of the first eternal truth: Everything changes, but the dawn always comes.

Half a shade after the sun disk pushed fully over the horizon, the Lioness seemed, impossibly, to shudder. Sounds emerged from under the ground that ricocheted around the still quiet crowd—vibrations that didn't make sense.

They had begun to murmur when the copper scarab emerged from the sand between the stone paws, hissing and clicking and gleaming in the sunlight. The people's silence held for one breath, two, before everyone reacted at once. Amatashteret watched from a short distance as some scrambled away in fear, some fell to their knees in shock or in reverence, and some ran to get a closer look. The engineers surrounded the scarab, lifting the copper wings to the right position and ensuring the steam pressure stayed at the right level. Once they gave the ready signal, she and the other chariot riders rolled past the machine, heading into the desert and upriver toward the capital.

She looked back at the massive scarab, watched the legs' deliberate movement as it walked on the stone pavement like a spider then switched to a sweeping, swimming movement when it reached the sand between the pyramids. The size, the weight, the fact that it wasn't perfectly built didn't keep it from moving along just as fast as the slow trotting horses.

Amatashteret had one small stab of regret that they hadn't been able to figure out how to make it fly. *Soon*, she told herself. If this worked, she and the Sisters would have many years to solve that puzzle.

Once away from the Library district, the chariots formed a wide circle around the scarab with Amatashteret and Kemanut in front. The engineers, smiths, and masons who didn't fit in the dozen chariots rode behind on mules, followed by the Khemetans who had seen the machine emerge. The group kept to the sand, but hewed close enough to the farmlands that people from villages along the bank of the river, alerted by excited criers, trickled out to watch them pass or to join. By the time the Ra-sun looked down on them from above, hundreds of Khemetans followed in their wake. And so they entered the capital on a wave of cheers and hymns that reached deep within the walls of the High House.

As planned, the chariots parted and the copper scarab reached the courtyard of the palace first. Amatashteret came to stand in front of it when she saw Yacob-

Hur coming down the long front steps, his white hot fury apparent even from this distance. She turned her back to him and took in the sight of the machine standing in the full sunlight. It towered over her, carapace gleaming yellow-red, outer wings up as if just about to fly, alive and vibrating. She looked at all the engineers and smiths and masons that helped build it, all the people fascinated and buoyed by it. This creation would change everything for her people. *All* her people. With that thought firm in her heart, she turned and faced the chieftain.

For many breaths he stood two arms length away, eyes jumping between her and the looming machine above them. Finally, he locked on her. "Speak, woman."

"After today you will never use that tone with me again."

He flinched as if punched, too surprised to form an immediate answer.

"Do you know what this is?" she said, arms raised to encompass the machine's presence. "No, I can see you don't. This is a scarab beetle. We Khemetans hold it sacred. It represents the celestial Kheper that brings the dawn, pushing it above the horizon to launch it on the daily journey across the sky."

"If you don't start making sense—"

"I'll put it in terms you can understand. The scarab is a god. I brought it to life."

That silenced him.

"Look behind me. Do you see all those women? They're engineers and metalsmiths. Together we designed and crafted this. Do you see all those men? They're masons. Together we built and sang this to life. Do you see all the people behind them? They know we're the ones who made that happen.

"Do you see the choice you have in front of you?"

A range of dark emotions passed over Yacob-Hur's face before he took a deep breath to laugh. "So I'm to give over all my power to you because you come back here at the head of a mob of peasants?"

"That isn't how this works," Amatashteret said. "Without balance, power dwindles away to nothing, just as with the Nile. Women and men rule together in Khemet. Why do you think the throne sits on top of Iset's head?" She pointed at the carving of the netjeret on the lintel surrounding the door.

"This is your choice: Join me, re-establish balance, and see the Black Land restored to glory."

"Or?"

At a signal from her, Neferu had the scarab take two steps forward.

"Get stepped on."

Fear and anger swirled in Yacob-Hur's eyes. "You harm me and you won't live out the day."

"Oh? Who will punish me? Them?" He followed her gaze to the upper balcony where three of the Amorite Patriarchs watched the scene below. "They came to warn you their patience is about to run out, didn't they? Or, that it has already."

From his look she knew her second guess was right.

"Show them you're wise enough to rule, not just strong enough to conquer."

"By giving in to a woman?"

She didn't respond. She waited. After a time his breathing slowed, his eyes fixed on the copper scarab, and his rational mind finally asserted control of his emotions. He still couldn't fix his mouth to utter the necessary words, only managing a hard nod of acquiescence.

Without speaking, she walked past him toward the High House steps. Before he could react to this, the engineers and smiths streamed past him to join her. Amatashteret waited at the top for them to coalesce around her, just as the masons moved to form a circle around the scarab. When Yacob-Hur finally came to stand beside them, the message was clear: I am protected. We are protected.

"Can you trust him?" Kemanut had asked in the hours before dawn. "Even if he agrees, can you be sure he won't take control back?"

"No. Never," she'd said. "We can never stop watching for him to betray us. He's not fit to be king in Khemet and never will be. We still need him, for now. Once we re-establish the kinswomen we can search for and anoint a king who has the respect of the Amorites and respects the ways of Khemet."

Even in this moment, standing before the High House as Kemanut announced her as the Great Mother, Amatashteret could see this future as if it already happened. Later, she would gather more women, the daughters and granddaughters of Khemet, to set things in order. Later, she would become the Superior Engineer and lead the Sisters of Seshet in creating more copper scarabs. Later, she would see her daughters take on these responsibilities and carry on her work.

For now, she placed her hand on Yacob-Hur's shoulder, accepted the regalia Kemanut brought out of hiding for her, took one last breath as Amatashteret, orphan and widow, and made her first official act as Great Mother and Queen.

❖ ABOUT-THE-AUTHORS ❖

New Zealand-born fantasy writer and podcaster PHILIPPA (PIP) BALLANTINE is the author of the *Books of the Order* series, and has appeared in collections such as *Steampunk World* and *Clockwork Fairy Tales*. She is also the co-author with her husband, TEE MORRIS, of *Social Media for Writers*. Tee co-authored *Podcasting for Dummies* and has contributed articles and stories for numerous anthologies including *Farscape Forever!*, *Tales of a Tesla Ranger*, and *A Cosmic Christmas 2 You*. Together, they are the creators of the Ministry of Peculiar Occurrences. Both the series and its companion podcast, *Tales from the Archives*, have won numerous awards including the 2011 Airship Award for Best in Steampunk Literature, the 2013 Parsec Award for Best Podcast Anthology, and RT Reviewers' Choice for Best Steampunk of 2014. Their first spinoff of the series, *The Curse of the Silver Pharaoh*, debuted at #1 under three different Steampunk categories on Amazon.com. They conclude the adventures of Books & Braun this summer with *Operation: Endgame*. Pip and Tee reside in Manassas, Virginia with their daughter and a mighty clowder of cats. You can find out more about them and explore more of the Ministry at **ministryofpeculiaroccurrences**.com and listen to their writerly podcast *The Shared Desk* at **theshareddesk.com.**

DAVID BARNETT is the author of a number of novels, including the Gideon Smith series (*Gideon Smith and the Mechanical Girl*, *Gideon Smith and the Brass Dragon* and *Gideon Smith and the Mask of the Ripper*.) His latest novel, *Calling Major Tom*, will be published by Orion in 2017.

K. TEMPEST BRADFORD is a speculative fiction writer by night, a media critic and culture columnist by day, and an activist blogger in the interstices. Her fiction has appeared in *Strange Horizons*, *Electric Velocipede*, and illustrious anthologies such as *Diverse Energies*. She's also a regular contributor to NPR, io9, and books about Time Lords. Visit her blog: **KTempestBradford.com**

CHAZ BRENCHLEY has been making a living as a writer since the age of eighteen. He is the author of nine thrillers, two fantasy series, two ghost stories, and two collections, most recently the Lambda Award-winning *Bitter Waters*. He has also published Chinese fantasy as Daniel Fox, and urban fantasy as Ben Macallan. He lost count of his short stories long ago. His work has won the British Fantasy Award and a Lambda Award. He has recently married and moved from Newcastle to California, with two squabbling cats and a famous teddy bear.

GAIL CARRIGER writes comedies of manners mixed with paranormal romance. Her steampunk books include the Parasol Protectorate, Custard Protocol, Supernatural Society, and Delightfully Deadly series for adults, and the Finishing School series for young adults. She is published in many languages and has over a dozen NYT bestsellers via seven different lists. She was once an archaeologist and is overly fond of shoes, octopuses, and tea.

SARAH CAULFIELD is a final-year Education, English, and Drama student at Downing College, University of Cambridge. She has been published previously by Lethe Press, Autonomous Press, Harmony Ink Press, Headmistress Press and Voicemail Poems. She was the 2015 and 2016 winner of the John Treherne Creative Writing Prize. The eldest of two children, she has lived in the United Kingdom, Poland and Germany and is from Blackpool, Lancashire.

P. DJÈLÍ CLARK is an Afro-Caribbean-American writer of speculative fiction. Raised on genres of fantasy, sci fi, horror and the supernatural, he felt a need for more diverse tales with more diverse characters drawn from more diverse sources. To that end, he put pen to pad and fingers to keyboard, seeking to Imagine, Dream and Create new realms to explore. You can find him on twitter at **@pdjeliclark** or at his blog at **pdjeliclark.wordpress.com.**

ROD DUNCAN writes alternate history novels set in the world of the Gas-Lit Empire. The first of these, *The Bullet Catcher's Daughter*, was shortlisted for the Philip K. Dick award. He has previously written contemporary crime, his novel Backlash being shortlisted for the John Creasey Dagger. Born in Wales, he has lived in Taiwan and Ghana but has been in Leicester since 1993. A dyslexic with a background in scientific research and computing, he now lectures in creative writing at DeMontfort University. To find out more about him and his adventures in writing: **facebook.com/gaslitempire** or **gaslitempire.co.uk**. Follow him on twitter **@RodDuncan.**

JONATHAN GREEN is a writer of speculative fiction, with more than sixty books to his name. He has written everything from *Fighting Fantasy* gamebooks to *Doctor Who* novels, by way of *Sonic the Hedgehog, Teenage Mutant Ninja Turtles, Judge Dredd* and *Robin of Sherwood.* He is the creator of the Pax Britannia steampunk series for Abaddon Books, and the author of the award-winning, and critically-acclaimed, *You Are The Hero—A History of Fighting Fantasy Gamebooks.* He also edits and compiles his own short story anthologies. To find out more about his current projects visit www.JonathanGreenAuthor.com and follow him on Twitter @jonathangreen.

Arriving from Denmark in 1995, ANNE JENSEN now lives and writes in Salisbury, England, taking inspiration from the ancient landscape (and the military installations) of Salisbury Plain. In 1992, she spent a year living in Cairo, and the impressions of that city remains with her still. She is currently working on a dark fantasy novel—taking time out to write 'The Internal' for this collection has been an opportunity to see again, in her mind's eye, the outlines of Menkaure, Khafre and Khufu on the horizon.

ZAN LEE's short fiction has appeared in publications such as *Asimov's Science Fiction Magazine, Alfred Hitchcock's Mystery Magazine, The Third Alternative,* and *Cemetery Dance Magazine.* Her stories have also been published in anthologies including *The Museum of Horrors,* which won the World Fantasy Award for best anthology. She won a first-place prize in the Writers of the Future contest, and one of her stories was shortlisted for the British Fantasy Award. She has a B.A. and an M.A. from Stanford University. She once lived in Egypt for a year, where she taught writing at the American University in Cairo.

JOHN MORALEE is the author of the crime novel *Acting Dead,* the zombie apocalypse thriller *Journal of the Living,* and the first book in a dystopian science fiction/fantasy series *The House on Willow Lane.* He lives in England, where his short fiction has appeared in magazines and anthologies, including *The Mammoth Book of Jack the Ripper Stories, Crimewave,* and the British Fantasy Society's magazine *Peeping Tom.* Several collections of his stories are available in physical and digital formats. They include the horror titles *The Bone Yard and*

Other Stories, the crime omnibus *Edge of Crime*, and the science-fiction collection *The Tomorrow Tower*. Find him at mybookspage.wordpress.com.

M.J. LYONS is a writer, game maker and professional nerd. He has contributed to dozens of publications, and writes a bi-monthly column with a colleague on lesser-known LGBTQ history, *History Boys*, for Canada's gay and lesbian publication *DailyXtra*. He has also contributed two episodes to *LongStory*, an episodic dating sim for young people, and contributed world building to an instalment of a modern day superhero tabletop RPG, *AMP: Year Three*. He lives in Toronto, ON with his partner and a sinister-looking cat.

GEORGE MANN is a *Sunday Times* Bestselling author, comic writer and editor. *The Affinity Bridge*, the first novel in the Newbury and Hobbes Victorian fantasy series, was published in 2008. Other titles in the series include *The Osiris Ritual*, *The Immorality Engine*, *The Executioner's Heart*, *The Casebook of Newbury & Hobbes* and the forthcoming *The Revenant Express*. George's other novels include *Ghosts of Manhattan*, *Ghosts of War*, *Ghosts of Karnak* and the forthcoming *Ghosts of Empire*, mystery novels about a vigilante set against the backdrop of a post-steampunk 1920s New York, as well as the original Doctor Who novels, *Paradox Lost* and *Engines of War*, the latter featuring the War Doctor alongside his companion, Cinder. Find more about him at **george-mann.com.**

CHRISTOPHER PARVIN is an author living in Lancashire who divides his time between writing, drawing, crafting and dreaming when not building shelves to buttress his hunger for books. After graduating with a degree in Creative Writing he has succeeded in the publication of several short stories and is currently working on his first novel.

NISI SHAWL is the Tiptree Award-winning author of the acclaimed steampunk alternate history of the Congo, *Everfair*, and the story collection *Filter House*. She's a founder of the Carl Brandon Society, and a Clarion West board member. She edits reviews for the *Cascadia Subduction Zone*. Her Guest of Honor appearances include WisCon in 2011, the Science Fiction Research Association in 2014, and Armadillocon in 2017.

BENJANUN SRIDUANGKAEW writes love letters to strange cities and the future. She has been nominated for the Campbell Award for Best New Writer and her debut novella *Scale-Bright* was nominated for the British Science Fiction Association Award. Her work has appeared in Tor.com, *Clarkesworld*, *Heiresses of Russ: The Year's Best Speculative Lesbian Fiction* and many more. Her second novella *Winterglass* is forthcoming from Apex Publications late 2017.

E. CATHERINE TOBLER has never been a widowed dwarfess fleeing sky pirates in the wake of a lavish opera, alas! Among others, her fiction has appeared in *Clarkesworld*, *Lightspeed*, *Interzone*, and on the Sturgeon Award ballot. Her Folley & Mallory novels now encompass four volumes and she is surely at work on another, for steampunk Egypt never sleeps!

TIFFANY TRENT is the author of eight young adult books, including the award-winning novel *The Unnaturalists* and its sequel *The Tinker King*. Born and raised in Roanoke, Virginia, she has stayed true to her Appalachian roots with a deep interest in the natural world and folklore, which is apparent in both her fiction and nonfiction.

ABOUT-THE-EDITOR

MATTHEW BRIGHT is a writer, editor and designer who often wonders exactly what order those words go in. His short fiction has appeared or is forthcoming in publications such as Tor.com, *Nightmare's Queers Destroy Horror, Steampunk Universe, Harlot Media, Clockwork Iris, GlitterShip, Queen Mob's Teahouse* and others. He is the editor of several anthologies, including *The Myriad Carnival, Threesome, A Scandal In Gomorrah* and *Gents*. He pays the bills as a book cover designer, and lives in Manchester, England.

Published anonymously in three volumes in 1827, when the author was only seventeen years old, *The Mummy!* is, as she describes it herself, a strange, wild novel that—to an audience nearer her future than when Loudon imagined it—is filled with striking similarities to our modern world, including a form of the internet. But it is also filled with brilliant flights of fancy: her court ladies wear hair ornaments of controlled flame; surgeons and lawyers may be steam-powered automatons; people holiday by moving their entire home on rails. The visionary technological setting contrasts with a morality seemingly gone awry as it falls to the reanimated mummy Cheops to try to find a role in this corrupted society. A lost curio of Victorian futurism waiting to be discovered, *The Mummy!* is as bizarre and entertaining as it's premise promises—and more.

AVAILABLE IN PAPERBACK AND EBOOK.